# Safe Haven

## by
## Nita Hughes

ISBN 978-0-6151-8035-9

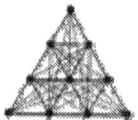

Pyradice Publishing markets products and services
that focus on educational and inspirational topics
(visit: www.PyradicePublishing.com).

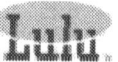

This book is printed by Lulu on recycled paper
(visit: www.lulu.com/nitahughes).

For a current listing of the author's work
or to download a press kit, please visit:
www.NitaHughes.com

# ACKNOWLEDGEMENTS

Many thanks go to my husband, Douglas, for all the detailed work he does to make sure that everything is ready to go to press, as well as the support and encouragement to create that he fosters.

Always I am grateful to my Mom, Audrey Davis, for a lifetime of nurturing growth on all levels; and to my daughter, Kim Brady, for her keen eye and salient input to the text; and to my son, Kristopher Gerbracht, as avid a reader and enthusiastic a giver of feed-back as anyone could ever want.

Finally, I wish to thank all the many people with whom I worked at Security Pacific Bank, particularly those in the International Private Banking world, which provided the inspiration for the background of this story.

# ONE

Amanda Evans replaced the receiver and stared into space. A sudden chill gripped her. Not a rumor had rippled through the bank's grapevine. Such silence was unheard of. She shoved her chair back from the desk, nearly upending a delicate jade statue on the credenza.

She turned the intricately carved sculpture slowly in her hand, reminded of how she'd chosen such pieces of Asian art for their beneficent energies. Honoring the age-old tenets of feng shui was critical to her success in attracting Asian clients seeking a safe haven for their wealth.

She'd made the most of it. The waters of the bay flowing towards her window, red touches in the decor, goldfish to consume any bad luck, and wind chimes, even if no breeze but the air conditioner blew-- all were skillfully designed to attract prosperity. Even her desk was positioned so its feng shui, literally translated as Wind and Water, conspired to assure an unimpeded flow of success and harmony.

Amanda grimaced. No amount of good feng shui had vanquished her growing anxiety. "Better to brave the lion in his den." She moved towards the door, added emphasis underscoring her words. "The sooner the better."

As if on cue, her secretary's raised voice announced her failed attempt to stop Amanda's boss, Nigel Taylor, in mid-stride with an offer of coffee. Amanda reached the door as Nigel yanked it open, trailing her in its wake.

He dashed over to the window, pausing only long enough to say, "No time for small talk. Tell Karen to hold all calls. I don't want the conference room lines to ring while we're in our meeting."

"Everything's ready. Where's Chairman Sorenson?"

"He stopped to place a call. He'll be right here." Amanda picked up her notebook and turned. Nigel was already halfway through the doorway in his dash toward the conference room.

Something definitely had unhinged him, Amanda thought, studying Nigel as he walked away. She was shocked at his unkempt appearance as he turned to verify that she was following him. His bloodshot eyes pinned hers with an impatient stare. Nigel Taylor would no more look rumpled than James Bond—and never for a meeting with the bank's chairman. Nigel, known as a man who, even on the tennis court, returned serves without one lock of hair ruffled or one bead of sweat in evidence, was coming undone.

Throwing his briefcase on the table, he glanced nervously at the doorway as Sorenson approached.

"Have a chair, Ed." Nigel rushed to draw out the chair at the far end of the conference table, the action and words carrying an obsequious overlay. The silent solemnity with which Sorenson took his place, opened his briefcase and drew out a file, commanded the same frozen attention as a cobra poised to strike.

"Shut that door!" Nigel's outburst and wild gesturing to Amanda drew a slight frown from Sorenson. Registering it, Nigel's reddened face turned ashen.

"Shall we begin?" Sorenson directed his question to Amanda as she closed the door and took her chair. He began, poise intact, but with a grave emphasis coating each word. "It looks as though we have a serious situation brewing in the Philippines." Nigel's sidelong glance at Amanda implied it was somehow of her doing.

Chairman Sorenson looked down at his file, drawing out documents that seemed more than big-bank-official. "Fernando Alvarez, at United International Bank in New York, was arrested in Manila. Rumor has it he was helping a client launder money." He glanced at Amanda, his look taking the full measure of her response.

"Launder money? That doesn't make sense." Amanda responded slowly. "No international private banking officer would risk such a thing."

Nigel's withering stare refuted any such logic. Suddenly the reality hit her. Her counterpart at UIB arrested? A stunned intensity accompanied her renewed attention.

Sorenson's delivery resumed a 'nothing but the facts' rendition. "I put through a call to Mario Sanchez in New York just before I left. He assures me our New York office is clean."

Nigel glared at Amanda, unable to resist interjecting a fearful indictment. "It's the Philippine business that smells."

"What do you mean?" Amanda waited, sick at the thought that Mario, her counterpart in New York, may have thrown her to the wolves. She returned her focus to Sorenson, searching his eyes for the grace of full and rational disclosure. He looked from her to Nigel, giving a look that froze Nigel's face into a semblance of restraint. Returning his gaze to Amanda, Sorenson continued.

"There's reason to believe Fernando's client may be linked with one or more of yours." Nigel lowered his head, hands moving to brush away a bead of sweat trickling down his forehead.

"One of my clients?" Amanda's mind raced as she bit back the phrase 'no client of mine would be involved in money laundering'. "Who?" Her heart thudded as she waited for Sorenson's response.

"No one knows. They haven't yet released the identity of UIB's client."

Nigel turned to Amanda with a glare. "But you know how it is in the Philippines—all the money is in the hands of a few."

"What can we do?" Amanda kept her focus on Sorenson, waiting for his reply.

"We can't have Fidelity American Bank tainted by any connection with money laundering. UIB is fighting to keep it out of the press, to cooperate with the Feds and get their man out of the Philippines." Sorenson paused, studying Amanda solemnly. Nigel, who had sank deeper into his chair, like a balloon whose air escaped, couldn't resist the opening.

His features conveyed a mix of terror, disbelief and self-importance. "That's their problem." Nigel's voice resumed a tone of complete assurance as he looked up at Sorenson and back to Amanda. "Mine was to assure Chairman Sorenson I'd have you cancel your Manila trip. We can't risk having our bank tainted in this mess." His firm tones punctuated the finality of such a decision.

Sorenson looked at Nigel with an expression that didn't quite cloak his impatience. "I don't agree."

Nigel stared in complete bafflement. One lock of blond hair dislodged and pointed towards his left eye as he shook his head briskly. "But...it's too dangerous. Any problems could finish us." Amanda waited; her steady focus fixed on Sorenson.

"We've gone over all of the bank's Suspicious Activity Reports." Sorenson hesitated, looking down at one of the forms in front of him. Amanda listened, mentally ticking off her 'nothing to report' responses on the form she filed each month for her department. "Are your Client ID Forms up to date?" Sorenson held his gaze steady as Nigel threatened what looked to be an incipient heart attack.

Amanda wavered between telling the chairman what he wanted to hear or telling the truth. There wasn't any option. "To the extent that corroboration is obtainable, I've documented each depositor's history and sources of funds." She waited into the silence; unable to judge how such an answer was being received. "International clients provide only as much information as any given banker needs to know, of which very little can be completely verified."

"Having done my stint in International years ago, I know only too well that there isn't any such a thing as a Philippine audited financial statement worth the paper it's printed on." At Sorenson's words she felt her shoulders lower an inch or so from their protective rise around her neck.

Sorenson continued. "Knowing that, I want you to continue business as usual and proceed with your trip. To do so not only advertises our bank's innocence, but allows you to do some deeper digging on their home soil."

"Their? Do we have some idea of who represents exposure for our bank?"

"Not yet. That will be chiefly up to you to determine." Sorenson watched as her eyes widened. "We may, with your help, be able to short circuit any indictment descending on FAB. Are you willing to do this?" Sorenson was as intently focused on her reception of his words as she had been on his. His eyes took on an earnest expression before continuing.

Nigel nervously twirled his pen. Impatient at Amanda's struggle for an answer, he couldn't resist coaching her. "It'll save your neck as well as that of the banks, you know."

Sorenson directed a scathing look at Nigel. Returning his focus to Amanda, he enunciated each word firmly. "Be assured you need not agree to such a trip."

"Of course I'll go."

"Good. We should have clearer guidelines after my meeting tomorrow with United Bank's chairman and the federal agencies involved." He studied her closely before continuing. "You have a brief window of time before the fallout hits Fidelity American. For now I'd like you to go over each client ID form with a fine-tooth comb." He began to reinsert the documentation into his briefcase, halting Nigel's, "Of course." with a dismissive glance as he returned his focus to Amanda. "Nigel will present copies to me for review with the various agencies involved. If we can connect any client of yours to Fernando's, that'll narrow your focus. If not, we count on you and our Manila office to gather all the evidence you can, for or against, during this trip." Sorenson closed his briefcase, stood and extended his hand to Amanda. "We'll be in touch." The handshake was firm but the words neutral of reassurance.

"I know you have business in San Francisco—he'd turned to Nigel—let me know how it goes. I'll see you tomorrow in LA"

Nigel shadowed Sorenson out to the elevator. Amanda's secretary, Karen, rushed up with an "important phone call", saving Amanda from lingering during their exodus.

The phone call wasn't critical, but Amanda gave it all the attention her fragmented focus could allow. By the time Nigel returned she had hung up and returned to the conference room to stare at the uneaten French pastries and cold coffee. Nausea stirred.

Nigel charged back into the room, slammed the door and began pacing. "Whatever his game-plan, we can't afford a single misstep. Not with the FBI, the CIA, and you name it—everybody's involved." His glare as he turned to Amanda was iced with fear. "It's essential. You must produce a clean bill of health for each client."

So much for beneficent feng shui, Amanda thought, as the impact of the meeting began to fully sink in. She shivered as she turned to Nigel. The image of her colleague rotting in a Manila jail took on a frightening reality. She shook her head as she gave voice to the unthinkable. "I just can't believe Fernando would become involved in money laundering."

Nigel stopped his pacing and looked at Amanda with a gaze blended of exasperation and earnestness. His response was delivered slowly in a tone of voice disarmingly solemn and weighted with concern. "Believe it. From the way Sorenson is approaching this, Fernando's involvement is only the tip of the iceberg." His jaw clenched. "Never for one instant lose sight of what's at risk."

The moment of silence that followed was palpable, broken only by the soft gray rain that blew against the windows. Amanda felt frozen, less by the degree of seriousness their meeting had revealed, than by the disastrous implications implicit in Sorenson's top-level meetings. The urgency with which he flew from LA headquarters to her SF office was unheard of. "Never fear, Nigel. I promise you nothing could make me risk spending even one night in a Manila jail, so don't...."

Nigel grabbed at her deliberation, using her words to etch his fears even deeper. "So don't" is exactly what I need to get across to you." Nigel drew himself up to a commander's stance as he moved face to face, piercing her gaze with his. "Don't overlook the slightest detail of information on your client ID forms." Nigel's stiff upper lip wavered, a look of horror replacing it. "Don't leave any avenue for Fidelity American Bank to be accused of accepting dirty money." He froze, speaking haltingly, his words seeking to follow the scenario to its logical conclusion. "Sorenson wouldn't be above throwing someone to the wolves." His voice took on a sudden confidence. "And his scapegoat won't be me."

The pointedness of his conclusion left Amanda reeling. Stunned by Nigel's crassness, she wavered between falling to the mat or coming out swinging. One look at Nigel convinced her that any words would fall on deaf ears. He returned to his theme, as if in repeating it, his security would be guaranteed.

"Don't, for God's sake, do anything that will jeopardize the future of our department. I want you focused on one thing only." He struck one balled up fist against his other hand to emphasize his edict. "Review all of your client ID forms, and by God, each one of them had better end up looking holier than the Pope!"

Amanda carefully unclenched her jaw, deciding her best response for now was to lighten his paranoia. "I'll do what I can to make them appear second only to God."

"They'd better be. I intend to x-ray them before Sorenson gets his eyes on them." Nigel gave a swift look at his Piaget watch and pulled his briefcase forward. "I have a meeting at the Hyatt at noon"—his mouth curled in impatience—"an interview with some chap to head up our Cayman Islands Group. I'll be in touch later this afternoon."

It was Amanda's turn to be stuttery. Dozens of questions surged to the fore as she followed in Nigel's wake. She launched one swiftly through the closing elevator doors.

"Dare I let Karen or Mai in on this?"

"Say nothing." Nigel held the door from closing. His eyes nervously scanned the hallway before they came to rest on hers. "Dare?" He spit it out like venom sucked from a wound. "If you only remember one thing from this mess, it's never... ever... dare!"

# TWO

She headed back towards her office, deep in thought. The potential for her hard won surroundings being destroyed stopped her in her tracks. She glanced around. The reception area gleamed with an aura of money. Tall blue and white Ming Dynasty style vases, filled with tree-sized pussy willows, sat on one end of a deeply polished mahogany credenza. Exotic goldfish glided soundlessly around a cut-glass bowl on the opposite end. The soft Italian leather couch swirled in a freeform "S" around matching mahogany coffee tables displaying the latest Financial Review, Euromoney, and The Economist. Everything was designed to convey serenity and security to her wealthy and cautious clients. Nigel's departing blast, like a tornado, seemed to circle threateningly about the room.

"Don't you dare." She got it, she thought as she reached the door of her office. Don't dare jeopardize the bank. Don't dare jeopardize the department. Don't dare reveal any client as anything but lily white and pure. By all means, don't dare put Nigel Taylor's job at risk. What she most wanted to dare, she thought, was to tell him what he could do with this job. She drew a deep breath as she settled into her chair, glancing out of the window at the Embarcadero clock tower in the distance, returning her focus on the facts.

An international private banker arrested for money laundering in the Philippines? In spite of the unsettling implications, she didn't, strangely enough, feel frightened. Anger was her predominant emotion. How dare Nigel imply she'd be the one to be sacrificed in this mess? Her initial reaction was one of concern to validate her clients and protect her department. Anger had swiftly rearranged that agenda. "Scapegoat? Me? No way." Her words made their way through clenched teeth. An image became crystal clear. Whatever it took, she vowed to vindicate her professionalism and her self.

Karen popped her head into Amanda's office. "Mai's waiting and Rob Bennet called. He had a client cancel and wonders if you're free to join him for lunch today."

Amanda hesitated before answering, deciding she needed to break away. "Please call him back Karen. Find out when and where and tell him I'll be there." Karen turned to leave. "And ask Mai to step into my office please."

As Mai walked in, Amanda couldn't help but compare her to the efficient, low-key personality of Karen. How well matched on the intensity scale, she thought, were Mai Wong Lee and Nigel. Mai was outspoken, energetic and doggedly committed to success. Usually graceful, however, Mai nearly stumbled in her haste to enter Amanda's office. Amanda had noted that lately Mai seemed to waver between a state of panic, excitement, anger or sulks. "What is it Mai?" Amanda watched as Mai hesitated at the door. "Close the door and take a chair."

Mai glared petulantly back at the office staff as if annoyed at the denial of a visible forum for her dramatic outpouring. To handle her was one of Amanda's most challenging management skills. On the other hand, she held fast to the belief that hiring Mai was one of the best decisions she'd ever made.

For all of Mai Wong's posturing, she was a great sales performer, with an incredible technique of "boss-ladying" the clients in a manner that left them convinced that she had the perfect solution to all their investment needs.

"Would you like a cup of tea?" Amanda turned to the teapot on the credenza behind her.

"Can't think of tea now." Mai hesitated, drawing a breath to begin her account, but choosing not to sit down. Amanda studied her. Mai was unusually tall for an Asian woman, with a body well suited to her cheongsam, the traditional body-hugging, slit-skirted dress favored by all Chinese women able to wear them. Her arms glittered with gold, as did her fingers. Amanda knew the rings and bracelets weren't adornment alone but a totally mobile and dependable source of safety. The tenacity that had allowed Mai to escape from Communist China and create a life of abundance in San Francisco left Amanda speechless with admiration.

As if sensing Amanda's line of thought, Mai looked over at the clock and turned to Amanda with a torrent of insistent pleas. "You have to do something fast. Mr. Chan will be here soon. I afraid he take his five million away. He not listen to me. He say only talk to you."

"Start from the beginning Mai, slowly please." Amanda knew Mai had to be reined in by the rapidity with which her command of English was unraveling.

"I recommend open for him our Eurobond portfolio. Much better for him. The rates too low on his certificates of deposit." Mai's index finger and thumb widened and pinched together in illustration. The bright red nails accented with circles of gold distracted Amanda. Glitter and Mai were synonymous, she thought, eyes moving to Mai's gold threaded scarf. Not for me, Amanda thought, glancing down at her serviceable, but admittedly drab, wool suit.

As Mai described her successful sale of a Eurobond account to Mr. Chan, Amanda anticipated what had happened to sour its success. "I never tell him he always earn fourteen percent. This month he say account only five and a half percent. He very angry. What can we do?" Mai's face suddenly turned pale. "I lose my bonus if Chan money goes."

"Bring me copies of his latest statements. When do you expect him?"

"Twenty minutes. He say he close account." Amanda's focus had quickly veered to another person that would be displeased, Don Emilio de la Serna, who had referred Mr. Chan.

"Leave Mr. Chan to me."

Mai bolted out the door, like a prisoner unexpectedly reprieved. Amanda's thoughts went back to Don Emilio. Y.A. Chan's business was worth going the mile for, but the fact that Don Emilio would be incensed on hearing of Y.A.'s dissatisfaction, was unthinkable. Y.A. and Don Emilio, apart from being friends, were partners in many large business ventures.

She thought back to the memory of her first impression of the rich and powerful Don Emilio. The short, smiling man had disarmed her with an image combining the soul of Don Quixote in the body of Sancho Panza. Such an illusion belied his lifetime's quest for power and wealth. Still charmed by his magnetic warmth, Amanda had grown increasingly wary, as tales of his being the power behind the scenes in the Philippine government, surfaced. He wasn't a man to alienate.

Fortunately she didn't have to. Mr. Chan walked in just after Amanda finished perusing his statements. He was visibly agitated, but inherently polite, as he accepted a cup of tea and listened to her explanation.

Amanda gently and thoroughly began to explain the vagaries of the currency markets and their impact on his Eurobond portfolio's yield. One look at Mr. Chan's face told her he understood the reality, but his fear of loss prevailed. She'd already arrived at the solution and began to lay it out.

"This is what I recommend. We can switch your Eurobond portfolio into a managed portfolio with a mix of conservative investments such as money market, U.S. Treasuries, and Certificates of Deposit of staggered maturity dates."

Mr. Chan relaxed back into his chair, a slight smile playing around his mouth. "An old man like me gets confused with these new things." His humble deprecation was belied by the astuteness of his next remark. "It was what I planned to do by moving my account to one of my other banks." Shrewdness shone in his next comment. "But

I know you will better their rates, Miss Amanda. You work it out now please."

"I'll call our portfolio manager." Amanda dialed Sam Adams, using her speakerphone line to include Mr. Chan and clarify his instructions.

Sam's deep baritone carefully enunciated each requirement, finishing with a solid vote of confidence. "Will do. You now have the perfect conservative portfolio, Mr. Chan. More importantly, you have a great banker, Amanda Evans, to monitor your investments."

Amanda hung up the phone, thinking what a good dog and pony act she and the head of their Financial Management Group made. She turned to a smiling Mr. Chan.

"Sorry I take up so much of your time." He arose from his chair assuming an apologetic and appreciative semi-bow. "After I return from Hong Kong we go to Flower Garden for dim-sum, yes. You please to send my new account statement to Miss Li in your Hong Kong office." Mr. Chan's voice had its decisive edge back as he moved to go.

"Certainly. I'll take care of it." Amanda walked him to the elevator, wishing him a safe journey. No sooner had the elevator closed then Karen rushed up to hand her a phone message.

"You're on for lunch with Rob in twenty minutes. He said he's over that way so he'll meet you at the Bristol Cove." Amanda smiled, noticing that Karen had delivered her comment with a shade of 'hope it will help' consolation.

Before Amanda could reply, Mai rushed through the door, a deep frown clouding her brow. "Mr. Chan not take his money away, did he?"

"No, Mai." An almost visible wave of relief allowed color to return as Mai smiled.

"What...?"

"We'll go over it later. I'm off to lunch."

"One moment of your time please. It a personal matter. Very important."

Amanda hesitated, glancing at her watch. "I can give you five minutes now or more after lunch."

"Now." The look on Mai's face mirrored Nigel's panic.

The minute Amanda's office door closed, Mai spoke hesitantly. "I think not good you go on your next trip. Paper say shooting at Americans near Manila Hotel. I looking like Filipina. Better I go. Yes?"

Amanda let out a slow breath before responding. "Mai, you of all people, know how the press exaggerates anything in the Philippines. Why this sudden concern?" Her gaze directed a firm "Let's come clean" look directly into Mai's eyes. The look challenged her to confirm Amanda's growing suspicion that a conversation with Mario in New York had prompted Mai's histrionics. Amanda watched the build-up in Mai's acute anxiety as her English fragmented further.

"No, not stories papers tell. They always wrong, I know." A sheepish look spread over her down turned face as she continued. "It my fortune teller. She say danger coming. You must..."

"Enough doom and gloom." Amanda interrupted. "We won't discuss this any further." Amanda reached over, picked up the Chan file and handed it to Mai. "Did Y.A.'s credit cards arrive? He leaves tomorrow for Hong Kong. Will you make sure those cards are delivered today?" Mai nodded glumly as she turned to go.

Amanda pushed back from her desk. She couldn't get out of the building fast enough. Hitting a stride more conducive to power walking, she blindly aimed in the direction of Fisherman's Wharf, away from work, clients, and crises-- away. Hoping to outdistance Nigel's bombshell, she pressed on, drawing deep breaths of the sea air to clear her mind.

A few blocks later Amanda began to reclaim her composure enough to notice she had continued way beyond the restaurant itself. The walk back allowed time to examine the implications of her upcoming trip to the Philippines. Anxiety flared, for her clients, her staff, and her career. But so did determination. Her jaw was set and her step firm as she approached the Bristol Cove. She deliberated over whether to share with Rob any part of her morning's drama. Nigel's ringing dictum not to reveal a word to anyone, not even to colleagues, left her no option. Her professionalism cloaked any sign of turmoil as she approached the restaurant.

Amanda grinned as she entered its elegant cut glass doorway. Rob amazed her with his knowledge of the best place, the right thing to order, and the exact moment to abandon an old restaurant for a new favorite. He also knew the entire bank's, as well as the City's, latest gossip. It was the latter that cemented her decision to say nothing.

The maitre d' indicated Mr. Bennet had yet to arrive as he led her to one of his best tables. In spite of her impulsive hike in the opposite direction, Amanda was amazed to discover she was early. Good, she thought, time enough to switch gears.

She thought of Rob Bennet and his place in her life. They'd known one another for two years. Gradually their bantering camaraderie led to comfortable lunches that graduated into candlelit dinners. A couple of months ago, after sharing an exquisite bottle of champagne in celebration of Rob's latest corporate coup, they fell into bed. She frowned at the memory. As for his apparent virility, put to the test it had left her stunned, displaying all the warmth of an automaton. If lovemaking were ranked using a restaurant rating, she frowned, it would barely have made one star. A second into this memory, Rob walked through the doorway. Quickly putting a smile on her face, Amanda studied his entrance objectively.

He was almost too handsome. Cut from the macho movie hero mold, he was tall with sandy hair, blue eyes, lean and muscular from years of exercise. His athletic body accommodated itself wonderfully well to the perfectly tailored suits his position required.

Amanda watched as the maitre d' smiled a broad welcome. With a flourish, he led Rob to their table; not departing until assured that it met with Mr. Bennet's satisfaction. She smiled at Rob's impact, not only on the maitre'd, but on the females in the room. He magnetized their attention as he passed by.

"Hope you haven't been waiting long?"

"Just got here." Amanda smiled as he took his chair, thinking how much his voice added to his appeal. It was richly overlaid with echoes of faint Southern charm. He studied the wine list and she studied him, contrasting the personal Rob with the professional Rob.

Watching him at his job, Amanda had seen the steel his velvet accent cloaked. Throughout the bank he was known to be unrelenting, even merciless, in the way he negotiated leveraged buy-outs and debt-equity swaps in Fidelity's favor. Amanda secretly thought of them as 'funny money' deals. Rob could never convince her that debt and leverage were how one got ahead, both in the business and the private world. Whenever she tried to apply such actions to an individual, it seemed a sure course to bankruptcy. Still, it worked for him. Way out in front on the corporate fast track, it was clear that he was capable of staying the course to the executive suite.

"How does a crisp Riesling sound?"

"Perfect." She smiled up at him, trying to reflect her friends' awe at her great good fortune. What's wrong, Amanda wondered? Why doesn't my heart leap at the thought of him? No elevator feelings stirred. Just pride at being with him, respect for his business acumen, and pleasure in his company.

He looked up from the menu. She forced herself into a semblance of composure, mentally replaying her relationship mantra, "Give it time." Suddenly she felt absolutely famished.

"Well, what do you think? Do I pick them or do I pick them?" he said. "Nothing but the best and all for you." His expansive mood disarmed her. She smiled and turned to admire the room.

The Bristol Cove was known for seafood and impress-your-biggest-client lunches. Its elegant interior belied the fact that it was an old, harbor-front warehouse. With the freshest produce and seafood, a spectacular view of sailboats, and the Bay Bridge's span to Oakland, Amanda wished it a lasting success in the fickle world of City dining.

Their waitress approached the table, her smile wide and wreathed in dimples. She fluttered and fawned over Rob, giving a coquettish imitation of Bernadette Peters, whom she vaguely resembled. An uplifted arm teasingly brushed back a willful spill of red hair as it coyly highlighted her petite but voluptuous form.

Rob appeared to take no notice as he casually ordered a Hop Kiln '83 Riesling with oysters on the half-shell to start. He beamed at Amanda in a playful way, as if he were a boy escaping the serious intensity of his working world.

"Why so pensive? The rain stopped but you still look as though a fog hovers over you."

"I didn't know it showed." She shrugged, put her real concerns on hold and decided to share instead, the Mai incident. "I was thinking of Mai. Her actions lately have really been off the wall. She caught me just as I was leaving for lunch and proceeded to tell me of her fear that danger might befall me if I go to Manila." As the words left her mouth, Amanda frowned, convinced that Mai's premonitions were something more than psychic, maybe as pragmatic as overhearing Nigel's news. Her thoughts were interrupted as their waitress placed an elegant array of oysters between them.

"You know better than to listen to Mai. She's drama personified." Rob's expression conveyed complete dismissal of anything so far fetched. "Put it out of your mind and enjoy these perfect oysters." He raised his glass in a toast meant to finish the topic once and for all.

Amanda was torn between a desire to put the issue aside and a longing for some disclosure of the more pressing concerns coloring her mood. She compromised. "I know that's generally true, Rob, but it's unheard of for Mai to have any hesitation about traveling anywhere. Not for herself or for me." Amanda forced a light tone of dismissal. "I guess it stayed with me." Glancing up, she quickly bit back any further revelation as one of her Filipino clients walked in and discreetly smiled her way. The Bristol Cove was fast filling up with the power-lunch crowd, more eager to land the deal than enjoy the excellent bouillabaisse. A whiff of the large bowl being placed on the table beside them brought Amanda back to the world of their physical surroundings.

The dramatic view of San Francisco Bay was accompanied by the lapping sound of water hitting the pilings that supported the restaurant. The staggered levels of table seating assured everyone a captivating view. It also guaranteed each a good look at his or her fellow diners and, with the room's excellent acoustics, a good chance to eavesdrop on conversations. Amanda was unable to curb Rob's next comment.

"You know your Filipino clients look after you from the moment you arrive until your departure. As long as you're scrupulous about handling your business dealings in the Philippines with discretion, you can forget Mai's off the wall omen." He put his glass down as he raised his voice. "Call Manila and check with Miguel or Paco so you can put your mind at ease."

Amanda winced. Her client's names seemed to reverberate throughout the room. "I'm sure you're right." She'd pointedly lowered her voice. "Let's change the subject. Let's talk about you." It was his favorite subject, guaranteed to defuse the moment. "I hear you're working on a big debt-equity swap in Mexico. How'd you manage that?" Her voice took on an added level of encouragement.

Rob took the bait. He began a complete recap of the negotiations. "That situation last week with HM Capital had me thrown for a minute. It looked as though we might be relegated to the also ran category but I came up with new structuring no one could resist." Rob actually licked his lips as he relished the memory. "The guy from HM didn't know what hit him. I had to argue my case with senior management for dropping our offer so low, but with the compensating balances I tied up, we'll be profitable." He grinned as he speared the last oyster. "This deal should attract more such business to the bank."

Rob was momentarily interrupted as the waitress cleared away their appetizer and took their entrée order. As he continued to explain its intricacies, Amanda focused her thoughts on his intensity. For Rob, deal making was an almost holy pursuit, the art of negotiation demanding more skill than composing a concerto. The motto of the day in the banking world was: To win is all. It seemed to apply, not only for Rob and the banking world, but also for many of the new breed of businessmen.

Amanda's sea bass was delectable, white and flaky to the fork, a fitting testament to the success of the restaurant. She enjoyed each mouthful, savoring the artfully arranged baby squash and leeks that surrounded it.

Rob hadn't let his bouillabaisse interfere with his build up to the successful conclusion of his story. His eyes flashed as he cut to the chase, exulting at the response of senior management to his success in landing the business.

Amanda leaned into his gaze, drawn by the aliveness radiating from him, but heavy with her own remorse at not feeling heart-sinking, joyous warmth in response.

Rob's voice broke into her reverie. "You know the new guy I told you about-- Lyle Carter? He's coming up for his first inspection tour of his Northern Empire. How about I try to line him up for lunch, just the three of us? It'll give you a chance to size him up." The playful Rob suddenly vanished. A hint of worry colored his expression as his tone deepened. "Rumors are flying hot and heavy about his arrival on the heels of Dave Edward's sudden departure. Everybody's anxious to know what's up."

Sensing his intent to expand his own take on the puzzle, Amanda rushed in. "I'll have to get back to you on that. Nigel's in town." She bit back their chairman's name; "I may be spread pretty thin."

"Nigel certainly keeps you on a short leash, if you ask me. And speak of the devil." Rob nodded in the direction of the entryway.

Amanda turned to follow his glance, surprised at the sight of Nigel. He was accompanied by someone who was turned away. She decided it had to be the man he was interviewing for the job in the Caymans. She swiftly turned her head back towards her plate, hoping Nigel would be steered in the opposite direction and not notice her.

No such luck. She cringed as she heard Nigel's voice ring out. "Rob Bennet." Nigel moved towards them. "This place must be as good as they claim if you're lunching here." He turned a pleased look of discovery spreading over his face as he said: "And Amanda, how fortunate." Amanda looked up, pasting on a weak smile. "There's someone here who's anxious to meet you." Nigel gave a slight half turn to allow his companion center-stage. "Amanda Evans, Derek Ashton, the new manager of our Cayman Islands Group."

A hand was extended in which two of Amanda's could disappear. She mumbled a response to his "So good to meet you." Dark hair, cut somewhat long in the European style, emanated a seductive whiff of cologne as he leaned down to shake Amanda's hand. She felt a slight rush of vertigo, grateful for a moment to fully take him in as he turned away to be introduced to Rob.

Derek Ashton was tall, much taller even than Rob. He not only had the height, but the breadth of his shoulders filled his expensively tailored suit. His bearing suggested someone more suited to stepping off the cover of the latest Gothic romance novel than into any bank. A sudden cleft in his chin appeared as he turned and smiled at Amanda.

*God, did he just ask me something*, she wondered? "I'm sorry, Mr. Ashton. Will you repeat that?"

"I asked if the news of our upcoming trip hit you as surprisingly as it did me."

"Our upcoming trip?" Amanda's jaw dropped as she turned to Nigel. "OUR upcoming trip?"

"Hold everything." Nigel fidgeted, turning to glance at the waiter patiently holding out a chair at a table nearby. "I'll explain everything after lunch—say three o'clock in your office." His sheepish haste to leave was aborted by the ice in Amanda's steady glare. Recovering his balance, he turned to aim his parting shot. "Sorenson thinks it's a good idea for you to have a partner."

*"Partner" be damned*, Amanda thought as she watched Nigel firmly walk away. Derek glanced back with an upraised eyebrow and gave a slight shrug before turning to respond to something Nigel had said. "Baby-sitter" is more like it. Amanda felt a heavy wariness overtake her.

# THREE

Rob's voice broke her silence during their walk back to the office. "Some 'partner' if you ask me. I'm not sure how I feel about your heading to the Philippines with that guy." For one brief second Amanda thought, in spite of his lightness, that Rob may care for her more than she suspected him to be capable of. His next comment punctured that balloon. "So what gives with Sorenson so involved?" A real energy colored his voice as he leaned in for the whole story.

"Sorenson involved?" She grinned up at him with a look of incredulity. "Hardly; Nigel was just passing the buck to cover for his having blindsided me." Rob's disappointed but resigned expression told her he'd bought it. As they approached one of the bank's waiting elevators, Amanda felt grateful that it was packed with the after-lunch crowd.

"Get back to me about lunch with Lyle Carter?" She nodded her agreement in farewell as he squeezed through the door's closing at his floor.

Amanda hurried out of the elevator at the next stop, quickly curving towards the ladies room before anyone could corral her.

Glancing in the mirror she was surprised that her dark, willfully unruly hair, needed little taming. The wild surges of her morning should show some outward effects, she thought, as she hastily dabbed on lipstick and headed towards her office.

Sitting down at her desk she began riffling though the little green slips of phone messages. Karen popped her head in the door. "I have your travel agent on hold. She's confirming your hotel reservations. Are you staying at the Mandarin in Manila and the Regent in Hong Kong?"

"Mandarin, yes, but our new client, Mr. Wong, insisted that I try the Shangri La next time I'm in Hong Kong." Amanda hesitated, the memory of her surprise 'partner' intruding. "Go ahead and book it if it's available. If not, let me know."

Karen nodded. "Will do." Her smile, as she turned to leave, conveyed a 'business as usual' relief.

"Thanks, Karen. And hold all my calls for the rest of the afternoon."

Amanda frowned, wishing she could have been as easily sold on business as usual. She picked up a hefty stack of Client Identification Forms and files that Karen had placed on her desk. She felt her anxiety build. One forty-five, she thought, and Nigel due back at three o'clock.

Focusing with a vengeance, the balance of the afternoon was spent pouring over her Client Profiles. She grimaced at the number of clients that came across as sketchy under scrutiny. Repeated notations such as, "Referred to IPB-SF by Brad Gregory, Manager of Manila Office", "Prominent in the Philippines", "Various business interests,", "Known to—so-and-so, who has two million on deposit with FAB", etc. All seemed damning in their brevity. More damning yet was her sense that one of them may well be linked to Fernando's money laundering scheme. Most owned, or were involved with, several businesses-- but all of them completely legitimate? The more she looked the more they appeared, not just sketchy, but a long way from God. The memory of Nigel's edict made her glance at the clock.

She was startled to see it was nearly four with still no sign of Nigel. Amanda picked up the phone's intercom line. "Karen, any calls from Nigel?"

"Yes, but he said not to interrupt you." She laughed. "Actually he said, "Tell her to keep at it until seven AM tomorrow."

"Seven AM?"

"He said he'll be in at seven to go over them with you before he departs for LA." Karen studied Amanda's solemn look. "About your Sorenson meeting this morning..." Karen hesitated, before she blurted out a worried, "It was OK, wasn't it?"

"I'm sorry, Karen. Step in my office and I'll fill you in with whatever I can."

Amanda swiftly decided to tell that part of the truth that was soon to be evident. She replaced the receiver and closed the last of her files. Karen walked in, tablet in hand.

"What's up?" Amanda turned away from Karen's direct but guileless look.

"I haven't had time to absorb it all myself. "Amanda deliberated over her next words. "You've heard about Nigel's search for someone to head up the Caymans?" She waited as Karen stood silently at attention. "Well, he's found someone, right here in San Francisco. Nigel arranged for this fellow, Derek Ashton is his name, to meet with him." Amanda rushed to keep at bay the shadow of disbelief stealing over Karen's expression. "We can expect Ashton to come round, maybe as soon as tomorrow, to meet the staff. It seems they may want me to take him along on my Manila trip."

"Hire in one day and leave Saturday for Manila?" Karen raised an eyebrow. "That only gives him three days to get a visa." Her quizzical stare challenged Amanda.

"Somehow I don't think that's a problem." She decided to emphasize the positive spin running through her mind as she reviewed her client ID forms. "His knowledge of offshore trusts and companies should be a big asset." Amanda's words were delivered with a disarming smile. "Anyway that's it; nothing to be concerned over."

Karen gave a wry look and shrugged, seemingly deflected by Amanda's response. "Great. Oh, and the Shangri La is confirmed." As she turned to go she handed Amanda three green phone messages. "These just came in."

Amanda laid aside the one from Vivian Nova who said she'd call her at home tonight. She frowned as she stared at the remaining two. One was from Brad Gregory, manager of their Manila office, and the second from Miguel Santos, a client also in the Philippines. Pretty early in the morning, Manila time, she thought as she glanced at her clock, picked up the phone and began to dial.

She counted on Brad Gregory to put a more realistic spin on the news of the day. While she couldn't come right out with it, knowing the danger of tapped phones in the Philippines, she hoped she could tease out of him any knowledge of United Bank's fiasco in the Philippines. It definitely would go a long way to reassure her if sophisticated, smooth, unflappable Brad made light of it.

Doubtless he couldn't discuss the money laundering scandal, but she'd at least probe him for an update on the general situation in the Philippines. As manager of the Manila office, he'd know if things were heating up politically. The Philippine press in the U.S. gave mixed messages. "A surprise coup was in the works", or, "Marcos will prevail". She hoped to get a full update from Brad, especially on the NPA. The New Peoples Army was a Communist rebel force sprinkled throughout the islands. It was rumored to be growing in opposition to Marcos' rule and, if not the trigger for a coup, one of the biggest sources of unrest. Right now the NPA seemed small potatoes compared to her becoming enmeshed in money laundering. She counted on Brad to have some answers.

She listened to the unending ring of Brad's phone, hesitating before hanging up and dialing Miguel.

The line crackled its threat to go dead. Just as Amanda moved to disconnect she heard Brad's voice—faint, but there. She rushed full tilt. "Brad? It's Amanda here, returning your call. Something's happened and…"

The emptiness of any response silenced her. Brad's voice finally penetrated, "Amanda? Amanda? Are you there?"

Amanda hesitated at the sudden thought that his private line might be tapped. "Brad, I… I mean, I just wanted to..."

"Stop right there. Without spelling it out I know your concerns. Mine are equally strong." An endless moment of silence passed before he continued. "The United story is all over Manila. We're under a microscope. I wanted to let you know upfront that I intend to call Nigel and urge him to cancel your trip. There's simply too much at risk."

"It's not like you to sound so, so...." Before Amanda could finish her thought, Brad interrupted.

"Don't underestimate the seriousness of this business. Any U.S. bank in Manila, with private banking reps, must lay low until this blows over."

"But..."

"But nothing; take it from me—that definitely means canceling your trip."

Amanda held the receiver away at the volume of Brad's response. As it waned, she enunciated slowly: "Sorenson doesn't agree."

"What?" Brad's voice held a mix of disbelief and...something else. She listened closely, hesitating to call it fear. "He can't mean it. Nigel's got to talk him out of such a risk."

"You really think...?"

"Trust me. It's too dangerous. I must reach Nigel immediately. Goodbye." His disconnect was so abrupt that Amanda hadn't time to let him know that Nigel was in San Francisco.

Amanda slowly replaced the receiver, stunned by the intimidation in Brad's voice. His response convinced her that she needed to talk to Miguel. Miguel Santos was more like a brother than a client, a brother light in spirit, big in heart and as savvy as they come. He adored Amanda, and the feeling was mutual. She could hear Miguel's laugh at anything or anyone in Manila representing any danger to her. She held that thought to deflect her growing anxiety. Without hesitation she dialed Miguel's number. The ringing seemed as interminable as her call to Brad. As she once again was about to replace the receiver, a voice sounded.

"Hello? Is anyone there? Who's calling?" The voice sounded unusually abrupt.

"Miguel? It's Amanda here." Amanda paused, not at all certain from the tone of voice that it may not be someone else who had answered.

"Amanda? I'm sorry. I was on my way out to the car when I thought I heard the phone." His tone softened. "It's good to hear your voice."

"Thanks for returning my call. I'm counting on you to fill me in on the situation over there. My trip's being readied, but I'm getting feedback that…" She hesitated, suddenly registering his opening comment. "I'm sorry Miguel. You're on your way out. I'll call you at a better time."

"My people will wait' remember?" Miguel's emphasis chided her lack of memory of Filipino time. "I'm more concerned by the anxiety in your voice."

Amanda hesitated, phrasing each word carefully. "Brad thinks I should postpone my trip. He says the situation's too volatile." Amanda waited into the silence for Miguel's expected guffaw, finally adding, "Can you give me any encouraging words?"

Miguel's response lacked its dependable lightness. "What can I tell you? The atmosphere here is more tense than usual. Everyone's wondering who's leading in this dance between Marcos and the U.S. If it were just Reagan it would be a sedate and gentle minuet sweeping Ferdinand right back into another long stay in Malacanang Palace. Rumors are growing, however, that a couple of factions may cut in, changing the tune, if not ending the music."

Miguel's metaphor drew Amanda up short, reminding her that he wasn't speaking to her from his apartment in San Francisco. "Miguel, can you talk?"

"Last I looked this phone was clean, Amanda. But, with the Philippine Phone Company currently controlled by one of Marco's cronies, who knows what kind of electronic tabs they're keeping on me. I say come ahead. I can put you in the picture more fully then. Meantime, don't you be losing any sleep over the endless soap opera here. It's nothing that can affect you."

"I know I must sound a bit paranoid, but... Amanda halted, "Anyway, you don't know how happy the thought of seeing you makes me. Forgive my interrupting you."

"No worries. I'm on stand-by if you need a trusty airport shuttle service. Let me know. Ciao." Miguel hung up.

Amanda stared at the phone. Relief at Miguel's closing note of reassurance fast faded, leaving frustration and shock in its wake. A chill went through her as she realized that no one could, or would, level with her.

* * *

Her journey home was made in a paralysis of highway hypnosis. As she exited the off-ramp to the Marina District she released a long drawn out breath. Her apartment was one of six in a patrician old building, just three houses up from the harbor, near the Palace of Fine Arts. The prominent curve of its graceful cupola hove into view. She felt a little frisson of peace. After her evening run she often sat among the gardens, soothed by the weeping willows, serene pond, and friendly ducks. No run tonight she decided as she pulled into her garage. To be alone within the comforting confines of her home was all she wanted right now.

She paused as she entered her apartment, casting her glance about as though seeing it through a stranger's eyes. It greeted her with its casual mix of comfortable furnishings and islands of clutter. She headed towards an overstuffed sofa of rich cranberry and gold chintz, easing into its piled up pillows. Letting out a sigh, she continued her scrutiny. A worn leather chair drawn up to a passable copy of a Biedermier desk brought a smile. Its beauty was nearly covered by stacks of papers, but the scent of flowers emanating from the colorful bouquet it held, filled her nostrils. Impatient at being ignored, the piece de resistance in the room languidly met her eyes with its golden ones, stretched out one paw and yawned.

Amanda's beautiful, longhaired, calico cat was the love of her life. Never having been allowed such a pet in her childhood ('too messy, killers of birds'), she adored and was adored by her furry roommate. Fortunately Oedipus was also adored by her next-door neighbor, who lovingly tended to him in Amanda's absence. Better than you do, he seemed to say as he gave her an accusing eye and meltingly slipped over the edge of his favorite napping spot, a large fringed ottoman that had seen better days.

She walked over and scooped him up. "Well my friend, so much for your welcome, and just when I counted on your purr therapy." She stopped to straighten a watercolor, leaving Oedipus to jump from her arms. Her walls held a few good copies of French impressionists, an original etching of a European countryside castle and a friend's self-portrait. As her glance completed the room's circuit, the realization that she needn't whisk out of sight the tumble of books on the tables, or the scrunched up lap robe that lay where it had fallen last night, prompted one long sigh of peace.

Her eyes lit on the blinking red light of her answering machine. She hesitated before pressing the play button, not willing to invite any jarring notes into her peaceful haven.

She listened to Nigel's voice booming out. She glanced at her watch. Six fifty. "Amanda, are you there? I'll see you tomorrow morning at seven. Have those client ID forms ready to go. Ashton will join us at nine thirty." She hesitated, deciding she needed a big glass of red wine right about now.

The second call was from Rob. "Amanda. Just wanted to let you know I invited Lyle Carter to lunch Friday and he's accepted. Hope you can join us. Let me know." Strange, Amanda thought, unwilling to identify the edge to his words as 'fear'.

The third message was from Vivian Nova. "Hi sweetie; I'm off for dinner with a major hunk. Call you at the office tomorrow. Big news." She waited until the machine clicked, rewound and reset, staring at it a long time, willing her disrupted peace to return.

A glass of red wine and some warmed up pesto pasta served to bolster her energies enough to return her calls. Neither was in. She left a message that she'd returned their calls and could be reached after seven AM in her office. Her initial gratitude at bypassing any long conversations failed to stem the incessant circling of her thoughts.

Their demands claimed her focus throughout the endless night, always returning to the echoes of Nigel's inference that her neck was in the noose. She was determined to see it through, baby-sitter and all. She clenched her jaw in anger at Nigel's having blindsided her on the Derek Ashton decision. For that matter, she thought, why hadn't Sorenson mentioned the likelihood during their meeting?

Still wide-awake at three AM, she took her turmoil out to the kitchen, hoping to still it with a cup of chamomile tea. The warmth of its steamy, soothing scent helped to ease her. Oedipus followed her into the kitchen and onto her lap, allowing Amanda to softly stroke his thick fur.

The action prompted her thoughts to scan for someone to act as a sounding board. But who, she wondered? Not Rob, or anyone in the bank, she decided. Apart from being cautioned against any such discussions, Rob was too caught up in his own problems. Her friend Vivi? At least Vivi would rise to the occasion, most likely suggesting an outrageous resolution. She smiled at the likely scenarios, concluding that Vivian Nova, apart from being the very opposite of discrete, was a client of sorts as well, and therefore, potentially taboo.

Her parents? They would only remind her that they didn't want her in this business anyway. Nope, she decided, not lover, family, friend, nor colleagues, and certainly not casual acquaintances.

Staring out at the night sky, stroking one 'baby' while taking ownership of another not so gentle one, she watched a brightly glowing Venus rise. Two hours later it dimmed, leaving only its dramatic memory underscoring her firm decision. She stood up, stretched and announced her vow to Oedipus and the first rays of dawn. "This is my baby alright; ready or not."

# FOUR

It was five thirty AM when Amanda pulled into the bank parking lot. Its eerie emptiness took on a surreal, film-noir image in the darkness of predawn; gray, ominously cold, and empty. Intermittent lighting cast treacherous canyons of dark shadows. Amanda warily exited the safety of her car, intently directing her vision full circle to capture any movement. Once committed, she forged ahead, dismissing the prickly feeling between her shoulder blades as she darted towards the elevator. It stopped at the lobby, a reminder that she couldn't enter her office before or after normal business hours without the guard providing special access.

Ernie, the night watchman, rushed over. "I haven't seen you at this hour in months now. Getting a head start on rolling out the red carpet for this new guy, Lyle Carter, right?"

Lyle Carter? She glanced at Ernie, forcing a smile. "Not really Ernie. I just wanted to clear the decks a bit before my next trip." Amanda managed to hold her smile just until the elevator door closed. The speed with which news got out had never ceased to amaze her.

Amanda switched on the office lights, the copier and the coffeepot, and checked the fax machine. Pages had billowed out and scattered onto the floor. She gathered them up, gave a cursory glance at the Hong Kong Office origination and dropped them on her desk.

No tea for her this morning, she decided as she prepared a cup of freshly ground Jamaica Blue Mountain coffee. She savored its revivifying impact as she reviewed the faxed messages.

She skimmed the first few paragraphs of a call report from Elizabeth Tai Li, the manager of IPB-Hong Kong. It concerned a meeting with one of Amanda's Filipino clients, Raphael, 'Raffy', de la Serna. Although most of her male Filipino clients had a nickname, Raffy seemed to fit the junior De La Serna better than Raphael. Raffy epitomized the art of the rake. Famous for his sexual prowess, he was adored by women, admired by men and forgiven by most. His family was too powerful to cross. Amanda frowned at the realization that Raffy seemed a bit too aggressive lately in moving to assume his father's mantle. He may have inherited his father's savvy, but not his integrity.

She continued to read Liz's notations on the call report: "Picked up bank statements, discussed rates, etc." Not until page two did the import of what was being said register. Raffy was involved in a real estate deal with Y.A. Chan that involved a ninety-five million-dollar sale of Y.A.'s hotel in Guam to the De La Serna group. Several of the faxed pages were copies of the sales contract, the architect's drawing, and the terms of the sale. Amanda focused on the current and intended ownership, scrutinizing just how title would be held. Both were offshore companies, one in the Bahamas and the other in the Netherlands Antilles. Looked like what was known in the trade as a 'Dutch Sandwich,' an effective use of two tax havens to obscure legal, tax, and ownership issues.

Interesting deal on the surface of it, Amanda thought, but she hoped Raffy didn't expect her bank to provide him with financing. Not even for the son of her richest client, Emilio De La Serna. She wasn't about to fight for funding on commercial real estate in Guam, not after her recent uphill battle to push through a residential real estate loan program for international clients.

She thumbed through to the last page. Raffy wanted her to bring the real estate documents. It was the urgency that caused Amanda to re-read the request. Heavily underlined, a notation to the effect that his father, Don Emilio, urged Amanda to oblige worried her. It definitely lacked credibility. A hand written addendum from Raffy was affixed to Elizabeth's thorough call report. "Amanda—please note that the condition of the sale directs that the proceeds, ninety five million dollars, be remitted to your bank until such time as we have need of them. My father insisted. He is very ill but he looks forward to your visit, as do I. Thanks for your assist."

Liz had nearly as much contact with Y.A. Chan and Raffy de la Serna as Amanda did. Her 'gut level' reaction would be meaningful. Amanda paged through again, looking for, but not finding, Liz's personal commentary. After a quick calculation, she decided to try to reach Liz at home.

On the sixth ring a breathless Liz picked up the receiver as Amanda shouted, "Hello?"

"Amanda? Finally we get to talk, even if it is at home. I just walked in the door from dinner with a client. What's up?"

"I got your fax from Raffy regarding his real estate deal with Y.A. Chan. Anything more you can tell me about it?"

"Not really. The photos of the hotel, its cash flow statement and the contract all looked routine. Raffy said his SF lawyer is drawing up the actual loan documents." She hesitated. "Is there something more behind your question?" Before Amanda could respond, Liz's voice took on a conspiratorial tone. "I mean, about your trip—you're obviously still coming. I'd have thought the arrest would have caused enough concern to postpone it."

"I'm surprised to hear you already know of it."

Liz's full-throated laugh filled the room. "You know any such news in Manila spreads fast to Hong Kong." Liz's tone segued to solemnity. "It's bound to ripple through headquarters soon. Don't tell me they aren't coming unglued back there."

"That's putting it mildly." Amanda caught herself, remembering Nigel's admonition. "I mean, naturally it's causing some fall-out, especially since it happened in the Philippines." She hesitated.

"Fall-out is putting it mildly. I'd just loved to have had a look at Nigel's face when he heard."

"He panicked, wanted to cancel my trip, but..."

"But?"

"Sorenson insists I go and business as usual."

"Business as usual, huh?" The doubt in Liz voice deepened.

"Well, except for a bit of extra digging to verify source of funds." She rushed on, uncomfortable at saying too much. "You know; flesh out the gaps in my client ID forms. You can imagine how skinny some of them are."

"Can I ever." Liz quickly turned serious. "No one in Asia is lily white and pure, certainly no one who is rich...." She hesitated before adding, "But, in terms of the Philippines, it's truly a different ball game."

"What do you mean by that?"

"A country in economic turmoil, an ailing leader, panicked politicians—all fertile ground for money laundering."

"So what do you make of this surprise arrest? What's really going on?"

"Rumor has it the whole thing is a set-up to get Reagan to take notice of Marcos and assure continued U.S. support. Just a little diplomatic strong-arming, that's all. A few days will prove it."

"A few days, right. As in during the exact time I'm there."

The silence grew. Liz responded haltingly. "You should be alright as long as you keep your eyes open and don't take any risks."

Amanda heard Karen shout out "Good Morning, early bird!" She and Liz must have been talking well over an hour, somehow ricocheting away from the initial focus of her call. She glanced at the clock: nearly seven AM.

"Back to Raffy's hotel purchase, Liz .I'm not comfortable hand delivering any kind of papers in the Philippines right now. I'll try to reach him, but, should he call you, let him know we talked and I'm happy to courier his loan docs direct to our Manila office."

"Makes sense to me."

"I'm also sending you a statement on Y.A. Chan's new account. Could you call him when it arrives?"

"Sure. I'll probe a bit, see what more I can unearth on this real estate deal. For that matter, any information I can provide on your Hong Kong clients, let me know."

"Thanks, Liz."

"You'd do the same for me. Hang in there." Liz's pragmatism was therapeutic. "See you soon." Amanda replaced the receiver firmly.

Karen popped her head in the door to let her know that Nigel arrived and had headed for the conference room to use the phone. Amanda picked up the file of copies of her Client ID forms and walked towards the conference room. Just as she was about to back away from its closed door, Nigel opened it, frowning as he motioned her in.

"Well, what did you come up with?" His question challenged her to respond in any way but "We're looking good."

Amanda sat down, spread the copies on the table and began in a matter of fact tone. "The good news is we've documented most of the deposits in terms of the banks and accounts from which they originated." She paused. He looked at her with the anticipation of one hoping for a rabbit to materialize out of a hat.

"But, as you know, large amounts transferring from solid banks don't guaranty the original source of the money as clean." Nigel jumped up, ran to a window, swung around and pierced her with a gaze of incredulity.

"Any banker knows by the time it hits a major U.S. bank, the dirty money has been tumbled with legitimate money." His delivery held an implicit "Idiot" between every word.

Amanda took a minute to pull her punches before continuing. "Right, Nigel. That's why it gets back to the only real validation is tracing money laundering at its source. The climate in the Philippines right now is exactly the time when the dirty money gang will move fast and loose for one last sweep."

"And?"

"And it should make it easier for me to separate the wheat from the chaff. If my clients are involved, now's the time it'll surface, and I'll be there to spot it."

"As long as you haven't..." He hesitated at the word 'haven't' as Amanda glared at him, biting down so firmly she feared for the enamel on her teeth. "I mean 'don't' get roped in to it."

"Haven't, don't, and won't." Her words came out like bullets. Amanda shot Nigel a look that caused him to slink into his chair and look up sheepishly. She wasn't through. "If you have any doubts on that score, why don't you come along instead of, of..."

"Instead of...?" The lilting accent caused Amanda to turn towards the partially opened door that framed the Cheshire cat grin of Derek Ashton. He slipped through, drawing the door closed and extending a hand.

She ignored it for the length of time it took to finish her statement. "Instead of a stranger, someone my clients haven't met and won't feel comfortable around." Taking a fleeting touch of his still outstretched hand, she combined the gesture with a motion towards a chair. He remained standing. Undaunted, she pressed on. "I don't mean to discount your skills, Mr. Ashton, but they can't outweigh the fact that, as you are a stranger, it's sure to silence my clients."

Nigel came to the defense. "Derek's a senior officer of Fidelity American Bank, the head of our Cayman Islands Group and your colleague. What more of an introduction could your clients ask for?"

Amanda glanced from Nigel to Derek; the one looking smugly challenging, the other amused but open. "Granted, they'll give him the benefit of a doubt. Even be eager for his products. But comfortable in leveling with him? Not by a long shot."

Nigel gave a quick look at his watch. "Smoothing that over, I leave up to you, Amanda. Derek is going." He reached for the file of client ID forms. "And so am I. I have another meeting with Sorenson at four. I can't miss my plane. I'll review these enroute." He tossed the file into his briefcase, opened the door and began heading towards the elevator. Stopping in mid-stride, he turned to catch Amanda's stare. "Stay near a phone. Sorenson may have questions."

"That's what we in Dublin would refer to as being 'in a bit of a swivet." Derek Ashton's voice took her by surprise, but not half as much as his unexpected nearness as she turned.

"Oh, well—" She was torn between defending Nigel and resisting her unwanted 'partner'. Chalking the warmth in his tones up to being Irish and well versed in 'blarney', she stiffened and pointed towards the coffeepot and pastries. "Help yourself. I'll bring in the original copies of the forms he took, along with the files. You'd better start to get acquainted with my clients."

She left him with stacks of files and walked back to her office. Hours later, he was still at it. She looked in, begrudgingly giving him credit for turning to with a seriousness she hadn't expected. "It's nearly two. I'm ordering a sandwich from the deli. Can I get something for you?"

"Thanks, no." His tone was brusque as he glanced up. Nodding down at the diminished stack of files, he moderated his explanation. "I'm getting towards the end of these and want to press on."

Derek's gaze, as he looked from her to the client files, held an intensity that caused her to feel defensive. She turned to leave, stopped by his request. "But, about these clients—" He reached for a group of files, pulling them towards him. "I'd like to go over a few things with you." Her look held him. "Sorry, I don't mean that as peremptory as it may have sounded." His Irish elfin accent was back. "Not this very minute. In fact, I have another meeting shortly, so how about sometime tomorrow?"

Amanda felt the atmosphere became pricklier as he stared, waiting for her response. "Nine o'clock, here in the conference room. We need to get started on a strategy." She turned to go, stopping abruptly as she looked down at his bulky briefcase. "Any documentation materials you have on trusts, please leave them on my desk when you go."

"Will do." He'd already turned back to his task, oblivious to the testiness of her stare at his brief response.

Undaunted, she turned her attention to the blessed numbing of mail, phone calls, rollover deposits and lots of coffee. She was too focused to glance up when her door opened. Rob's voice startled her.

"Hey you, I knocked twice. I ran into Karen in the hallway and told her I'd hand deliver your lunch." He held out a brown paper bag.

"Such intensity calls out for relief. How about you take a break for a quick cup of coffee with a friend?"

Rob's entry had pulled Amanda from the depths of concentration on the office's monthly report. Like a scuba diver surfacing too abruptly, she took a few seconds to decompress. When she did, she was shocked to discover the strange look on his face. It nowhere matched the jocular tone of his offer.

"Well, I'm really over-coffeed, but I'll share my juice and sandwich with you. Have a chair." She pointed to the small table and chairs in one corner of her office. "You look as though the roof had fallen in."

She spread out her grilled cheese sandwich, motioning for him to take a half, looking up when no move was made. Rob shook his head, released a long drawn out sigh and began. "The roof has fallen in. You know about Dave Edward's abrupt departure and replacement by Lyle Carter?"

"Yes." Amanda nodded, suddenly remembering the grapevine gossip. "Something to do with a loan loss, right?"

Rob's eyes seem to go away, lost in some internal landscape he'd never encountered before. "I tried to contact Dave at home with no luck. Yesterday the story began to leak out. It seems he was discharged over a loss of eighty million dollars on the approval of a loan that had been declined by Credit Review."

Amanda choked out her response through a mouthful of sandwich. "Not Dave; he's Mr. Straight Arrow himself. He wouldn't try to push through a declined deal."

"God, Amanda, you just don't know the pressures we're under. The name of the game is to get big deals on the books at all costs. With deregulation due to hit London soon, Dave was angling for a chance at heading up the bank's new division there. He needed to prove he could run with Europe's merchant banking hot shots, so he had to keep up the Division's totals."

Amanda studied Rob. Gone was the smooth Southern drawl confidently espousing the value of winning at all costs. His brow was furrowed, his eyes riveted into the distance. One finger nervously tapped the desktop. She rushed to reassure him. "That's all the more reason he wouldn't be so foolish as to fund a declined loan."

"Unless it wasn't declined—and it wasn't. I should know. I was in on the whole deal."

"You?"

"Me; although I wasn't in on its finalization. Still, Carter's here as a hatchet man and heads are bound to roll. Damned if I'll let one of them end up being mine."

"Yours? Why; you're the backbone of that department. That's unthinkable." She reached over to take his hand.

Rob looked through her. His face darkened and his brows scowled in dismissal of her reassurance. "Don't breathe a word of this. The grapevine's in high gear already. "

"I promise. Maybe you'll feel less anxious after your lunch with Carter tomorrow."

'That's just it. He just called me to cancel." Rob's face drained of color as he pushed his chair back and rose to leave. "Thanks for listening."

"I know it will all work out." Amanda felt the emptiness of her words, but pressed on out of frustration. "Try to get some perspective. You're a solid banker, who'll still be around when the Carter's of the world are forgotten."

Rob gave her a scathing glance. "Get real, Amanda. It's the world of the risk takers. Look around you. You don't notice many conservative bankers around any more, do you?"

Stung, Amanda knew better than to reply with anything more than an icily polite silence as she walked him out to the elevator. Rob was equally silent until the doors opened. "Right then, Amanda. I'll call you."

"Sure Rob." Shoulders squared, Amanda returned to her office. Instead of support for herself, she felt the added weight of Rob's situation.

She looked down on her half eaten sandwich and reached to sweep it into the wastebasket as her phone rang. Nigel's timing was dead center aimed to catch her testy "Hello", a brusqueness to which he proved totally oblivious. He pressed on, not letting her get a word in edgewise.

"I reviewed your client ID forms. I'm sending them back with asterisks against those that need the most work. Do what you can to shore up the holes before you go." He hesitated. "By the way, I just got off the phone with Brad Gregory. His office is off limits for any of your client meetings."

"Off limits?"

"Yes; that is, apart from his agreement to meet with you and Derek after you arrive." He rushed on, changing the subject. "How are you and Ashton hitting it off?"

"It's not about his hitting it off with me or me with him. It's about his hitting it off with the clients--- in or out of Brad's office." She paused, adding a more positive spin. "But his trust products may help us dig deeper when I get to the Philippines."

"Yes, yes, that's all fine and good. Just remember, no slip-ups. I've convinced Sorenson no dirt will land on our bank. Don't let me down."

"Rest assured I won't take any chances."

Nigel's tone took on added intensity. "Remember: our team is depending on you. One false move and Sorenson could ax the entire department. Think about it. I know I can count on your coming through for us." Nigel cleared his throat into the silence. "Well then. You've got a lot riding on this trip. Don't risk it."

Stunned, Amanda hung up the phone. "That sneaky bastard. He really has my number", she said out loud. Although her jaws had clenched, her eyes were opening. A pattern was beginning to take shape. Images from the past superimposed themselves on current relationships, "There's a good girl, Annie; don't upset your father", "Don't you dare." "Consider others." "We're all counting on you."

"Here you go." Derek's voice pulled her out of her reverie. She stared as he walked over and placed a packet of documents on her desk. "Your homework for the night; I expect you to have it memorized by morning."

"What?"

His hand moved in a slight salute. "Now, now; not so stroppy." He grinned and turned away. As he walked off her hands tightened into a grip strong enough to suddenly snap her pen in half. "Damn" she spoke it louder than she thought.

"And now you're talking to yourself. Shall I reserve the little white jacket?" Karen's entrance and comments short-circuited Amanda's intensity. "You didn't let Nigel get to you, did you? Or this Mr. Ashton?"

"Sorry, Karen, I didn't hear you enter. I will take a lot more than Nigel's frenzy to push me over the edge. She intentionally slid over the "Mr. Ashton" part. "What's up?"

"Vivian Nova is on the line."

"I'll take it, along with another cup of coffee please." Karen rushed off as Amanda reached for the phone, forcing some brightness into her voice.

"Vivi; where are you? I got your messages yesterday."

"I'll explain everything. I'm right around the corner at the Hyatt Regency. I'm meeting with a client in ten minutes, but how about dinner at 'Entré Nous', say six o'clock? We can get well lubricated before I let you in on my big news."

"Everything's big news with you, Viv." Amanda laughed. "Can't you tell me over the phone?"

"No. Just say you'll be there."

"Sure. I'll be there. I'm ready for just that kind of a break."

"Great. Six it is then, at ' Entré Nous'. Ciao!"

Karen entered, placing a cup of coffee and a copy of Amanda's itinerary on the desk. "I've confirmed your flights and most client calls verified." Karen hesitated, a frown coating her features. "Except for one; I couldn't reach Emilio de la Serna."

"Not to worry Karen. I'll call soon after I get there."

Karen hesitated as she turned to leave. "I never thought I'd feel like giving La Nova a hug, but I owe her. She's managed to bring a smile to your face."

Amanda's smile broadened as Karen closed the door. A generous comment, she thought, given that Karen thought Vivi a prima donna times ten. Amanda tried chalking Vivi's bold, brassy, bossy manner with Karen to 'cultural differences', but Karen wasn't buying it.

No matter, Amanda thought. She counted on dinner with Vivi to pull her out of a sudden lethargy. As much as she'd tried to put a good face on it, she was worried. A bubbly conversation with Vivi should take her out of herself. She returned to categorizing her client ID forms as "Passable', 'Borderline' and 'Downright Invisible'. Amanda was still going at top speed when Karen's voice reminded her of the time.

"I'm out of here. It's nearly quarter to six. Best not to let the Brazilian Bombshell cool her heels waiting."

"Right you are, Karen. She's apt to be whisked away. Another few minutes with these files and I'm off. Good night."

Amanda readied her client's files to lock away, when something struck her. The De La Serna file was missing. She jumped up to see if Karen, or perhaps Mai, still remained in the office. Silent, lights out, desks empty, drawers locked, no one around.

Looking in any unlocked desks or credenzas, she remembered Mai's mention of the Guam hotel deal and concluded that Mai had some need of it. She determined to put it out of her mind until morning or she really would be 'stroppy' by Friday.

Karen's joking comment was more prescient than she knew, Amanda thought as she walked into 'Entré Nous" to find Vivi surrounded by the cocktail hour crowd or, at least the masculine half.

"Darling." Viv made way through her admirers, kissing Amanda on both cheeks, and holding her at arm's length for a long look. "What happened? You look ghastly."

Viv, on the other hand, looked radiant, Amanda thought. Her hair, a newly white-blond, shoulder length fall of sheen; her skirt and sweater expensive and beautifully cut to mold a figure made for film. Her smile was oversized as if still focused on the camera's audience. As the star of "Viva Vivi" in Brazil, she'd mastered all her best angles. Although 'curves' was more the operant word, Amanda thought, observing the entire room's focus. Vivi's successful television show was long since discarded, 'my former life darling,' in favor of her current role as a successful designer of women's lingerie.

"Thanks, Viv. If we can find a quiet corner I'll fill you in."

Amanda sipped her glass of wine slowly, editing any full revelation of what lay behind her own, was-it-really-that-frazzled-look.

"I've been thrown a bit of a curve. My trip to Manila is going to be more challenging than I'd expected. I'm leaving Saturday and..." Before she could elaborate about having a new employee along on the trip, Vivi broke into a squeal of delight.

"Great! That's just perfect." Vivi reached over and took her hand.

"What makes that 'just perfect'?"

"My Texas client wants me to fly to Hong Kong to meet their design team. I'll have to be there a couple days, so I can meet you in Manila. Just think of the fun we can have. We'll set Manila on fire!"

"Fun! Sorry, Viv; but put the idea out of your head. There's no room for fun on this trip. It's all business from the second I land to the second I leave."

"Well then, you can introduce me to some of those Filipino textile gurus and I'll place some orders for my fabrics." She paused to emphasize her point. "See. It'll mean more business for you, right?"

"It's out of the question. I'm going to have a new bank employee along." Amanda watched as Vivi set her little chin in a pleading moue of disbelief.

"Don't be such a party pooper. Live for now is what I always say." Seeing the look in Amanda's eyes as she squared her shoulders, readying her response, Viv hesitated. She glanced around as she raised her voice. "OK, I'll drop the subject for now; but just think it over, sweetie. It couldn't be more perfect timing."

* * *

Amanda couldn't stop thinking about it during the drive home. Derek Ashton was baggage enough. All she needed was Viv to show up in the midst of an already incendiary trip. In spite of Amanda's firm reply, "No way, Viv, and no need to think it over. It can't happen this trip, timing or not", she felt the knot in her stomach grow. Amanda knew Vivi well enough to remain nervous. With anything Vivi wanted, she was like a dog with a bone.

# FIVE

"How many of these annual reports do you need to take for your trip?" Karen placed her armload of materials onto the table. Amanda smiled at the pride Karen took in preparing everything just so. Her smile dimmed as she remembered Brad's refusal to allow her any use of his Manila office for client meetings.

"Let's try to lighten the load a bit this time. Annual reports are better left behind except for those sent on to Hong Kong. Do we need to buy any gifts?"

"We're all right in the gift department." Karen delivered her announcement with a little extra punch. "We had four hundred dollars remaining in last year's marketing allotment." She smiled a broad 'cat that ate the canary' smile. "When the memo came out about cuts in this year's marketing budget I stocked up on chocolates, and scotch. That big carton in the stock room should supply your next couple of trips."

"What would I do without you?" Amanda watched as Karen turned back to remove the annual reports. She thanked the day she'd hired her. She was small, attractive, spoke both Mandarin and

Cantonese, and somehow quietly present as part of the team from the first day, turning out to be efficient and cheerful as well. Karen's annual salary review was due out next month. That was one budget that wouldn't be cut.

Karen turned with a smile in the direction of the diminished stacks. "These should be much more manageable." She paused as a serious, listening intensity suddenly erased her grin. "Hmm; I think someone's in the reception room. If it's Mr. Ashton, he's early." She hurried away to greet whoever it was.

Amanda rummaged through her desk for the list she'd made of her most likely prospects for trusts. She wanted Derek to review those client files first. Her search proved fruitless. The contents of her desk, like the rest of her, she thought with a wry grin, had somehow begun to go slightly out of sync. She found it just as her phone rang. "Mr. Ashton is here to see you, Miss Evans. Shall I show him in?"

"Stall him if you can. Offer him coffee or tea and some of those croissants I picked up from 'Le Patisserie.'" Amanda replaced the receiver, grateful for a few minutes to compose herself. She'd just time to draw a breath and arrange her notes when the door opened.

"Thanks for your offer of coffee, but I've had my daily quota hours ago. I even brought bagels as a peace offering." Derek held out a large white pastry sack. He seemed to fill the doorway. "I'm ready to get down to work." Derek's words went right over her head. Her visual senses were so fully engaged that she stammered as she offered him a chair.

Amanda stared, trying to remember when, or even if, she had ever seen a man so impeccably dressed. His suit looked expensive; but almost too studied, she thought, staring at the silk pocket-handkerchief.

Quickly composing herself, she turned toward the credenza and picked up her files. She halted, momentarily thrown by the sight of the "De la Serna" file on top, wondering how and when Mai had replaced it. "These are the clients I'd like you to review first." She hastily shoved the files into his hands, remembering Mai was on client calls in San Jose for the day. "Let's go into the conference room and I'll give you a rundown on each client." As Derek took the files from her hands, she ignored the hot-cold feel of her flesh as his hand made contact.

Derek seemed not to notice. His manner was totally professional as he headed towards the conference room. "Let's get down to business." He sat down, opened a file and began to read. Amanda sat quietly, observing his intense focus. His eyebrows went up slightly, mouth pursed as he turned the pages.

"Just what do you mean by the statement that 'Chi-Chi' Amparo is one of the uncrowned kings of the Philippines?" Derek gave her an inquiring look. "I'm sure it has meaning for you, but I need clarification in terms of what that would mean in our discussions with him."

"Well, the gossip in the Philippines is that Chi-Chi has become very close to Imelda Marcos ever since her husband has taken ill." Amanda looked up from the file as Derek threw back his head and let out a full-throated laugh.

"What, and not the handsome U.S. actor the tabloids have such fun publicizing?" Amanda smiled, surprised at Derek's awareness of some of Manila's more titillating gossip.

"Hardly—although I hear they may have business dealings with some of the wealthy Americans he introduced her to." Amanda decided to use this opportunity to give Derek a sense of the culture and its love of rumor. "In the Philippines it's hard to separate the truth from the tales. Filipinos love gossip. They can take a germ of truth and dramatize it beyond any semblance of reality. Each new rendition adds a further embellishment according to the skill of the teller. Every Filipino wants the reputation of possessing the highest wit." She looked to see how Derek was digesting such information. His look was unreadable. "You'll see." She smiled at the image of the crowd at the cocktail lounge of the Manila Peninsula where the art was most eagerly practiced.

"If that's the case, how do you decide who's telling the truth and who isn't?" He looked at Amanda with a penetrating stare that disconcerted her. "You've described all of your clients, Marcos cronies or opposition, in a favorable light. Aren't there any bad guys in your book?"

Amanda hesitated. "How can I pass judgment? So much of what I've seen and heard is admirable."

"How admirable can it be to contravene the laws of a country by removing millions of dollars?"

Amanda hesitated, her cheeks flaming at his remark. "I can't answer for their actions." She lifted her chin higher as she locked his eyes with her steady stare. "As for my own involvement, I had difficulty at first with the moral aspects. The bank's explanation was more pragmatic. They reminded me that neither the bank nor I were involved in taking money out, but only in providing accounts for those wanting to remit funds." Amanda watched Derek's impassive face as he listened and waited. "It was the clients themselves that convinced me that removing their family's assets was the only moral position to take in a country with such an immoral government."

Derek stared out the window. Amanda recalled the anguish she'd experienced in arriving at such a rationale. Most of her clients made light of politics whatever side they supported. They all agreed that the political situation left them no choice but to remove assets to the U.S.. She looked up to find Derek studying her with a questioning look to his fixed gaze. She rushed to qualify her explanation. "I know when the government changes they'll reinvest the money back into their country."

"In one breath you tell me all of your clients are saints, even the ones involved in the current government. In the next, you say the actions of the Philippine governing body are immoral. Which is it? Isn't the government made up of responsible human beings, some of them your customers? These clients of yours are the most prominent families in the Philippines. Who, if not they, are accountable for the imbalance in that country?" Derek stood up abruptly, took a stride towards the door, turned on his heels and stared at Amanda with a look of disdain. "There are so many poor, so few middle-classes, and so much wealth—all in the hands of these same families. Why, it reminds me of the Southern gentlemen of your Civil War. How noble and gracious they were as they lived so opulently by the sweat of their slaves."

Derek's voice had risen. He fought to bring it under control, to lighten it with his next comment. "Oh well; who am I to say? Certainly Great Britain's problems and politicians are not above reproach. I was just trying to understand how a country such as the Philippines, whose people you describe as warm and caring, can have so many problems. I guess I'll have to reserve judgment until I see the situation firsthand."

Amanda's look had darkened. She jumped to the defense of her clients. "Where do you get off being so holier than thou? You're in exactly the same type of business, eager to go there and convince all of the country's corrupt rich to hide their money with you in the Caymans."

Derek's grin widened. "Guilty as charged. You win. Mea culpa. What say we declare a truce and I treat you to lunch in Sausalito? I promise you the only conversation allowed will be of your beautiful city." With that he gave a slight stretch and walked over to the window. "It's a great day for a ride on the ferry."

Damn, Amanda thought, it was hard to be angry with him, even while still simmering at his unexpected indictment. "Count me out. Since we're leaving tomorrow, I'm working straight through until time to go home and pack."

"Right, then; and I'll continue reviewing these files." His all-business face was back as he returned to his notes, looking up as she left to add, "We'll have fifteen hours of flight time to go over these."

Amanda quickly found herself embroiled in a last minute check of everything she would take with her as well as everything being forwarded. Satisfied she'd pared back to the minimum and her monthly report was completed, she glanced at the clock. It was nearly four. She wandered out into the lobby area to find Karen. "Is Ashton still hard at it?"

"No. He took a call and ran out the door around one thirty. But he left this though." Karen held out a sandwich, with a look that said it all. "He said to let you know that he had an appointment and would see you tomorrow at the airport."

Amanda shrugged as she handed the sandwich back to Karen. "Why don't you call it a day and head for home?" She picked up two large envelopes; one marked 'Hong Kong' and one 'Manila'. She held them out to Karen. "On your way out would you place these into the courier mail?"

"Sure. That reminds me, something just came in." Karen stepped out, returning with a packet marked 'Personal and Confidential'. One look told Amanda it was Raffy's real estate documents. She motioned to Karen.

"Hold off sending the courier mail while I attach a note to Brad." Amanda jotted a brief, 'Call Raffy for personal pick-up' message, attached it to the front of the packet and inserted it into Manila's courier mail.

"That should do it."

"You sure there isn't anything more I can do?"

"Nothing, thanks. Just head on home and have a fun weekend. I appreciate everything you've done. I'll call you at the office on Monday."

Karen gave Amanda a quick look of concern as she turned away. "Try to get some sleep on that long flight. Good luck."

Amanda wrote a brief list for Mai to follow up on some loose ends on Monday. Satisfied that her materials and itinerary were in order, she turned to the notes on her calls. She'd made enigmatic and, hopefully indecipherable, notes regarding information she needed to supplement her client ID forms. A long, drawn-out yawn persuaded her to wrap things up and head for home. Locking the conference room door, she frowned in puzzlement over Derek's having left so abruptly, without a word to her.

The slow Friday night drive home allowed too much time for thoughts to circle endlessly in a futile quest to try to identify her nameless uneasiness. When she finally reached home, a long bath, a light dinner and a few phone calls were all she had energy for. Sleep ambushed her the minute her head hit the pillow.

Saturday flew by, consumed with last minute minutiae. She tided the house, prepared a care package to give to the cat sitter and double-checked her packing. Satisfied everything was accomplished, she rang Rob to confirm his offer to take her to the airport.

"Oh, right; we're having dinner." He hesitated, his voice absent-minded, as though he was fumbling for something. "Our reservation isn't until seven. I'll come by at six thirty."

Funny, Amanda thought, frowning as she hung up the phone. He gave the distinct impression he'd totally forgotten dinner and her flight. She tried to put it out of her mind. The phone rang as she moved her last piece of luggage into the entryway. Derek Ashton's voice rang out with a brisk and breezy message to let her know that he'd be tied up until departure, but not to let the plane leave without him. She hung up, suddenly appreciating Rob's steady reliability.

* * *

Rob was reliable but silent during their short drive to 'Ernie's.' It wasn't a companionable silence. If Amanda didn't know any better, she would have described his emotional tone as 'surly'. Whatever it was, he wasn't responding to her attempts to make conversation. She began to take it personally.

"What's wrong? It's not like you to be so quiet."

Rob's look silenced her. His jaw was clenched and his eyes were focused so far inward that any assumption of her involvement was made trivial. His hands gripped the steering wheel with such force as to graphically demonstrate the term 'white knuckles'.

Her repeated words finally penetrated his total preoccupation. He made a conscious effort to focus his attention. His usual sparkling blue eyes were as cold and gray as leftover winter snow. An almost malevolent aspect quickly vanished as he noticed her beside him. "It's not you, Amanda. It's this Carter business." With that, he completely disappeared into whatever avenue of thought his last comment presented.

Shocked to find themselves so quickly at 'Ernie's', Rob pulled into a parking spot in the garage alongside and sat staring into the distance. Amanda halted her move towards opening her door.

"Look Rob, we don't have to have dinner. We can go directly to the airport. They feed us shortly after take off anyway. I can't enjoy dinner with you off somewhere in your private pain."

"Oh God, Amanda, I'm sorry. I promise you a rain check." Rob's relief shone through his whole being as he turned towards her. "You pick the place; anywhere you like. Right now I need time to sort this situation out." A swift U-turn out of the restaurant's parking lot accompanied Rob's words.

Before she could reply, they were headed up the on-ramp of the freeway and towards the airport. Amanda's muttered response, "Sure Rob, if you really don't feel up to it", was absorbed into the black hole of their drive. Rob's jaw was still clenched, his driving purely automatic, but skillful enough to have them quickly at the airport. With one movement he was out of the car and had flagged a porter for her bags.

Amanda knew it was useless to try to communicate but she couldn't leave for two weeks without trying to make some sort of contact. As they embraced automatically she blurted out. "Rob, anything I can do, let me know."

"Sure, sure; have a good trip. I'll call you." This last barely loud enough to register as Rob was already half way into the car. She found herself walking dazedly towards the ticket counter, surprised at not seeing the usual crowds of Filipinos lined up with huge, twine-tied cartons of personal goods awaiting the flight to Manila. She recalled her first sight of such quantity and quality of boxes. She'd feared the plane would never take off.

There was one advantage to being so early, she thought, deciding to use her gift of time to review her itinerary. Amanda headed towards the Red Carpet Club. Philippine Airlines had a shared arrangement with United Airlines.

She was buzzed into the club's hushed environs, surprised to see so few passengers waiting until she noticed the departures board. The next international flight, hers, was over two hours away. Great, she thought, the quieter the better.

Convinced a shot of caffeine might help, she carried a cup of coffee into one of the private cubicles, arranged her briefcase on the desk and withdrew her itinerary. Her usual objectives were increased deposits, but for this trip offshore trusts or companies would be her focus—at least her overt focus. She shivered at her real mandate—to verify the nature of her largest client's wealth.

Reviewing once again the features and benefits of setting up an offshore trust started her thinking of Derek Ashton. She'd been shocked at his abrupt departure yesterday, calling to say he'd meet her at the boarding gate. Derek the Devious, she thought, surprised by how skillfully his brashness obscured any real disclosure.

Apart from revealing nothing about himself, he'd never once asked for any brochures, product information, account opening documents, etc. Strange, she thought, given we're both working for the same bank and I'm actively helping him sell trusts to my clients. Why doesn't he show any reciprocity?

With these thoughts she let her mind wander away from the forms in front of her. It quickly followed a fantasy path, creating an image of what Derek's life was, had been, or might be. The thought of spending the next two weeks in close proximity sent a sudden emotion of excitement through her. She had traveled in the company of other colleagues, male and female, and, although many pleasurable dinners and drinks were shared, she always went to her room alone. Word quickly got around, establishing her reputation as 'strictly business.'

Even her relationship with Rob was totally circumspect in so far as work versus personal went. Although the grapevine was a prescient vehicle of information, no gossipy tidbits were ever bandied about at the mention of her name. Only such descriptors as, 'Great relationship manager, hard worker, pretty and friendly, but somewhat aloof and probably not political enough to crash the glass ceiling.' Knowing that there was never any slander or dirt, she intended to keep it that way.

The thought of the grapevine decided her to use it to help unmask the enigmatic Mr. Ashton. She'd have to be indirect in order to deflect suspicion of any personal interest in him. Maybe have someone else broach the subject?

As intriguing as this line of thought was, sleep overtook her. She woke with a start, barely registering the announcement: "Philippine Airlines Flight 237 to Manila is now boarding".

As she rushed to the gate, the sight of Derek Ashton brought a quick flush to her face. Amanda lowered her gaze, searching her purse for her boarding pass.

"I was about to come looking for you. I thought you might have found it hard to break away from your dinner date; maybe even decided Manila could wait." Derek smiled teasingly, took her briefcase and swiftly steered through the gangway into the Business Class section. "Quite frankly, I barely made it myself. Although I requested a seat assignment next to yours, I ended up two rows in front of you." Tucking their bags safely in the overhead, he turned to scan the coach section of the aircraft. "With my height I intend to head on back into the farthest recesses of the tourist section and pray to find an empty center row. I suggest you do the same if someone comes along and you can't curl up here and sleep."

He glanced around, lowered his voice and raised one eyebrow in mock surprise. "Strange to see so many 'holiday' travelers clustered in the Business and First Class Sections, aye?" Derek made sure that Amanda was settled in, complete with pillows, magazines and blankets. "Comfy? Great! Well, say one for me. I'm headed back to Coach. If you don't see me back here in two minutes, I've lucked out and crashed for the night. I'll look you up when they do a wake up call. Hope you can manage to get a little shut-eye, me love." Amanda glared in response. "Cat got your tongue, Mandy?" Derek said as he reached across her to grab The Economist magazine.

Amanda visibly jumped as she responded. "Let's start out on the right foot, Derek. The name is Amanda. Don't call me "Mandy" unless you don't want any response."

"Amanda is it? A bit stiff for me; but right you are; I do consider 'Mandy' too teen-age prom queen for your personality.' He looked reflective. "You strike me as much more the 'Anne' of a thousand days persona—or of two weeks, perhaps? Well, we shall see. Sleep well."

He headed away before she could respond, thinking, *So much for strategizing our joint calls. Not an auspicious beginning, given that he obviously never intended to go over them on the plane.* Resigning herself to slumber, she plumped up her pillows, positioned them behind her back and neck, stacked her magazines on the center seat and sent out vibes that no one would sit beside her. If they did, she'd pop on her headset and close her eyes.

She felt fiercely protective of this time away from everyone, free from any demands. Knowing her itinerary would be a grueling one, the sanctuary of the plane was her last cocoon of peace. She intended to keep it that way. She had little patience for passengers that assuage their anxieties by talking a mad streak to a complete stranger for the entire flight. Courtesy required she not be so totally rude as to ignore a seat partner for the entire trip. She always made a point of being interested during the last hour of flight time. Discovering a fascinating fellow traveler was rare. More often than not she was saved from endless hours of crashing bores.

So far, so good, she thought, as no one appeared to claim the seat alongside her. She let herself savor the thought of curling up for a good long sleep. She cast her eyes about for anyone on the flight she might know. Often one of her clients would be on board, although usually in First Class. She'd lucked out once and had the pleasure of experiencing the only 'beds' in any airline's First Class Section. One of the senior officials of PAL, a co-member with Amanda in the Philippine-American Association of San Francisco, happened to be on board. He had smoothed the way for her to enjoy the luxury of a nearly empty First Class. She savored the memory.

Still smiling, she turned and was startled. A man seated four rows behind her, across the aisle, was staring intently in her direction, a piercing stare of malevolence. She had the distinct feeling that he'd been involved in this focus for some time. Before she could get her bearings, he moved quickly to open the overhead bin for a blanket.

The thought of possibly knowing him, or of his knowing her, was eclipsed by the look. His expression was not one of pleasant recognition, but a fixed and undiluted stare of pure hatred. *But it couldn't be, she decided. Maybe he thinks I'm someone else. Could I have imagined it?* She took a second to glance back, feigning interest in adjusting the air vents over the top of the seat alongside of her.

Now he wasn't showing any interest in her direction at all. In fact, he was covered by the skimpy airline blanket and was turned aside in a distinct posture of sleep. *I must be hallucinating, she thought. Damn Mai's prophecies.* She snapped off her light, determined to escape such thoughts in sleep.

It was a long night, full of fitful tossing, cramped legs, constant interruptions by the dinner service, passers by, movie screenings, and the softly cheerful assistance of an attendant addressing someone close by. The more Amanda urged her body to relax and sleep, knowing the hectic pace of the day to come, the more wide-awake she became. Frustrated, she decided to cooperate with the inevitable, convincing herself that resting was as good as sleeping.

With the first blush of dawn she ventured to the galley for a cup of coffee, choosing the one in the rear of the tourist section in order to look for Derek Ashton. He seemed to have lucked out with a full stretch of seating in the center section all the way back in the rear of the plane. Amazing-- with all the commotion of early risers, he was still slumbering with the sweet abandon of a baby.

The considerate part of her was careful to keep her voice low as she accepted her coffee. The other part, which seemed to be surfacing more lately, wanted to dump the cup directly on Derek's oblivious head. On second thought, she decided to grab the opportunity to study that head. Wisps of dark-brown hair curled across a smooth un-furrowed brow, trustingly facing the cabin's roof. The area around him was unnaturally neat and tidy. His shoes were lined up just so, with not even a magazine or newspaper jammed into the seat-pocket. The anal-retentive type, she concluded.

That thought, or her fixed gaze, must have penetrated his sub-conscious. He began to move his hand up to his eyes. Amanda swiftly dashed into the nearby lavatory. She did the best she could to wash up, put on fresh make-up and ready herself for the day.

She longed for a few minutes in her hotel room after she arrived, but doubted such luck on this trip. From the moment she walked into The Mandarin Hotel in Makati on her first trip she found clients waiting for her—at seven A.M. A typical day that often didn't end until midnight. She couldn't hope for anything different this time and knew it best she prepare for the worst. Actually, past experience had shown that, once the day began it seemed to roll on quickly, erasing the worst of her jet lag. When she finally did hit the bed she'd sleep soundly enough to re-charge for the coming days.

She took one last look in the mirror before she braved Derek's Irish bonhomie. Her black and white knit suit, a 'St. John's' indulgence, had survived beautifully through her restless night. She counted on it to stand up to anything, even the heat of a Manila day. Fortunately, most of her time would be spent in air-conditioned automobiles, spacious air-cooled homes, or the Arctic-cooled air of Manila's 'In' restaurants. She smiled at the thought and exited confidently, only to run into Derek, standing in the aisle, patiently waiting his turn at the lavatories.

"Well", he said, smiling as he eyed her up and down. "You look raring to go. As soon as I match your results, I'll come up front for a run-down on our day. See you shortly." He moved forward, next in line for the WC. "If they come by with breakfast, will you order me an extra orange juice and lots of coffee? Thanks, love." Amanda bristled at his parting remark. It was, she supposed, as mindless an expression as a Yank saying, 'Thanks, guys.' But that didn't wash. The truth of the matter was that he was really beginning to irritate her before their trip had even begun. Her conviction grew that his casual insouciance, warmth and friendliness were all a front. That veneer is just too damn perfect. She determined to penetrate it.

By the time he walked up, she had her own mask of perky professionalism firmly in place. She beamed a bright smile. "Good Morning. At least, I guess its morning, although our body clocks will say differently."

"I would have thought yours was accustomed to it by now." Derek slid into the seat beside her, smiling up at the approaching attendant who cheerfully accommodated his request for double juice and triple coffee. "I travel so much I'm actually beginning to like airline coffee. My body seems to thrive at thirty thousand feet. It can't function properly without a few time zone changes each month." Noticing Amanda hadn't commented he went on. "Ah well, it's probably good for us. No time to settle into routine and get stale."

'Routine' and 'stale' were appropriate descriptors as the ghastly coffee was followed by a breakfast mummified by microwaves.

Amanda picked at her omelet, finally pushing it aside in favor of the warmed over fruit. In spite of the lackluster food, after having finished a bran muffin and forcing down several cups of coffee, she felt her disposition improve. She decided to lay the ghost of the night before by confessing her paranoia to Derek.

"Derek, did you happen to notice a man sitting across the aisle about four rows back?" she began. "Just on the left as you walked towards me. Small, a Filipino with large dark eyes, sitting alone?"

"Now why would you think I would notice anyone, and certainly not a man, when I was approaching you?" His reply was playful as usual, but she returned to her subject.

"No, seriously, he was staring at me last night in such a way that I feared for my life. I've never seen such a look of hatred. At first I thought maybe I knew him, or perhaps he mistook me for someone else. Then I decided I must have imagined it because of, of…"

"Because of what?"

"My assistant, Mai Wong Lee—you met her at the office—has been filling me with prophecies of disaster for this trip."

"Prophecies? It's too early in the morning for such balderdash."

"Anyway it's not my imagination. This morning, although I walked past him, he studiously avoided any eye contact. I mean, he deliberately lowered his face."

Amanda reacted to Derek's raised eyebrow of disbelief. "I'm not misinterpreting it. He acted like he didn't want to see me, or to be seen by me. What reason would he have to feel such animosity towards me? I've about decided to go back there and ask."

Derek's response took Amanda by surprise. Gone was his Irish rover's banter as his voice took on a commanding tone. "Amanda, whether you know it or not, you've really let this bizarre talk of Mai's get to you. You have to snap out of it. The poor guy was probably thinking of someone waiting in Manila. You admitted how passionate and emotional a people the Filipinos are. He might be headed towards a particularly hellish set-to with someone when he lands. It has nothing to do with you. It was just a coincidence that you turned to face him when the thought was going through his head. Don't let such an incident color your day." Derek's reasoning was so forceful and persuasive that Amanda began to feel like an idiot.

"You're right. I sound paranoid even to myself. The combination of Mai's comments and not enough sleep must be getting to me." She looked up as the flight attendant took their trays, turning back to Derek with a grin of relief. "I feel really foolish now."

"Well, good; those thoughts ought to help bring you back to earth. Just in time, since it looks like we're starting our approach. Before we touch down, can we go over our first couple of meetings?" Derek's switch to a more professional role provided the focus Amanda needed to chase away the thoughts, if not the emotions, as they prepared to land.

She lowered her voice as she began, "Our first client is Ambassador Antonio Ramirez, an easy first call. The ambassador goes by his middle name's diminutive, which is "Paco". He's a gentleman of the old school and one of my favorite clients. He's usually waiting when I arrive, but not this time. Paco's recuperating from minor surgery and will meet us at his home, but his car and driver will be at the airport."

"All well and good, but apart from being one of your favorite clients," he gave Amanda a look blended of tease and gentleness, "just what sort of business is this Paco involved in?"

"Several as usual; he's currently an ambassador to Spain from the Philippines, on the board of a major airline, and the chairman of a shipping company. Much of his time is spent between Manila and Madrid—actually more Madrid since the death of his wife last year."

Amanda was reminded of just how much Paco had seemed to fall apart without his wife. Where he used to look a fit forty, suddenly he seemed more like sixty, although only recently celebrating his fifty-third birthday.

"He has a son in a Switzerland finishing school and a very spoiled sixteen year old daughter who is terribly protective of him. And of her own inheritance, I suspect." Secretly Amanda thought that the best thing for Paco would be to fall in love with one of Makati's wealthy widows, maybe even re-marry. After having spent the last few years watching his wife die of cancer, he deserved happiness.

Amanda pressed on with her description. "Since his wife died, Paco has been visiting the sick, donating money to the hospitals and enlisting others to do likewise." She paused. "Paco is so kind, why..."

"Wait a minute," Derek interrupted, "you make this chap sound like a saint. I know it's important to know the personal background but do get to the money part. What does he have with you? Do you know what else he has in the U.S. or Switzerland? Any trusts?" Derek had pen poised to jot a few reminders.

"Oh God, put that pen away!" Amanda lowered her voice another notch. "I forgot to mention the most important 'Do's and Don'ts' about business in the Philippines. We need to get that covered before you leave this plane."

"Better be quick then," Derek responded as the wheels touched down on the runway. Touched and touched and finally decided to stay. Amanda's attention was distracted momentarily by the unusually precarious landing. She let out a long-held breath and continued.

"Rule Number One is 'Never take notes', or only cryptically and never with the name of a client. Rule Two is 'Never refer to their deposits or any assets whatsoever.' Leave them to decide when, where and how it shall be referred to. Rule Three is 'Never refer to any business matter over the hotel phone, or any phone.' Follow the lead of the caller, and if you are doing the calling make indirect references to meeting them. When you call the U.S. or the office never mention any business dealings." The plane jerked its way into an arrival bay. As they waited for the gangway to move into place Amanda leaned closer to Derek's ear for one last admonition. "Remember that this is a foreign exchange control country whose laws prohibit the irregular removal of money offshore. Anyone assisting such illegal activities is apt to find oneself spending time in a Manila jail."

"Hold on there. Remember that my business is offshore trusts, and these rules you mention govern my dealings with client's daily. You can depend on my observing the rules of the game. My notations would take a cryptographer to decipher." The doorway opened as passengers positioned themselves for a quick exit. Derek moved his massive bulk to fill the aisle. Reaching down to take her hand, he smiled. "Now lighten up, we're here!"

# SIX

Their approach to Manila Airport brought back vivid memories. Amanda remembered her first arrival, giant butterflies in her stomach, perspiration streaming down her face, and wrinkled linen skirt clinging to her legs. Some caused by the suffocating heat, most due to fear that the immigration agents would see through her 'tourist' disguise. Hester, wearing her scarlet 'A', couldn't have felt more graphically exposed than Amanda did as she approached Immigration. Poised to 'confess', hands anticipating handcuffs, she steeled herself for whatever Kafkaesque fate awaited corrupt foreign bankers. Anxiety grew to fear of fainting as she reached the head of the line.

The agent had routinely processed her through without so much as lifting his head from the hypnotic slap of stamp on papers. All that drama for nothing, she thought. Not one question or a 'Good Morning, Welcome to Manila' interrupted his bored routine.

Amanda had fished for a tissue to dry her dripping brow and fought back an impulse to giggle. She had walked in a light-hearted fog over to the carousel off-loading her flight's endlessly circulating luggage. Light-heartedness suddenly turned to light-headedness.

Monsoon-type heat and humidity, coupled with exhaustion and fear, sent her slumping down onto the floor's cool marble surface.

How mortified she'd felt. If it hadn't been for the grace and ease that Paco exhibited in rescuing her at almost that very second, she might never have made a second trip. He had all of the 'sure cures' close at hand. Their use, aided by her embarrassment, brought her sheepishly smiling, up on her feet. Before she could register the impact her ludicrous arrival had made, Paco had dispatched her luggage and had her resting in his cool Mercedes. What heaven to slowly sip a proffered iced kalamansi juice, letting its tart orange-lemon-lime flavor sooth her senses. Paco lessened her embarrassment by assuring her that her arrival response wasn't uncommon.

Her gauche beginning seemed funny and far away, she thought, as she and Derek made their way smoothly through Immigration and out into the baggage area. As Derek focused on each bag as it dropped, Amanda discreetly looked around to study the disembarking passengers. She wanted one more look at the man who had fixed her with such a fierce gaze, if only to assure herself that it truly was her imagination. In the broad light of day he was probably an innocuous fellow, happily being met by wife and family. She clung to that thought, puzzled when she couldn't spot him in the milling crowd around the baggage carousels.

The carousel's circling seemed to be interminable in its patient transport of endless lines of twine-tied boxes. Most boxes, Amanda learned, contained disposable diapers, miscellaneous baby products, strollers, and copious quantities of liquor. Even if duty was collected in Customs, the buyer's rationale was that the total was less than the cost of good Scotch or Bourbon in Manila. Customs agents expected to have their meager incomes supplemented by arriving Filipinos who made certain their passage through was suitably oiled with good old U.S. dollar greenbacks. Amanda wasn't quite sure how this was accomplished. Somehow it must be during the exit routine but it certainly wasn't obvious. By that stage she was keeping an eye on the exit areas, trying to spot Paco's driver. Her train of thought was broken by Derek's exclamation.

"Isn't that your bag coming around now?" Derek's tone seemed a bit abrupt and impatient. She smiled, thinking how much his British Empire efficiency was going to be put to the test in the Philippines. His luggage soon followed hers, and they quickly passed through the 'Nothing to Declare' line. They had snaked through the curving passageway into the Waiting Area when Amanda saw and heard Eduardo, one of Paco's drivers, calling her name.

"Miss Amanda, how happy I am to see you." His wide grin radiated a warm welcome as he shook Derek's hand and efficiently gathered their luggage. Soon they were seated within the cool, clean oasis of the Mercedes limousine's spacious back seat. The luxurious transport was just a sample of the good life in the Philippines.

*Damn, she thought, I didn't have a chance to look for my mystery man.* Everything had moved so fast from the moment the luggage arrived. Abandoning her concern, she rested her head against the ubiquitous doily-covered seat back. Entering the outskirts of Manila, she watched Derek's expression turn grim. Waves of repugnance washed over his face as each block of ram-shackle buildings, tumbling in motley stages of disintegration, greeted their progress. The crowning affront came as they approached Manila's morning traffic jam. At each slowing of their automobile they were approached by heart-breaking figures. Most were women and all emaciated and gray with caked dust. Many carried a ragged bundle of crying baby, which they thrust up against the windowpanes of the car.

The first time Amanda confronted such a sight, grief and sorrow overcame her. She wanted to open the window and give to each until her money was gone, but the driver wouldn't hear of such a thing. His callous explanation stung her almost as much as the sight of the poor women and children.

"You must not encourage them. They are breaking the law to approach cars in this way. Do not even look at them or they will follow our car as far as they can."

Paco had added, "I know how you feel. Manila has its poor people as does New York and every big city in the world. The difference in the people you see here is that their assumed poverty is a racket used to avoid work. The money you hand them ends up in the pockets of men whose goal isn't food. There will be opportunities for you to provide charity in more effective ways." Amanda had outwardly nodded understanding, but her anguish remained. Remembering those feelings, Amanda decided to plumb Derek's depth of compassion. "How does the poverty level here compare to what you see in the Caribbean?"

His look verged on the incredulous. "In the Caymans there is always full employment for those who wish to work. If they've completed what you would call their High School levels, they can find work in the many offices and businesses that support the financial community. Even those who do not finish school find jobs in service areas or in farming." He glared at the beggars. "Our police officials would never stand for such blatant displays of begging. These people would be behind bars in no time."

Amanda unclenched her teeth and formulated her response. "Here in the Philippines there is such a vast layer of poor whose children cannot attend school, or even have a school to attend. The struggling middle-class sacrifices everything to see their children through to the highest school levels." Derek's silence pushed her to an attempt to make him understand the culture. "Good jobs are scarce. Only those with the highest academic achievement are fortunate enough to find employment."

It suddenly dawned on Amanda that Eduardo might overhear her in spite of the glass barrier between them, bulletproof glass, itself a commentary on the current rebellion in the society. She lowered her voice with her next comment. "You and I have so much compared to these people". She looked up into the deep brown eyes and dirty face of a young boy holding a grubby pack of Chiclets against the windowpane. Impulsively, she pressed the button in order to lower the glass and hand him a U.S. dollar. Quickly several others elbowed him away, angry when Amanda's efforts were thwarted. She glanced away, shamefaced at the realization that the windows were centrally locked from the front.

They soon neared Makati, the financial hub of Manila. On first impression, from the cool confines of a Mercedes limousine, it appeared to be straight out of Southern California. McDonalds,

Kentucky Fried Chicken outlets, palm trees, broad boulevards and architecturally ambitious commercial centers lined the broad expanse of Roxas and Puyat Boulevards. Upon exiting the car however, ones nostrils would expose another layer of reality, a fetid scent that surrounded such luxury. Just out of sight lay crowded alleyways teeming with the smell of rat-infested garbage, urine, and sweat-drenched workers. The Mandarin Hotel, as they neared, quickly erased such knowing. It was a welcome sight, Amanda's preferred home away from home. She had chosen it originally for it's proximity to her bank's Makati Office, but she returned for its service and serenity. Eduardo pulled smoothly into the foyer area and quickly opened her door.

"I'll see to it that your bags get up to your room, Miss Amanda, and wait for you at the entrance at nine o'clock. The Ambassador is expecting you at half past nine." Eduardo was always punctual, so Amanda luxuriated in the thought that she would have nearly one full hour to unpack and to gear up for her day. She looked around as she approached the registration desk, pleased to see that all remained exactly the same.

The smiling clerk greeted her by name and handed her several messages. While waiting for her credit card's return, she glanced up at the three massive and beautifully carved Asian gods looming serenely over the lobby. Carved of magnificent mahogany, their height soared almost up to the level of the mezzanine section. The intricacy of the woodcarving, with its rich gleam, highlighted their serene gaze and cast an aura of calm and endurance upon the elegance of the foyer. The lobby was quiet this time of the morning. She liked that it seemed always to maintain certain decorum, even during the cocktail hour. Most Makati hotels were noisy, gossipy, hotbeds of intrigue and activity day and night.

Derek had completed his check-in, but was staring with surprise and consternation at a message that the clerk had just handed him. "I have to get to a phone that I can depend on for privacy. What do you recommend?" His look broached no delay or discussion.

"After our meeting with Paco we're scheduled to go by the office for an overview of our itinerary with Brad Gregory, the Manager.

Brad has a private conference room available for phone calls or meetings. You can use the Swift line in there."

"That all sounds well and good, but I can't wait until ten thirty." He frowned as he glanced down at a watch that showed two time zones. "That would be nine thirty on the East Coast. Impossible! Let's stop there first." Derek turned in the direction of the main entryway, ready to bolt out the door.

"Hold on. It wouldn't solve the problem to go over there now. You may find some of the staff on hand, but Brad won't be in the office 'til nine or later and he's the only one with the key to the private conference room and the Swift facilities." She thought for a moment as the bellhop gathered their luggage onto a cart and handed them the key cards to their rooms. "What you could do is return the call from your room and let them know to await a call from you sometime between nine thirty and ten tonight."

Derek took a second to mull over her solution. "If that's my only alternative; but they aren't going to like it." He said it with a finality that didn't invite any comment and walked briskly towards the elevator.

What a relief to step inside her hotel room and be alone, if only for what amounted to forty-five minutes now, Amanda thought. The sight of the room's interior still had the power to impress her, especially the bathroom. It was bigger than any standard room at a luxury U.S. hotel. It wasn't just its size but the luxurious pink-veined marble floors that continued right on up the walls. Thick, soft, white terry robe, baskets of luxury soaps, bubble bath, two telephones—of all things, she thought, two phones in the bathroom. She tried to imagine the use of both.

The room was elegantly furnished with rich mahogany built-ins, a comfy chair and ottoman, a covered pot of warm tea and an overflowing basket of exotic fruits. She quickly counted the mangoes. She learned to identify and enjoy all the strange new fruits, but she had a positive addiction to Philippine mangoes. In her opinion they were unequaled anywhere in the world for their sweetness and delicate flavor. Whenever she finished the ones in the basket she made certain to re-supply them, usually directly from one of her client's trees. Her room always smelled of mangoes. During her first trip one of the hotel's cleaning ladies, seeing the remains of five mangoes consumed in one day, shyly cautioned her about a rare and exotic disease that could occur from eating an overabundance of mangoes. Amanda only half believed her until a client confirmed that mangoes had a fruit acid in their skin that could irritate the lining of the throat and cause muteness. No such luck; she never once had the excuse of canceling a meeting due to an excess of mangoes.

Amanda quickly had all of her clothes hanging on the padded hangers. Some would require pressing. She dialed Housekeeping. Her knit suit would do for today, but it was a relief to know that everything else would be perfectly pressed, awaiting her return. No hotels in the world, she decided, could compare to Asian hotels. The service was abundant, excessive and exemplary. She'd heard that this particular hotel's staff to guest ratio was two to one. An added plus was their unobtrusiveness and friendliness. Amanda always left a sizable tip to supplement the room staff's meager salaries.

Settling comfortably into the large chair, she began to review her messages. A covetous glance at the mangoes would have to do for now, she decided. Paco is sure to have many delicacies, including mangoes, awaiting them. Most of the messages were of the vague, 'Welcome to Manila' type, indicating she should call to arrange a visit to their homes while staying here. Many of her clients operated on the "manana" principle, a carry-over from their two hundred years of Spanish rule. They preferred a loose arrangement whereby Amanda would call when she arrived and plans could then be made to best suit her busy schedule and theirs. Never was there a sense of rush or difficulty or inconvenience.

All such arrangements would be made so smoothly and with such little apparent fuss and bother that she felt singled out for special treatment. She soon discovered this was true of all of their handling of appointments. Each person was treated as a guest whose consideration and comfort was all that mattered. What a refreshing change from the practical, purposeful approach of the U.S., she thought. It made one feel absolutely catered to and treated as a beloved friend. It was easy to fall into a sense of being on holiday and really visiting 'family'.

As genial as they were, however, each client made certain that his or her objectives were addressed, privately and pointedly. The astuteness of their questions soon disabused Amanda of the belief that they were at all casual about business. On the contrary, even the wives were extremely well informed as to what was happening in the financial world. The women of the Philippines were, in Amanda's experience, equally as shrewd, if not more so, as their distaff side.

Amanda smiled at memories of her gauche misconceptions of Asian women in general and Filipinas in particular. She harbored the stereotype of their being pretty but servile, adornments only to their powerful men. What a surprise to discover the marvelous composite of womanhood the Filipina turned out to be. The Philippines, she discovered, was in many respects, a matriarchy. Not an overt one, but no less powerful in its women's affect on all aspects of society.

Amanda was surprised at the number of women who had completed higher levels of education. They entered government, law, medicine and business. Equally important was their impact on their children and their men. The Filipino male was outwardly the ruling voice in all matters, but the subtle influence of the female dictated and guided many of their actions. Although most of the men of wealth had mistresses, sometimes even more than two households to maintain, the wife exerted a profound level of influence. As the women aged, their power and confidence grew stronger and their bonds with one another, tighter.

This bonding created opportunities for social frivolity, gossiping, afternoons of Mahjong, and the usual round of parties. It also involved participation in spiritual retreats and charitable activities in the community. Amanda had accompanied women to hospitals, orphanages and children's welfare organizations. She was awed. They didn't just write a check or organize fund-raisers. They washed sores, read to children, donated clothing and remained involved. Why couldn't such an evolved group of women bring pressure to bear to change the governing structure at the highest levels?

The phone derailed her thoughts. Expecting Rob, her cheerful "Hello" quickly diminuendoed into a "Be right down" as Derek answered. One glance in the mirror, a quick slick of lipstick to transform her down turned lips, and she was out the door.

Derek was pacing the lobby as she stepped from the elevator. "I hope you're ready for a busy day." Amanda said as she walked towards him.

"I'm accustomed to long days." He responded with abrupt impatience and not a trace of his usual Irish whimsy.

Eduardo was waiting in the foyer's parking area. He jumped to open the car doors for them. The morning continued hot and humid, but the cool interior of the car and the thought of seeing Paco, lifted Amanda's spirits. Eduardo skillfully left behind the streets of Metro Makati and entered the hallowed exclusivity of Manila's wealthiest residential district, Forbes Park. As with many exclusive residential areas worldwide, one couldn't see the homes for the surrounding walls. Eduardo took a back way into the property and pulled up to its guard-gated entrance. The compound's guard was no one she remembered seeing before, but he smiled a friendly greeting as the massive iron gates swung wide. They drove slowly through what had to be a runner-up to Eden. The profusion of orchids and roses and flowers of all descriptions overwhelmed her senses. Fountains splashed everywhere, their soft spray reflecting myriad rainbows. The sound of exotic birds in cages, chorusing with their free cousins, created a delightful cacophony of song. Their music, with the mingling scents and colors, intoxicated her senses.

Paco's compound housed four lavish homes built for various family members, and yet no feeling of clustered living existed. Eduardo pulled slowly past the perfect little family chapel as he drew up to the massive portico entryway.

Amanda caught sight of Paco, standing in the doorway, smiling his familiar warm greeting. Unexpected was the servant holding his arm as Paco carefully descended the entryway stairs.

"Amanda, my dear, how good to have you here again! How lovely you look, as always! He gave her the warm Filipino 'abrazo', with two light kisses, one upon each cheek. "And this must be your colleague, Mr. Ashton. Welcome to the Philippines. I hope this shall be your first of many visits." Derek extended his hand as 'Paco'' reverted to a more Western greeting and held out his hand in a firm clasp. "Do come in and relax. I know how brutal that long flight can be. Would you prefer the terrace or the lounge?" Paco turned to Amanda with a pleased grin. "Ana has laid out a morning merienda for you with your favorites, plenty of mangoes and her special cheese bread."

Amanda gracefully wrapped her arm through Pacos' to aid him with the steps. "Ana remembered how I devoured her cheese bread. It's heavenly." Amanda thought of the birthday gift she had in her purse, an aromatic box of Paco's favorite cigars. She turned to him. "If it isn't too warm for you, could we sit out on the terrace? I love to look out on your magnificent orchid garden."

"Of course, my dear; your choice will please Ana. Those orchids are her children. But it's Jorge, our gardener, who shares her labor of love." As they entered the terrace area, Paco's spinster sister, Ana, appeared with a face wreathed in smiles. Her role in her brother's household was an important one, especially since the death of Paco's wife.

"My dear Amanda, how happy I am to see you again". Ana's voice held musical warmth and sincerity and her scent radiated her favorite 'Tea Rose' cologne. Her face recalled the stereotype of a cozy, maternal 'Auntie', although her dress was expensive and tailor-made. She wouldn't be caught dead in an apron. When Amanda first met Ana she was fooled by her 'Tia' persona and almost missed the shrewdness behind her warmth. Amanda recalled how Ana had given her a discreet but thorough scrutiny, not only to ascertain the level of wealth and appropriateness exhibited by what Amanda had chosen to wear, but, more importantly, the manner in which Amanda interacted with her brother Paco. Amanda had since learned that Ana considered herself to be the 'keeper-of-the-gate' insofar as her brother was concerned. Any and all women, especially attractive women, were considered suspect in their designs on her brother until proven otherwise. Apparently Amanda had soon eased any fears as to her designs on Paco. Amanda genuinely cared for him, not only as a client and a friend, but almost as a paterfamilias, a kinder and gentler father image. Ana, once reassured, quickly warmed to her. Their mutual love of flowers and Amanda's appreciation of Ana's cooking, cemented a sincere friendship.

Ana gave Derek a proper welcome as she led them onto the terrace. "Mr. Ashton, as soon as you and Amanda have had a chance to rest and enjoy a cool drink, I have a special treat for you. You may be surprised, but I have managed to cultivate my own English garden, complete with some lovely Irish heritage roses that are just in bloom."

Derek was gracious, although a bit aloof, Amanda thought. He acknowledged their conversations smoothly enough, but it seemed as though he was preoccupied with his own internal ones. As soon as they took a chair on the terrace, a servant appeared with a choice of drinks. Amanda was torn between the delicious kalamansi juice, so rich in sweetness and Vitamin C, and the creamy coolness of the milky green mango juice. She opted for the latter. Derek and Paco chose, in spite of the early hour of the day, a Scotch and water.

Derek seemed to hesitate over the water part as he glanced discreetly at Amanda. Ana's eagle eye rarely missed a trick and she quickly commented, "You need have no fear of drinking the water here Mr. Ashton, at least not in our household. All our water is boiled and steam distilled, even that which is used to wash the vegetables and fruit."

Amanda seconded that with a brisk nod of her head and a big gulp of her drink in affirmation. "I've never felt a moment's queasiness. I eat everything, but nothing as wonderful as Ana's cheese bread." Ana quickly brightened, but declined at the suggestion that she join them in a drink.

"I'll make certain the prawns are ready. Please relax and enjoy yourselves." She smiled and headed into the houses' cool interior. Although the terrace was a bit warmer than the house itself, Amanda was surprised at how pleasant it felt. The breeze, the orchids, the soft splash of the fountains, even the cool expanse of marble at her feet, eased her into an almost hypnotic state of repose.

A state ruffled by Paco's comment, "Well, how are things going in the U.S.? What do they think of the latest developments in the Philippines?"

"You just stole my lines," Amanda laughed. "I'll go first, if you'll bring me and Derek up to date on how things look from your perspective."

Paco grinned somewhat sardonically at this request as he replied. "You know I will, although neither of our views is apt to agree with what appears in the U.S., or the Philippine, press." He smiled encouragement and gave her his rapt attention.

Amanda began a recap. "The general consensus is that President Reagan wants to try to find a way to aid President Marcos in making some sort of a graceful resolution to the turmoil here. He's been getting a lot of pressure lately though to concur with his senior advisors. They claim Marcos no longer has the ability or the support to maintain the leadership of his country." She grinned and reached up to accept a second glass of juice from an extended tray. "Each time it appears that Reagan may acquiesce to his advisors, Marcos highlights the increasing size and danger of the NPA or some catastrophic situation that only he can subdue. Reagan wants to buy that, but Marcos' failure to follow through with the snap election—promised for this year—has disenchanted him."

"Disenchanted him? I think it tied his hands. As much as he and Marcos are pals, I think it has painted your President into a corner." Paco took a long pull at his drink before he continued. "It must have been the final straw after August thirteenth when the opposition tried to have President Marcos impeached." He looked from Amanda to Derek for their reaction.

"Such actions don't leave much room for any support for Marcos." Amanda put down her glass and glanced up at Paco. "How do you read it from your end?" As Paco turned away to reach for a newspaper, Amanda took a moment to study Derek. He'd remained silent throughout their exchange, alert to their conversation but unreadable.

Paco paused to point to a headline in the Philippine Press: 'Laxalt Sphinx-like Upon Return to U.S.'. Paco turned to Derek. "I know you must be aware that your President Reagan has recently sent Senator Paul Laxalt to Manila. Since his return to the U.S. the Filipino rumor mill has been working overtime. Conjecture is running the gamut, but

I feel certain that some pointed suggestions, if not ultimatums, were given. Suddenly the opposition here has formed a 'secret' group called RAM, he smiled sardonically, "the Reform Army Movement." He looked over at Derek. "The atrocities Marcos claims for the NPA have been more than matched by the brutalities of the Philippine Army."

"I thought Marcos had firm control of the Army." Amanda turned, shocked to hear Derek chime in at last. Paco gave him a wry smile as he turned to pour them each an inch or two more of scotch.

"Not any longer. Enrile and Ramos, who head RAM, have usurped President Marcos control of the Philippine Army."

"That would suggest Marcos is on the way out." Derek gave Paco a solemn look. "The key to his meeting strong opposition has been his ability to retain solid leadership over the Philippine Army. Am I right?" Derek waited for Paco's reply.

"Rumor has it that the primary requirement Laxalt discussed while here was a firm directive that Marcos get rid of Fabian Ver as army chief-of-staff."

Amanda interrupted. "But just this past week I read an article in the San Francisco paper saying Reagan wasn't going to insist on Ver's complete removal from power." Amanda looked puzzled as she turned back to Paco.

"Your President, my dear Amanda, still seems to want to handle Marcos with kid gloves. He and Imelda certainly did a good job of establishing a personal friendship with your President and his wife."

"Friendship or not, the tide looks to have turned once Laxalt arrived." Derek stood up and gave a little stretch.

"Right you are; enough to get Marcos to set a date to carry through with a snap election."

"He agreed?" Amanda gave Paco a disbelieving stare.

"Of course. Marcos is convinced this election will prove to liberal critics in the U.S., and to dissenters in the Philippines, that he has the full support of the people."

"What a laugh." Ana's comment surprised them with her chuckle as she walked in to announce their merienda was served. "Enough of such talk for now; it will spoil your appetite. Eat first and continue later on a full stomach."

The table seemed to groan under its array of all the best of Filipino cooking. Amanda scanned the dishes for her favorites. She intended to enjoy them to the fullest. All too often her clients entertained her at the latest restaurants, all chosen for their French, Japanese, Italian or American style menus. Without Ana's delectable repasts she would never have come to appreciate the variety and delicacy of Filipino cooking.

The discerning Pinoy, as the Filipinos called themselves, took the best of their multi-cultural mix and produced cuisine for the Gods. The seafood, Amanda thought, was the very best. She'd never known there were so many types of shrimp, more than twenty in the Philippines. Her favorite fish however was lapu-lapu, the grouper. The magic of coconut, Malay spices, vinegary sweetness, chilies, lumpia (spring rolls) and lomi (flat Chinese noodles) wafted their aromas through the room. Amanda felt her stomach reminding her of its readiness as her mouth watered in anticipation.

"Please try these sugpo sa aligi, Mr. Ashton." Ana ladled a generous serving of tiger prawns onto Derek's plate and turned to Amanda. "I made enough of your favorite cheese bread to take back to your hotel room."

The conversation had turned to compliments on the various dishes, mention of the upcoming memorial service to be held in Paco's chapel, and jokes about his birthday. "Do open your gift, Paco." Amanda, noticing that all had finished their food, extended a ribbon-tied package. "It's time."

Paco proceeded carefully as he un-wrapped the box. "Perfect timing I should say." He drew out a cigar, pressed it gently, turning it about in his fingers before cutting the end and lighting it. He drew a long, satisfied inhalation. "Thank you for your thoughtfulness, my dear."

"And I'll thank you for your thoughtfulness, my dear brother, in taking that cigar right out to the terrace." Ana gently motioned him in that direction. "I'll bring your coffees out to you."

'I'm glad you like it, Paco." Amanda smiled happily at his genuine delight as they all rose to adjourn to the terrace. Amanda turned back to Ana. "Oh, Ana, I almost forgot. I have a box of chocolates for you." She reached back into her bag and offered the familiar box to a smiling Ana.

"I'll add these to the coffee tray, my dear." Ana walked back towards the kitchen as Amanda turned to head towards the bathroom.

"I'll be right back with you," Amanda said as she turned to Derek. He surprised her by turning to follow her down the corridor.

"When do we get out of here? I need to get to a phone."

"Business, remember? Now is the time to join Paco and sound him out about a trust. That's what you're here for, right?" She gave him a quizzical stare.

"Right you are." His answer was accompanied by a swift about-face as he turned away and headed back to the terrace.

# SEVEN

Derek wasn't the only one who needed to get down to business. Amanda returned, finished her last bite of mango and rose to join Derek and Paco on the terrace. "Where shall I put these?" Juggling two used glasses, she turned to Ana.

"Amanda, my dear, remember you are in the Philippines now. Don't even think of lifting a finger to help clear away. Maria and her team have it down to a fine art. Not another word; off with you."

Amanda smiled and turned back towards the terrace. Paco was discussing something rather heatedly. She hesitated just out of view, concerned by the vehemence in his voice and only relieved when she identified the topic as politics.

"The election will be a total farce. Vote buying and ballot box stuffing is the way the democratic process works in the Philippines." Paco seemed to recognize the disenchantment in his tone as he turned to Derek in apology.

"Forgive me, Mr. Ashton. I don't wish to give you the wrong impression on your first visit to the Philippines. There are many honorable people in our government. Even in our army. People who were appalled at the assassination of Aquino and the disgrace it brought to this country." At that remark Paco began to get up, very carefully, from his chair. His look quickly changed from one of righteous anger to one of abject sorrow.

Derek rose to offer him his arm. "Please, no need to apologize. Is there no chance that the opposition can marshal enough support to prevail?" Before Paco could reply, Amanda walked up and offered her arm to him.

"I think I arrived at just the right time. Perhaps we'd better leave that question for another time." She eased Paco back into his chair. "I don't want you to get overtired from our visit."

"Nonsense; it does me good to vent my spleen a little, but I'm sure you'll get your fill of Philippine politics from your other clients. Even so, I'll answer Mr. Ashton's question and be done with it."

"Hope for the opposition? It would take a miracle. Maybe Cardinal Sin, the leader of the Catholic Church in the Philippines and one of the strongest supporters of the opposition, can use his prayers to bring about such a miracle. In the meantime, let's discuss some more pleasant subjects." He beamed a look of genuine appreciation towards Amanda.

"I was pleased at the results of the treasury portfolio you suggested, Amanda. I'm also looking forward to learning more about your Trust Company in the Caymans, Mr. Ashton." He turned to Derek with his all-business demeanor firmly in place. "What can you tell me about the safety and privacy of offshore trusts?" Paco settled back into his chair with a warm smile of receptivity and attentiveness.

Amanda was impressed at the ease with which Derek reviewed all of the features and benefits of an offshore trust. The examples he used were specifically tailored to Paco's needs. Derek knew, of course, that Paco's children were warring over who would get what and actively obstructing any new wife coming along to divide their spoils. The Ambassador may be the most skillful of diplomats, but he was putty in the hands of his children, especially his daughter, Angelina. Derek also was privy to Paco's concern over the close liaison that his Angel had formed with a notorious playboy, a man known to live off of the largesse of the women in his life. With this knowledge, Derek focused on discreetly highlighting the ability of a trust to allocate how much, when, where, to whom, and in what circumstances, money would be paid out over the lifetimes of his beneficiaries. The ease, the privacy, and most importantly, the ability to retain control over his money and his businesses even after his death, was beginning to make an impression on Paco. He listened carefully, never taking his attention off of Derek's words.

Although no commitment was made on the spot, Paco took a packet of trust documentation from Derek and announced, "I'd like to go over this with my attorney. In the meantime," he turned to Amanda, "I've notified my New York bank to wire you an additional deposit of three hundred thousand dollars to place in a new certificate of deposit for one year at the best rate you can give me." He smiled companionably as he rose. "I know you have a busy day ahead of you, but you will humor Ana with a walk through her garden before you leave. She is counting on it."

"Of course; we'd love to." Amanda beamed her delight as she steered Paco out of range of Derek's annoyed stare of impatience. "We can't meet with Brad for another forty five minutes anyway", she enunciated clearly in Derek's direction.

It must have worked. Ana seemed to have warmed to Derek during their walk through her gardens. Derek's enthusiasm over her English roses brought a blush to Ana's cheeks. The combination of superb food, soothing scents of the garden, and their host and hostess's warm receptivity, all established a strong sense of optimism. Their leave-taking was as warm as their arrival. Paco reminded her that he expected to see them again, if not before, at least at lunch on the day of their departure, when he would accompany them to the airport. *How fond she was of him, she thought, and how much his warmth as an individual colored her attitude towards her Filipino clients.*

Some of the wind went out of her sails during the drive back. She shook herself as if out of a dream into the reality of her purpose during this trip. She stared intently out the window, resolving to look beyond liking them and deeper into the nature and source of their money. Paco's, she knew, was verifiably old money, inheriting most via a long lineage of Spanish grandees. The three hundred thousand was peanuts and doubtless clean, given its long rest in his New York bank.

"Where did you go? I've asked you twice what you thought of my handling of Paco." Derek's question penetrated. She looked up, her expression mixed with contrition and chagrin.

"Sorry. You were brilliant, a big hit. They liked you and they loved your products. Congratulations and let's discuss it later." She nodded in the direction of the pane of glass behind the driver's head.

"Good. How close are we to the office?"

Amanda laughed. "Let me amend that. You could have blown it during the garden walk when you glanced at your watch after ten minutes had passed."

He barely acknowledged her little dig. From his anxiety to get to the Manila office she knew that her client calls would test his patience. His business persona, she'd discovered, was to be short and to the point. She gave him a puzzled stare that questioned why his time in the Caymans hadn't mellowed him.

The parking lot of the bank was full, but Eduardo pulled right up to the front entryway. The heat nearly overcame her as she stood at the car door saying thank you and good-bye to Eduardo. Derek had already reached the lobby and was waiting impatiently at the opened elevator door as she walked into the over-air-conditioned foyer.

"Mabuhay, Amanda!" Marisa sang out her greeting as she unlocked the office door and embraced Amanda. The staff gathered around to chorus their greeting. Amanda introduced them to Derek, who impatiently shook each one's hand. Undeterred, she extended two large boxes of chocolates.

"I brought one each for the front office staff and the back office operations team."

Marisa had already opened a box. "The chocolate here just can't compare." Amanda responded to their welcome, feeling a sense of being 'home'. Her smile quickly faded however as she glanced at Derek.

He obviously didn't share in her delight at the group's welcome. His look was one of barely concealed impatience. "I thought Brad

Gregory would be here." He glanced at his watch. "I have a call to make— a call that is past due by seven minutes."

"Mr. Gregory is in his office. I'm sure he'll be right out." Marisa's voice held a note of uncertainty, glancing at the set of Derek's jaw as he fought to restrain his irritation.

Brad's not having been there to greet them was unusual, Amanda thought as she turned to Derek. He'd obviously reached the end of his patience.

"I need to use a private phone line right away. Point me in that direction." His request had no sooner left his mouth than Brad walked in.

"Speaking of phones, forgive me, but I had a call that couldn't easily be terminated." Brad extended his hand. "You must be Derek Ashton." Derek's responding handshake seemed abrupt, dismissive and annoyed. Brad seemed not to notice. "I'm eager to hear more about your corner of international banking. Why don't we step back into my office and leave Amanda's fan club to their chocolates."

Derek terminated Brad's friendly line of patter. "I need to make a call first. If you'll show me to a private line, I'll be happy to fill you in just as soon as I get this call off my plate."

"Sure thing; follow me." Brad's attempt to run him through the tie line codes for an international call was quickly aborted.

"I can handle it. Thanks, Brad. Be with you shortly." Derek was already dialing as he darted a pointed look at Brad. "Please close the door."

"Well then, Amanda," Brad's smile vanished as he led her into his office. He pulled out a chair, motioning her to take a seat. "It's just us for a few minutes." His look was laced with incredulity. "What on earth decided our chairman to let you come out on this hair-brained mission? And why did he agree to this new –and rather testy guy, Ashton— tagging along?"

Brad's sources must have been exhausted if he still had questions about such an action, Amanda thought, as she decided to make short work of any explanations.

"Sorenson decided the money-laundering brouhaha in New York warranted a show of confidence in our bank's activities here in the

Philippines. Business as usual is our bank's path of confidence, but with Derek's trusts as a means to discreetly validate any doubtful client assets." Amanda noticed a strange look come over Brad's face.

"Sure, but they only put what they want in their trust, remember." Brad's look discounted any such a solution.

"True, but a scrutiny of those assets would provide certain linkages to confirm sources of funds." Detecting a further disclaimer, Amanda rushed to defuse any more resistance. "In any event, Sorenson expects you to give us carte blanche at any in-depth information you can obtain." As Brad smiled, turning his hands up in surrender, Amanda rushed to acknowledge him.

"You've always been such a big help. I want you to know how much I appreciate it."

"Well, yes, but..." As Derek entered the room, Brad bit back any further elaboration. "Let's hold off on that discussion for the moment, shall we?"

Derek settled in beside Amanda in the larger of the two leather side chairs, and accepted the proffered cup of tea. Sipping it slowly, his eyes roamed the room. Amanda tried to take in everything through Derek's eyes. Apart from looking annoyed, Brad was looking especially good, she decided. She remembered when she'd first seen him, several years previously. He'd had that worn look of a man who was self-destructing. His florid face, thinning hair, expanding waistline and chain smoking, all belied the fact that he was only forty-one years old. She'd heard of his divorce and the rumors of his having become involved with a Filipina nearly half his age. That last bit of news really didn't surprise her. With the many charms of the Philippine women, she marveled that any expatriate banker remained married to their hometown wives.

Younger or not, it seemed Brad had found the right person in Carolina de la Serna. His second marriage definitely seemed to agree with him. Amanda was struck by how clear and confident he appeared. The real surprise was that Carolina's family had approved of the wedding. The De La Serna family was one of the oldest, wealthiest, and certainly the most powerful, in the Philippines. It was rumored that even President Marcos was careful to cooperate with anything a De La Serna wanted. The entire country had been shocked by the news of the beautiful and eligible Carolina marrying a gringo. Not just a gringo, but a lowly manager of a U.S. banking office. What was even worse, a divorced American. The unthinkable had happened, setting tongues to wag.

The gossips couldn't lay the cause on the usual early pregnancy, Amanda thought. Caro's first-born arrived one year to the day of their wedding. Amanda smiled in Brad's direction, convinced that both the office and his new look were due to his beautiful wife.

Carolina Gregory was clearly Brad's pride and joy. One look around the office confirmed the fact. Large blown-up photos nearly covered one wall. Photography was Brad's passion, and Caro his favorite model. She smiled out from every corner of the office; young, beautiful, vivacious, exuding the self-assurance of one who knows the world is hers for the asking. Her unusual blond hair, sparkling eyes and assured manner suggested she might have been a top model or an actress, had such a thing not been unthinkable for a De La Serna. The closest Caro ever got to stardom was her reign as "Miss Manila" and her debutante ball.

As Brad refilled Derek's tea, Amanda studied him. Although he looked lean and fit, she noticed a strange look that came and went when he felt unobserved. It vanished the moment he turned to her.

"If you like those photos, wait until you see the latest shots I took of Caro and the baby."

"I can't wait."

Amanda had met Caro only briefly when she accepted Emilio's invitation to a family gathering at their summer home in Bagio two years ago. Amanda's friendship with the elder De la Sernas had grown close, but Emilio's children, Raffy and Caro, had been strangers, always away at school in Switzerland. Brief or not, it was enough time to become intrigued by the girl and puzzled by she and Brad's unlikely pairing.

"Well," Brad's voice brought her back, "...now that Derek's returned we can get a bit better acquainted." He studied Derek's face closely as he asked. "How do you find your first visit to Manila?"

"Almost too gracious, these Filipinos." He patted his taut midriff. "If I'm not careful I'll gain ten pounds." Derek's remark stayed Brad's hand as it reached for the box of chocolates Amanda had placed on the coffee table.

Brad turned away from both chocolates and Derek. "Thanks for your thoughtfulness, Amanda. Not only for the chocolates, but the scotch is always appreciated."

"It's a small token of my pleasure at your help. I could never function here in the Philippines without you and your staff and all they do for me"

In the space of a minute the look on Brad's face turned solemn. "Along those lines Amanda, we need to finish our discussion now that Derek's here." Turning his back to Amanda, he aimed his comments directly to Derek. "As you know, I've been filled in by senior management. They are concerned by the suspicion the arrest has cast, not only upon this office, but all Offshore Banking Units in Manila." His confident expression segued into a scowl. "Somehow they've got the idea that President Marcos is trying to move a large quantity of money. Whether or not that's so, our bank mustn't be implicated whatsoever."

He stopped. A look of anxiety surfaced as he continued; his inflection strengthening. "You must appreciate my position. I can't afford to have the slightest attention cast on my office." Brad jumped up, pacing the length of the office as though to escape.

He turned to face Amanda, gave a slight shudder and continued. "We must be extra-circumspect during this time. I must insist that this be your only visit this trip." Brad studied Amanda's incredulous look. "That doesn't mean we won't work together on this thing. We'll meet at the house for dinner and discussions—but no meetings here. Should you need any routine documents sent on to Hong Kong, you can leave them with me then." Brad registered Amanda's dumbfounded look of shock, glancing over at Derek's silence. "I don't mean to play hard ball. I'll do all I can to help you both expand your client information, just not here at the office. I've decided that the fewer rich Filipinos seen going in and out of here, the better."

"Yes, of course, Brad; somehow we'll have to work around it, as strange as it feels." Amanda's response mirrored Brad's intensity. "'Strange' seems to be the key-note for this trip." She hesitated but rushed on as the images flooded her mind. "The strangest thing happened to me on the flight here. I may be paranoid, but given your own caution, I'd appreciate your take on this."

Derek had been quietly observing their interchange. Suddenly he sprang from his chair, nearly upsetting the tea service. "You can't be serious, Amanda. Not your mystery-man story. I thought we laid that ghost." Derek smiled dismissively as he cast Brad an 'indulge her' look.

Undaunted, Amanda began her tale of the staring stranger on the flight. Trying not to editorialize, she recited it in an as matter of fact a manner as possible. She even punctuated her concluding remarks with, "You'll probably second Derek's opinion that I'm reading entirely too much into the man's stare."

Brad muttered something that sounded like 'Cool arm.' His teacup rattled as he sat it back in its saucer. "What did this person look like? Would you recognize him again?"

"I'm not sure. I tried to get a good look, but he was asleep or turned away whenever I walked by. I thought I'd see him at the baggage carousel—but I never did. He was Filipino, maybe thirty-five to forty, black hair and, I can't be sure of the height, but he seemed to be of slight build. All I really noticed was his piercing stare. It was filled with hatred." Unable to interpret the look on Brad's face, she pressed on. "Why do you ask if I'd recognize him again? He couldn't have any real focus on me or he'd have lingered in the baggage area; right?" Amanda's voice rose as she waited for Brad's reassurance.

Finally, after what felt to Amanda like the length of time between doctors giving a verdict of terminal illness, he looked fixedly at her and said, "Well, you certainly could have been imagining it. The extra intensity of this trip could have fired your imagination." He gave a little grin and a dismissive shrug to accompany his explanation. "You know how the Filipinos are. They take such pains to put a good face on everything that their anger rarely shows. The chap was probably just using the anonymity of the plane to express anger towards his boss or wife. You just happened to turn and catch him at it. I wouldn't let it get to you; after a good nights sleep everything will look different." As Brad finished what sounded to Amanda like a too-pat prescription for a slightly hysterical female, Derek broke in.

"I'm sorry if I discounted your feelings, Amanda." He turned to Brad. "Brad and I don't doubt that he frightened you. But you yourself said that if you were really his target, he would have pursued it further. I agree with Brad that a good night's sleep will erase the whole thing."

Amanda resented Derek's jollying her up, but decided to reserve judgment. *They're probably right, she thought, a good night's sleep would change my entire perspective.* Amanda felt her lingering irritation begin to wane.

Derek's hail-fellow-well-met attempt escaped Brad, whose face resumed a solemn demeanor as he anxiously returned to his own agenda, reiterating the need for them to run every action, question and concern by him. Amanda wondered how, given his veto of any further visits to the Manila banking unit.

Brads voice penetrated her questioning thought. "I'll be sure to coordinate with you periodically—at the house, your hotel or another area other than the banking office."

Derek interrupted. "Let's get down to business then. What can you tell me about the principal players in the Philippines, especially those that might have you most concerned?"

Amanda listened with grudging respect as Derek skillfully grilled Brad. "Let's start with your analysis of the individuals we'll be meeting during this trip." Derek pulled his chair closer to Brad's and drew out a list of their client calls. "You know this playing field well. Amanda seems to feel that all of her clients are above reproach, but given your concerns, I'd like to hear your impressions. Could any of these individuals be implicated in money laundering?"

Brad rose to walk to the door and close it before turning back to respond to Derek's question. "I don't necessarily agree that Marcos is moving money, but that doesn't mean that something fishy isn't going on involving some one of these clients." He lifted the paper for a closer review of the list of names.

"Who might you suspect and how should we handle our scrutiny of their assets?" Derek glanced over to Amanda who had stood up as Brad read over the list of names. "The sooner we can identify clients, even those who may only be indirectly involved, the better." Derek leaned closer to Brad with the intent air of someone deferring to greater wisdom, and waited, hanging on his reply. Amanda waited, but with chin raised and shoulders squared.

Brad adopted an air of professional detachment and neutrality. He seemed to want to distance himself, and yet, as he glanced over the list of Amanda's client calls, he quickly went from statement of fact to editorializing, to downright gossiping. Amanda gave a sardonic smile as she observed how living here had gotten to Brad. He actually warmed to the more salacious tidbits he imparted.

"Take Miguel Santos, your next appointment. He's no saint. Excuse my play on words. He bears watching. He's sitting on a crisis situation that may make him more than willing to cooperate with whatever it takes to break the logjam. The governments withheld payment to all the sugar growers for two years now, but Miguel seems to be targeted for some particular punishment. His anti-Marcos sentiments don't go down very well and the NPA is infiltrating his workers." Brad looked up at Derek as he issued his smug verdict. "Keep your eyes open with this fellow. He'd be high on my list of those who bear watching."

Amanda leaped to her friend's defense. "Miguel wouldn't be caught dead helping Marcos or any of his cronies." Amanda's voice raised a few decibels. "He pays his workers out of the family money. That certainly wouldn't indicate someone ready to move money out of the country. You're barking up the wrong tree there." Amanda heard the accusation in her voice and felt her face reddening.

"Hold on, Amanda." Derek reached over to touch her arm. "I know how protective you feel about your clients, but Brad's just giving his opinion, which is exactly what we asked for. Let's hear him out."

Amanda shrugged off his arm as Derek nodded to Brad to continue. It took all her willpower to swallow her indignation, but she managed to at least cover it over with professional attentiveness. She felt her veneer crumble more than once as Brad's comments on each group of clients stirred her proprietary defensiveness. Each statement marshaled her silent rebuttal, sparked more by emotion than reason. *These are my people, my clients, my friends, ran her thoughts. How dare you dismiss them so glibly?* She nearly missed Derek's question.

"Amanda, what say we try to reschedule this last chap, Chi Chi Amparo, until the latter part of our trip? I'd like to get a better feel for Santos before our meeting with him. Can we safely contact a client to reschedule from the hotel's phones?"

Amanda didn't want to reveal the extent of her preoccupation. The comments concerning Miguel had caught her up in thought. She decided she must have checked out of the conversation before the Amparo comment. She briskly responded. "The hotel phones are fine as long as the conversation is brief and couched in terms of a social get together." A commendable save, she thought, making a mental note to find out more about exactly what Brad had implied about the Amparo group.

Brad glanced impatiently at the clock. "I'm running a bit late for my golf date at the country club." He looked a bit sheepish. "I know, I know, but my client is one of the banks biggest, and if I have to play a lot of golf, so be it." He laughed, using this gambit to deflect a look of anxiousness that colored his words. Rising, he began their move in the direction of the lobby, where he deftly intervened in the staff's attempts to lionize Amanda. They barely had time to reiterate their thanks when two chimed in and asked when they would next see her.

"Amanda is fully scheduled with appointments," Brad answered. "In fact, she tells me we won't be seeing her again during this trip" Disbelief and puzzlement fleetingly crossed Marisa's face.

Amanda determined to put a good face on it. "Busy or not, I couldn't do it without you, Marisa." She turned, hands outspread. "All of you. Thanks again for your help. You can ask them to contact me at the hotel if there are any clients calling for me." A farewell as glum as the greeting was exuberant, followed them out the door.

Derek took Amanda's arm as they left the smooth concrete of the parking lot to navigate the dirt lot between the office building and the hotel. Amanda felt a mix of anger and gratitude for his assistance. High heels made the crossing difficult.

The contrast between the glossy facade of the new office building facing Roxas Boulevard with the debris-strewn lot behind it was representative of the country as a whole. Fortunately the distance was short and by far the quickest way to get back to the hotel. She turned to Derek, "Thanks for the assist. Crossing the main street, with cars coming at us from all directions, would have taken forever."

Derek was silent until they reached the foyer of the hotel. "Well, that was interesting. How accurate do you think Brad's information is?" He turned to an Amanda who looked ready to have at him.

"Hold on there." Derek softened his question. "I'm trying to reserve judgment as to the accuracy of Brad's information. I must admit his commentary sounded as emotionally biased, and far less kind, than yours."

Amanda's response was clipped as she looked up and smiled at the approach of one of the hotel's desk clerks. "Yes, it certainly is hot. But you'll get used to it in a couple of days".

"I was just headed up to your room, Miss Evans. The phone hasn't stopped ringing with messages for you. I was sure you would appreciate having them just as quickly as they come in." The hotel employee handed her an envelope. One glance told her she'd have her next hour cut out for her in returning phone calls.

"Thank you" she said as she handed him a thousand pesos. She turned in the direction of the elevators, discreetly hidden behind the far wall of the lobby. Ignoring any response to his ill-timed questions in the lobby, she turned to Derek while they waited and said, "I'll have to be the one to return all of the calls and try to reschedule those meetings intended for the banking office. We do need to talk before our lunch with Miguel." Amanda glanced at her watch.

'Yes we do. I have a few questions."

She looked up, confronting Derek's serious stare. "It's now ten past twelve. Since lunch with Miguel isn't until two, how does a get-together in the bar area at one sound? It will be pretty deserted this time of day so we should be able to deal with it then."

"Sure, if you think that'll give us enough time. Meanwhile I need to deal with a few things myself. How is the fax service in the hotel?"

The arrival of the elevator halted her response. "The service is usually pretty reliable, but be discreet in the wording. All of the top hotels are rife with informers. It's a lucrative way to supplement their incomes." She recalled Brad's comment about a dinner party at his home. "If you can wait until dinner at Brad's, he can send your faxes much more safely from his office."

"Hmm, maybe."

"It's up to you, but if you do send anything from the hotel make it as obscure as you can." The elevator door opened and they both headed swiftly towards their rooms.

Derek hesitated as he put his keycard in the lock. "Fine; I'll hold off on my faxes until Saturday at Brad's. You needn't fear I'll put you in an unsafe position." He grinned up at her. "Matter of fact, I'm beginning to find this whole cloak and dagger thing a bit of a lark. See you in the bar area at one. Ciao!"

Amanda let out a large sigh of relief once inside her room. She kicked off her heels, fell onto the couch and began to riffle through her phone messages. Rob's name on the top of one of them indicated he'd try to call her back at midnight. Good, she thought, knowing it would be midnight before she settled into her room for the night.

"That should make it around eight AM his time," she murmured aloud. The memory of his strange behavior returned. He would have been in the office at least an hour when he called. She hoped whatever had him devastated may have been resolved.

She returned to her review of the other messages. Most of her favorite client's names appeared. Not all of them represented million dollar clients. Some, although connected to the mega-wealthy, were only marginally defined as 'high net-worth' themselves. She discovered early on that, since they comprised part of the 'families', she couldn't refuse to accept them as clients

Furthermore, she thought, smiling as she dialed, many of them, like Cisco here, are such delights. The maid who answered recognized her voice.

"Oh, Miss Evans, please hold. Mr. Lozano's right here, waiting for your call"

Cisco's warm tenor radiated delight at hearing her voice on the other end of the line. "You simply cannot stay away from the charms of the Philippines.... or are they my charms perhaps? How long are you here for and what does your busy social calendar allow for your greatest admirer?"

"I can't wait to see you and Cia. How's the new baby? I'm really looking forward to seeing her. How about tomorrow afternoon or sometime over the weekend?"

Cisco seemed to have his calendar in front of him, "How about tomorrow? I have a Japanese restaurant that I want you to experience. I can send my car and driver round for you. The baby won't accompany us, but photos will. How does two o'clock sound?"

"Perfect, Cisco." She chuckled softly. "I loved the birth announcement. Natasha is it? I should have known you'd give your daughter a Russian name. Now you have Sasha and Natasha. I can't wait to see her photos tomorrow." Amanda hung up the receiver with a smile of anticipation.

The remainder of the calls went with surprising ease. Only one had to give a tentative OK to her suggested time and location. Interestingly, she thought, those clients accustomed to meeting her within the confines of the bank didn't question her change of venue. Many seemed delighted to plan a meeting over lunch or dinner. Relieved, Amanda quickly annotated her appointment book, making note of the fact that over half now would be in client's homes. Good, she thought, Derek can get a better feel for the culture and the clients by visiting their homes.

She finished twenty minutes early and rang Derek to suggest he meet her as soon as possible down in the cocktail lounge. She grabbed Miguel's gift box of chocolates and headed out the door.

Derek was sitting at a small table in the far corner of the deserted bar area. He seemed pensive and lost in thought. Her nervousness at having a newcomer accompany her suddenly surfaced. She recalled Nigel's strange ambivalence. Although Nigel had hired him, even giving lip service to Derek's impressive background, he seemed nervous about her laying her cards on the table concerning this trip. The memory of his last admonition returned to her. "Be careful. Don't go overboard on filling this Derek fellow in. Let him help you, but play your cards close to your chest."

*Derek is definitely an enigma, she thought as she neared his table, but presumably trustworthy.* She was reminded of the Scottish Sean Connery as Derek directed a winning smile her way and stood up to greet her.

"How'd your calls go? I must confess that I put my feet up for a bit of a snooze." He reached to pull out a chair. "Will this table suit or do you prefer a banquette?"

"It's perfect, and the calls went remarkably smoothly. A good sign, I hope, for the rest of our trip. You might want to note your calendar as to the changes. The only one I left open is Chi Chi Amparo." She handed Derek her calendar. He quickly lined through and made conforming changes to his appointment book.

"What do you make of Brad? He didn't seem to like the looks of several of your clients."

She hesitated, smiling up at the waiter approaching. "I'll have just a pot of tea, thank you."

"A beer for me."

As the waiter walked away, Amanda turned a look of surprise towards Derek. "That Brad would believe for one second that one of my clients could be implicated in money laundering really frosts me, especially given that many were referred by him."

"He's just being ultra-cautious. As Manager of an offshore banking office, he must walk a fine line avoiding any prohibited activities."

"I'm just sorry that you had such a cool reception, especially after my telling you how helpful Brad always made things for me."

"You needn't apologize; it adds a bit of excitement to our trip. In the meantime, it would be helpful if you would address each client in light of Brad's comments." Derek hesitated, lowering his voice before mentioning the name. "Take this Miguel Santos, for example. I know you're very close to him, but I would strongly suggest you reserve judgment regarding disclosing your real mission here." Derek felt her bristle and quickly softened his comment. "No offense meant. Just better we err on the Doubting Thomas side. You know our British motto: 'Least said, soonest mended'?"

Amanda's silence prompted him to change his tack. "Enough said. Now, how about giving me your read on Miguel's position in light of Brad's commentary."

"Where can I begin? Miguel has a home in San Francisco's Marina district. He's usually there the legal limit of 180 days a year, so I see him often." She smiled fondly as she continued. "Miguel has two sides to his personality. One is a throwback to his college days and his love of the theater. He's a drama buff, a closet intellectual, cloaked under a lighthearted, offhanded manner. He keeps involved in the world of the arts by owning the majority share of the biggest theater group in Manila, as. well as investing in some of the Philippines' top films."

"And his family?"

"He's the hard-working scion of one of the oldest and most respected families in the Philippines. The Santos family has had large sugar holdings in the Negros province for centuries. Brad was right in saying that the government has withheld payments to the sugar owners, along with payments for other commodities, but Miguel's managing to pay them somehow. To diversify, he's recently bought several prawn farms in Ilo Ilo."

"It must be getting to be a big strain, financially, for him."

"His biggest worry right now is the NPA. Playing on their fears and using this whole crisis of non-payment, they have been very active among the sugar workers. The attacks on the fields and the farm buildings have been increasing. Miguel hasn't been to San Francisco for some time in order to keep a close watch on developments at the farm."

"He sounds a fascinating person. It would be tempting to sound him out on any rumors; but I hope you resist."

Amanda's response was a brisk rebuttal. "Miguel's no fan of the Marcos crowd. He'd be the last one to help him launder money. On the other hand, he's high enough up in the ruling strata to know if such rumors are baseless or not." She noticed Derek's frown. "Don't worry, I promise to hold off. Not because I have any doubts concerning Miguel, but we don't need the repercussions such revelations could provoke."

Derek looked relieved. "I can see where that'll be a tall order for you. Now I know why you're such a hotshot relationship manager. You seem to take each client to your bosom as a life-long friend. You worry more over their money than your own." Derek smiled up at her and changed the focus of their conversation as their waiter approach.

"Would you care for a refill on your pot of tea, Miss Evans?" With a shake of her head, Amanda rose to go. "We really should be headed out to the lobby. Miguel's the exception to the rule and is always on time." Amanda no sooner got the words out when she glanced up to see Miguel approaching them.

"Amanda! I almost didn't see you, hidden back here in the deepest corner of the bar. It's not like you to indulge so early. Do I place the blame for your dissipation at the feet of your colleague?" Miguel embraced Amanda with a quick kiss on each cheek, while turning to extend his hand to Derek. Amanda made the introductions, watching Derek's covert sizing up of Miguel.

Miguel was dressed comfortably with the informal formality of the Philippines barong tagalog, the loose fitting white embroidered shirt. Derek seemed overdressed beside Miguel, or at least over- warm for the sultry tropical heat. Miguel stood a full head shorter than Derek did, although he was considered tall for a Filipino. In any country Miguel would command attention. His full head of wavy brown hair curled fashionably long and framed sparkling black eyes, magnetizing one's admiration. Until, that is, one's eyes moved to the raised scar running from his left ear down onto his cheek. His rich and cultured baritone softened questions that might arise at its sight. Their mellow tones, hinting at his past involvement with the theater, riveted one's attention, especially when punctuated by his deep, uninhibited laugh.

Derek's handshake was returned with a distinctly less formal one as Miguel commented, "You show good taste in your choice of a watch. The one you are wearing is the top of the Rolex line, but if you value it, I suggest you keep it in the hotel's safe-deposit box until your departure. Or, do as I do and buy a cheap watch for donating to our active community of thieves—especially in walking into the Mikado." He laughed to lighten his words. "It's not only become the latest popular destination for wealthy diners but the favorite venue for thieves."

Derek seemed to ponder Miguel's suggestion as he hesitated briefly before drawing himself up to his full six feet, four inches. "Thanks for your bit of advice; but for now I'll take that risk. Somehow, I think any thief would get more than a run for his money if he decided to tackle me."

"As you wish; my driver does double duty as a bodyguard, so we shouldn't meet with any problems." He gave Derek a slow once-over and grinned. "I don't doubt for a moment that you could more than handle yourself in a fair set-to. However, our thieves are notorious for the hit and run approach. Just the other day, one of them jumped on a jeepney bus carrying a sack dripping blood. It was filled with fingers and hands—complete with rings, watches and bracelets still attached. They are masters with the machete."

It was Derek's turn to let out an explosive laugh as he responded. "Thanks, Miguel. After that bit I'm a little less certain about retaining my watch, but definitely sure to lose my lunch when I recall your graphic description. What say we compromise? I'll pocket the watch for now? Maybe I can pick up something during my stay that will prove less attractive to thieves—and to tales of disaster."

# EIGHT

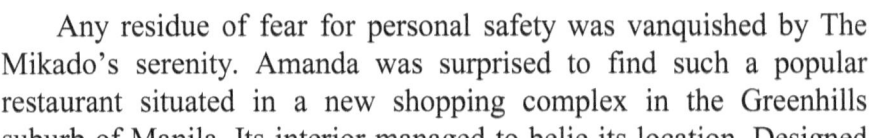

Any residue of fear for personal safety was vanquished by The Mikado's serenity. Amanda was surprised to find such a popular restaurant situated in a new shopping complex in the Greenhills suburb of Manila. Its interior managed to belie its location. Designed as though suspended on an island of water, the soothing sound of waterfalls eased all anxieties. Amanda smiled up at Miguel, beaming her approval. "If the food lives up to the ambiance, this will definitely become one of my favorite restaurants."

"Wait until you sample their seafood. I hope you're a fish fancier, Derek. I can recommend any of it, especially the sushi." He glanced over at Derek's faintly doubtful expression. "Not to worry. It's even more hygienic than any you would find elsewhere in the world, since their fish comes from those aquariums in the back." Miguel leaned down to whisper sotto voce in Amanda's ear. "The prawns, of course, are the world's best, since they come from my prawn farms in Ilo Ilo!" Miguel's laugh was echoed by their waiter's barely disguised chuckle.

"You couldn't ask for a better recommendation than that, could you waiter?" Derek asked as ordered the prawns. Amanda wasn't hungry, but followed their lead and ordered prawns. Both Derek and Miguel began with scotch whiskies. She nursed a green mango juice as she settled in for a warm round of gossip and local color update.

Miguel never failed to amuse her. He seemed to be going out of his way this time. Maybe for Derek's sake, she thought, although he seemed to enjoy pulling Derek's leg a bit. Macho rivalry, she felt, smiling as it dawned on her that the witty verbal dance they were doing had something to do with her. She decided to try to deflect it before it escalated.

"Miguel, give it to me straight. What's the story on the snap election? "

He grinned as he shrugged his shoulders and lowered his voice. "That's a tall order to address over lunch, but, since you sound so earnest, I'll give it my best shot." Miguel's jaw firmed, his breath let out on a long drawn sigh as he responded.

"Marcos has to go through with the snap election. Reagan and his advisors are looking for evidence of overwhelming popular support for him." Miguel's long pause prompted Amanda to fill the void.

"But what about Cory's possible run for office? I hear…."

"Cory Aquino is determined to stand against him on the ballot but, whoever his opponent, it's destined to be a cleverly orchestrated charade ending in a shoo-in. You know how complete Marcos' control of the ballot count will be."

"Is it true this Cory person is just a housewife?" Derek's eyes widened with disbelief.

"Not 'just a housewife'; she's a woman whose husband was assassinated as he returned to his county to try to counter Marcos corruption. She's spunky. Unfortunately…"

"Unfortunately she's wasting her time. Sounds to me like your typical banana republic; all this strum and drang to validate a pre-determined outcome." Derek placed his glass on the table with the same emphatic energy his voice conveyed. "But why now? The U.S. has wanted a snap election for a long time. There must be a deeper context to his timing."

Miguel looked about the room before continuing. The waiter was nowhere in sight. The other diners were clustered to the smoking end of the room, leaving their area relatively private. And yet his tones were muted as he continued.

"Bear with me while I flesh out the context of his actions. First, there's the issue of his deteriorating physical condition. He can't control his bladder, let alone his country." Miguel turned to Amanda. "Excuse the coarseness. The truth is that Imelda virtually runs the country in his stead. She's convinced the army is in their corner and will assure the success of his re-election."

"Is it true that some changes in the army's leadership are in the wind?" Amanda waited for Miguel to verify Paco's account.

"The army is vulnerable right now. They are unpaid, nervous about Marcos' failing health, and ripe for an overturn." Miguel stopped as he registered Amanda's wide-eyed look.

"But..."

"But" is right, Amanda, and an emphatic 'but' it is. The consensus is that nothing will happen except more of the same, i.e., an election outcome keeping Marcos and his army intact."

"I begin to get the picture," Derek said. "A strong crow from the cock affirming he still rules the roost. It brings the army to heel, convinces the U.S. he is still the man to back, and vanquishes the opposition."

"You got it; a grandstand play on all counts—and destined to work, mores the pity."

Miguel hesitated, watching the waiter calculate whether or not to approach them. He gave the waiter a subtle nod. All conversation halted as their water glasses were refilled, their orders delivered, and the waiter took his discreet leave.

"But enough with the view from here, Amanda; what do you hear back in the States?" Miguel continued.

"The U.S. papers seem to be giving the situation a wide berth, watching and waiting as the gauntlet is thrown down for Marcos to undergo a snap election." Amanda reached down and drew out documents from her briefcase. "Except for this San Jose newspaper." She handed the paper to Miguel, who smiled as he read the front page. "Its editor is a Filipino who's been doing a series of exposes on the corruption of Marcos, as well as hurling accusations at President Reagan for being too weak with him."

"And right he is. I know Hernando, the editor. He's a straight shooter, but at risk if he ever returns to the Philippines. During his last visit to Manila he had at least four pair of eyes on him all the time." Miguel frowned as he looked around. "For that matter, he's almost equally at risk in San Jose, especially since this article accuses Marcos of bleeding all of the country's wealth—the fabled Yamashita's gold included—out of the Central Bank and into numbered accounts in Switzerland.

Miguel's statement rang in Amanda's ears. "Miguel, please don't think I'm catching the Filipino paranoia, but I need your advice on something having to do with this trip. I don't know whether to take it seriously or not." She paused, wanting to frame her account in as balanced a perspective as possible before continuing. She looked up and caught Derek's eye.

His stare was almost, but not quite, as menacing; more a firm 'Stop' message being transmitted. It suddenly dawned on her that he was concerned she'd reveal too much of what Brad had confided.

She laughed to break the tension. "Derek thinks I'm imagining things to be so haunted by a strange man on my flight over." Derek visibly eased back into his chair, a look of barely tolerant exasperation directed her way. Undaunted, she began to recount her episode on the plane.

Miguel listened to her description intently, without the slightest trace of his usual whimsical smile. Even Derek's raised eyebrow and muttered "Overactive imagination" as she finished, didn't deflect his focus.

Miguel chose his words carefully. "Amanda, I know you've heard of some of the superstitions the Filipino people still believe in. There is one that may fit the episode you described. It is called 'kulam'. The person using it is called a 'mangkukulam'. It is a belief that certain people can cause physical illness by a stare. This sorcery is usually only practiced because of a belief that the other person has, or will, create an intolerable offense."

"Me?" Amanda choked on a prawn, stopping mid-bite.

"Calm down, Amanda. You'd be the least likely person to create any offense. I've seen you go overboard to avoid any friction, large or small, even when it involves your own discomfort. So relax, it's highly unlikely that it was an incidence of 'kulam'. My guess is the same as Derek's. I don't believe that you imagined it, only that it was directed at someone else, maybe his wife or business partner. You simply turned into its path."

On that note he broke into a smile. "Please erase that frown, Amanda. I don't mean to worry you, but I knew that if you polled anyone else you'd wonder why I didn't level with you. Superstitions are rampant here, as you know. Even the educated have been known to carry an 'anting-anting' just to be on the safe side." His smile conveyed the absurdity of his next comment. "One of the more far out rumors concerning Marcos is that he actually had an 'anting-anting' inserted in his back by Bishop Aglipay."

Derek let out a snort of disbelief. "I thought I'd heard it all. What on earth is an anting-anting?"

"They're believed to be magical talismans assuring their owners invincibility." Miguel caught the deep look of contempt that flickered across Derek's face. "I know, I know; you have absolutely no belief in that sort of thing, and I agree with you." He turned to Amanda with a look blended of casual but concerned protectiveness.

"Even so, I think I'll have my driver bring round an extremely powerful amulet for you to wear. I'll choose one pretty enough to hang from a ribbon around your neck or out of sight if you wish. It can't hurt. Wear it, as a token of my affection and appreciation."

Amanda glanced from Miguel to Derek, armoring herself against a look of derision on Derek's face. She was surprised by his look and shocked by his words. "Go ahead, Amanda; what harm is there in it? I've been known to wear a copper bracelet a client from Mexico gave me when I mentioned I was having trouble with arthritis from years of playing rugby."

"I don't believe we are really having this conversation, but it's clear I'm outnumbered." Amanda laughed gently and turned back to Miguel. "OK, if you send a 'what's-it' over I'll wear it to humor you two, but not a word to anyone else." Amanda turned a conspiratorial look at Derek. "Think what that would do to my corporate image." Derek laughed and Amanda and Miguel joined in. The residue of tension was released.

"Gone troppo is what we'd call it." Derek said, glancing down at the newspaper Miguel had placed on the table. "Best not to leave this around, I expect."

"Right you are." Miguel turned to Amanda. "Mind if I keep this?"

"Not at all." She glanced down at the other item in her lap and placed it in his hands. "I nearly forgot these chocolates."

Miguel carefully took both paper and chocolates and placed them in his briefcase. "I'll savor them both."

The remainder of their luncheon conversation was filled with lighthearted pleasantries. Over coffee, Miguel quickly discovered his and Derek's mutual love of golf. Amanda was shocked when Miguel got Derek to agree to a day of golf at Plaza Verde Resort. But not half the shock at the coincidence of her having an appointment to meet a client there that same day, an appointment Derek had no awareness of.

Lunch concluded with Miguel giving each of them a warm abrazo and reminding Derek of their game. He turned to Amanda. "Be on the look-out for someone to deliver your new necklace. Just promise me you'll wear it!" Miguel looked deeply into Amanda's eyes until she nodded agreement.

As Miguel's car and driver pulled up, Miguel hurriedly made arrangements with the driver to pick them up at their hotel for the hour and a half journey to Plaza Verde Resort next week. Settling into the drive back, Miguel smiled as he invited Amanda to join them in their golf game or alternatively, to just lie by the pool and catch a few rays.

Amanda bristled. "Remember what I'm here for, Miguel. The bank expects me to work, not lie around a pool at a resort."

Miguel shrugged. "Some day I'll persuade you to adopt the Filipino credo, "Live now, Work later." I'll wager you could get a lot of work done around the pool at this resort. All of the big money in Manila will be there, including my favorite aunt who wants to discuss business with you. So, work and play, OK; conscience clear?" He gave her another quick embrace as the car pulled into the hotel's portico. "Until then; Ciao!"

Since the expected car and driver belonging to Engineer Lopez was not waiting in the hotel's entryway, Amanda and Derek decided to run up to their rooms to check for messages. During their brief elevator ride Derek commented on how much he had enjoyed the lunch with Miguel. Amanda remained silent, turning aside to hide a small 'I told you so' smile.

There were several messages under Amanda's door and two telexes from the office. The telexes were general in nature, only asking her to call two other individuals who would like to 'show her around on her holiday in the Philippines." Amanda couldn't help but wonder if their ruse was really necessary. With all the gossips congregated in the Manila Peninsula Hotel each day, everyone knew not only who was in town, but where and often with whom they were meeting. Still, she was sworn to do her best to protect her bank, herself and her client's secrecy.

She reviewed their agenda for their next meeting with Engineer Lopez. 'Nonnie' was a prominent attorney in Manila and on the board of the Makati Stock Exchange. He made no bones of his partiality to the existing government since he enjoyed such an important role in their economic arena. Amanda reminded herself to caution Derek to maintain neutrality in any discussions. It turned out she need not have had any apprehension. Derek handled the Lopez call and all those that followed with impressive skill and discretion.

Amanda had willingly let Derek take the lead in his presentation of the features and benefits of offshore trusts and companies. It quickly became clear that, not only were many clients already familiar with offshore centers and their tax and anonymity benefits, but they often had companies already established. Her competition's calling officers had obviously not been sitting on their hands, but they hadn't clearly explained their uses. Derek saved the day as he probed to discover that many of the clients weren't getting full value out of the companies they had, especially given the thousands of dollars per year the average client spent in fees.

Armed with the personal rundown that Amanda had provided, Derek skillfully tailored the additional uses to be made of them, such as providing for care of children with on-going health problems; (Sr. Panay and his retarded daughter), and the establishment of business continuity trusts (various clients). Amanda was struck by how maintaining control of their hard won businesses, even from beyond the grave, had enormous appeal.

Not much room for levity presented itself during the day's trust presentations, Amanda observed. There was only one occasion when Amanda had to muffle a gasp of either horror or humor. Director Cruz, who ran one of the largest corporations in the Philippines, shocked her when he revealed his concerns.

"Mr. Ashton, how would you handle the trust assets in a case where one of his beneficiaries may kidnap the trustee, claim his death, and try to have the assets of the trust disbursed?" He gave as an example the case of a friend's son arranging the kidnapping of his father in order to come into sizable assets needed to pay the son's gambling debts.

Derek kept a straight face as he explained that the trustee was the Bank, not an individual, and therefore beneficiaries were powerless to disrupt the trust structure as originally set up by the founder. Furthermore, he emphasized, actual death has to be confirmed before any distribution is made.

Strange what money could do to parent-child relationships, she thought on the drive back. One of the opportunities her job provided was an in-depth look at the super-wealthy. She found it fascinating to try to isolate the common denominators. Wealth could certainly buy, if not happiness, then at least privacy, freedom and power. She questioned whether the old adage, 'It's better to be poor but happy', had any basis. Why was money equated with discontent? She couldn't see poor people demonstrating much happiness in their lives. Better rich, she supposed, and yet society's focus on greed and acquisition dismayed her. So what then constitutes a genuine safe haven?

Their day had run from eight AM until eleven PM, but, tired as they were, they decided to recap the day, preview tomorrow's schedule, and let down over a nightcap. The Mandarin's bar area was almost empty, except for two small groups of people clustered around the piano bar. They found a quiet corner where they wouldn't be overheard. Derek ordered a cognac, Amanda, red wine. The minute the waiter headed behind the bar, Amanda decided to broach the subject that had filled her thoughts since their last meeting. She began by using the tale of the 'kidnapping by your children' scenario to open a philosophic discussion with Derek on the pros and cons of wealth.

"I know that money doesn't guarantee happiness, and obviously, lots of money can produce greed, but at least it can protect you from having to toady to anyone. Take Jacqueline Kennedy, for example. She had a whole island and a yacht in the middle of the ocean to keep her far from the madding crowd." Amanda let out a long sigh.

Derek grinned and took a slow sip of his cognac. He placed the empty glass down carefully on the table and studied her. "Not so strange that Amanda Evans should focus on that aspect of wealth. You've chosen a career where your success depends on your ability to deal with demands from people all the time." Derek pulled his chair closer to hers and reached out to take her hand. "Does the Queen of Relationship Managers need to identify her own needs?"

Derek's sincerity and his gentle touch took her by surprise. Confused, Amanda didn't trust her response. She turned her head away to focus on the group across the room. Someone in the group was staring at them.

All previous concerns vanished as she turned back to Derek. "That man over at the piano bar with that group. He looks like the man on the plane. At least, I think it's him. Can you tell?" Derek turned aside. "Don't make it obvious, but I'm sure he was looking at me. I think it's the same man." Amanda knocked her drink coaster onto the floor in her haste to turn and cast one more covert glance at the man.

Derek was more direct. He rose from the table to exit the room on a path that would take him right past the piano bar. The group continued to chat among themselves or hum along with the pianist. No one appeared to pay attention to Derek's passing, even when he turned and directed his gaze at them, giving more than a cursory glance at each individual. He acted as though he might have been looking for someone he knew as he smiled and headed in the direction of the men's room. Amanda greeted his return with an eager, questioning gaze.

"Well, was it him? Could you tell?" He motioned her to lower her voice.

"I can't be sure because I didn't get a good look at him. One of them could fit the general age and description. In fact, two of them could." He glanced away and back at her. "Let's face it; probably half the Filipino male population under forty could fit that description. The only thing I'm sure of is that we're both exhausted. Everything and everyone will look different in the morning. What say we turn in before the witching hour?"

"I guess you're right. It must be sleep deprivation and jet-lag that's getting to me." Amanda rose and started walking towards the elevators, surprising Derek by her speedy recant and willingness to call it a day.

"Are you certain you'll be able to sleep? Promise me you'll not count strange men instead of sheep?" He said as he turned to her after stepping out of the elevator. "I'll be happy to stay with you awhile until you're drowsy. I've been known to talk anyone into a coma without even putting half a mind to it."

Before Amanda could quite register his intent, they'd reached the door of Amanda's room where Derek turned her face up to his. She was taken aback at the look that filled his eyes.

"Derek, I—" Her feeble attempts to respond were stopped by the warmth of his lips, silencing all words and all thoughts. A weightless, melting into eternity feeling left her sinking towards the floor when he abruptly broke contact.

"Forgive me, Mandy, me love. I guess it was your looking so helpless there, or, my being weakened from jetlag myself. Say you understand and I'll let you go off to bed."

Amanda's voice sounded like someone deep within a well. "Forget it, Derek; it never happened." She heard herself coolly making arrangements to meet for breakfast in the hotel's coffee shop at seven thirty. With a brief 'goodnight' she was behind her locked door, bracing herself against it and releasing her withheld breath. Her heart was beating too fast. Anxious to discount the last few moments, she compulsively snatched up the scattered messages protruding from under her door. Had it really been just one day in the Philippines?

Amanda riffled through her phone messages looking for Rob's name. She missed his call, she thought, feeling vaguely responsible after that incident outside the door. Amanda distracted herself with a long cool shower. She was just getting into bed when the phone rang. She quickly grabbed it, reassured at hearing Rob's solid baritone. It took her a couple of seconds to register the anxiety that coated his words.

"Things are crazy back here. Carter's called a meeting this afternoon to announce a complete reorganization. Rumor has it many heads will roll."

Amanda was stunned by the fear in Rob's voice. "Surely not yours?"

"Who knows? Edward's firing over funding that large loan..." The line went silent except for a strangled sound from Rob. "I worked with Edwards on that deal. Granted, not at its conclusion; but—" He hesitated. "By the time you return, I may no longer be part of Fidelity American Bank". He tried to make the comment light, but Amanda heard the shock in his voice.

"Rob, there has to be an explanation for it." Rob's silence prompted Amanda to try harder. "Who would be better than you to help Carter get to the bottom of things? This whole mess could turn out to be the making of you." Amanda waited. But, if anything, Rob's response was even more doubtful.

"Carter intends to expose everyone involved." His voice reflected his bewilderment. "Anyway, I thought I'd better fill you in before this afternoon's meeting. You're bound to hear something through the grapevine, even in Manila."

"Whatever it is, you'll handle it fine. I know you."

"Thanks, Amanda. One way or the other, I'll call and let you know the outcome." Rob's voice had regained some of its firm confidence.

"Sure, Rob. Good luck." She turned her head into the pillow, suddenly feeling the depths of her exhaustion. Rob's total lack of any mention of concern for her contrasted with Derek's strange behavior and unexpected tenderness. More serious concerns of the 'who, how and why' of which client was connected to the money laundering scheme swiftly vanquished personal concerns, including sleep.

# NINE

The ringing went on forever. Fighting a cocooning fog of sleep, Amanda groggily sat up. She stared around at unfamiliar drapes, puzzled by the source of the ringing. A slight dizziness of jet lag reminded her that she was in a hotel in Manila. Lifting her phone's handset, she frowned. Slowly turning her head, her ears registered the source of the incessant ringing. It was coming from Derek's room.

"What time is it?" she muttered, glancing at her travel alarm. "Five o'clock!" Amanda yanked the covers determinedly over her head. The ringing ceased, as did the likelihood of her going back to sleep.

Tossing her pillows against the headboard, she grabbed a book, willing it to lull her back into slumber. Her focus wavered as predawn thoughts claimed center stage. *Dangerous 'To Do's', images of the strange man, Nigel shouting, "Don't you dare", Brad's Keep away";* All commanded her attention.

Open-eyed reality returned and with it, a frown of puzzlement. Phone… Derek's phone…Derek…suddenly reminded her of last night's kiss as she brushed her fingertips across her lips, jumped out of bed and shook off any further examination except that of the phone ringing The sound continued from next door, indicating he must have left his room. But where would he be going at this hour? More importantly, what was he up to, she wondered?

She headed for the bathroom, deciding to shower, dress and go down to the café for a cup of coffee. "And the gooiest pastry around." Speaking aloud to her mirror image, she willed such simple clarity to follow her through her day.

Dressed and ready to go, she unlocked her door, stooping to pick up the morning paper wedged beneath. A message dropped from its folds: 'Parcel delivery for you at reception'. The concierge greeted her as she walked off the elevator, cheerfully locating a twine-tied parcel as she waited at the desk. As she turned to go he retrieved a message that had just come in confirming Brad's dinner party in her honor. She stashed the package in her handbag and headed towards the coffee shop.

Poised to enter, she hesitated and looked around. The coffee shop was open but still semi-dark and nearly empty. Suddenly she spotted Derek sitting in a far corner. She'd barely taken her first step when she noticed he wasn't alone. A large cluster of decorative palms obscured his companion's face. She moved out of Derek's line of sight as she studied his companion who'd suddenly turned to motion the waiter.

Amanda choked. It was the man on the plane! Praying she hadn't been noticed, Amanda silently backtracked to the elevator and the safety of her room. Her heart was pounding in sync with her racing thoughts as she fought to develop a plausible explanation. A rush of adrenaline, with its fight or flight affect, filled her with anger. She grabbed the package she had dropped on the bed and ripped at its wrappings.

Miguel's amulet! How extraordinary it seemed as she turned it in her palm. It was strangely shaped, a tree-like piece of stone, light in weight and luminescent in its refraction of light as she moved it. Feeling a bit foolish, she decided to loop her gold chain through and wear it as a necklace inside her blouse.

Whether it was the remains of her rage or the comfort of her hidden talisman, she was calm when she headed back to the coffee shop for their scheduled meeting. Derek was all smiles and light-hearted banter. "How'd you sleep? I feel great, slept the night away right on through 'til dawn."

"Wish I could say the same, but—" Amanda had to bite her tongue not to burst out in rage at having seen him with her nemesis earlier. Instead, she aimed her most charming smile. "Guess I'm just excited about the day. It'll take me awhile to catch up on sleep, but I feel fine."

"And well you should. You were an apt pupil yesterday." He lifted his coffee cup in a toast. When she failed to react, he seemed to try harder with the humor.

"My jokes aren't getting to you this morning, are they? My guess is you've let the situation in Manila and the rumors from head office begin to spook you. "

"Maybe you're right." She chose to let him think it.

"If you let every rumor get to you, your effectiveness will go downhill. You have more immediate concerns."

"Exactly—like my ordering of breakfast." Amanda turned to the waiter. "Coffee and a pastry, something with cinnamon, raisins, butter… the works"

Derek gave her a puzzled look as he ordered "just coffee". She choked on the image of the breakfast he'd already had. Catching her look, he redoubled his efforts.

"Come on now, let's see a smile. I won't be with you to jolly you up during your next appointment."

Amanda's questioning stare prompted his reply. "I'll be locked in my room waiting for an important call from the Caymans. But you'll do fine. I fully expect you to have sold an offshore trust when next we meet." Gulping down his coffee, he turned to watch her finish hers.

Noticing his silent stare, she hesitated. "Right you are then. It'll give me a chance to see if I really have mastered your pitch on offshore trust and companies." She brightened her next words. "If I don't see you here at one o'clock I'll head on to my next meeting." She gathered up her pastry and headed back to her room. A quick "good luck" was all the conversation shared as she closed the door behind her, leaned against it and muttered, "What is going on around here?"

The meeting with the Villarreal's went well—phenomenally well. She'd managed to lay the ghost of the sight of Derek with the man of the evil eye, at least for the duration of their meeting.

Vic didn't appear to notice anything amiss. He seemed to be in high spirits, regaling her with jokes on their drive to the club. Amanda found herself falling into the easy atmosphere of work cloaked in fun by the natural ebullience of the Villarreal family. Vic's driver swiftly pulled up to the Jockey Club where Dina greeted them from a table groaning with a lavish merienda. The perfect mid-morning meal did wonders to restore her balance.

Her trust presentation was received enthusiastically, especially the feature that allowed it to provide protection for the continuation of Vic's businesses. "I plan on making a trip to Miami late in February. Let me take those documents and I'll route by the Caymans to go over them with this guy Ashton while I'm there." He glanced around to survey anyone within earshot of his next remark. The table he had requested provided perfect privacy. "For the moment though, I have more pressing concerns to discuss."

Amanda soon learned why. He lowered his voice and drew his chair closer as Dina smiled her encouragement. "I've just closed the sale on one of our manufacturing plants and want to deposit the proceeds with you. It'll take at least three weeks until closure, so the twelve million won't stay in the account for long but..."

"Twelve million? In U.S. dollars?" Her decibel level was low enough but her dramatic delivery prompted Amanda to glance around to be sure she'd drawn no attention.

"U.S. dollars yes, but most of it moving into another investment within thirty days."

Her mind was racing. Any deposit that large would have to involve senior management. The thought of receiving twelve million in new money was both elating and suspect. The amount, the speed with which it would wash through the account, the rumors of money laundering, all rang alarm bells. She composed a look of friendly acknowledgement. "How exciting for you; tell me more."

"The exciting part isn't so much the sale. I've been trying to unload the furniture manufacturing side of the business for awhile now and finally got a good offer. It's the new investment opportunity that's the exciting part." He hesitated, studying her reaction intently as if expecting her to interject. "But maybe you've already heard that part from Raffy de la Serna?"

Amanda hesitated, remembering that Raffy and Vic were cousins. "Not yet." She smiled. "We're meeting at Plaza Verde this week." Vic gave a broad grin as she prompted him. "So why don't you steal his thunder and let me in on it?"

"Plaza Verde, you say? Then maybe I'll see you there. As to letting you in on it, I'm still in the dark myself. Raffy's called a meeting to outline the deal." Vic turned to each side and lowered his voice. "It must be something big to interest the Hong Kong crowd that's flying in."

"Knowing Raffy's exuberance, it's sure to have wide appeal."

Vic registered the implied 'but'. "Not to worry, Amanda. You know me, the tortoise side of the family. I'll examine it six ways to Sunday before I decide. For now, all I know is that leaving twelve million in a deposit account, even a CD, isn't a good investment. If Raffy's deal doesn't wash, I have a line on another business opportunity that will require a major portion of those funds." Dina, silent throughout, smiled and gave his hand a little squeeze.

Amanda's thoughtful expression prompted him to add, "Don't worry though. I'll try to keep whatever isn't needed on deposit with you. I have no complaints, so you'll just have to put up with me for awhile." He laughed as he ordered a round of champagne in celebration. Before she clinked glasses, Amanda added an important caveat.

"One thing, Vic; I'll have to run it by senior management before any decisions are made. The total amount, even if the bulk of it doesn't remain long, will warrant several units having input. Anything you can give me on the sale will help."

"Sure thing; I'll have my accountant run you off a copy of the escrow documents and drop them off at your hotel.

"That'll help. Is it the factory in Bagio where I fell in love with a mahogany dining set?"

"It is. Place your order now if you're serious."

"No; I was just curious."

"Well then. Here's to your coming up with the best deal." Vic raised his glass. "I leave it in your hands. It's at least three weeks off yet." Vic seemed relaxed and confident as he and Dina turned to discussions of family.

Amanda was anything but relaxed. She was on a fear and excitement high when Vic and Dina dropped her back at the hotel. *Just wait until I tell Nigel,* she thought. No one had ever brought in twelve million in new business from one client. Wariness suddenly overcame her enthusiasm. *Where the money's coming from may be legit,* she thought, *but where it's headed is the key. And Raffy holds that piece of the puzzle.* The meeting at Plaza Verde Resort seemed to be shaping up to more than just sunbathing.

Approaching her hotel room, she noticed the edges of a sealed envelope protruding from under the door. Stepping inside, she retrieved it and two phone messages. She kicked off her shoes, sat down at the desk, opened the envelope and drew out two telexes. It took her a minute or two of rereading the first to absorb its message.

It was from Nigel. His message, even more strongly, cautioned her to use extra circumspection in the handling of all of her visits. Her heart sank as she deliberated over calling him at home. *Just wait 'til I launch my blockbuster,* she thought. She read on to the end.

He insisted she call him Friday night via Brad's home number to discuss something that had come up. She figured Brad must have called Nigel with his version of the seriousness of the situation to prompt Nigel's bizarre postscript: "URGENT! I worry about the hepatitis epidemic there. Is there any threat to your health?"

She pulled a lock of hair distractedly, frowning at the weird phrasing of Nigel's message. *He would have made a lousy spy,* she thought.

"Epidemic is right—of drama and deception." She spoke aloud, pausing for a moment as her unspoken thoughts surfaced. *I'm a banker, not a CIA agent. Intrigue was not what I bargained for.*

She quickly tore into another telex from her office. It was from Mai who commented on the office briefly and reminded Amanda of her willingness to fly out to replace her in Manila. Amanda flung the telex aside. What's come over Mai, she wondered; usually she looks forward to playing queen of the office while I'm away? She made a mental note to call Mai tonight.

The cumulative effects of the day, first Derek, then the windfall deposit prospect from Vic, and now Mai; all left her in an agitated state. What next, she wondered? What's next, she decided as she picked up one of the green phone messages, was returning the call of her most important client, Don Emilo de la Serna.

'My dear Amanda; it is so good to have you here." She hardly recognized the labored words as coming from the dynamic Don de la Serna. "I look forward to seeing you." His voice weakened to where Amanda could barely make out his next words. "Brad's; meet you before party. Six o'clock?"

The sound of his voice as he struggled to get the words out stunned her. "Of course, but are you certain you want to do that? I'd be happy to come to your home."

"No. I must be there." An echo of the old Don wavered in the strength of the 'must'.

"And I will be there for you. Six it is, Friday at Brad's." Amanda knew that Brad and Caro's home was in the De La Serna compound and the Don could leave should he not feel up to it. A guttural sound issued from the receiver as Emilio labored to say something more. She could make out only one word, "Raffy" before his voice failed.

"Rest my dear friend. I'll be there; six at Brad's." She hung up after his pained goodbye, crumpled the note and blinked away the stinging behind her eyes. Glancing down at the second message, her spirits lifted to read that her last appointment of the day had cancelled. She jumped when the phone rang. Derek's irritatingly cheerful voice let her know he would be waiting at the elevator in ten minutes.

Their afternoon luncheon with Cisco and Cia Lozano had been rescheduled for the Manila Hotel. The gossip had reached Cisco's ears that Amanda had lunched at his planned restaurant, The Mikado, yesterday. The Manila Hotel's restaurant was usually one of her favorites, but lunch passed with Amanda fighting a sense of distraction. Fortunately Derek carried the ball. Amanda was grateful for his success and their obvious charm at his tales.

Lunch passed in a blur of excitement over pictures of baby Natasha. Amanda commented enthusiastically but barely ate anything. Cia noticed Amanda's preoccupation. "Is it jet-lag getting to you, Amanda?"

"I'm afraid so. Everything's starting to blur right now." She forced a brighter expression and turned her attention onto Derek and Cisco's conversation concerning trusts. The birth of their new baby had focused both Cisco and Cia on assuring the well-being of their new family. Amanda watched as Cia memorized every detail, knowing that in the end she'd be the primary decision-maker.

Amanda realized she'd checked out a bit when Cisco turned to ask if she'd like any coffee, adding, "I'm glad we could make this lunch because we'll have to miss your party at Brad's. The baby's had some congestion in her chest. We're going to take her in to visit her doctor tomorrow afternoon." He turned to Derek. "I'll take these documents and call you next week before you leave." Turning back to Amanda he repeated his regret at not making her dinner party.

"First things first; if Natasha were my baby, heaven and earth couldn't distract me if she weren't feeling well." Amanda's response brought a big smile to Cia. She offered their car and driver to drop them back at the Mandarin. Amanda gratefully accepted. Two and a half hours of a late lunch had caused her energies to wane.

Derek seemed pensive during the trip back. He even stumbled a bit over their names as he said farewell and watched impatiently as their car pulled away. He turned to Amanda as they walked into the lobby. "What I could really use is a warm bath and a solid night's sleep." He looked down at his watch. "It's quarter to five. How would early dinner, say seven, sound to you? We can round it off with a stiff nightcap and an early night."

"I'm tempted to crash right now." She looked up at him, anticipating what he was about to say. "I know. It's best to hang in there until Manila bedtime if I expect to overcome my jet lag. So dinner at seven it is."

Derek gave a look mixed with satisfaction and concern. "You really look fagged out. I'm worried about you. If there's anything you want to talk about, we Irish not only have the proverbial gift for gab, but I guarantee you that I am considered equally great as a listener."

"Thanks, Derek. It's just exhaustion. Nothing a good night's sleep won't cure." She punctuated her words by walking quickly through the hotel entryway. As she aimed towards the elevator she turned to add, "Perhaps room service would be best." No sooner than those words had left her mouth than she remembered her resolve to discover what he was up to. "On second thought, let's stay with Plan A, early dinner and early night. In the meantime I'm going to put my feet up so I'll be less 'fagged' as you call it when I join you for dinner." They rode up in silence. "See you at seven then", she called out as she headed for her door, closing it on Derek's puzzled stare.

Entering her room, she kicked off her shoes, glanced over to the phone, and blessed the gift of no lit up message light. The thought of a bath filled her senses with anticipation. She'd finish by curling up under the bedcovers with a "Do Not Disturb" sign guarding her door

Sedated by the warm bath, Amanda fell back onto the bed, reviewing the highlights of her day. Her thoughts turned to the Villarreal's twelve million-dollar deal and the fact that she'd never made any mention of it to Derek. Nor had she discussed her success in handling the trust presentations. After the breakfast episode she decided the less she revealed to him the better. High on her list were verifications, not only of deposits, but also of Derek Ashton. In the meantime the twelve million—three weeks away or not—had to be discussed with Nigel. But not until after the Raffy meeting, she decided, when she'd have more answers to Nigel's questions. For now she'd give a call to the office and speak with Mai.

Karen answered, saying Mai was out on a client call, and although Nigel's panic was growing by the day, all was well. She called out a 'Hello' to a customer, prompting Amanda to interject an abrupt 'Talk to you later then; goodbye'.

Having decided to put her feet up just for a few moments, suddenly Amanda found herself fighting up from a deep sleep to peer out at a clock saying seven PM.

She managed a quick application of fresh make-up in record time, tossing on a soft cotton skirt of deep purple with a lighter violet sleeveless top. She was out the door exactly at seven twenty. Derek's bright glance told her she must have managed to repair her earlier impression.

"You look decidedly non-bankerish. You must have grabbed a little shut-eye. Just what the doctor ordered, I'd say." He took her arm and guided her into the dining room. Out of habit Amanda scanned each table, expecting her 'mystery' man to be lurking among the potted palms. When she saw that only six tables were occupied and none of them by anyone she recognized, she relaxed. A candle on the table cast just the right warmth through its pink globe as soft music filled the background. After the first glass of a delightful white burgundy she felt a celebratory mood fill her at the delightful secret of her day's mix of success and suspense. Her eyes sparkled with invincibility as she parried Derek's every bon mot. The chilled papaya soup was liquid heaven and, along with a perfect Caesar salad, warm garlicky bread and more wine, she felt her confidence expand.

"It's amazing what a little nap can do. You are positively radiant, Amanda."

Derek reached across the table and took her hand. A sense of an electric shock caused her to draw it back in surprise. Derek's reaction was just as abrupt. His voice took on a distinct firmness as he continued.

"Well then, shall we review the output of the day and strategize for tomorrow?" His manner was as business-like as she had ever seen.

"Please no, Derek. Let's just not be working for at least an hour or two in a day. I really am enjoying unwinding." Amanda was gambling that 'in vino veritas' might drag some personal revelations from him. She punctuated her remark by reaching across the table and giving the hand that seemed about to snap the stem of his wineglass, a light touch.

The time seemed to flow past in a wine drenched haze of conversation that somehow managed to pry out of Derek at least a key piece of personal background.

"I was married…once." He hesitated as she waited for him to go on. "My wife died in the crash of a private plane bringing her from the Grand Caymans to a small, private island in the Bahamas." His voice was strangely hollow as he continued. "She was to have joined me at the estate of one of my client's to help celebrate his fiftieth birthday." He took a moment to look up and away with a focus entirely inward. "I'd gone over earlier to handle some private business dealings with the client and was eagerly awaiting word of her arrival. The plane disappeared off the radar over an empty stretch of water." Derek's eyes looked haunted by the image. "Planes and boats kept up their search for days, but no sign of the plane was ever found."

"Oh Derek; I'm so sorry." As the words left her mouth she knew how hollow they sounded.

"It nearly drove me over the edge. I quit banking, bought a sailboat and sailed around the world."

Amanda hesitated at adding any further comment. Six years ago or not, the wound was still open. Derek had quickly turned to studying the menu while Amanda studied him. That might explain part of his erratic behavior, she thought. He was extremely charming, but only in the most superficial of ways. Might that also explained his moodiness, she wondered? She was on the verge of feeling sympathetic when the image of Derek in the company of her mystery man suddenly returned. Nothing could explain his breakfast with such a man. Especially after Derek had lobbied so strongly with his theory that the man was just an unfortunate stranger and her fears totally ungrounded. The fact that he hadn't revealed a word of such a meeting decided her to lay low and continue her observations before confronting him.

After they both had ordered, Amanda changed the conversational direction, drawing Derek out about how he'd happened to apply for work at Fidelity American Bank and what he had done earlier. He dismissed that topic with a simple account of Nigel's job search for a

Cayman Islands Manager. Sorenson knew of Derek through a friend of his and recommended him as someone who had operated a successful offshore bank for over fourteen years.

Derek looked up, saying he hadn't been able to decide whether or not it was a good decision to go back into banking. "I had expected, once having decided to leave the world of banking, that I'd never return.                                                                                                       "

Amanda shook her head. "But why then?'

"I needed to get back into the traces." Their dinners were served and Derek saw his chance to change the subject. "I really don't know much about Fidelity American Bank, its business or its politics. I'd appreciate your filling me in." His comment led them into a long discussion of the current climate transforming all banks. The ease with which he opened to the subject decided Amanda to reveal at least the puzzling wording in Nigel's telex.

Derek paused. "From what little I know of Nigel, I'd reserve judgment. It sounds as though Brad may have put him into a paranoid mode."

"With the arrest of the New York banker, both Nigel and Brad have grounds for some paranoia." Amanda felt suddenly defensive of her team. She put down her fork and shoved her plate away. "Money laundering's a serious business."

"More serious is convincing the right banker that it can be done with no one the wiser." Derek glanced at her half-eaten dinner, took another large forkful of fettuccini and watched as Amanda turned a cautious eye over the room. He fully expected her to veto any more banking talk.

"Please go on, Derek." She'd crossed her fingers under the table before continuing. "Believe it or not, although I know in theory about money laundering, I've really never experienced it first hand." Amanda listened closely, the memory of him with his breakfast partner coloring each word she took in.

"There are so many ways to make dirty money look as though it came from a legitimate business. The large transactions and the variety of businesses and accounts through which money can be transferred are done in such a sequence that by the time it reaches your department it appears to be clean."

"Make it simple; an A B C of laundering money example, easy enough for me to absorb."

Derek smiled. "I'll try. So much of any really big money has been tainted—unless it's old family wealth; and even that may once have started off as shady. For example, one of your most illustrious young president's came from a family whose earlier generations are reputed to have earned considerable wealth by dealing on a large scale with illegal transactions during prohibition." He looked studiously into her eyes. "But let's use an example of a more modern scheme of setting up a business that looks, on the surface, like a company that would be expected to deal in large dollar amounts—like a jewelry store business. Accounts are set up in various locations under various business names, all of which are 'owned' by offshore corporations. Using money that has originated in illegal ways, say, for example, selling clandestine goods—like armaments— to third world countries, deposits can be washed in and out through the jewelry stores without suspicion, all the while using what seems to be authentic bills of lading or the like. By the time anyone recognizes—including the bankers that are handling the store accounts—that the jewelry stores have gone out of business, the owners have lots of money sitting in a Swiss bank and their erstwhile clients are cruising the Aegean on their yacht."

"Wow, it sounds so intricate to lay a 'genuine' looking web to bait the banks for handling the accounts." Amanda shook her head.

"As intricate as that set-up step is, the more serious one is to build a relationship, ideally with a noble, naive banker, and then lure him or her, always with apparently legitimate deposits. A warm relationship guarantees them an easier conduit for expanding their less than honorable pursuits."

Amanda bristled at what she perceived as an implicit insult to her own professionalism. She drew a deep breath before she replied. "No one can ever con me, Derek Ashton. I know my customer or prospect before I commit to accepting new money. We don't just take anyone's say so." She looked firmly into his eyes, enunciating each word carefully. "My intuition is so keen that I would smell anything rotten—a person or a funny money deal—from way off."

Derek smiled. "Don't get your dander up. I'm not attacking you. I meant the 'him' or 'her' descriptor of the banker simply as a generic reference. I'm sure you wouldn't act without being very certain as to the source of the money."

As his assertion rang on the air, Amanda gulped at the thought of having sandbagged any mention of the twelve million in new money from the Villarreal's. She must have revealed something of what she was thinking. Derek reached over to her.

"Hey there; you checked out completely. I don't think you heard a word of what I last said."

"I'm sorry, Derek. I just remembered that I have a call coming in and a few things to catch up on before I call it a day. What time do you have?"

"Nine thirty. We still have plenty of time. How about a wee dram of good whiskey? I noticed they have Glen Livet in stock. "

"Well, all right, just one and then I must be off." Their order was taken and the liquor lived up to its promise. The buttery liquid left her feeling gently mellowed.

Derek lightened up as well, telling her a funny joke that the Filipino doorman had told him as he waited for her in the lobby. She laughed all the way up to her room. As she turned to say goodnight, Derek pulled her into his arms. She didn't resist and he didn't explain. His kiss was far more intoxicating than any Scotch liqueur. The separation from his mouth seemed a most grievous loss. It left her with a floating, unbalanced, otherworldly feeling.

When she could focus on his voice she heard, "Sweet dreams, my Mandy" as he turned and headed for his room. She stumbled into her room, leaning up against the closed door to catch her breath. It took her a minute after entering her room to register that her phone was ringing and finally to lift the receiver.

"Hello. Hello? Is anyone there?" The voice repeated.

After what seemed like ages, she answered, "Rob? Is that you? "

"Of course it's me. I got in the office early and thought I'd try to catch you. Are they keeping you working long hours?" She started to respond but he'd already moved on. It dawned on her that what she'd hoped was concern, maybe even a little jealousy, was simply a conversational opening. He rushed headlong into the focus of the call, which was to let her know that he not only was saved from the guillotine but stood a good chance of being a key player in the new regime.

"Carter changed his tune when he became convinced I hadn't signed off on the loan." His voice took on a mix of self-importance laced with undercurrents of concern. "He wants me to work to identify those involved in the loss. Not only will they be out, but a big cutback is in the works. 'Lean and mean' is the new motto."

Amanda was shocked at how quickly he had memorized the new party line and how eager was his desire to implement it. The current buzzwords tripped off his tongue like the litany of a devout monk.

"Well, say something. Congratulate me. Are you still there?" His tone was impatient.

"Yes. I'm here. Congratulations. I was thinking about all the people whose careers will be impacted."

Rob responded defensively. "That sounds like you, always the bleeding heart. Anyone displaced would be deadwood to the new corporation." He seemed to warm to his news. "Speaking of deadwood, Nigel had better shore up his organization. If even a ripple of anything distasteful hits the ears of Lyle Carter, Nigel will be first out the door. "

"IPB's a success. It's already as lean and mean as any department, especially when you do a cost-benefit analysis."

Noting her voice turn cool, Rob had a quick rebuttal. "Even so, Carter won't stand for any kind of negative press from any department and rumor has it that yours is positioned for a headline-breaking mess." Rob's voice was so merciless and Amanda's silence so pregnant with anger that he finally broke the impasse with some softening of his indictment. "I'm sorry to be worrying you. I know you won't do anything that might involve any negative press. "

He interrupted as she fought to clear her throat and respond. "Not to worry, Amanda. I haven't said anything to Lyle yet, but he's bound to ask my opinion sooner or later. You can count on my support. Whatever happens, I'm sure you'd land on your feet."

"What are you getting at?"

"Just do your job and return as soon as you can." Rob tried to put cheerful warmth into his words.

Amanda had all she could do to muster a lukewarm finish to a call that left her shivering with an internal chill. "I'm happy for you at the outcome of Carter's meeting. I know you'll do a great job for him."

"Thanks, Amanda. I knew you'd understand."

"Just one thing, Rob, promise you'll not let me be blind-sided if anything is in the works concerning my group." She hesitated while positioning her next phrase to lead him away from any scent of problems. "All is going well here. No problems."

His reply sounded distracted. "Great. I've got to go now. Take care. You hear?" His southern accent leaked through his closing phrase. It was only when she hung up that it hit her that he had completely avoided responding to her request to keep her informed. Fair's fair she thought. I certainly did some fast tap dancing to lead him off the trail of anything out of place here. Serves him right though, she decided, thinking of just how smug he'd sounded.

The phone rang again. Oh good, she thought. It must be Rob saying not to worry about a thing; he'd keep her posted and never do anything to pull the carpet out from under her. But it was Mai's voice on the line, asking if she was doing all right. In spite of the anxiety lurking beneath Mai's persistence, Amanda cut to the quick with a firm, "Yes Mai, everything's fine."

"If you say so; clients say problems very bad in the Philippines. "

Amanda broke off any such dialogue over the hotel phone lines. "I can't discuss anything further."

"Sorry, I…" Mai's voice faded and the line went dead. Amanda replaced the receiver with mixed emotions. Her anger at Rob's veiled threats caused her to respond a bit heavy-handed, she decided. And yet, never had Mai come up with such an off-the-wall, insistent request. She picked up the phone and called Karen, hoping for some clues to Mai's behavior.

Karen added more fuel to her confusion. "All I can tell you is Mai looks like death warmed over. She ran out of the office after talking with you. Didn't even say when she would be back. She's never acted this strange before. How about you? I didn't get to ask you earlier. How's everything going over there? From the way Nigel's chomping at the bit...."

"I'm fine. Everyone back there seems to be over-wound. "

"Part of it is the sudden news about cutbacks."

"Let me know if anything reaches your ears concerning our department. As to Nigel, I just telexed to let him know that I'll fill him in on Friday from Brad's.

"Good. I know Nigel's always hyper; but I swear if you were to tell me he's sacking us all and leaving his wife for an English countess, it still wouldn't add up to the intensity of his phone calls these days."

Amanda laughed at Karen's outrageousness and assured her she'd keep in touch. The laughter lingered, but with a manic touch that threatened to segue into tears of rage.

# TEN

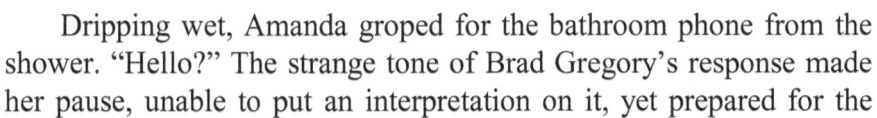

Dripping wet, Amanda groped for the bathroom phone from the shower. "Hello?" The strange tone of Brad Gregory's response made her pause, unable to put an interpretation on it, yet prepared for the worst.

"Plans have changed for our dinner party. Caro took her father in for a check-up yesterday; his blood pressure is sky high. They've given him something to lower it, but he's supposed to remain quiet and under constant monitoring for the next day or two."

"Oh Brad, I'm so sorry. Of course the party is off." She hesitated, fearing the answer to her next question. "How is Don Emilio doing?"

"The prognosis looks good. Actually good enough that the party's not off, just postponed. Don Emilio insists we go ahead with it. Caro's already calling everyone to reschedule for Monday night."

"'Monday night?"

"It's definite. He wants you to meet with him before the party. He's waiting for me to confirm with you and get back to him."

"Of course, Brad. Can I talk with him?"

"Not now. Give him another day or two before calling. Maybe he'll reveal more to you. He puts a good face on everything for Caro's sake."

"Maybe; meantime, Monday looks fine. Will you fax the change of plans to Nigel for me? He's counting on a phone call on Saturday night."

"Will do; got to run now."

Amanda hung up with a heavy sigh. Her shock at the news of Don Emilio quickly changed to fear. Ignoring the prickly feelings, she dressed and turned to her schedule for the day: four meetings, two during the morning and two during the afternoon, one a late lunch at three o'clock. None involved any stated focus, but most were interested in hearing about offshore trusts and companies. She decided Derek could handle the weight of the day's presentations. Her job would be to listen closely and to obtain verification of additional assets to be deposited. Derek's products, she grudgingly admitted, were widening the opportunity, as well as expanding her totals.

Expanded totals reminded her of the twelve million from the Villarreal sale. She'd lain awake designing a strategy to verify where they were headed after FAB. Raffy had only allowed for a half-hour meeting at Plaza Verde. If he didn't open the topic, she would. Fortunately the check from the sale wouldn't actually be in hand for three more weeks. That should give her time to do her due diligence, notify Nigel and begin the approval process.

The day went by in a whirlwind of success, starting off with the reassuring parcel placed in her hands as she left the hotel, copies of the escrow documentation from Vic.

Derek's presentations went extremely well. He charmed everyone with his knowledge, experience, and easygoing humor. She was surprised by his knowledge of the Philippines. His enthusiasm for their country won her clients hands down. Three out of four arranged for Derek to establish an offshore company, taking the trust documents to discuss with their attorneys. Their fourth call promised an additional four hundred thousand-dollar deposit when his deposit with another bank matured at months' end.

Driving through the busiest section of Manila, in a Mercedes with driver, courtesy of their last client, Amanda turned to Derek. "Since when did you become an expert on the Philippines? Been burning the midnight oil?"

Derek's enigmatic grin couldn't contain a bit of boasting at the results of their day. "Now that I've done your job for you, maybe we can ease up a bit, do a bit of sightseeing or some such thing. How does that sound to you? You've the look of an overblown balloon about to burst its tether"

Amanda laughed. "Sightseeing; not likely, but it does remind me that Miguel called this morning to confirm your golf date: Friday at Plaza Verde."

"Friday; isn't that Brad's dinner party?"

"It's postponed. Don Emilio has taken a turn for the worse." Amanda's silence failed to hide her anxiety.

"You're not going to rest easy until you see him; any chance?"

"Not until Monday. I'm hoping to get to talk with him tomorrow, certainly before we leave Friday morning."

"So you changed your mind on the sunbathing bit?"

"Not really. Miguel's lined up his aunt for me to call on and talk to while there." She smiled, grateful to escape into lightness. "But I suspect his real goal is similar to yours—to get me to lounge by the pool."

"What about the schedule for Friday; are there any meetings for us to cancel?"

"I'd left that whole day for Don Emilio."

"Great" the decks are cleared for Miguel's and my conspiracy to try to get you to relax."

She hesitated over sharing word of her meeting with Raffy. "I've arranged to call on one of the resort's owners as well as Miguel's aunt." She laughed. "So, business conversations notwithstanding, it should fill your prescription perfectly."

Their driver pulled up to the front entry of the hotel. Derek and Amanda waited until they were in the lobby, alone at the elevator, before picking up their conversation.

"What revisions did you make to our calendars with the change to the party?"

Amanda glanced in the direction of her room. "None for Friday, but there have been changes tomorrow. Thursday's looking pretty light. Stop in for a minute and we can go over it."

Seated alongside one another at her desk, Amanda began to compare calendars. "Tomorrow's lunch with the Lopez family was our primary Thursday meeting. They're open to substituting a quiet chat on Monday night at Brad's party." She pursed her lips and hesitated at the next name, Chi Chi Amparo. "Chi Chi heard I'd be in Plaza Verde over the weekend and called to schedule a meeting there."

"You're holding out on me about this sun business; three meetings?" At this rate I'm going to have to give up my golf game."

"Trust me; I can wing it on my own. I wouldn't want you to miss your golf."

Derek began studying her with a solemn intensity. It caught her off-guard to find his clown facade obscured by such solemn scrutiny. "Put your mind at ease; I'm looking forward to a day out on the links. It's you I'm concerned about. Let me say it one more time. Unloading worries can create clarity." He reached to close his hands around hers. "Feel free to use me as a sounding board."

Amanda felt her resolve waver. "You may be right, but I'm not sure there's anything to get a grip on yet. Until I am, I don't want to dump on you." Temptation to do just that moved dangerously close. Wary, she awaited Derek's response.

"Not another word. It's settled." He stood up and walked towards the door. We'll celebrate our timeout with a pre-dinner cocktail where you can say as much or as little as you choose. Say eight o'clock in the lobby?"

Amanda nodded, a shiver going through her when the door closed. Suddenly her mother's voice rang in her ears. "Such shivers, Amanda, are caused by someone walking over your grave."

She shunted such thoughts aside by returning three messages left by clients and confirming her Monday-Tuesday schedule. By resetting her Monday morning meeting for later that afternoon, it would allow time to return from her weekend at Plaza Verde. Her clients seemed genuinely happy to see her succumbing to the Filipino way. One suggested he'd see her at Brad and Caro's and would then take a few minutes of her time to review banking matters. Amanda marveled at the ease with which they accepted rescheduling.

Having made the changes, she let her thoughts return to Don Emilio. Tomorrow she'd check with Brad or Caro and, with any luck, talk with Don Emilio. She stared out the window, trying to put the pieces together. Somehow Raffy held the key. His recent grandstand deal making would never meet with his father's approval, she thought, as she heavily underscored questions to ask Raffy while in Plaza Verde. Confidence surged at having her own agenda clarified and held secretly in reserve.

Totally absorbed, nightfall forced her to turn on a light and notice the time, seven fifty. Her yes to cocktails meant her suit would have to do. She made one concession by letting her hair down. Out it tumbled from its tightly anchored chignon. She tied its tumbling mass loosely back with a black and white chiffon scarf and removed her suit jacket. She hesitated as she stared at her anting-anting, so blatantly revealed against the expanse of her white blouse. Her hands went to the back of her neck to unclasp its chain and then hesitated. It looked rather lovely. She softly stroked it in her hand and watched as it picked up the light. On second thought, either Derek will make her feel foolish or one of the Filipinos may recognize what it is. Not wanting to go into any explanations, she unclasped the lock and placed it on the bedside table.

Approaching the lobby area she hesitated in the shadows as she glanced about to spot Derek. Once burned, twice wary, she thought. The thought and her new habit refreshed her rage at his puzzling betrayal with her man of the evil eye. *How could I ever think of confiding anything in him?* She squared her shoulders and headed for the far corner of the lobby lounge. Derek was addressing a waiter. Turning, he announced that he'd requested a special order of her favorite wine. His broad smile, filling his eyes as well as his wide mouth, quickly vanished as he took in the grim set of her own mouth, the rigidity of her chin.

"What's happened? You look as though you're prepared to lead a march against the Mongol hoards." Derek tried to tease out a smile as they walked towards the cocktail lounge. "Maybe I should have ordered a jeroboam of champagne instead—something heavy-duty to thaw you out."

Amanda hesitated. "Sorry, Derek. But this thing with Sr. De La Serna has upset me." She suddenly stopped any reference as the waiter arrived to pour the wine.

Lifting her glass, she resolved to mask her motives and unmask his. "A toast; let's drink to our success today and to a worthwhile trip for both of us!"

Derek raised his glass, looking bemused but undaunted. "If you agree to a refill, I'll agree to keep to neutral conversation."

"Fair enough; I'm a bit over-tired and over-wound. I'm sure I'll adjust." She gave her head a toss as if to aid in accompanying such an adjustment. "And, speaking of adjusting, Miguel is an excellent golfer. I do hope you're prepared."

"It's been awhile since I've played golf—too busy with rugby to get a game in anymore." Derek smiled companionably. Amanda noticed the tiredness in his eyes. Catching her look, he reached across the table to pat her hand. "You'll see; a day in the sun will have you in tip-top form."

Amanda resisted any flippant reply. She allowed the dark, cool seclusion of the lounge, the glow of the candles and the warmth of the wine to enfold her in a moment of peace. Her serenity was short lived. Their waiter approached with a message in hand.

"Mr. Derek Ashton? Your caller insisted I locate you immediately and give you this message." He smiled apologetically at Amanda as he pressed a note into Derek's outstretched palm.

"Why is it that problems always come up when you're away from the office?" Derek's face registered a mix of urgency and exasperation. "I expect my Cayman team to know how to run the shop without any hand holding by me. Is there any privacy on any of these hotel phones?" His last question burst forth with an intensity that brought Amanda wide-awake.

"Most likely the room phones are tapped, not always, but sporadically, yes." His glare told her that answer wouldn't do. "Perhaps the phone booth near the restrooms may be 'clean'. You'll have to weigh the pros and cons."

Derek glanced again at his message. "I'll need to take that gamble." He nearly upset his glass in his haste to leave the table. She watched his rapid lunge toward the restroom.

Amanda contrasted such intensity to his Irish rover cover. "Cover"? The word shocked her at the speed with which it surfaced. It was quickly followed by the sobering thought of his potential to compromise her with any such rash calls. She turned to seek out their waiter, anxious to pay the bill and follow Derek. He was nowhere in view. She located a piece of paper and wrote a terse note to the waiter to charge the check to her room. Ripping off the bottom half, she quickly scribbled a second note. "Derek: Do not refer to anything that may compromise us!" She dropped the first note on the table, folded the second, gave one more glance around the room and headed toward the restroom phones.

The area was empty. She headed for the gift shop, remembering the phone booth discreetly hidden behind it. Derek was there. She stopped in the shadows, noticing how deep in conversation he seemed. Something about the way his body angled itself away from any possible interference, and the intensity of his focus on the call, resurfaced her doubts. *Who is Derek Ashton--friend or foe?* The question kept running through her thoughts as he turned with a glare. Catching sight of her, he quickly assumed a reassuring look and placed the receiver hastily on the hook.

"Drat all! Why is it axiomatic that, the more you need to get through, the harder it is? I've been trying every which way to get this bloody call through, with no luck." He shrugged and walked towards her. "Perhaps you're right and I'm better off waiting.'"

His attempts to blur his intensity, almost, but not quite, deterred her. "Look, Derek. Let's get one thing straight. I can't have you going off half-cocked on the phone and putting me in jeopardy." She shoved her note in his hands, turned swiftly and was in the elevator before he could respond.

Amanda headed for her room, snapped on the light and moved toward the bathroom. She stopped before she reached it and stared around the room. Something wasn't right. Her eyes raked the corners of the room, doing a quick inventory of chair, table, dresser, and... They stopped to linger on the bedside table. Her anting-anting—it was gone.

# ELEVEN

Thursday passed in a blur. Amanda sank into a well of grief when Brad informed her Don Emilio wasn't able to talk with anyone. Caro's comment in the background rang in her ears. "He can't talk because they're killing him with all those ..." The abruptness with which Brad hung up echoed in her thoughts throughout the day.

Derek kept his distance, sensing her remove and willingly carrying the ball on their client calls. Only during their drive back to the hotel at day's end did he attempt to break her silence. "Look, I'm sorry about last night. I want to assure you I won't do a thing to put you or the bank in any jeopardy."

*Like not having a rendezvous with my 'imaginary' menace for instance?* The thought served to solidify her resistance. She bit back any discussion of Don Emilio, responding as to a non-person. "Yeah well...." Her dismissive shrug and minimal words silenced him until they reached the hotel.

"Look, try to get a good night's sleep."

She felt her buttons getting pushed at the patronizing echo to his words, but resisted. "That's exactly what I intend to do." She looked back at him after she'd put her key-card in the door. "Miguel will pick us up at seven thirty. Good night."

Intentions aside, a good night's sleep wasn't in the cards. Amanda shook herself out of a nightmare filled with images of her missing anting-anting. "What?" She shouted as she struggled up from her dream. Vivi was in it, calling her name. The dream images slowly faded, but not the sound.

"Amanda? Open the door. It's me, Vivi."

*No, it can't be,* Amanda thought as she staggered towards the door. She listened carefully at the doorway as its shaking confirmed her waking nightmare. A louder knock followed and along with it a more insistent: "Amanda. It's me; Vivi." Amanda slammed open the deadbolt lock, jerked the chain off and yanked the door open.

"Thank God you're here. I'm exhausted." Vivi moved into the room, tossed her suitcase towards the closet and collapsed onto the extra bed. Amanda's silent stare brought her to an upright position. "I know; but before you give me a lecture let me explain." She hesitated, never for a moment taking her eyes off Amanda's reaction. "I mentioned to my Hong Kong client that a good friend was in Manila. He said that, should I consider going there, he had a good contact for me." Vivi spread her hands wide. "It being the weekend, I figured I'd come ahead just for a few days, meet this guy, and get the lay of the land; and...."

"And?" The word came out iced with import.

"And...stay out of your way, I promise." Vivi gave a slight smile. "You'll see. A little fun over the weekend and I'll clear out." She got up from the bed, moved to Amanda and clasped her in a warm embrace. "I'm sorry. Can't we just make the best of it now that I'm here?"

Amanda swallowed the "How could you...no phone call, no consideration...indictment running through her mind. She looked at the clock's hands turning to three o'clock. "I'm scheduled to leave in five hours. Let's turn in."

"Leave? As in go back to San Francisco?"

"As in go to a resort three hours north of here?"

"Great. I could use a weekend in the sun?"

Amanda groaned and switched off the light.

* * *

"What kind of a hotel is this anyway?" Amanda buried her head into the pillow, unwilling to come fully awake. She shook herself, turned to one side and froze as she listened.

"Not a sign of bubble-bath!" Someone was in her bathroom and complaining loudly. The loud "Damn!" with its Brazilian accent reminded her of Vivi's late-night arrival.

She groaned and looked over at the clock. Twenty past seven. She staggered out of bed and aimed her body in the direction of the bathroom, keeping her eyes semi-closed.

Vivi remained oblivious to Amanda entering the bathroom, stubbing her toe against the bidet and collapsing on the toilet. Amanda let out a sibilant expletive as she projected her voice in the direction of the bubble-less tub.

"Vivi, at seven thirty I'm being picked up by one of my clients, Miguel Santos, to drive to Plaza Verde. If you want to go, we need to be ready in ten minutes."

"Now you tell me?" Vivi yanked the shower curtain back and rose full-length from the tub like Poseidon's handmaiden, ready to confront whatever lay outside her watery domain. "Of course I want to go. What in the world would I do hanging around here all day?"

Amanda was about to mention 'Mr. Client you're supposed to contact,' but didn't want to rekindle either her disbelief or her anger. She hesitated, her attention drawn to a Vivi sidetracked by the mirror and her close scrutiny of her naked body. Looking for signs of sagging, I bet. Fat chance, Amanda thought ironically, glaring in Vivi's direction.

"Viv, for the last time, if you're going with me, we need to be walking out that door in ten minutes. And I need to get in that shower for at least four of them. Amanda stepped out of her nightgown and into the shower. She turned the faucet full blast to "Cold" and let her pores reach the semi-frozen consistency of ice cream before she decided she might be able to face the day.

Vivi was standing in front of an array of cosmetics rivaling Macys's, Amanda thought, while marveling at the fact that Vivi was dressed. One of them, at least, might appear on time.

Jetlag seemed to make Vivi's feral-cat green eyes brighter and her cheeks pinker, both highlighted by an aqua silk shorts set. It's not fair, Amanda thought, as she caught a glance of her own eyes in the mirror. She groaned as she saw that the only pink reflected seemed to be that rimming her eyes.

Vivi grabbed the phone on the first ring. In a soft, sighing mix of happy, sexy, little-girl-lost voice she breathed "Hello" to an obviously startled Derek. Amanda grabbed the phone.

"Derek? The 'who's that voice' is that of my friend Vivi. She flew in unexpectedly from Hong Kong last night." Amanda turned and directed a pointed reply in Vivi's direction. "Yes; just for the weekend. So we'll be four and we'll be late." Amanda hesitated as the sharp remembrance of her missing anting-anting returned. "Would you tell Miguel it shouldn't be more than twenty minutes?"

Viv grabbed the phone as Amanda started to end her call. "I'm ready; I'll be right down to join you for coffee and get acquainted. Right then--Ciao" She took one last glance in the mirror, flicked a trace of lipstick off the edge of her pouting mouth and disappeared out the door, trailing an echoing "Ciao" behind her.

Amanda immediately went down on her hands and knees and examined every inch of the floor. A thorough search of drawers, closet and every item of clothing, convinced her that her anting-anting had truly disappeared. Anxious to get down in time to talk with Housekeeping, she threw on her purple cotton skirt and a tee shirt, grabbed a sun hat, tossed a few things in a suitcase and headed for the elevator.

During the ride down she puzzled over the why, how and who of her vanishing anting-anting. Who'd want to take something so obviously of no value? When the elevator door opened she headed straight to Housekeeping. She might have saved her breath. No one had seen or taken or reported such an item. "We will certainly question our evening staff, Miss Evans. If it's in the hotel we shall locate it."

Amanda held back her disbelief, thanked them and headed to the coffee shop. She knew exactly which direction to turn as she entered. She simply followed the sound of Vivi's laughter. Viv was in her element with two attractive, intelligent and mesmerized men. Maybe not quite at the total mesmerized state, she thought, as they both looked up when she approached.

Miguel studied her as she hesitated alongside their table. "You look as though you need more than caffeine to set you up for the day." As he drew out her chair, he flicked his hand in a gesture that brought the busboy bearing a steaming pot of coffee.

"Thanks, Miguel; I'm so sorry to have kept you waiting." Amanda punctuated her message as she looked up at him. "I've been madly searching for a piece of jewelry that I seem to have lost. It's brand new and it simply vanished." Miguel's eyes darkened.

Determined not to be cut out of whatever the drama seemed to be, Vivi added her two-cents. "You brought valuable jewelry after warning me that's a 'No-No'?"

Miguel pushed his chair back. "While you have breakfast, I'll go talk to the hotel's management." He turned to Amanda. "Don't worry about a thing. We have plenty of time to make our golf schedule if we leave in, say twenty minutes? I'll meet you in the lobby."

Derek looked from the departing Miguel to Amanda. "What was that all about? Missing jewelry can probably be sorted out with housekeeping."

"Well, good", Vivi said, glad to have settled something that didn't focus on her. "I'm going to use the time to stop at the ladies room." She flashed Derek one of her "don't forget me" smiles and walked briskly towards the exit.

Assuming her best imitation, Amanda jumped up and, tossing a smile to Derek, said, "Well good, because I'm using this time to go for some mangoes and yogurt and maybe even one of those sinful cinnamon rolls."

Derek raised one eyebrow and, giving a sardonic smile, turned his attention to his copy of their agenda for the weekend. As Amanda returned he asked, "Would you like me to join you at any of your meetings? If so, I'll get a sense of what our golf schedule looks like so I can be there."

"No need, Derek. I can handle any questions on trusts. Thanks anyway, but let's try the Filipino approach to business. You enjoy your golf game with Miguel while I enjoy meeting his Aunt Florencia."

"I'm counting on you to sell one of them a trust. Miguel and I will drink to your success after our game."

"What time will you finish up?"

"We'll probably be on the links most of the day. Will Vivi be all right being alone?" His last remark was delivered as Vivi approached.

"You won't find me grieving over not being able to join Amanda to sip tea with some old lady." Vivi punctuated her comment with a slight frown and a glance around he room. "However, I think you're a spoilsport for not taking me along and teaching me the game of golf." Seeing a lone businessman staring her way, she smiled, carefully enunciating, "I guess I'll just have to work on my tan at the pool until Amanda finishes up with Miguel's auntie."

"Very good." Derek glanced pointedly at his watch and motioned the waiter for the check.

"Thank you sir, but Mr. Santos took care of it," the waiter replied as he pulled out Amanda's chair.

As they entered the lobby, Amanda glanced over towards the desk at Miguel. He was deep in discussion with the manager. A look of shock came over her as she got a look at his face. Miguel's easygoing smile had been replaced by a steel-jawed look of focused wrath. She felt sorry for the manager. His ashen face seemed poised for an even more physical punctuation of Miguel's communication.

As Amanda hesitated, Vivi blithely sailed over in Miguel's direction with a cheery challenge. "Miguel, I'm ready if you are." Fortunately her near-sightedness gave him a moment to compose himself before Vivi could see what Amanda had seen.

Derek seemed oblivious. He'd headed to the concierge's desk to pick up his messages. He turned and, looking pleased at something they revealed, walked amiably towards Miguel. "You ready to get out-golfed by an Irishman?"

The manager looked grateful at the distraction. He humbly repeated, "You can depend on me. I shall attend to it promptly, sir."

Miguel turned to Derek, friendly Filipino smile in place, "Overconfidence will do you in, my friend--- prepare for your defeat". He smiled at Amanda and Vivi, offered each an arm and headed out the door. "I couldn't want for more delightful companions in what looks to be a very special day."

The drive to Plaza Verde passed quickly. Amanda and Miguel sat up front discussing his aunt and the most likely focus for Amanda's discussion with her. Vivi, who sat alongside Derek in the backseat, was giving him the not so subtle third degree as to the women in his life. Amanda strained to capture his response. Derek was lightly deflecting any specifics, but charmingly enough to keep Vivi in a playful mood. When they seemed to be deeply engrossed in such give and take, Miguel turned to Amanda with a serious, through low-pitched, comment.

"Something's going on. The hotel manager was terrified at the mention of your missing anting-anting. He clearly knew who, why and where."

"He did? But then...."

"I put the fear of God into him; so you just may find it reappears. If so, don't wear it." Miguel's voice had grown in volume. He turned to make certain Vivi and Derek remained oblivious. Hearing laughter, he lowered his voice.

"They can reverse its effect. I thought when I gave it to you it would ease your fears over a simple case of mistaken identity. Now I'm' sure your suspicions are valid. Someone wants to shake you up. Have you any idea who and why?"

"None; but I'm glad someone finally believes me."

Vivi's voice suddenly piped up from the back. "What are you two up to? It sounds serious. Not a lover's tiff, is it?"

"I should be so lucky!" Miguel laughed. "No Vivi; believe it or not, there is one topic even more serious than love--money. But I promised a carefree day, so forgive me; I'll leave that topic for later." He grinned and started pointing out some of the features of the rural area they were passing through. Amanda became entranced by the contrast to Metro Manila.

Derek turned his face to the window and soon was asleep as they drove through several small settlements of farm laborers. Curious faces turned in their direction as they slowed to navigate dusty lanes filled with children, goats and dogs. The looks they gave the passengers of an air-conditioned automobile that cost more than the entire village would make in a lifetime, were ones of solemn, guarded inspection. Amanda smiled broadly at a dark-eyed girl shyly staring, and was rewarded with a toothy grin. Its after-image lingered.

Miguel broke into her thoughts. "We're about ten minutes from Plaza Verde. You'll begin to see bungalows through the trees."

On schedule, they entered a world of bright green, landscaped lawns and gentle rolling hills dotted with waving palm fronds and riotous shades of bougainvillea. Amanda tried to make out the few homes not obscured by landscaping and private courtyard gardens, but caught only glimpses of red-tiled roofs amidst the green. A golf cart putted across their path and the cart's driver smiled and waved, restoring a sense of anticipation.

Vivi burst out laughing as they slowed for their approach to the winding circular drive to the entranceway of Playa Verde. "What gives?" She pointed in amazement at the sight of several jeepneys making their way down the drive as they delivered residents and their luggage to their bungalows. "Why on earth do they have all those shiny silver horse statuettes on top of their jeeps? Does it represent how much horsepower their vehicles can deliver?"

Miguel laughed. "Close, Vivi; but horsepower the owner can deliver—not the automobiles." He paused as the driver tipped his hat in Vivi's direction. "It's an outward display of the owner's virility."

Vivi let out a hoot. "I can see I'm going to have myself some fun, since golf isn't the sport of all the males around here."

Derek, glancing her way as they exited the Mercedes, laughed as a stooped, ancient driver alighted from his jeepney. "Perhaps you may be in for a bit of wishful thinking, Vivi." Derek's rejoinder caused Amanda to burst into nervous laughter as they walked into the lobby.

"Do my ears deceive me—Amanda Evans laughing?" They all turned to see who had entered their conversation. "Are you really here to relax, Amanda?"

"Raffy." Amanda was swept into a quick embrace. "I didn't expect to see you until later."

"'What kind of a host would I be not to have met you at the door? I'm pleased it could work out..." His broad smile segued to sorrow "....what with father and all. Meantime, here I am. And here you are, and with two men no less." He paused and fixed his gaze firmly on Vivi. "And one goddess; please introduce me to your special friend. Miguel, I know. Como esta, Miguel?" Raffy held out his hand to a less than enthusiastic shake by Miguel and returned his focus to Vivi.

Amanda broke the tension. "Raffy, meet my friend, Vivian Nova. Vivi, Raphael de la Serna." Raffy's gaze was fixed firmly on Vivi as he addressed her outthrust hand with a slight bow and a light kiss.

*Oh, oh, pure dynamite*, thought Amanda. Raffy's reputation as a notorious womanizer flashed in front of her. Most of the beauties of Manila, married or unmarried, had either shared his bed or dreamed of doing so. Amanda understood why. Raffy was tall for a Filipino, nearly six foot, slender, with liquid black eyes and a full head of dark hair cut in the European fashion. *All that certainly; but also he is very, very rich and powerful, Amanda thought; quite the aphrodisiac. The frosting on the cake however, was Raffy's eligibility. At thirty-two, he was still unmarried.*

Derek's slight cough brought Amanda back to reality. She nervously turned to correct her oversight. "Derek Adams, manager of our Cayman Islands Trust Group; Derek, please meet Raphael de la Serna."

"So you're the chap I've heard mentioned?" Raffy smiled. "Perhaps, since I now intend to make Brad's party after all, I might bend your ear with a bit of business that night?" He turned back to Amanda. "Meantime, I've made certain your arrangements were suitable. You each have the best accommodations, bungalows right on the beach, adjoining one another."

"I understand you've an important meeting lined up." Amanda studied Raffy's eyes as they fought to erase his surprise.

"Right you are. It'll consume me for most of the day, but as soon as this meeting is out of the way, our even more important meeting can take place. Will you all join me for a pre-dinner cocktail in the lounge; say six-thirty?" He turned to Amanda. "Right after our meeting at six, if that will work for you." Re-directing his glance to Vivi, with a look of abject apology, he added, "I'd love to make it dinner as well, but business calls."

"It would be our pleasure; I'm sure, Mr. De La Serna." Vivi's reply was soft and breathless.

Derek seconded the acceptance in his no-nonsense way. "Count me in."

"Count me out. I have other plans." Miguel's clipped rejection had everyone turn.

It startled Amanda, but didn't surprise her. She had always known that Raffy and Miguel were in different political camps. But more importantly was the gossip surrounding Miguel's sister, Hortensia, and her unrequited love for Raffy. It was the scandal of the day two years ago when Hortensia suddenly joined an order of Catholic nuns. That put an end to everyone's certainty that one day the families would be united through marriage.

"Well then. It's settled." Raffy had turned away from Miguel. "I'll look forward to seeing you at six, Amanda. And you, he nodded in Vivi and Derek's direction, at six-thirty." With a slight motion toward the bellman, a jeepney driver appeared; ready to deliver them to their bungalows. Raffy saw them on-board, wished them a pleasant day and, with a glance at his watch, headed swiftly aw.

Miguel turned to Amanda, his expression more relaxed. "I'm going to take a run up to my Aunt Florencia's house right away. She'll be awaiting my arrival. How about I meet you back here in thirty minutes Derek? We'll just make our tee time." He spoke with Amanda before he clambered into an awaiting jeepney. "I'll call your room when I get there and let you speak with my aunt to confirm your meeting." Nodding in Vivi's direction, he added, "You should have some time to enjoy the sun."

"I can't wait." Vivi said with a glance towards their jeepney driver.

Derek chimed in. "See to it that Amanda goes in the pool as well."

Before Miguel's jeepney headed away, he rushed through his remaining good-host instructions. "Enjoy your lunch, but hold back some appetite for dinner. They have a great chef in the main dining room." With that they went their separate ways, Miguel in one jeepney, Derek, Vivi and Amanda in another.

As the jeepney pulled up into a driveway, the sight of their bungalows took Amanda's breath away. It was the dream of a tropical paradise made real. The bungalows were all facing an incredibly azure and emerald ocean, with powdery white sand coming almost to their doorway. A span of green grass, dotted with bougainvillea, birds of paradise and hibiscus encircled the bungalows. White shutters were thrown wide on each, giving an illusion of living outdoors.

Derek seemed not to take a whole lot of notice as he headed towards the farthest one. "You know where to find me; I need to get a call out of the way before playing golf."

"Party pooper; I thought we'd each compare our digs. I insist on a rain check." Vivi's words trailed wistfully in Derek's wake without his responding with as much as a word of agreement.

She shrugged her shoulders and turned, frowning, to Amanda.

"Never mind; let's go for it." Amanda said. They each popped in to have a quick look at one anther's quarters. Opulent in a casual way, both units were different in layout but equally luxurious. Amanda most loved the hammock on her lanai, wishing she could remain in it the entire stay. Her bedroom was seductively inviting— dominated by a king-size bed covered in white and enshrouded with abundant draping of white mosquito netting. The furnishings were natural wicker with brightly flowered chintz cushions ample enough to disappear in. The kitchen area was a treasure trove of delights, everything from fresh orange and mango juices to a variety of fresh fruit and, incredibly, a bottle each of the finest of French wines and champagne.

But the bathroom was the biggest surprise of all to find in a beach bungalow. The overall design wouldn't find fault with a maharaja. The centerpiece of the room was a huge circular bath-cum-Jacuzzi, big enough for six at least. Surrounding it were separate doors leading to individual bidets, toilets and walk-in closets. Adjoining the bathing area was a dressing room fit for a movie star.

Vivi smiled as she kept up a running commentary. "Wow; get a look at the TV built in opposite the tub. Oh no, two TV's! I guess that's so each bather can see the program." She laughed at the very idea of watching TV while bathing a deaux. "Did you see all of those makeup lights in the dressing room? It looks like these bungalows are designed to spend most of ones time in the bathroom."

Vivi, whose Brazilian home had been in Architectural Digest, surprised Amanda with her lack of restraint but not her risqué addendum: "How about, 'take a meeting Raffy; my tub at four!;" Vivi's exuberant laughter drew a smile from Amanda, but a sobering thought quickly followed with a silent prayer for Vivi to keep her behavior within bounds.

"Let's get down to unpacking so we can check out the pool." Amanda's comment prompted Vivi's quick departure with a breathless, "I'll be unpacked instantly. See you soon."

Amanda swiftly put away her few clothes, soaking up the joys of her little haven. As she finished and entered her living room, the phone rang. It was Miguel.

"I thought you may have been abducted by your jeepney driver! How are your accommodations?"

"I think we've landed in a rajah's seraglio, South Seas style." Amanda laughed as she looked around and wondered if all this might be conflict of interest. If bank policy says that employees may not accept gifts in excess of fifty dollars in value, where does this fit in? She put a lid on that thought for the moment as she registered Miguel's comment.

"My aunt is clamoring for the phone."

"Hello, my dear Miss Andrews; welcome to Plaza Verde. The way my Miguel has described you, I'm sure we shall be family from the first moment. I wonder whether we might arrange to get together for merienda this afternoon, say around four o'clock. I would love to ask you to lunch, but my Mah Jong group meets today." She laughed as she whispered her guilty secret. "I am passionately addicted to Mah

Jong. Even the thought of lunch with the Pope couldn't deflect me from my game. Not only that, but I'm sure you would like to have some time to yourself to relax." Her voice was warmly coated with the mellifluous accents of Spanish and Tagalog.

"Four o'clock is perfect. I can't wait to meet you."

"Very good, my dear; your jeepney driver will know the place by my name. In the meantime, do please intend to relax."

"Thank you. I shall." Amanda replied, adding, "I have a six o'clock appointment scheduled, but that should give us nearly two hours."

"That is perfect for me; see you soon."

Amanda hung up the phone, glanced at her watch and whispered a silent: "Thank you." *That's just what I needed, she thought, a bit of time to rehearse a strategy with Raffy—but at the pool.* As she looked at her almost empty closet, she decided to stop at the resort's shop and buy a bathing suit. She smiled, taking a moment to flop down onto the hammock and gaze at the ocean. *Maybe this really could be a carefree interlude, she thought, holding momentarily at bay the conflicting incidents that continued to nag loudly for her attention.*

# TWELVE

"Miss Evans, are you in?" Amanda tumbled out of the hammock in a daze.

"Out here on the terrace." Amanda staggered towards the door.

"Sorry to disturb you, but the gentleman insisted that you receive this message immediately." The hotel employee offered a sealed envelope.

Amanda ripped the envelope open, thinking Nigel had tracked her down. She stared, unable to take in the words. Black, scrawled lettering, heavily underlined, read, **"You won't get away with it. Leave before it's too late."** Amanda's hand shook as she looked up. "Was this message hand-delivered or taken over the phone?"

"We would have transferred any calls to your room. A gentleman left it with the front desk"

"Who is this gentleman? Did you see him? Is he staying at the hotel?"

"I'm sorry. I don't know." The man seemed impatient to go. "The front desk clerk gave it to me along with other deliveries for our guests. Will you be sending a reply for me to take back?"

"No, but I'll return with you. Give me a moment please." Amanda turned away, out of the bright sunlight back into the bungalow's cool interior. Disbelieving, confused and angry, she found her teeth tightly clutched, not in simple anger but in rage, thinking: *How dare someone accuse me of, of—whatever it is they think I've done?* She felt violated and vengeful. Grabbing her purse and room key, she slammed the door and walked toward the waiting jeepney.

"Amanda, where are you going?" Vivi shouted as she ran towards the jeepney. "You weren't going to leave for the pool without me, were you?"

"No, Viv; I have to run up and see the manager. I'll meet you at the pool in—" She looked at her watch, remembering she'd have to buy a swimsuit in the hotel shop. "Thirty-five minutes."

"No need, I'm ready now; I'll hitch a ride with you." Vivi was up on the jeepney's front seat as quickly as the tightly wrapped sarong covering her bathing suit would allow.

"What's up; the room not opulent enough, the wine gone bad—?"

"No." Amanda wasn't about to get into it, not with the driver all ears. Actually all eyes and ears from the look he was giving Vivi. "Business, Viv. Resort or not, I'm here on business."

Amanda's impatient response seemed to have gone over Vivi's head. Her focus was on a man headed down the path in the direction of the pool. He laughed as—so fixated was he on Vivi's smile—he stumbled, looked up and gave them a slight salute.

Viv pulled out a compact, scanned her face, and leaped off the jeepney before it had come to a complete halt. "I don't want to miss a minute of my swim. See you when you get there." With a quick "Ciao", Viv was off.

Amanda walked briskly to the front desk, trying unsuccessfully not to sound imperious with the young Filipina at the desk. "Were you the one who took this message?" She held out the envelope and watched as the clerk scanned it. "Can you describe the gentleman who left it?"

The clerk looked nonplussed as Amanda held back the message itself, offering only the information that the envelope was addressed to her. "Sorry, Miss Evans, but I only arrived ten minutes ago. Do you wish to speak with our manager?"

"Yes, I do. Right away, and with anyone else who may have been working the front desk during the past hour." As the girl walked off Amanda turned full circle, hoping to catch a glimpse of the author somewhere in the lobby. Only one person, a young man patiently picking dead leaves off of hanging plants, was in view.

"My name is Eduardo Curzon. I am the manager of Plaza Verde. How may I be of service?" The man's tone of voice matched his posture, filled with enough heightened importance to make up for his short stature.

Amanda moderated her response; she needed his cooperation. "A message was left for me by a man who dropped it by the front desk, insisting I get it immediately. It must have been sometime during the past hour. I was wondering, since it was unsigned, whether whoever accepted it may be able to identify who it was, or describe him to me."

"But of course, Miss Evans, the person at that time would have to have been Pablo Vicente." He called to a clerk working at the rear of the front desk area. "Pablo, would you give me a moment, please? Do you recall a gentleman giving you an urgent message to be delivered to Miss Evans, sometime during the last hour or so? She would appreciate your help identifying him."

"He seemed in a big hurry. I was checking in a large party of Japanese golfers at the time. He dropped the note off quickly, didn't give his name, said to deliver it immediately, and rushed away. I didn't get a good look at him. The man was well dressed; but not a guest of the hotel though, I'm certain." He paused as his mouth pursed in thought. "Strange; but he was carrying a heavy coat in this heat."

"Yes, yes, but what did he look like—young, old, Filipino, Japanese, American?" Amanda leaned across the desk, physically trying to urge his rambling comments to focus.

"Maybe mid-thirties—or he could have been in his early forties? Filipino maybe, but I didn't get a good enough look at him. He shoved the envelope at me, insisted it be delivered promptly, and was gone as fast as he appeared." Pablo turned to his boss, the hotel manager.

"Even with twelve guests waiting to register, I can assure you that I had it sent it to Miss Evans bungalow immediately."

"Miss Evans isn't faulting you, Pablo." Mr. Curzon smiled broadly. "Thank you for your help. If anything more occurs to you please be sure to inform Miss Evans."

The manager turned to Amanda, hands held out, face up in an "I've done all I can" manner. "Let me know if I can be of any further assistance. Try not to let this subtract from the full enjoyment of your stay at Plaza Verde." He shook Amanda's hand, smiled with a certain restrained professional condescension and turned back to his office.

*Now what?* Amanda thought, feeling diminished and impotent. Her anger had nowhere to go except action. Deciding to go the pool and swim as many laps as it took to clear her thoughts, she headed in the direction of the sign marked "Hotel Shops".

She quickly chose a suit in midnight blue; a simple cut designed to handle serious swimming. She put it on and, at the last minute, added a sarong.

*Maybe I'll see him around the pool* Amanda thought, hesitating as she entered the pool complex. Few men of any description were at the pool. She spotted Viv lying face down on a lounge, sound asleep.

Grateful for no conversation, she put her things down and dove into the water. Its coolness was a balm to her over-heated thoughts. She was exhausted but clear headed after swimming twenty laps. Viv had just turned over to apply suntan oil and squinted into the sun as Amanda approached.

"Finally; you're here." Vivi stood up, twisting to aim the bottle of lotion at the furthest reaches of her back. Amanda couldn't help but smile as the few men there all came to full attention. Their eyes held the studied fixation of an eagle spotting prey. Vivi wore the soft, inward smile of one that knew her art and just how far she could go with it.

Amanda turned away, drew up an empty lounge chair and aimed it to deflect the glare of the sun. Although it altered the direct alignment with Vivi's lounge chair, Viv didn't seem to notice as she turned her chair around to face Amanda, giving her a solemn look

"I'm bummed. I called the referral my Hong Kong guy gave me and he's out of town." Amanda waited. Vivi's voice assumed a business-like intensity. "Can you line up anyone in the textile or accessories business for me to see while I'm here?" She stopped, not even waiting for a response, as she turned to study a woman passing in front of them. "Did you get a look at the shell work on that woman's belt? I could save a lot of money ordering accessories like that while I'm here in the Philippines. How about it; who can you line up for me?"

Amanda hesitated for just a beat. Vivi's energies and the steamroller way in which she presented her demands, left no room to broach any argument. "Let me repeat what I told you before I left. I'm here on bank business. I have an intense schedule. 'Don't even think of joining me,' I said. Now here you are." Amanda gave her an incredulous look. "Don't, for one moment, expect me to focus on your business needs."

Vivi's expression wavered between petulance and shock. "My word, Amanda; I've never seen this side of you. I feel like my pet kitty cat just turned and scratched me."

"Exactly; you stepped on my tail big time, Vivi. Don't do it again."

"Alright, alright; I got it, but calm down. I have to go back to Hong Kong in a few days. In the meantime, how about we arrive at a truce?" Vivi's appeal, couched in the most sincere of tones, eyes moist, ended with: "Friends; right?"

"A friend who needs her space right now, Viv. I have to go over some notes."

"Right you are. I'm famished anyway. Think I'll head on over and check out the cafe." Viv jumped up with the eagerness of a student whose detention bell had rung.

"I'll try to join you, but it may be awhile." Amanda's comment trailed in Vivi's wake.

Spotting a shady, corner table, Amanda gathered her belongings and moved. Refreshed by her swim and energized by the clearing of the air with Vivi, she began to examine the series of bizarre incidents.

She reached into her bag, pulled out her note pad and began to jot down the sequence of events, starting with the man on the plane. Replaying his every action, she felt increasingly convinced that he must be the author of the threatening message. But why? Frustrated at too little to go on, she left one mysterious male to dwell on another.

Her notations concerning Derek were pro and con. Just as she seesawed up at his caring actions toward her, so did she abruptly crash into rage at the image of his breakfast with the 'figment of her imagination'. She underlined his name with a mental reminder to grill Nigel for more background. Until she unearthed what Derek Ashton was up to, damned if she'd do anything that would tip her hand. She flipped the page over and penciled: "Mai"

Comments concerning Mai were covered with question marks. Amanda stared out in the distance, convinced that Mai somehow had more going on than simple anxiety surrounding this trip.

Unable to come up with any specifics, she turned her focus onto her clients. The top name on her list was "Raffy". Her notes highlighted questions concerning his current project and today's big meeting. Even more important was his Guam hotel deal and how it and the Villarreal factory sale dovetailed. Less specific, but more intense, would be her need to probe for details concerning Don Emilio's sudden illness.

Sidetracked by her stomach's rumblings, she was surprised to find it was forty-five minutes since Vivi had headed off to lunch. She tied her sarong around her waist, gathered up her notes and headed toward the lobby. Amanda walked into the coffee shop, hesitating as she searched the room.

Vivi was sitting alone at a far table, stirring her drink vigorously and glaring in Amanda's direction. "What's with these men in the Philippines anyway?" She'd begun her comment well before Amanda had pulled out a chair. "I thought they had an eye for women, but you wouldn't know it from the dead pan faces in here—a bunch of pansies if you ask me."

This last comment was pointedly and a bit too loudly, directed to the approaching waiter. Amanda blanched in anguish as the young man's demeanor was momentarily shaken. His expressive face warred between any one of a range of suitably defensive comments.

"I see your friend has arrived. Would you care to order now?" He glanced at Vivi, settling for a look of not-so-faint disdain before turning to Amanda.

"Yes, thank you. I'll have the cold seafood salad and an iced green-mango drink, please." Amanda turned, squaring her shoulders and fixing Vivi with a steady gaze that held exasperation.

"Make that the same for me." Vivi's response was curt as she reluctantly gave quarter.

Amanda turned to Vivi as the waiter departed. She was torn between a 'How could you?' lecture and a save your energy to greater affect, attitude. She opted for straight down the middle.

"Viv, let's get one thing clear about the Filipino male." Amanda lowered her voice. "They are very proud—and very vindictive when their egos are wounded. Your comment was totally uncalled for."

"Jeez, Amanda, what's with you? I only meant you wouldn't find a Brazilian man so cool."

"Cool they're not—just subtle and skillful when it comes to seductions. Filipino men like the art of the conquest to be indirect and drawn out—whatever their sexual bias. Any more slings at their sexuality and you just may find yourself in hot water."

"I hear you."

"Good, then let's enjoy our meal." Amanda directed an extra wide smile at their waiter as he placed their food in front of them. She turned to with undiminished appetite before renewing her focus on each person in the room. One glance and she could discount most as vacationers, complete with sun lotion, children, maps and tour guides.

But a table of two men drew her attention. She studied as best she could without being obvious, the one facing in her direction. He was an attractive man of indeterminate middle age, dressed in an expensive business suit, with no overcoat in view. He never took his focus off the words of his tablemate, who in turn, never glanced her way. She determined to wait them out until she could catch sight of the other man.

Meanwhile the waiter returned with their check. She studied his nametag as she smiled up at him. "Armando, those gentlemen just across the room; they look familiar to me, but I just can't place their names. Do you know who they are?"

"Sorry, Madame, but I'm afraid I can't be of any help." He seemed to reconsider his clipped response as he added, "They aren't staying at the hotel. Perhaps they may be attending one of the conferences. Shall I inquire?"

"No; I'm probably mistaken. I appreciate your trying to help. The seafood salad was delicious."

Amanda slowly turned her attention to the bill but, deciding to wait out her stay until the other man turned and she could catch sight of him, she hesitated; "I'd love a cappuccino please, Armando."

Vivi gave her a puzzled look as the waiter left to bring it. "You can't really want hot coffee in this heat?" She raised her eyebrow and pushed her chair back. "I'll wait for you at the gift shop. I need to pick up some more suntan lotion."

As soon as Viv walked off Amanda brought her attention back to the table with the two men. The man who faced in her direction caught her staring at him. He turned and whispered to his partner, who cast appreciative, but non-mysterious, eyes her way.

Amanda blushed, grabbing for the cappuccino that had appeared. After one or two desultory sips she pushed it away, signed the check, and with eyes downcast, strode swiftly past their table and headed towards the lobby.

"Miss Evans, there you are. Another message just arrived." Eduardo Curzon, the hotel's manager, smiled broadly as he efficiently presented the envelope. "I thought perhaps it may be from the same person."

Amanda thanked him, took the proffered note and turned away. Hands shaking, face pink, she unfolded the message.

"My dear Amanda," the message read, "I've arranged to have my own driver, Asuncion, pick you up at your bungalow at a quarter to four. I so look forward to meeting you." It was signed: Florencia Santos.

Amanda turned to the manager. "Thank you. It doesn't require any response."

"If there is nothing more I can do for you then, good day Miss Evans." He walked away with a look that said he hoped to have no more such meetings with this particular guest.

She caught his look, gave herself a mental shake and hurried towards the gift shop. A bored looking Vivi was paging through magazines. Relief filled her eyes as they headed for the nearest jeepney.

Their brief journey was completed in silence. Vivi sighed and said "I'm ready for a siesta," as the jeepney pulled to a stop. She gave a big yawn as she headed towards her bungalow, saying, "Don't wake me if I'm still asleep when you return from your meeting."

Amanda nodded and hurried towards the welcoming coolness of her own bungalow. She longed to stretch out on the soft white bedspread. But—she froze, staring at the bed—someone had mussed the edges. She was certain she hadn't left the dust ruffle tucked up into the mattress. Glancing around, her eyes caught sight of an opened drawer, its contents scattered. Grateful she'd left her passport and airline tickets in the safe deposit box back at the Mandarin Hotel, she ran to check on her appointment book, kept wrapped within her lingerie pouch. Her appointment book, while not taken, was out of its protective cover and clearly missing pages. Every page for this trip was neatly ripped out. She cursed her oversight in not having taken it.

She tried to resurrect exactly what her notations would have revealed. They were cryptic as always on any trip to the Philippines; but indecipherable, probably not. *Certainly not by anyone intent enough to persevere,* she thought.

Suddenly vulnerable, her dream hideaway felt ominous. Actions that had seemed curious and upsetting turned swiftly to calculated and threatening. After the initial shock, Amanda found her emotions changing to deep anger. She considered calling in the hotel's staff or the police, but hesitated, knowing that either wasn't an option. Not with Nigel's edicts to keep discretion at the maximum. Whatever actions she took would have to be, not only discreet, but hers alone.

As she dressed for her appointment a half-formed thought kept nagging at the edges of her consciousness. The ghost of some not quite registered awareness kept trying to get her attention. She replayed every comment, and each person's actions, during the day. A discreet knock on the door short-circuited her thoughts as Aunt Florencia's driver announced his arrival. During the brief drive her thoughts kept circling around the facts, trying to fit the pieces together. The more logic she applied, the more everything faded into shadows, like one of those pictures with a hidden image only seen by offsetting one's vision.

# THIRTEEN

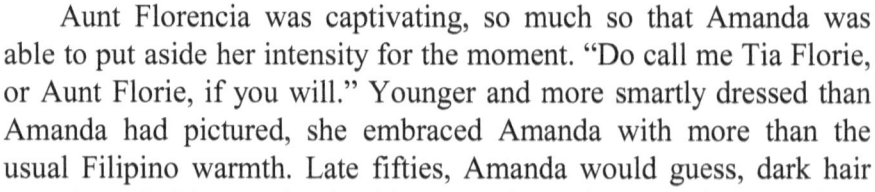

Aunt Florencia was captivating, so much so that Amanda was able to put aside her intensity for the moment. "Do call me Tia Florie, or Aunt Florie, if you will." Younger and more smartly dressed than Amanda had pictured, she embraced Amanda with more than the usual Filipino warmth. Late fifties, Amanda would guess, dark hair smartly styled into a simple chignon and wearing a cool cotton dress that wouldn't look out of place in downtown New York.

"My Miguelito considers you one of his closest friends. I feel I know you already, my dear. Come; allow me to give you a tour of my little cottage."

Amanda's ease deepened as she passed through each room. The decor was simple, all restful sea green and blue and comfy, with books everywhere. A piano with photos of family and friends and a seascape were the only focal points to draw ones eyes away from the heart stopping view of the ocean.

After their tour of the house, Florie led the way to the sanctuary of the garden. Its terrace provided a perfect view of a waterfall cascading gently among ferns, into a koi pond. The peace and warmth,

Amanda thought, clearly reflected Aunt Florencia's own energy. They approached a large coffee table surrounded by two wicker chairs, one of which held a gorgeous, chocolate Siamese cat. He purred as he glanced contentedly at Aunt Florie with his cool blue eyes as she lifted him gently. "Now there; do have a chair, Amanda."

"And the cat if I may?" Amanda took the languid bundle from Florie's outstretched arms. Stroking its fur brought Oedipus to mind. "You are as much a beauty as my cat."

"A spoiled beauty I'm afraid. Aren't you, my little "Lian?" Aunt Florie smiled as she offered Amanda a tall glass of frosty kalamansi juice. "It is spiked with just a little champagne, my dear. It keeps the sparkle in my eyes and gives a lift to the appetite." She raised her glass in the direction of a table that groaned with delectable tidbits.

Amanda banished any mention of not being hungry, smiling as Aunt Florie brought a light assortment back to their coffee table. After taking the proffered plate, she put it aside and looked over at Aunt Florie. "I understand you have some questions—"

Florie stopped her in mid-sentence, popping a delicate morsel of shrimp on toast into her mouth, running her tongue over its last crumb. "Please my dear, one must leave any thought of business until one's physical appetites have been satisfied."

Amanda smiled, thinking there'd be no knitting antimacassars in her dotage for this auntie. After they had both consumed some of each delicacy, Aunt Florie put aside her glass and began: "You've arrived at just the most perfect time. I'm feeling exceedingly prosperous today since I was the biggest winner at our Mah Jong game—thirty-six dollars!" She poured another healthy dollop of champagne into their glasses. "My doctor says a little won't hurt me. Please begin." She beamed in anticipation, eyes sparkling and only then, in the slant of the sunlight, betraying a hint of tiny laugh-line wrinkles.

The Filipino approach was illustrated by Florie's technique. It wasn't that they didn't acknowledge the world of business. Every question Florie asked erased any doubt as to her financial savvy. She quickly moved through her banking issues while adding asides on world politics and economics. The difference lay in the emphasis on life, family and relationships.

In support of that thought, Florie ended her banking concerns with a surprising question. "How do you find my Miguelito this trip, Amanda?" She stopped the gentle stroking of the cat, which had made his way back to her lap, and gave Amanda a searching look. "I am very concerned for my boy."

"I'm not sure what you mean. He does seem preoccupied." She hesitated. "And tired—now that you mention it."

"He's exhausted alright. But it's more than that. I thought he may have revealed to you something of what's worrying him."

"We haven't been able to talk much this trip, not yet anyway." Amanda's voice turned solemn. "But I'm worried as well." She stared at the fountain, her thoughts recalling exactly what prompted her concern. "Lately, when he's teasing me, it feels forced, as though his emotions are miles away from such light comments. What do you think might be concerning him?"

"Definitely it involves the NPA, who've been infiltrating his sugar workers, along with increased concern for not having been paid for his sugar crop for two years now; the usual worries. But that isn't what's on his mind lately. Whatever this new thing is, it must be something he feels he has no control over. When I ask him what's wrong, he says 'Nothing', and changes the subject fast. I'd hoped he may have told you what's troubling him."

"No. But then again, I've arrived with a colleague, so we've really not had much alone time." Amanda hesitated, looking deeply into Aunt Florie's eyes. "If he does share any confidences, you know I couldn't reveal them." She watched a film of sorrow quickly cloud Florie's eyes. "But I could let you know that everything's alright." Amanda took Miguel's aunt's hand. "I'll make time to talk privately with him at Brad Gregory's party." She hesitated. "That is, if he attends the party. He didn't seem fond of being in Raffy De La Serna's company, so maybe he won't show." Amanda looked down to stroke the cat that nuzzled at her ankles. When she looked up, she was surprised to see tears running down Aunt Florie's face.

"Please forgive an old woman her sorrows. Your mention of Raffy brought back all the pain of 'Ortie's' heartbreak. The kids were about to publish the bans when Raffy abruptly announced his decision not to wed." Florie reached into her dress pocket, pulled out a tissue and wiped more tears away. "Ortie was devastated. She entered the church. Miguelito will never forget or forgive Rafael."

Amanda was surprised at the freshness of the pain. "I'm so sorry; but what about Raffy's father? How did he react?"

"You will see the old man on Monday night. Don Emilio's health has failed so quickly—and all to do with his son if you ask me." She reached over and snapped off a bloom, tearing its leaf and holding it up to Amanda. "With help from these plants—or others like them—a perfect blend that only a mankukulam would know."

"But surely his doctor..."

A sharp snort accompanied her reply. "A doctor—humph! They don't know what to look for."

"I am seeing Emilio on Monday. What should I look for?"

"Look in the whites of the eyes for a yellowing and under the fingernails, dark spots."

"Would Miguel know?" Amanda hesitated. "And do you think he'll show up?"

Florie reached over and took her hand. "No and yes; he wouldn't miss any party on your behalf. It would be an insult to you and to your host, Mr. Gregory."

"Will you be there? Amanda stopped, suddenly remembering their discussion of business. "Any questions that might occur to you after I leave today, I could answer then."

"Not me. I intend to stay put here awhile. Speaking of business," Aunt Florie smiled a 'guess what hand it's in?' smile. "I've been waiting for two things. To meet you and to have my deposit with another U.S. bank mature. What kind of rate can you give me on a one year deposit of one million dollars?"

Amanda's spirits rose at the unexpected windfall. She paused as she considered just how much she could improve the rate. "I can offer you at least fifty basis points higher than the going rate."

Her offer brought Aunt Florie's laugh lines into play. "It's yours." She refilled their glasses as she insisted they cement the transaction with one last celebratory glass of champagne.

Amanda's mellow buzz had begun to vanish as she returned to her bungalow. She hesitated, warily scanning the area for signs of anyone nearby. Gingerly, she opened the door on a room as pristine as she had left it. She decided to hold back any mention to Nigel of her missing appointment book pages or the threatening letter. His knowing wouldn't help and his panic could aggravate her situation. In practical terms, her missing pages of appointments could be replicated from Derek's.

Amanda anticipated Derek's reaction to those missing pages, expecting it to peel back his mask a bit. As to the threatening letter, she decided to play her cards close to her chest.

Shifting her thoughts into neutral, she quickly showered and threw on her dependable cotton skirt and top for her meeting with Raffy. The vivid purple highlighted her brunette coloring and accented her bloom of tan. She was dressed and ready with ten minutes to spare before the jeepney arrived.

She took one last look to make sure every lock was secure before she closed the door to head over to Vivi's. As Amanda approached Vivi's bungalow, she heard sounds of frustration, emphasized by something striking the door. "Is it safe to enter?" she shouted through the open window.

"Damn it all, Amanda; come in and help me find something to wear tonight." Vivi's desperation was evident by the clothes flung about on every surface.

Amanda picked up a black linen dress. "This. Wear this. With your tan and coloring, it's perfect."

Vivi held it up, took a long look and, turning slowly, said, "You're right; it's perfect."

"Good, then I'll expect to see you at six-thirty cocktails." She turned as she heard the sound of the jeepney pulling up. "I'm off to my meeting."

* * *

Raffy seemed unusually distant and, just as surprising, gone was the obligatory embrace. "There's a small conference room in the back where we won't be disturbed." He turned, walking swiftly in that direction.

"At last;" he said as he closed the door. "Thirty minutes isn't going to do it, I'm afraid." He walked over to a small sofa, sat down, opened his appointment book and spread a document alongside it on the coffee table. He motioned for Amanda to take a seat beside him. "I wanted to go over two things; first, my father, and second, this deal I'm working on." He looked up as Amanda waited. "My father's health, as you'll see on Monday, is failing fast. I have to deal with all his business interests." He looked up, staring intently into Amanda's eyes. "All of them. In fact, if there is anything—anything at all—that you may need to discuss with him, it should be run by me."

Amanda's thoughts raced with the intent implicit in those words. "I'm hoping it's not as bad as you think."

"It's worse. Monday will erase any such hopes."

"At least it will help clarify any special instructions he may have concerning the handling of his accounts." The look in her eye became all business. "Until it does, I'm not, as you know, at liberty to run by you any discussion involving his banking relationship."

Raffy's eyes turned to steel, as did his voice. "I'll remember that when it's me that holds the purse strings." He turned away, removing his appointment book and the ashtray from the table, as he spread out architectural drawings for Amanda's viewing. "A purse that will be considerably increased by this project. Have a look. A state of the art conference center, incorporating the world's largest auditorium, concert stage, art and music theaters, parking for sixty thousand cars and…" He glanced up, waiting to hear or see excitement from Amanda.

"Wow; it looks twice the size of the Dorothy Chandler Pavilion in Los Angeles. But where do I fit in?" She listened closely for his response.

"Not to finance it. Today's meeting with the investors proves there's money to burn." His eyes gleamed. "Knowing Imelda is interested is collateral enough for them."

"And me?"

"Soon I'll have power of attorney on all of father's accounts. I'll be moving some cash into this project. The rest I'd like to put up against a CD secured loan." He looked closely into her eyes, studying her response. "Your department does do cash-secured loans, right?"

"Yes, but..."

"But only with collateral owned by the borrower? Not to worry. That's being handled."

A chill went through Amanda as she thought, *His father dies; he milks investors of mega millions so that Imelda can have another puff project built, and—*. Her heart missed a beat. *The project was a perfect front to launder money!*

Raffy glanced down at his watch, giving her a moment to collect herself before responding. "Raffy, it's not the right timing for any commitment on the part of Fidelity American."

"I gave you a chance." He hastily gathered up his papers and moved towards the door. "We'll talk more about this later. I need to make a phone call." His: "—meet you in the cocktail lounge" was shouted back from the hallway.

Stunned, Amanda sat for a few minutes, fighting the bile in her throat. "You snake," she whispered, with as much venom as the reptile. The thought of her meeting with the Don sent shivers down her back until she remembered his insistence on meeting Derek to discuss a new trust. Relief flooded her. A new trust could definitely protect his assets and maybe even his life.

As she jumped up excitedly from the sofa, she looked down to see Raffy's appointment book fall at her feet. He left in such a hurry he's forgotten it, she thought as she scooped it up. She put it in her purse, deciding to give it to him over drinks. She actually had a smile on her face as she neared the entry. Vivi, who'd just walked into the lobby, headed her way.

"You look great, Vivi." Viv smiled at Amanda's praise, linked arms and moved through the lobby.

"Where did all these people come from?" Amanda whispered as they pressed through the crowded cocktail lounge.

"All I've seen thus far were moms, children and a few stuffy men." Vivi gave an appreciative smile as she tallied the ratio of men to women. "But these men are gorgeous, even in those ridiculous shirts."

"It's called the 'barong-tagalog', Amanda replied. It's considered tropical formal."

"Well, they do look cute, I guess." Vivi's eyes flashed approval, drawing an echoing response from several men, including Derek's, as they entered the room. Derek's expression conveyed amusement as he and Raffy rose from their chairs.

Raffy, all amiability now, smoothly swept Amanda and then Vivi into a warm Filipino embrace, followed by his graciously extending chairs, both angled nearer to his.

"Well, Miss Nova, what brings you to the Philippines? Good fortune, I hope, as it is surely mine to have you here."

"Good fortune I have plenty of, but good friends few, Mr. De La Serna. I was in Hong Kong on business and decided to visit Amanda in Manila." She gave one of her quick downward glances, swiftly drawing her gaze up, eyes wide as she gazed deeply into his. "I'm so glad I did."

"I hope you will like what you see and return often. Please call me Raffy." They held their look before Raffy coughed and turned to Amanda.

"Here's to a toast to my great, good fortune at having the pleasure of your company." As Raffy touched his glass to Amanda and Vivi's, pausing there, he missed Derek's smothered hint of laughter. Amanda gave him a subtle 'Mind your manners' stare. She could have saved her look. Derek obviously wasn't about to let this opportunity go by.

"Raffy, you've heard of the fame of the Irish for dishing the blarney? Somewhere along the line a leprechaun must have been added to your gene pool. A toast to that magical gift from the Emerald Isle, and to its new master!" Derek grinned wickedly as he raised his glass high.

Raffy hesitated for just enough time to flash Derek a cool glance. Before Amanda could register their parry and thrust, Raffy's look transformed itself to one of amiable good will. "To kissing the

Blarney Stone as it's never been kissed before!" From that moment on Raffy seemed to outdo himself with warmth, wit and charm. Although the charm was generously extended to Derek as well, the subliminal message seemed to be: "I'm nobody's fool. Don't mess with me ".

Amanda felt a chill, knowing how easily a Filipino could feel insulted and the lengths to which they would go to redress such actions. She tried to deflect Derek's dangerous gaffe as she turned to Raffy. "I'm convinced the real "Luck of the Irish" is in not being at the receiving end of their appalling sense of humor." Amanda laughed with what she hoped was a clear-the-air lightness.

For all her skills at throwing water on fires, it was Vivi who saved the day. Intentionally or not, she began a concerted effort to enchant Raffy. Effortlessly, she had him eating out of her hand, staring dazedly into her eyes, and hanging on every word that left her mouth. Bewitched is what I'd call it, thought Amanda, amazed by the ease with which Viv had charmed a man used to having females hang on his every word.

Their waiter's approach terminated the spell. "Sr. De La Serna, your party asked that I let you know he is waiting in the dining room."

"Where has the time gone? I've a meeting in the boardroom right now. Sorry, but I really must go. Please give my apologies to Miguel." Raffy turned to Amanda, speaking softly. "I need to continue our discussion. I'll call you to schedule a time." He turned to Vivi, taking hands he was obviously reluctant to relinquish. "I'm sorry to have to break away. Enjoy your dinner. I will call and make certain my country charms you. Ciao."

It was only after he'd gone that Amanda registered his unheard of omission in not having mentioned what a pleasure it was to have met Derek Ashton—or her oversight in not giving Raffy his appointment book. Rather than run after him, she decided to leave it with the desk.

Derek paid for the drinks and he, Vivi and Amanda headed for the dining room. Miguel was deep in conversation with a man who seemed annoyed at their arrival. He abruptly pushed his chair away, turned and headed towards the exit before they could be introduced. Amanda was near enough to make out his parting comment. Although uttered in a confidential tone, it seemed barely civil and vaguely ominous. "Not a word to anyone—and don't be late."

Miguel arranged his features into one of pleasurable expectation. "Well now, we're all here; primed with the heartiest of appetites, I trust?"

Vivi gave Miguel a friendly "You bet" response, with a smile only half the wattage recently spent on Raffy.

Oblivious, Miguel pressed on. "The food is superb and the desserts are manna from heaven." Amanda studied him, wondering why she hadn't noticed the worry etching his forehead and the deep shadows under his eyes. She reached out to touch his hand. "I promise to try to do justice to the dinner even though your aunt Florie stuffed me. You were right. We connected right away."

"You, Amanda, would connect with anyone." Her "not everyone" response was short-circuited by the waiter who'd walked up to take their order.

Amanda had spotted Derek's glance at Miguel and his raised eyebrow in her direction. She determined to safeguard Miguel from any of Derek's barbed witticisms, especially after Derek's recent and willful baiting of a major client.

Derek had no hesitation where food was involved, betraying his ancestry and his size with his order of the largest steak, double potatoes and a pitcher of beer. Amanda stayed with Miguel's recommendation of the fish and a Caesar salad.

Miguel ordered very little, pleading a large lunch. Derek loudly guffawed. "What do you mean, a large lunch? A beer and a hot dog on the golf course should have been worked off before the fourteenth hole. Especially the way you played. He's formidable." Derek raised his glass in a comradely gesture. "When did you begin the game; when you were three?"

Miguel smiled. "It was a freak day, trust me." He turned to Amanda. "How was your day?"

Amanda began with, "Nevertheless, my congratulations Miguel." She glanced Derek's way and catching him and Vivi deep in conversation added, "My meeting with your aunt was great. Thank you for arranging it."

"My pleasure; she told me she's opening an account with you. She's not a pushover you know, for all her easygoing facade." Suddenly Miguel gave her the sort of in-depth scan she had recently given him. "Your success ought to have brightened your spirits a bit, but something's eating you. Want to talk about it?"

Derek turned his attention away from Vivi to comment. "She's probably still in a tiff over my ribbing of Raffy-boy. Let's call a truce, Amanda. Maybe I was a bit out of line, but Mr. Charmer definitely rubbed me the wrong way."

Vivi drew a deep breath before coming to the defense of Raffy. "You were none too friendly, you know." She softened her delivery a bit. "Funny maybe, cute, of course; but anyone could see those hackles rise." She reached out to stroke the hair on Derek's forearm.

Amanda's response came as a dash of cold water on any playfulness. "The De La Serna family is a very important relationship for me, Derek." She lowered her voice as she glanced around before continuing. "Remember my mentioning that Filipino men have thin skins, even hold grudges and seek revenge when their egos are involved?" She lowered her voice to a whisper, determined to make her point. "Raffy has the thinnest." Miguel's silence, his penetrating look, stopped Amanda like a bullet. Her words rang in her ears, as Miguel would have heard them: *"Filipino men, holding a grudge, wanting revenge. Hortensia and Raffy and Miguel and* ... She turned to Miguel to explain. "I didn't mean—it's just Raffy and—"

Derek turned from one to the other. "What gives with you two? Looks like I'm not the only one to put my foot in it."

"She hasn't put her foot in anything." Miguel put his arm around a stricken Amanda. "No offense meant, no offense taken. I know exactly what you mean—what you both mean: Raffy's a jerk, but not to be messed with." He went on to explain briefly to Derek the heartbreak Raffy had caused his sister, even his desire to seek revenge. "Revenge is part of our culture. What did a president of yours once say, 'speak softly and carry a big stick'?'

"Point taken; I'd be out for blood if some bloke harmed a sister of mine. But I've had it with discussing Raffy for the moment. The chemistry between us was way off from word one." He turned to

Amanda. "I'll try to mind my P's and Q's." He raised one eyebrow and changed the conversation abruptly. "What's on the agenda for Saturday?"

Before Miguel had time to respond, Vivi yawned, saying, "Count me out for any early morning activities. Once I hit my bed I intend to remain there until checkout time. In fact, I definitely hear my pillow calling." With that she rose, prompting Derek and Miguel to stand.

Vivi kissed both men good night with a sleepy, lingering sigh. Amanda noticed Derek move closer to her clinging embrace, almost in spite of himself. An unexpected twinge of pain surfaced. Amanda turned away.

Their waiter, staring in Vivi's wake, approached their table with a note for Derek. Derek glanced at it quickly. His jaw tightened, chin firmed and voice hardened as he rose from his chair.

"Would you excuse me? Something's come up. I'll try to get back in time for coffee. If not, I'll see you at breakfast."

As Derek raced away, Miguel turned to Amanda with a quizzical look. "You'd never make a good actress. The dark look on your face tells me you feel about Mr. Ashton something akin to what I feel about Raffy. Has Derek done you wrong?"

"Done me wrong?' Where do I begin?" At that moment their waiter brought the dessert menu. "A cappuccino, if you have it."

Miguel seconded her order and looked around. "The place is filling up with late diners. Let's take our coffees out to the pool where we can talk in private. You look as though you're about to cry or scream if what you're holding in doesn't come out."

Settled into a poolside chaise, coffee warming her spirits, she turned to Miguel. "You know I can't really—.

He stopped her in mid-sentence. "I know. You can't say anything about clients, their money, or their business dealings. That's obvious, and that isn't what I mean. What I see in your eyes is more like fear or desperation. Which is it?"

Not stopping to edit her comments, she found herself telling him about today's threatening note, her ransacked room, the missing appointment pages, even discussed Derek's secret breakfast meeting with her man with the evil eye.

Miguel remained silent throughout her account. Only his intensifying grip on the arm of his chaise betrayed his anger. He spoke slowly and evenly, measuring every word. "God-willing, someone is just trying to scare you off, starting with the missing anting-anting. Whoever it is, I mean to help you get to the bottom of this." He looked intently into her eyes. "In the meantime, I'd feel better if you would consider shortening your trip—or at least staying with someone. I'm sure my aunt would have you in a minute. What do you say?"

As convincingly as he tried to reassure her, she read worry and anger, thinly veiled behind such a suggestion. Fighting a sick feeling in her stomach, she said. "I can't just leave. Trust me, I can't. I'll be as safe in the hotel as anywhere. Derek is there and—"

He finished her sentence for her. "—and that's what you're afraid of. Derek is there with your strange man on the flight and Derek is running off now to God knows where. What do you know about him anyway?"

Amanda suddenly felt a sense of having revealed too much. "He comes highly recommended. I can't fault his knowledge of trusts."

"Maybe—but from what you've told me, I don't trust him. Promise me that if you change your mind about moving from the hotel you'll let me know. I can have you safely behind the family compound's walls in a minute."

"I won't change my mind, but thanks anyway." Noticing Miguel's look, she rushed to reassure him. "I'll take care; you can count on it."

# FOURTEEN

Miguel, seemingly pacified, led Amanda to a jeepney, saying goodnight with no further warnings. Relinquishing any attempt at sleep, she entered her bungalow and brewed a pot of tea. In the midst of its boil she remembered Raffy's appointment book, still in her purse. She picked up the phone to call the front desk. With every unanswered ring her curiosity grew.

Maybe some clue lies inside. Removing the appointment book, she carefully opened it to the current week and began scrutinizing the notations. Her own name was down twice this past week, with today's underlined and accompanied by a strange notation: the words "Status?" and "Control?" "Both heavily underlined. She read the notations surrounding it, paging back through the previous week, noting the initials 'M.W.' appeared with 'Anxious' and 'M.S.'— Handle ASAP', written alongside. What could that stand for? Oh, my God! How could I have missed this one? Her meeting today with Raffy included the notation, 'Call M.W. re development'.

Laying the book aside, she focused on anyone she knew by those initials. A sick feeling descended as M.W. and Mai Wong surfaced at the same time as M.S. for Miguel Santos. A mix of anger, fear and confusion filled her. Confusion won out. Surely, she thought, Raffy knows many Filipinos with the same initials. She returned to the book in the hopes that further scrutiny would erase any doubts. Many notations of back-to-back meetings, abbreviations and other initials appeared. She stopped, incredulous. 'Derek A.' underlined, with five PM on the day they arrived at Playa Verde. How could he have met with Derek? And why; and why didn't Derek let on that he had an appointment with him?" The image of their seemingly 'first' meeting returned. *Great ruse that antipathy scene, she thought, gagging at the memory.*

One last slow scrutiny of the most recent notations concerning her: 'Amanda, Status? Control,' destroyed any decision to reserve judgment. Making a quick copy of all the notations, she glanced towards Vivi's bungalow, hoping to see a light on. One A.M. or not, she could use a friend right now—even if all they discussed was a postmortem of the evening. It was completely dark.

"Just as well to heed the 'let sleeping dogs lie' maxim, especially where Vivi is concerned." Amanda muttered, remembering Vivi's emphasis on getting her beauty sleep. She took her tea, headed back to bed and a night of restless sleep.

\* \* \*

Sun streaming in woke her at eight. She jumped up, wondering why no one had called to get together for breakfast. Quickly throwing on last night's skirt and top, she headed for Vivi's bungalow to see if she was still asleep or had gone to breakfast and left her a note.

*Strange, she thought, Vivi's door was partially open.* Amanda called her name, stepping inside to find Vivi gone. And, either her bed hadn't been slept in or the maid had come awfully early. Curious, she opened the closets and drawers. Empty.

Must have awoken early, packed, and went to check out before breakfast, Amanda decided, looking for a note. At no sign of one, she called for a jeepney and headed for the lobby, expecting to find the three of them having breakfast.

Derek and Miguel smiled a bright greeting as she approached. "Where's Vivi?" Derek asked, looking around.

"Getting more beauty sleep?" Miguel added with his best imitation of Vivi's voice.

"What do you mean, 'where's Vivi?' She's not with you? Her clothes are gone and—she looked in frustration at their dumbfounded stares—Could she have gone to the main dining room?"

"She couldn't have been there. Miguel and I checked and they're not serving breakfast today in the main dining room." Derek turned to Miguel. "Let's go up to the front desk and see what they know."

Mr. Curzon's professional smile wavered briefly when he spotted Amanda at Derek's side. "Vivian Nova? No message has been left by Miss Nova." He quickly flipped through the registration files. "There is no indication that Miss Nova has checked out and no breakfast was charged to her room this morning."

"Oh my God!" Amanda turned to Derek and Miguel. "Someone should have gone with her to her room last night. Maybe she never got there."

"Hold everything. She must have gone to her room if her clothes are gone." Derek turned to the hotel manager. "We need you to do a complete search of all of the grounds and—" he began.

"And get the jeepney driver that took her to her bungalow last night." Miguel chimed in.

"Righto; and check with the night crew to see if they noticed anything. She may have come back to the lobby last night." Derek added.

"She may have had an emergency call." Amanda turned to Mr. Curzon. "Do you keep a record of any incoming or outgoing calls made from her phone?"

The look on the hotel manager's face warred between a knowing sneer of disdain, implying contemptuous familiarity with libidinous guests and their midnight peccadilloes, and a practiced look of concern for a client's well-being. "Did I hear you say that Miss Nova's room had not been slept in and that all of her personal belongings had been removed? Might I suggest that she had decided to leave early and return to Manila? I am certain you shall find her at your hotel, Miss Evans. In fact, she may be trying to call you at any moment." The hotel manager turned towards the telephone to punctuate his comment. With seeming prescience the phone rang, causing the manager to jump. Everyone held his breath in anticipation.

"Yes, certainly; you are interested in a room for two persons for four nights?" His opening conversation drew looks that had him hastily add, "Let me transfer you to our reservations clerk."

He turned back with a look of shock as he met Amanda, Derek and Miguel's eyes. Their looks told him to expect a cord around his throat if he didn't do something fast. "You may depend on my doing everything possible to determine the whereabouts of Miss Nova. Phone calls will be traced, employees questioned, taxi cabs called." He turned to Amanda. "Would you have me call your hotel, Miss Evans?"

"No. I'll take care of that myself."

"Very well; and how about contacting the police?"

Everyone looked at each other. Derek was the first to speak. "I don't think that will prove necessary. Let's take one thing at a time. We'll let you know after everything else has been checked out."

Amanda's look of shock had been replaced by one of anger. "If any harm has come to Vivi, I won't leave here until whoever has done it has been found." Another thought took hold, her forehead furrowing. "If this is one of Vivi shenanigans, I'll…" Her voice trailed off at Mr. Curzon's stare.

She turned back to Miguel and Derek. "I'll go to my room now and call The Mandarin to see if she's there. Then I'll call the office and leave word to have Karen fax us any personal phone numbers in Vivi's file." She gave her most reassuring look. "Just in case we need to contact someone back home."

"Stay in your room Amanda. She may call you." Derek turned his focus from Amanda to Miguel "Follow up with the manager on anything the employees may have seen. I'll be sure her phone calls are traced."

"Sure thing; I have an in with the cabbies. I'll check them as well."

"Very good; Amanda's bungalow will be our contact point. Any information should be relayed to Amanda the minute we hear it. Anything!"

"I'm off then." Amanda turned to find a jeepney driver waiting.

"I called him for you, Miss Evans." Mr. Curzon was at his most efficient. "An employee meeting has been called. Half of the staff will attend at ten AM and the other half at ten thirty. Even the night staff is required to attend." He addressed his concluding words to Derek. "If anything is learned, I shall call Miss Evans room promptly."

Derek and Miguel scattered, each to their own mission. Amanda's was beginning to take shape in her mind as she drove up to her bungalow. She leaped from the jeepney before it had come to a complete stop, dashed straight into the bungalow and grabbed the phone to call Manila.

"Why no, Miss Evans. I'm quite certain Miss Nova has not shown up." The manager of the Mandarin was polite, but Amanda wanted first-hand assurance. "Please go up to my room to see for certain. Also check to see if there are any messages from Miss Nova. Yes, I'll hold."

Amanda waited, hoping to hear Vivi's voice on the line.

The manager of the Mandarin returned. "Miss Nova is not in the room, nor is there any indication she had been in it."

"And messages?

"There is nothing."

"Please take this number down. I'd appreciate it if you would notify me if she returns or calls."

She hung up, dismayed but determined. Slowly she examined her images of Vivi since their arrival at Playa Verde. A hodgepodge of scenes presented themselves. Vivi demanding Amanda make contacts for her; Vivi complaining of the lack of nerve of Filipino men; Vivi petulant over not enough action and Vivi flirting at lunch and dinner. Amanda hesitated over her memory of the two men at lunch. What may have happened between Vivi and the two men was a blank. Whatever it was, Viv was in a giant sulk when I showed up, Amanda thought. She pulled out a tablet and penciled in: 'Determine identity of men. Get a list of all conference attendees and registered guests'.

Amanda paced, pencil twirling back and forth as a metronome to her thoughts. She headed back to the phone and dialed her office, leaving phone and fax numbers for Karen to fax her all phone numbers in Vivi's file.

As she hung up, she stood gazing at the phone. She nearly stumbled in her haste to get to Vivi's door. Leaving it open, she dashed into the bathroom. "Aha; I was right." One of the bathroom phones had a dab of lipstick on the mouthpiece. Vivi, or someone, must have made a phone call. No maid has been in. Amanda's thoughts raced in logical order. *Phone call; pack; leave in a hurry.* "Note; there must be a note." Amanda said as she grabbed for the bathroom trashcan. No note, but plenty of tissues with make-up. She looked around the room for a tablet. Finding none, she headed to the bedroom. If it matched her room, there was a message tablet inserted within a scalloped seashell holder alongside the bed.

The tablet was empty of any notation, but the top page revealed the ragged edge of a hastily torn page. Amanda took the tablet into the sunlight. White indentations appeared on the top page. They must have been written firmly, she thought. She could almost make out a heavily underscored word. "It looks like initials," she said, peering closely at the bone white tracings. 'H or A'; 'K or R'? She squinted in frustration before recalling a method to highlight them. "I'll run a light tracing of pencil over the depressed markings. "That's it", she said, running towards the kitchen. A pencil hung from a "Plaza Verde" magnet on the refrigerator. She positioned it over the tablet hesitatingly. Her thoughts warred between destroying evidence and determination to get at it. She gently but completely covered the tablet with a light back and forth pencil shading. A ghost of the letters H and K followed by MRA11 appeared.

"HKMRA11", she spoke aloud, wondering what it might mean. "Could it be a license plate number?" She peered closely. The K was slightly apart from the M. 'HK MRA11'; 'HK'? 'Hong Kong!', she shouted. It had to be Hong Kong. She followed a logical train of thought. *Vivi had a call from Hong Kong, a call from a client in Hong Kong, a Mr. MRA? She had to fly back, maybe?* "Fly back!" Of course; MRA11 must be a flight number!" Amanda grabbed the phone, pulled out the directory and dialed the airport.

"I'd like a record of all flights, particularly any encoded MRA11, leaving Manila for Hong Kong last night."

The response was matter of fact: "Four flights total, two last night and two before ten this morning; none bearing any flight number even close to MRA11."

"I want you to check whether a Vivian Nova was on any of those flights." She paused, her jaw set firmly. "Take however long you need. I'll hold."

The wait wasn't long. "No one by that name is shown on our passenger lists for those flights."

Amanda's frustration propelled her out the door and back to the lobby. Mr. Curzon was nowhere in sight. She glanced at the clocks over the reception desk: ten thirty-five. He'd be in the employee meeting, she remembered. Would Derek? No, she remembered that Derek was going to follow up on the phone calls and Miguel would attend the employee meetings.

She glanced at a notice board announcing a General Employee Meeting in the Dolphin Room and headed back to the conference rooms. She stopped. "Raffy", she thought, remembering his appointment book in her purse as she approached their meeting room. She decided to return it where she'd found it rather than reveal that she had picked it up.

Stealthily she entered the empty room, wedged it loosely among the sofa cushions and backed out, debating as to whether he could help them. The "De la Serna" name would light a firecracker under Mr. Curzon's commitment. She headed for a hotel courtesy phone.

"I'd like to speak with a guest, Raphael de la Serna. I don't have his room number."

"What?" Amanda frowned. "He's checked out? Last night? Thank you." She hung up, staring into the distance.

Convinced she should talk with Miguel, she turned and headed to the Dolphin room. A trail of employees passed her by, indicating their meeting had been a brief one. She approached the double doors of the meeting room, glanced in and found it empty. Turning away, she spotted a bank of telephones in an alcove.

Was that Miguel, she wondered? A man, with his back turned to her, had his head hunched down into the phone's mouthpiece. She approached quietly in case she was wrong.

"You heard me. Tell your 'jeffe' that if he so much as ruffles a hair on her body he will have me to pay." She recognized the figure as Miguel, but the tone of voice was so threatening that she quietly backed away.

Amanda's look as she entered the lobby caused Derek Ashton to rush towards her. "You look like the devil himself is chasing you. What are you doing here anyway? I thought you were staying in your bungalow."

She glanced at Mr. Curzon as he and a cluster of employees turned their way. "Let's go somewhere more private." Amanda headed towards the pool area, targeting a secluded garden bench as her destination.

"What's up?"

She proceeded to tell him of Vivi's note pad. "Obviously I thought it referred to a flight to Hong Kong. But there was no such flight number and no such passenger name."

"And no Vivi at the Mandarin, I'm certain." Derek watched as she nodded affirmation. "But we may have a lead. No incoming or outgoing calls were made to or from her room last night, except for one."

"A Hong Kong call, I'd be willing to guess; right?"

"That's the bummer." Her face fell. "It wasn't an external call. Someone called her from a house phone and they can't be traced, nor are they recorded." His face looked thoughtful. "Would you have called her from the lobby?"

"Not I; she said she needed undisturbed beauty sleep."

"Someone in the hotel called her room—but who?"

*You, or Miguel*, Amanda thought as she noticed him closely watching her. She described Vivi's pique over the men in the restaurant. "Maybe it was one of them."

"Maybe, but if they were here for any conference, no names are kept. I did get Curzon to print out a list of the registered guests. He resisted, but a little persuasion produced this." Derek brought forth a printout of hotel guests, along with a list of all the employees."

"What did the employee meetings turn up? Any jeepney rides late at night?"

"No, but according to Curzon, one of the night shift employees thought he saw a car drive up to her bungalow; a big Mercedes, he said."

Amanda turned in excitement. "Let's go. That would mean the guard at the main gate would have seen the car pull away and got a look at who was in it"

"Slow down, Amanda." Derek nodded as Miguel approached. "I'll let Miguel tell you."

"They said you had headed towards the pool." Miguel shook his head. "What gives?"

'You go first, Miguel." Derek said. "It would seem that the employee meeting turned up some interesting new information."

"Yes and no." Miguel's voice retained its echo of anger. "An employee had spotted a luxury car—Mercedes, he thought—driving towards the area of Vivi's bungalow, but the guard at the main gate saw no such car exit, with or without Vivi."

"And the taxis; were they called to go to her bungalow?"

"Nada, zip; there were no fares of any kind last night from Plaza Verde."

Derek turned to Amanda. "Tell him about the note."

Amanda described the enigmatic notations and her efforts at translating them.

"I agree with you," Miguel turned to Amanda with a more familiar tone of encouragement to his voice. "HK definitely sounds like Honk Kong. We know Vivi needed to return to Hong Kong, but do we know any specific person or hotel or phone number there?"

"I'm afraid not." Amanda regretted her focus on her own itinerary. "But Karen will be sending whatever numbers she can get out of Vivi's file."

"I say we don't hang around here." Miguel turned to Derek. "We'll have Mr. Curzon fax the phone numbers on to the Mandarin. We've checked phones, employees, taxi drivers and everyone registered here."

"Shouldn't we call in the police before we check out?" Amanda cringed as she looked questioningly from one to the other.

"The police be damned!" Miguel spit it out. "They aren't about to consider her missing for seventy-two hours and it's only been twelve at most. And it could leak out to the press."

"I agree." The latter seemed to have decided Derek. "We head back to Manila, leaving Curzon to watch this end and report anything to us."

"I second that." Miguel turned to Amanda. "My guess is that not a hair has been ruffled on Miss Vivi's head and we'll hear from her before the day is out. She knew our plans were to return to Manila, so let's head back."

"Amanda? Where'd you go? You look like you're a million miles away?" Derek's voice increased in firmness. "Miguel's right, you know; we can't do anything more for her here."

Amanda forced herself to look at Miguel. The echo of 'not a hair ruffled' had thrown her as though a rug had been pulled out from under her.

\* \* \*

Miguel drove. Silence filled the car. An obvious avoidance of conversation lent a stilted woodenness to infrequent and aborted attempts. Derek, arranging his massive bulk into the back seat, turned his face towards the window, attempting sleep.

Amanda stared out the side window of the front seat, resistant to talking to Miguel. Her silence seemed to break his hypnotic stare at the road ahead. He turned, lowered his voice to a whisper and gave a nod in the direction of Derek's turned head. "We need to talk; but I need to handle a few things before Brad's party. I should have something to tell you then." His look alone would have silenced her without the action that followed. Miguel's hand curled into the tightest of fists that he brought down with a slam on the dashboard. Any of the gentle sweetness remaining, of the Miguel she thought she knew, evaporated. She felt frightened, as though suddenly with a stranger, and a dangerous stranger at that.

"What goes on up there? Did we hit something?" Derek had come to full alert as he leaned toward the front seat.

With astounding rapidity, Miguel totally transformed, responding with a deprecating laugh. "Everything's fine. I just got carried away telling Amanda a little story." His contrite grin was distorted by the red gash of his twisted scar.

Although Amanda did her best to support his ruse, their conversation soon ground to a halt. Somehow the miles disappeared and they approached the outskirts of Manila. As they pulled into the driveway of the hotel, Miguel jumped out and hurried through his leave-taking.

"Count me out for dinner." He looked at his watch. "I've got to run. Let me know if Vivi calls."

Amanda stared intently into his eyes. "And vice versa."

"Right; if any of us hears from her, we post an all points bulletin." Derek held out his hand.

"And if not?" Amanda stared pointedly at Miguel.

"Put such thoughts out of your mind." Miguel said. As he turned to leave she gave him a questioning glance, obliterated by a quick embrace as he hurried to his car. Miguel's intense concern did little to erase the shocking images Amanda had seen of his dark side.

"Maybe we'll have good news when we get back to the room," she said to Derek as they entered the lobby.

He gave her a solemn look in return, his preoccupation deepening. "I need to handle a few things that will keep me in my room; so how's about a rain check on dinner?" She nodded and turned toward the desk.

The desk clerk assured them he would forward promptly any calls from Vivian Nova. "Great; that settles it." Rallying some of his old bon-homie, Derek turned swiftly towards the elevator.

Both walked in silence to their respective rooms. Amanda entered hers feeling as if she'd been away for ages. She returned her clothes to their hangers, pulling forward her one black suit, deciding it would have to do for Brad's party. Gone was her vow to treat herself to something new, not with Vivi vanished. *There'd likely be no party when Brad was told,* she thought as she turned to the phone, deciding to check on Don Emilio and then let Brad know right now.

The second her hand touched the receiver, the phone rang.

"Sweetie, you're back." Vivi's voice stunned her with its lightness. She actually giggled an aside that sounded like: "You devil. You're insatiable."

"Vivi; God damn it; where are you?"

"I'm in Hong Kong. It was late or I would have called you."

"But what? How? And why on earth didn't you leave us a message?"

"I'll tell all when I see you at Brad's party." She giggled. "I can't believe it. I think I'm in love." The sound of excited squeals blotted her hasty "Ciao sweetie."

*'Ciao sweetie' nothing*, Amanda thought as she slammed down the phone. No phone number, no hotel name, no explanation, and no sense of the chaos she had caused.

She picked up the phone and dialed Derek's room. Before he could finish his "Hello" she bombarded him with, "Vivi called. She's in Hong Kong. She's in love. She'll see us at the party Monday. Tell Miguel. I'm going shopping." She hung up before he could even respond.

Back straight, jaw set, eyes determined, she planted her footsteps firmly in the direction of the shopping complex adjoining the hotel. Their boutiques displayed the latest and most expensive fashions; all designed to woo the maximum dollars from wealthy tourists.

She approached an ultra-elegant shop displaying a cool expanse of marble and matching sales clerks. She would have backed out, but her eye caught at a lone mannequin wearing the most elegantly simple dress. It was one long flow of white, loosely fitted to outline every curve. A white circlet enclosing the neck fanned down in a latticework effect ending above the bust line. Amanda didn't stop to ask its price. She waited for the clerk to undrape the model and headed for the dressing room, a smiling sales clerk following with dress in hand.

"Madam, this dress was made for you", she exclaimed as Amanda walked out, staring in the mirror, speechless. "Your lovely tan, your shoulders, your long neck will look so beautiful with your hair up. But loosely, I think. Wouldn't you agree?"

Amanda hesitated as if expecting the creature in the mirror to respond. "I'll take it. And you're right, hair up it shall be. How much do I owe you?"

It took every ounce of will power to disguise her shock at the price. Even in Philippine pesos, she couldn't believe it could come to eight hundred U.S. dollars. Defiantly, she proffered her credit card.

Head held high, she felt a sense of power, not so much lent by the dress, but the dress as a result of it. It seemed preposterous to her that she could have worried so over Vivi. She cursed Vivi's romantic escapades. As she reached the lobby, she halted, frozen by an awareness that if it hadn't been for Vivi's disappearance she wouldn't have unearthed the clues she now had.

And certainly more questions, she thought as the elevator door opened to her floor. As she passed Derek's room, the sound of his voice raised in anger reached her ears. She halted at his door, straining to catch more than just his tone of voice.

"Not over the phone; I'll meet you in the bar at the Peninsula in one hour." She jumped at the sound of a slammed phone, backtracked away from her own door and softly moved to the elevator.

*Mystery number one: Derek Ashton, she tho*ught as she stepped out into the lobby and over to the house phone and dialed his room.

"I just wanted to let you know that, not only did I find a dress, but I'm going to have my hair done." She paused. "We'll talk of Vivi later." She set her jaw as she listened, thinking how easily he bought it. "Right, Derek; a nightcap sounds good. Ten in the lobby bar."

She hung up and walked quickly to the entryway. "A taxi please, to the Peninsula Hotel."

# FIFTEEN

The Peninsula Hotel was full. Early diners, steady drinkers and dedicated gossips held court in the central cocktail lounge. Its openness gave everyone elbowroom to gawk, separation enough not to be overheard and clear visibility to see and be seen.

*Much too clear visibility*, Amanda thought. She headed for the mezzanine area's news agency whose racks of books and magazines gave her a perfect vantage point. Semi-obscured, she could wait for Derek to appear and observe whoever joined him.

She didn't have long to wait before she spotted Derek's large frame threading its way towards two men at the far side of the room. Neither was the man on the plane, nor were they clients, she decided. Both jumped up as Derek approached. Amanda noticed that one of them was at least a generation older than the other was. Father and son, she wondered? The alertly fawning attitude of the younger suggested more one of chieftain and aide.

Derek was deep in conversation with the older one, his gaze firm, his face unsmiling. After a few brief words of response, the white-haired man turned a stern look towards the young man and gave a firm nod. The young man turned to the side, leaning down to draw out a parcel from alongside the table.

Derek glanced around, scanning the lounge before turning his gaze up towards the mezzanine. Amanda swiftly brought a magazine up in front of her face as she backed into the overhanging entryway of the shop. When she next dared to glance down, Derek was standing up, the parcel nowhere in sight. The two men didn't accompany him out the door, but the moment he exited they motioned for the check. Amanda hurried to follow, but by the time she walked out neither Derek nor the men were anywhere in view.

The driver had waited according to her instructions. She glanced both ways as she approached the car. No sign of Derek in the cars moving past. Momentarily frustrated, she used the drive to focus her thoughts on methods to examine Derek's briefcase and his strange parcel.

After the usual traffic jam, blaring horns, people dashing fearlessly in front of cars, the stench of exhaust and the raised voice of her driver as he opened the window to add his voice to the chorus, Amanda welcomed the sight of the Mandarin.

No sign of Derek in the lobby. She went over to the house phone and dialed his room. No answer. Before she could turn and head for the elevator, the concierge motioned her to the desk and handed her a fax from Karen and more phone messages. Her forehead drew into a frown, thoughts still on Derek as she headed to her room.

Another fax protruded from under the door. *Nigel.* She took it over to the sofa, tucked her feet up under her and began to read a simple message reminding her he'd call her at Brad's Monday night. She put it aside and examined her phone messages.

The name, "Emilio de la Serna", jumped out at her. She picked up the phone and dialed his number. It rang several times before someone picked it up.

"This is the De la Serna residence." The voice wasn't one she recognized.

"May I speak with Don Emilio de la Serna please?"

"I'm sorry. I have instructions he is not to be disturbed." Amanda bit back a response equal to the imperious tone.

"But he asked me to phone. This is Amanda Evans calling."

"Amanda Evans"; very well, Miss Evans, I'll leave word you called."

"Amanda? Is that you? I have it, Miss Esperanza." A dry and crackled cry came over the line. "Resting; drugged is more like it. My dear, I must see you soon. I want to—change trust. He…"

Amanda was shocked as the Don labored to get the words out. "Please Don Emilio, don't overtax your strength. Of course I'll see you, whenever you say."

"Soon; the party—Caro's."

"Very good; I'll come to your home before the party."

"No; at Caro's; six o'clock, before the party."

"Are you certain you feel up to it?"

"Yes." His voice seemed to grow in strength. "They keep me doped up, but Monday…" He halted. "I won't take."

Her heart gave a double beat in her chest as she heard his effort to get the words out. The depth to which the strength of his spirit had fallen stunned her. "Please, don't try to talk anymore. I will be there Monday, my friend."

"Before it is too late. Raffy…" A guttural sound issued from the receiver as Emilio labored to say something more. Someone took the phone back—the maid—a nurse perhaps?

"He must get his rest, Miss Evans. I have my orders."

"Of course." Amanda slowly returned the phone to its cradle.

She couldn't get the sound of Don Emilio's voice out of her ears. A sudden 'sick to her stomach' feeling overtook her. She glanced at her bedside clock: seven o'clock.

Maybe a little food, she thought, as it dawned on her that she hadn't eaten anything all day. She dialed room service and ordered soup and salad. As she listened for the trolley rolling down the hall she heard instead, the sound of Derek's return. Her thoughts turned to tactics to get into his briefcase and remained there, even as the room service table was wheeled in. She sipped at her soup as she considered asking him to bring some documentation forms to her, but quickly discarded that ploy as ineffective.

But not the idea of getting to his briefcase before whatever he put in it had disappeared. She finished her meal, ears straining to hear whatever sounds she could pick up from his room. Within minutes she heard his door opening and footsteps headed away. She opened her own door just enough to peer towards the elevator. He'd reached it, pushed the button and entered without so much as a backward glance. No sign of his carrying a briefcase. Good, she thought, he's probably gone down to dinner. She drew back into her room, trying to figure out a legitimate way to get access to his room. "The room service table. That's it." She exclaimed, hoping the idea taking shape would work.

She went to the phone, dialed room service and asked. "Would you please have someone come and pick up my dinner table? I'm in room seven one four."

She let out her breath. No questions as she gave them Derek's room number instead of hers. She quickly wheeled the table through her doorway and positioned it outside of Derek's room, listening for the elevator's sound. As she heard it stop at her floor she closed her door, moved in front of seven one four and smiled up at the approaching busboy.

"I thought I'd help you by putting the table out by my doorway." She turned back towards the door. "Oh no; I've locked myself out."

"Not a problem, Miss. I can open it for you." He drew out a master key and opened the door. "There you go. Have a good evening."

Amanda leaned against the closed door, heart pounding, as she glanced around the room. Hardly a sign of anyone's having occupied it, she thought as her eyes went to the desk area, scanning it for a briefcase—but finding nothing.

Holding her breath, she gently slid open the closet doors. She let out her breath at the sight of it sitting neatly alongside two pair of shoes. Leaning down, she prayed it wouldn't be locked. Surprisingly, the latch popped easily. A rubber-banded packet lay on top of documentation for trusts. She quickly removed the rubber band and opened the package, exposing numerous photographs. She riffled through them: photos of Miguel with people she didn't recognize, photos of her in her conference room meeting, her with Raffy and even the meeting with Miguel's aunt! She gasped at the next photo that showed one of the men from the Peninsula Hotel in conversation with the man on the plane. *Strange, she thought, none of the photos included Derek.*

She felt a chill go through her when she recognized the last item in the packet: her anting-anting. Her hand quickly drew away. "What is going on here?" Her whisper gained power at her rage and shock. She wondered how she could meet him for drinks in an hour without screaming out her questions. Her heart raced as she paged through the briefcases' remaining contents. Nothing further of an incriminating nature turned up. She quietly let herself out of his room and into hers.

Somehow she managed to compose herself. Even to the extent of arranging her hair in a fashion that should convince him she had gone to the hairdresser. As she began the final touches, the phone rang.

"Hello there, party girl. Bought a smashing dress, did you?" Derek's patter sounded forced. "I can't wait to hear about it over drinks." She decided to go along with his charade.

"And so you shall; see you downstairs in ten minutes."

Amanda was disappointed in her hopes that somehow he would reveal himself over a few drinks. The closest he came was his mention of Viv.

"So, what did she say? She went to Hong Kong just like that? How? And who's the lover boy?" He accompanied his question with fingers nervously twirling his swizzle stick.

"Your guess is as good as mine. You can ask her at the party." Amanda's impatience must have shown through.

"Tomorrow's Sunday; do we have anything on the agenda?"

"Nothing; I didn't think we'd hurry back from Plaza Verde. I plan to do nothing, except perhaps try out the hotel's spa." She hesitated over mentioning her phone call with Don Emilio, but instead decided to reveal her missing appointment pages and study his response.

"Something strange has occurred. I seem to be missing pages from my agenda. Could I copy yours?"

"Missing appointment pages?" His voice turned dead serious. "When did you notice they were gone?"

She watched his face closely as she told of her discovery while in Plaza Verde.

"What pages are missing?" Derek had pulled out a pen and began jotting her response down. Gone was any trace of lightheartedness. His brow was frozen into a look of intense concentration. "Do you remember if you'd added any personal notations against any of the client's names?"

"I'm not sure, but..." She hesitated, about to add that she'd acquired Raffy's appointment book by mistake, before quickly changing her mind. "I'm a bit paralyzed with thinking even one more thought." Amanda yawned and pushed her chair back. "I think I'm going to call it a day and turn in."

He seemed relieved. "Sure. Not to worry, I'll make you copies and leave them under your door. Let's meet over breakfast, say eight, to go over any thoughts about next week's calls." He glanced around the room, drawn by the sound of a large group that had just walked in. "I'll just stay for one more wee dram. Until tomorrow then."

Amanda turned as she approached the elevator, stopping to let it open and close as it moved upwards on its return journey. She remained behind. She quickly positioned herself to watch the main entryway, rewarded by the sight of Derek dashing out the door.

"Damn," she muttered under her breath, thinking: *to follow or not to follow?* She quickly moved out into the lobby and over to the doorman.

'Excuse me. Did you hear where Mr. Ashton was headed?" She gave a slight shrug and a smile. "He wanted me to call him when he arrived, but I'm not sure if I heard the Peninsula or the Oriental?"

"Sorry, Miss Evans. He grabbed a taxi that isn't one of the hotel's cabs."

"Thanks anyway." Amanda turned back to the elevator, resigned to having to turn in, like it or not.

* * *

Sunday flew by. Derek was a morose breakfast partner, scarcely touching his food and rushing off with a feeble excuse to 'do some work.' Amanda attempted to reach Mai at home, only to learn that she was out of town. Her thoughts wouldn't let go their endless circling around the M.W. initials and Mai's frenzy. She finally decided to follow through on the spa, swimming until the water obliterated all such thoughts. Heading straight from the pool to the gym, she peddled and rowed until her muscles cried out for relief.

Derek's 'work', she noticed, seemed to keep him away from his room the entire day. Grateful for dinner alone, she ordered pasta primavera, a half bottle of wine and a pot of tea. Whether it was the wine, the workout or the chamomile tea, she slept until dawn.

Monday morning gave her a chance to go over her notes and to try once again to reach Mai.

"Amanda? How you?" The concern in Mai's voice was underscored by her rapid fall into a more Pidgin English.

"I'm fine. What's been happening in the office?"

"Nigel call every day. I tell him office fine. Mr. Chan call; he so happy to sell hotel in Guam."

"Yes. To Raffy de la Serna, I hear."

"Raffy call to say he sending money from sale."

Before Amanda could respond with: 'Ninety thousand, I know' Mai rushed excitedly. "He sending nearly one million next week before you return."

"One million? Are you sure he said he's sending this money from the hotel sale?"

"Yes. He say so."

"Well then, I shall be sure to congratulate him tomorrow at Brads." Amanda's mind raced at the discrepancy, but covered her anxiety. "If any more amounts like that appear, Mai, please be sure to run them by Nigel."

"Not to worry. I do for you; happy all go well there."

"Right; remember to tell Nigel that I'm looking forward to his call."

Throughout the balance of the day Amanda's thoughts returned to Mai as Derek carried the ball with both of their client calls. Although the clients seemed interested in setting up offshore companies, nothing was about to happen on the spot until they ran it by their attorneys. Amanda couldn't help but feel a mix of puzzlement as well as regard at Derek's professional trust-officer persona. He parried the clients every question with thoroughness and charm.

*Nevertheless, Amanda thought, while back in her room readying herself for the party, tonight I intend to blow his cover.* "One way or the other" she said aloud as she grinned back at her reflection. She looked forward to grilling Nigel during his phone call, convinced that the bank grapevine should, by now, have surfaced something more on Derek's background.

Amanda had shared with Derek her scheduled meeting with Don Emilio prior to any of the other partygoer's arrival. He didn't balk when she insisted it must be a private meeting, saying only, "I'll go along for the ride. Early or not, I can chat a bit with Brad during your meeting."

Amanda smiled as she began her preparations for the evening, convinced tonight's party would provide some shape to the shadows.

"And speaking of taking shape..." She said, beaming at her reflection as she eased her new dress's cool, sleek whiteness over her head. Turning full circle, she admired the subtle mix of cool, yet classy sexuality that it bestowed. Just as she was applying the final touches, the phone rang.

"Are you ready to be escorted to your party? Your chariot awaits—extra horses and all." Derek's playful tone carried an echo of nervousness.

"I'm ready. With all that wonderful Filipino music and dancing tonight, I hope you're wearing your dancing shoes."

"Not only am I a great dancer, but I insist on proving it. Promise you'll save a dance for me?" Derek's change of voice, sincere and a trifle uncertain nearly disarmed her.

"I'm not sure how the evening will go, but one dance seems doable, as long as it's not the last. In the Philippines it's customary that the host has the last dance with the guest of honor." Reverting to lightness, she added, "I'm willing to take your word for your dancing skills, but, more importantly, how are you at singing? The latest rage in the Philippines is Karaoke. Just thought I should prepare you. They'll consider you a real spoil-sport if you don't join in."

Derek was back on familiar ground. "Have you ever known an Irishman who didn't like to sing? Although I'm afraid I only know the words to "When Irish Eyes Are Smiling." He laughed. "And none on tune. Ah well; what say I pick you up in ten minutes down in the lobby?"

"Ten minutes it is." One last hairpin to anchor her upswept curls and a simple pair of pearl earrings and she was ready. Exiting the elevator, she rounded the hallway into the open lobby to find Derek in conversation with Brad's driver. Both looked up in the same instant. Derek gaped.

"You look beautiful!" he uttered, completely caught off guard. He slowly walked towards her, for once seeming at a loss for his usual witty riposte. Amanda smiled and turned her head to receive a light kiss on the cheek, enveloping a stunned Derek in confusion and 'Bal de Versailles'.

Derek's unease was visible enough to bring a smile to the driver's face, who said, "You look very beautiful, Miss Evans. I'm glad I gave the Mercedes an extra special cleaning for this evening. Are you ready to go now?"

"Yes, Armando. I'm ready to go." Turning to Derek with a provocative grin, she added, "Let the party begin."

# SIXTEEN

Brad's home was part of Don de la Serna's compound. One glimpse of its luxury and Amanda wondered why Brad hadn't been transferred. His alliance with his most powerful client would seem to smack of conflict of interest.

The gate attendant seemed surprised at Amanda's early arrival, but quickly erased it with a warm welcome. As she rang the bell Amanda had a fleeting sense of regret that her entrance would be on an empty stage to a non-existing audience. Caro opened the door with a smile that seemed hastily applied. It quickly changed to one of amazement.

"Amanda, is it really you? You look absolutely stunning. No one will possibly believe you're a banker."

Amanda gave her a warm embrace, struck by the sincerity of Caro's response. In some intangible way, Amanda knew she'd just graduated to a female to be taken seriously by Caro.

"I decided to take a page from your book, Caro."

Caro smiled and held out her cheek to Derek. "And you must be Derek Ashton, the man most likely to be envied this evening." Derek's response was eclipsed by Brad's hasty entrance.

"Amanda, you look ravishing! Manila is bringing out the 'Grande dame' in you." Brad gave her a quick kiss on both cheeks and turned to Derek.

"Derek, old man, it's good to see you again. How are you reacting to the Philippines? I always find it very interesting to get a first-timer's unexpurgated opinion. But first, what's your poison?" He motioned to a servant standing at the ready with a tray of drinks. "I find the old rubric of 'in vino veritas' to be doubly powerful with one or two of my famous Philippine elixirs under the belt." Derek scrutinized the colorful concoction.

"Take care, Derek", cautioned Caro. "Brad's famous drinks have been known to promote either babies or knock down, drag out fights. I'd suggest starting with one so as not to offend Brad's efforts." Caro gracefully accepted hers, taking a slow sip from the frosty glass. "They really are seductively delicious. I swear he obtains his secret ingredient from the local 'mankukulam'. Come on Brad; confess. Just what 'gayuma' have you added to your specialty?" Caro looked at Brad affectionately.

"My darling Caro suggests that I've added a special potion to arouse passions. Little does she know but that's exactly how I captured her heart." Brad entwined the arm holding his drink around his wife's as they each sipped and he toasted: "To my love slave forever."

Derek and Amanda each took one, with Amanda making a mental note to ditch hers behind some plant at the earliest opportunity. All this talk of potions was too close for comfort. She needed to keep all her faculties keen without any major assist from alcohol.

Caro took another sip of her drink before putting it down and linking her arms with Derek and Amanda. "Father will be here shortly, but first I insist on giving you the full tour of our beautiful new home." Amanda smiled at Caro's seeming reconciliation to living in the family compound, a situation she had long protested. She soon discovered why.

No expense had been spared. Gleaming expanses of marble, a guesthouse and changing room opposite the enormous swimming pool and spa, lush gardens and a tennis court; all weren't unusual. The surprise came at the quantity and quality of artwork displayed throughout the house. Amanda felt a twinge of envy. The pieces displayed would more than warrant the extra guards she had noticed. The insurance alone must cost a fortune, she thought as she spotted one small Renoir etching alongside a Matisse.

"I never knew you had such a love of fine art." Amanda turned to Caro with an appreciative smile, fighting to keep a note of envy from seeping through.

"Daddy says 'what's money for if not beauty'? Anyway, it doesn't hurt that he's had both beauty as well as an appreciation in their value. His own walls are so full that he's constantly bringing new pieces to me."

Derek had been unusually quiet, apart from appropriate murmurs of appreciation. He seemed relieved when they reentered the living area and he spotted Brad among a cluster of newly arrived guests. Derek greeted him with, "Your home's delightful, but I was disappointed not to see your most valuable treasure; apart from Caro of course." Brad waited until Derek, who had paused for dramatic effect, continued. "Your new baby daughter; she must be an exceptional treasure if she is blessed with Caro's beauty and your acumen."

Brad gave a little laugh. "I wish I could have paraded her for all to admire, but she's been fighting a cold and needs more than her usual twenty hours of sleep. You're right though. She's a beauty. Sometime tonight Caro is sure to paper the party with photos." He laughed as he turned his attention to early arriving guests. "I'd like to introduce you to some dear friends: Ambassador Miguel Ramirez, his sister Ana, and Engineer Leon Cruz and his wife, Martita".

Paco gave Derek a warm handshake, acknowledging their having already met, as Ana smilingly offered each cheek to be kissed. Paco stood at arm's length, staring hypnotically at Amanda, while Derek exchanged introductions and small talk with the Cruz'.

"Amanda, my dear, you look stunning." Paco beamed as he took her by the arm to introduce her to the Cruz family.

A ring of the doorbell and shouts of delight announced that more of the De La Serna family had arrived. Amanda was surprised at the turnout of so many cousins and quasi-family—and shocked by Raffy's absence. There was a bit of pandemonium as at least twenty people approached en masse. But Amanda's eyes were only for Don Emilio, gently escorted by Caro. Amanda fought to keep her eyes from showing her distress at the sight of him. White hair, wobbling step, shrunken in stature, he approached slowly and only with the aid of Caro and a walking stick. It was unbelievable that in the few short months since they had last met, he could have deteriorated so.

"Lalo, please sit here." Caro gently lowered him into 'his" chair.

"Lalo?" Amanda started at the word. "Grandfather" would never before have seemed an appellation appropriate to him. He had always been a vivid Man of La Mancha type—active and impassioned. Now he appeared a wizened old man, lost within his too-large suit. Amanda approached, careful to beam a reassuring smile.

"Amanda, my dear," he said as she approached and tears began to cloud his eyes. "As you can see, I made it." He released Caro's arm and drew Amanda into a one-armed embrace, whispering: "We must steal away for our talk." No sooner had she nodded affirmation than family—each outdoing one another in their solicitations—surrounded him.

After graciously accepting acknowledgment from each, Don Emilio beckoned to Amanda. "You rival the angels. They shall blush when I tell them of you." His look clouded as he whispered: "Soon if my heirs' prayers are answered." He motioned to Caro to help him into the library.

After Caro departed and Amanda had closed the doors, she assisted Don Emilio into a comfortable chair and drew hers up to his, saying, "You'll outlive your sons and grandsons. I'll be sure to send you some of the latest 'stay young' potion the movie stars are taking." Amanda made a motion, drawing a package out of her purse. "And to make it palatable, I brought some of your favorite dark chocolates."

He stopped her. "I'm beyond any magic potions—or even chocolates. We must talk. Come closer, my dear." The tone of his voice had dramatically changed with this remark. One look at his eyes told her that social pleasantries were at an end.

"Something very important; I must discuss." His words held a mix of sorrow and anger. "I'm having serious doubts as to my son Raffy's ability to manage my businesses." Don Emilio hesitated, the subject obviously painful. "I've been hearing disturbing news concerning his involvement in business dealings abhorrent to the De La Serna name." Don Emilio, visibly straining at control, labored to continue. "I wish to set up a new trust. I would appreciate it if you and your Mr. Ashton could meet with my attorneys."

"Yes, of course, Don Emilio. Anytime you like."

"I told them you will call. Please schedule the meeting—soon."

She sensed the hollowness of any reassuring words as to his state. "Of course; I'll contact them right away."

Don Emilio sighed, the effort having exhausted him. "Very good my dear. Now I will have someone escort me home. I am feeling very weary." Amanda reached to offer him her arm. "Thank you, but I shall sit awhile. Please, if you would ask Caro to come and see me home."

Amanda felt her throat constrict as she leaned down to brush his cheeks with parting kisses. It was obvious that he'd pushed his scant energies to their limit. Remembering Florie's description, she stared deeply into his eyes—whites streaked with yellow—and took his hands. His trembling fingers revealed dark spots. She choked out the words. "Take care of you, my friend. I'll call tomorrow to discuss the meeting with your attorneys."

He closed his eyes and whispered: "Until then."

Amanda reentered the dining room, caught Caro's eye and relayed Don Emilio's request. Caro rushed to the library, Amanda lingering in her wake. She heard Don Emilio's angry greeting. "Where is that good-for-nothing son of mine? Didn't he know that we were all to appear promptly before nine thirty? It is now nearly nine o'clock. How dare he ignore my wishes?"

Don Emilio's voice crackled with rage as echoes of his former power filled his exhausted body with a surge of energy. Brad hurried to Caro's side to help lead his father-in-law to the front door. "Father, let me help you." Don Emilio assented, but the look he aimed at the arm that held him shocked Amanda into wondering: If he hated Brad that much, why did he agree to Caro's marriage?

"Tell Raffy to come to me the moment he arrives." Brad nodded, nervously attempting to soften Don Emilio's vocal exit. Suddenly a booming voice was heard from the foyer.

"Do I hear someone taking my name in vain?" Raffy, with all the command of a young Alexander, swiftly approached his father and the group who were aiding him. As he bent to place a kiss on each of his father's cheeks, he smiled warmly.

Don Emilio seemed to waver for a moment. "You may have my pardon for having raised you to be self-centered, but you were not raised to be rude and disrespectful." He glared at Raffy's vacant look. "Don't just stand there. An apology is owed to our guest of honor." Don Emilio turned and reached to take Amanda's arm in his.

Raphael fumbled a hesitant reply: "Amanda, of course. Forgive me; I'm sorry to be late. The blasted driver forgot to gas up the car."

"You bet he did. I was out there giving him a piece of my mind." The sound of Vivi's voice was only slightly less real than the sight of her, Amanda decided. An apparition of pouting red lips and tousled blond hair, wearing the same black linen dress she had worn at Plaza Verde, Amanda noticed. *Vivi and Raffy? Of course, Amanda thought* as Vivi effortlessly claimed center-stage.

"We ran out of gas in some ghastly barrio. You wouldn't believe it." Vivi glanced around to survey her audience, all of whom stared in disbelief at her shocking entry. "It took forever to fetch some." Her pretty pout melted into gawking disbelief as she gazed up and down at Amanda. "Is it really you? Where did you come up with such a dress?"

Don Emilio turned to Raffy. "And where did you come up with this young woman? We haven't been introduced. You are...?" Vivi glared up at Raffy as he rushed to make the introductions.

"She is an old friend of Amanda's, father—and a new friend of mine. Vivian Nova, I'd like you to meet my father, Don Emilio De La Serna. Father, Vivian Nova." Raffy quickly turned away from his father's lukewarm nod. He opened his arms to the gawking group. "Let the festivities continue. But first, I must insist, dear father, on having the honor of escorting you home."

Amanda was shocked by the devastating look Don Emilio turned on Raffy. Raffy had the good sense to hang his head. Silence filled the room. Don Emilio moved to Caro's side and announced firmly: "Come Caro, you may see me home. Goodnight Amanda. Until tomorrow." The sight of his back surprised Amanda. She could swear his stature had increased by several inches as he and Caro walked quickly past the wayward son.

Raffy stood silent, but only for an instant. Amanda studied his face. His emotions seemed to waver between shock, anger, hatred and vengefulness. *Everything but contrition, she thought.* By the time he spoke he was under control, his charm intact. "Forgive my father. He's not well. Please, let the music begin. In honor of Miss Evans," he said, as he offered Amanda a glass of champagne.

Derek, taking in every nuance of the interactions, walked between them, giving Amanda a pointed stare. "Do I hear music? You promised me this dance." His words were light enough, but his look translated as: "Let's talk". Before he could draw her away a maid rushed up to them.

"There is a telephone call for you, Miss Amanda—a Mr. Nigel Taylor. He called earlier but I told him you were with Sr. de la Serna and not to be disturbed. He said it was urgent." Amanda reassured the nervous maid and hurried off to take Nigel's phone call. As she entered Brad's private office and closed the door, the sound of dance music faded.

Amanda glanced at her watch as she picked up the phone, trying to read into the timing Nigel's urgency level. "Good morning, Nigel. Isn't it a bit early for you to be in the office?"

"I'm not in the office. I'm still at home. I've been waiting since bloody four A.M. to get this call though. You can't believe what's going on here." Nigel's voice carried more frenzy than Mai and Karen had led her to expect.

"I've heard some rumors," Amanda began, "but I was waiting for your call to know just how much to believe."

"Yes, yes," he pushed ahead. "The new guy out from New York, Lyle Carter— replaced Edwards—well, this guy's got acid in his veins. He's out to destroy all of Edward's old kingdom and establish his own. It's not looking good for International Private Banking. "

"But Nigel, we're so profitable. Why would anyone want to kill the goose that lays the golden egg?"

"Hmm?" He was silent for a long moment. "He's salivating to bring our profits under the control of one of his henchmen. He's begun scrutinizing all our deals with a fine-tooth comb, trying to build a case for new management." Nigel's tone had never sounded so intimidated.

"You've created what no one else had been able to do."

Nigel's voice had reclaimed its familiar firmness. "Maybe, but if we make one wrong move, we're dead in the water. That's why I'm calling you. What's going on in the..." He lowered his voice. "...money-laundering search? Our time-bomb could end up being those clients of yours. Any funny money deal unearthed now would be the death of us. Out with it; what have you discovered thus far?"

Amanda hesitated, deliberating as to whether or not to discuss any of her pent-up issues with him. Not just now, she decided. They were of the sort that he not only wouldn't be able to do anything about, but they may well serve to really push him over the edge. She isolated two items that might pass muster—business and Derek.

"I'm doing all I can to identify any client that might be suspect. Derek's trust products are a big help. I've gathered a lot more verification of the backgrounds of existing and potential deposits." She went on to tell him of the sale of the Guam furniture factory, carefully editing names and amounts. "Brad's agreed to inter-office the entire package to you. I won't give anything large, different or unverified, the green light without your blessing."

"Good. Use Brad to provide us any information he can dig up. "Be sure to give him the names of anyone under suspicion."

The 'anyone under suspicion' propelled Amanda into her next question.

"What about Derek? What more can you tell me about him?"

"What's that?" Nigel rode roughshod over her question. "I thought I heard a click on the line. How safe is this phone line?"

"Brad swears it's linked to his confidential line at the office. It should be clean."

Nigel wasn't convinced. "I'd best ring off. For God's sake, watch every word you say. I won't be able to talk to you again until you get to Hong Kong, and I want to hear nothing but good news."

Amanda set her jaw, surprised that her "Goodbye" cloaked the level of her frustration.

"Wait", she heard as she began to replace the receiver. "Let me talk with Brad, just in case you try to sidestep him as an ally in this mess."

Nigel's usual tact, she thought, barely controlling the force with which she placed the receiver on the table. Brad was deep in conversation with Raffy. At Amanda's approach their exchange came to an abrupt close.

"Brad; it's Nigel. He's holding to speak with you." Brad rose hesitantly. As he turned to glance back towards Raffy, Amanda detected a strange flash of worry in his puzzled look. She stared as he headed to take the call. It took her a moment to realize that Raffy had addressed her. "I'm sorry, Raffy. What did you say? My mind's still with the phone call."

"Nothing serious, I hope. Why don't you unload on Uncle Raffy? I owe you whatever I can do to bring a smile back to your face." He took her by the arm and led her over to a quiet corner. "First, let me apologize for being late and causing you concern over Vivi. She's enchanting. I made the impulsive offer that she join me in flying back one of my Hong Kong associates." Raffy gave her a mischievously contrite look. "We'd hoped to return before you knew she was gone. But—" He spread his hands and raised his eyebrow, laughing at the memory. "You know how she is. I was captivated."

"Well, we were worried. If she had only thought to have left us a note." The very reminder of the turmoil caused Amanda's voice to rise. Catching herself, she reluctantly relented. "Anyway, once her call came through, I was OK." Amanda turned to scan the room full of people. Most were dancing but Vivi wasn't among them. "Where is the lady in question?"

"She headed back to the pool house with your friend Derek. They've set up the karaoke machine out there. Vivi plans to wow them with her great singing voice." He studied her closely before continuing. "You look lovely, but worried. Come now: confess, dear Amanda, what is it? Not boyfriend problems, I hope. No. My guess is it was your call from the bank." His look turned more solemn. "Anything I should be worried about? If you need some more deposits, just say the word and I'll write you a check."

Amanda resisted bursting out with a 'like a million additional dollars from the sale of the Guam hotel'. She forced a smile. "I appreciate your concern, but it's not banking problems. You've met Nigel and you know how he can be sometimes. He's worried about the upcoming elections here. I guess I just reacted to the contrast his tone made to my party mood. It's really nothing. I'm fine, Raffy, but thanks anyway."

"Then let me put your mind and Nigel's to rest. Everything will remain status quo, trust me."

Amanda smiled. "If you say so."

Raffy reached for her hands. "Well then, now that your mind is at ease, I need you to put my mind at rest." He glanced around at the increasingly raucous crowd. "But not here. Let's step out on the terrace."

He steered her smoothly out the door and guided her towards a secluded bench at a distance away from the noise. "We need to talk." His voice had turned suddenly serious. "Remember the deal I showed you at Plaza Verde?"

With not even a trace of irony, he pressed on. "You've seen how much Father has declined. I'm concerned about his ability to handle his affairs."

Amanda bit back her response, deciding to watch, wait and listen. "Yes, go on Raffy."

"Something needs to be done soon. I've arranged to get power of attorney before he gets any worse." He lifted his palms upright. "He won't hear of it. He says everything is in order." Raffy turned his dark eyes, locking his gaze intently on Amanda's, "You have to help me. This deal is too critical to let it cool off." Amanda forced neutrality to her voice.

"Have you discussed your concerns over this project with your father?"

"I'm afraid he's not thinking clearly right now. He may even want to set up a new trust and upset all the work I've done." Raffy looked incredulous as he went on. "Maybe even set up some such thing with you and this guy, Ashton." Raffy's look pinned her with its intense mix of disbelief and questioning, before culminating in a beseeching plea. "Look, I know you have to keep everything confidential." He hesitated before playing his wild card. "Without actually telling me anything, if I guess at a few things can you just nod yeah or nay, or at least a nay if nothing is in the works?"

"A nay would be my only response. Just as with your business dealings, Raffy, I cannot say, nod or in any way reveal your father's business dealings. I can't. I won't. "Private" is the operative word in Private Banking" Her voice had risen firmly on the last words.

"She won't Raffy, whatever it is. Can't you take no for an answer?" Derek asked as he walked towards them, giving her the rare occasion to welcome his clowning. "Maybe what she needs is a little nourishment to shore up that resolve." He pulled Amanda around. "What say I waltz you in the direction of the buffet table?"

"I am a bit hungry, Derek. If you could prepare me a plate, I'll be along in a minute."

Derek glanced at the barrier of leaden silence that filled the space between Raffy and Amanda. "I'll hold you to that, or come looking for you."

Raffy had taken another tack. He gazed at Amanda with a contrite look. "I guess this is my evening for apologies. I know you can't say anything. I don't know what got into me." He glanced down and then up, turning on her a look of bleak despair. "I'm out of my mind with worry over father."

"I've never seen him so diminished." Amanda looked steadily into his eyes.

"Look, Amanda. I don't know how to say this, but I'm worried about you as well."

"Me?"

"Yes. There's something strange about this Derek guy. Just what do you know about him?"

She hesitated. "He's a solid trust officer who came highly recommended." She paused as he stared fixedly into her eyes. "He's done well, given that he is a stranger to the Philippines."

"A stranger who knows his way around, maybe even knows people here he shouldn't." Raffy swung around, walked over to the fireplace mantle and turned a baleful eye on her. "Look, you don't have to say anything, but there is definitely something fishy about this Ashton fellow. Let me do a little checking into him for you."

"That's not necessary. I'm sure that with his trust background, he would know people everywhere."

"You may be sure, but I'm not; especially as concerns his involvement with my father's finances." Raffy offered his arm to Amanda. "If anything interesting comes to my ears, I'll let you know." He looked around as they entered the living area. "It sounds like many have adjourned to the pool house. It seems Brad's alcoholic specialties have prepared the crowd for music and dancing. I'd better claim Miss Twinkle Toes Nova before her dance card is filled."

Derek approached, balancing a large tray of food and drink. He gave Raffy a long stare as Raffy rushed past, pointedly ignoring Derek. Raising his loaded tray, Derek made a motion as if to toss it towards Raffy's retreating back.

Amanda couldn't help herself. She broke into the giggles. "I guess I do need food after all. I get silly when I get hungry." *And when I get nervous,* she thought to herself, accepting a brimming plateful. After a few bites, she put her plate aside and stood up. "On second thought, I can always eat. What I really feel like is dancing. This dress hasn't been properly inaugurated yet."

"Well then, I'd better strike while the iron's hot." Derek folded her arm in his. "May I have this dance before you're lionized?" He swept Amanda in the direction of the dance floor.

She hesitated for less than a second. "Lead on."

"By the way, you were too absorbed to notice, but all eyes were on you when you returned from your call." Derek's seductive smile disturbed Amanda.

"Relax; it's just a dance." he said, drawing her close. She fought against responding to the romantic strains of a ballad, but by the time the number ended she felt herself hesitant to break from his embrace. He seemed equally reluctant, giving a slight tug of resistance as she broke away. She felt like a deer in a headlight as Brad walked up.

"Sorry old chap, but the next dance is mine. Brad briskly swept her into his arms, leaving her just an instant to flash Derek a bewildered look. In spite of all her efforts to match Brad's tempo, which seemed much too fast for the music, she faltered. Amanda was about to say something, when it became obvious that Brad wasn't really interested in dancing. His set mouth and purposeful spins propelled them towards the corridor leading to his office. "Amanda, we have to talk privately." With one urgent tug they were at the door to his study.

Amanda attempted to deflect his seriousness. "Well, if you say so, but isn't Caro going to miss her host, not to mention the guest of honor, who, may I remind you, has missed a good portion of this evening already?"

"Never fear. It shouldn't take long and we can get back to the party." Brad's comment seemed tinged with something heavier than sarcasm. Suddenly Amanda was all ears.

"What did Nigel say to put you in such a state, Brad? You know what a nervous-Nellie he can be."

Brad's expression teetered between incredulity and anger. He turned away. When he looked back it was with a look of intent seriousness. "Believe me, Amanda, Nigel wasn't overstating the seriousness of what's involved." He looked steadily into her eyes. "We need to discuss who you might suspect. Have you been able to narrow your focus?"

Amanda hesitated "What can I say? Nigel doesn't want any rock left unturned. He's most concerned over our new clients, or large, unusual transactions from existing clients." She proceeded to tell him of the Villarreal sale as well as Y.A. Chan's, asking that he not reveal the client's names or any of the information to anyone. "Not even to Caro," she added.

The last phrase seemed to register even more than the amount of the transaction. "What makes you think I'd discuss business with Caro?" Brad looked nervously about and lowered his voice. "Rest assured that anything you tell me will go no further than my ears." He stood up, walked to the door and turned with a take-it or leave-it expression. "Nigel insists we join forces; so what's it going to be? Are we a team? If not, from now on you're on your own."

Amanda felt encouraged by Brad's earnestness. She badly needed a trusted teammate. "OK; partners it is." She smiled as she reached over to shake his hand.

"We'll make a good team." Brad pursed his lips, appearing to go deep in thought before he continued. "We need to get together and go over anyone or anything you have concerns about." Before she could reply, he went on. "That reminds me, have you had any further experience with that strange man you mentioned?" He halted for a moment, a look of alarm coming over him. "You didn't stir Nigel up with such off-the-wall stuff?"

Amanda hesitated. "No. I know better than to unhinge Nigel, but—" She blurted out her confusion over seeing the man, or someone who looked like his twin, in deep conversation with Derek Ashton. Once begun, she felt enormous relief at sharing her suspicions with Brad. "I know how far fetched it sounds. I'm sure all this intrigue stuff is just a product of my over-heated imagination. Right Brad? Brad?"

Brad was staring at the doorway, mouth set in an expression of intense concentration. It wasn't his look that shocked Amanda; it was the face itself. It had suddenly gone white. She'd never seen anyone's color drain so completely as had Brad's. "Brad, what is it? Don't look that way. You're supposed to reassure me that I'm imagining things. Anyway, someone in senior management referred Derek, so he has to be on the up and up, doesn't he?"

"What did you just say, Amanda? Why didn't you tell me senior management assigned him? They don't usually get involved at that level." He stood up, looking anxious to bring their discussion to a close. "As to trusting him, I think it's best we don't trust anyone right now—but each other."

"Right; but..."

Brad broke in. "How about lunch on Wednesday? We can meet at Aloha Breweries. Since it's one of the De La Serna companies, I'll arrange for a private dining room where we won't be disturbed."

"Wednesday lunch can work for me."

"Fine; we can do a complete analysis of anyone you consider suspicious. I'll see to it you get all the verifications you need." Glancing at his watch, Brad hurried her in the direction of the doorway. "Now let's get you back to your party. Oh, one other thing, I suggest that you say nothing—not a word— to this fellow Ashton."

Amanda's sense of relief and her own concerns over Derek had her agreeing. *As uncertain as I feel right now, she thought, it's important I keep aligned with Brad and his office staff as a support group.* "Brad, you don't know how much I appreciate your help."

Brad seemed relieved as he turned to detour by way of the kitchen, leaving Amanda to make her way back to the living room. It seemed as though they had been in consultation for ages, but one glance at the clock revealed it to be only twenty-five minutes.

Before she entered the living room she restored her smile. It was soon echoed in the smile of Miguel Santos as he approached with widening eyes. "Sorry I'm late. For a moment I thought it was a vision approaching. Goddess or mortal, will you dance?" He swept her into a friendly embrace.

Amanda responded with an equally flirtatious remark: "By all means. This goddess is overdue for a little dancing." As he skillfully drew her into the seductive steps of a tango, her flippancy turned to amazement. "You never told me what a great dancer you are?"

"There's a lot you don't know about me."

"So, tell me, dear friend, what other secrets are you keeping from me?" Amanda regretted her lighthearted response as she glanced up. She feared for his answer if it were even one half as grim as his look.

# SEVENTEEN

The double entendre seemed to hang in the air, deepening the solemnity of Miguel's response. "It's not I who's keeping secrets from you, Amanda," he repeated. "But there is someone who is—serious secrets that could put you in jeopardy." Amanda stopped dancing and stared in disbelief. "Keep dancing and smile," Miguel murmured, leading her toward a doorway that led into an enclosed sunroom. Scrutinizing every corner, Miguel moved straight for a cushioned chaise, well out of sight.

"What kind of a statement is that? What I need is substance, not scare tactics." Amanda stood up. "Who is it that would 'put me in jeopardy'—and why?"

His eyes narrowed, eyebrows corrugated as he whispered in response. "Don't panic. I just don't want you blindsided. Taking people at face value could prove your undoing." He pulled his chair closer. "Listen carefully. If you have some sense of what's going on, you'll be ahead of their game."

Amanda squared her shoulders as she gave Miguel an unwavering stare. "What have you found out?"

"I've been able to confirm the broad outline and some of the players." He studied her expression before continuing. "A steady stream of money is being laundered; lots of money, allegedly Marcos money, but his cronies are adding theirs to the total. I know some of the local players involved, but I want to nail the top dogs and many are not Filipinos." Miguel hesitated, weighing his words. I need your help on that." Amanda's eyebrows shot up.

"How could I be of any help, and why are you risking such a perilous undertaking?"

"Why? They're raping my county of all its assets!"

"And how could I help?" Amanda frowned, wary of his answer.

"I suspect they are using U.S. banks—Fidelity American among them—but I need proof."

"We" need proof, Miguel. If Fidelity's involved, I'm involved. What makes you think the trail leads to FAB's involvement?"

"I'm not at liberty to say as yet, but I'll know soon—very soon. When I do, I'd like your help with confirmation." He looked around the sunroom, straining as though someone approached. Scowling, he turned, seeming to deliberate before he continued. "It's important that you know that your involvement could put you in danger."

"From the look on your face, Miguel, I doubt that anyone involved that deeply are amateurs at what they are doing."

"No, they play for keeps—and with powerful colleagues able to whitewash their trail. The more I look, the more frightening the connections become. Any attempt to cut through would be like slicing off one tentacle of an octopus."

Amanda shivered. "More would simply grow back on."

Miguel looked thoughtful as he began walking back and forth, muttering softly under his breath. "That's it!"

"That's what?" Amanda turned an impatient look at him.

"A phrase I overheard—'The Kraken'—a mythical beast with many arms." Miguel stared beyond her, lost in thought.

Amanda shook her head and glared at him. "Enough of such suspense; I must have some idea just who this Kraken is. What, where, how and why could it involve me?"

Miguel took both of her hands in his. "Not yet. I understand that you want to know, but, trust me, its better you aren't involved any more than you already are."

"Damn it Miguel, if what you've learned involves me, I need to know. At least tell me if you found proof that any of my clients are involved?" She watched as Miguel's expression vacillated between disclosure, reassurance and fear. "Out with it. What do you mean by 'danger'? Maybe enough that I'll decide to call Nigel and quit. No job is worth risking whatever's caused that look on your face."

Miguel walked over to the door, opened it slowly, looked around and closed it before walking the periphery of the screened room. Satisfied that no one was in earshot, he stopped in front of Amanda, taking both her hands in his. "What you don't want to do is overreact."

Overreact? Fight or flight suddenly became real for her. She did neither for the moment. Instead she drew a deep breath and listened closely as he continued.

"Quitting would tip their hand that someone is on to them. If you think you can handle it, it would be far better that you act normal, but—and this is critical—use extreme discretion as to what you say or do. Don't trust anyone. I can't be sure of the identity of all involved, but of those I have traced, a trail leads to you."

Amanda jerked her hands out of his "You mean to tell me that whoever this group is, they may be involved in irregular money transfers laundered through my department?"

"More importantly, the trail suggests you are being set up as a scapegoat. You'd be the perfect foil to deflect attention away from who and what is really going on."

Amanda spun around and began pacing. She gave Miguel a look of incredulity. "A scapegoat! If that's anything like a sacrificial lamb, I'm out of here!"

"They need to throw a spotlight on someone and with something convincing enough that all focus on the real perpetrators is extinguished. As to danger, I doubt they'd risk an American banker actually meeting with foul play."

Amanda stared in incredulity at a setting that should never allow for the words 'foul play' to reverberate through it. The room was reassuringly cozy, with its soothing collection of soft wicker lounges, colorful throw pillows and potted palms moving gently in the tropical breeze. The door leading back towards the living room leaked happy sounds of music and laughter.

Miguel had caught the look on Amanda's face and rushed to reassure her, shaking his head. "It's unthinkable. Marcos needs the U.S. to support him with whatever grandstand play he intends to put in place. So, don't worry. Just act natural; but, until I've established the identity of the kingpin, don't confide in anyone, especially not in your new teammate, Derek. What do you know about him anyway?"

"Not enough, obviously. The story I get is from Nigel. He claims someone in senior management personally recommended him—and Derek does know his trust business; I'll give him that." She paused before deciding to go on. "Still, all along something has seemed fishy." She began to fill Miguel in on what she had seen.

Miguel listened, his intent look escalating into one of black rage. As Amanda described seeing Derek at breakfast with the man on the plane, he leaped up, slamming his hand against the back of his chair. "Describe him again—slowly."

Amanda repeated every frame of the episode, studying Miguel's reaction as she did. He gave the distinct impression of memorizing every feature while running through his mental rogue's gallery of Filipino thugs.

"I'll get onto just who this character is." Miguel's statement carried a certainty that should have caused Amanda relief and not the shiver that overcame her. "Is there anything else you want to tell me?"

Amanda hesitated. "Nigel and Brad, I mean, shouldn't they be called in on this? If what you've discovered is true, I'll need to get them involved soon. They're the ones who'll have to weigh the consequences to the bank and make the decision as to what my actions, if any, should be."

Miguel's expression told her more than his words that followed. "Hold off for now. Any undue reaction from them could tip our hand and cause those involved to go to ground. I'll be happy to give you the green light to notify them. Once I've verified my information, that is. If I'm correct, it shouldn't be much longer. In the meantime, I see no need to panic them just yet. It could upset the whole apple-cart."

"How soon do you expect this drama to play out? Remember, I'm only here for another week before I'm off for Hong Kong."

"Before then; I'll not be able to lay it all out for them, but I'll meet with whomever they feel appropriate. Once that happens, it'll be important we both get well away from the Philippines."

Amanda turned a puzzled look directly into his eyes. "Why are you willing to go out on a limb for me? I know just how easily problem people can be eliminated in the Philippines. The whole thing with Ninoy Aquino's death was a perfect example. If you really do target the people behind this Kraken thing, it won't matter where in the world you are—you'll meet up with a sudden accident. So why risk so much?"

"You're right. It's not pure altruism." He drew her gently by the hand, leading her towards the door to the garden. "We both need a little fresh air." They walked out onto a path leading towards the rose garden. Amanda rushed to keep pace with Miguel's long strides. He moved as someone pursued until they reached the cool overhang of a rose arbor where he slowed and turned.

"I have my own reasons. Don't ask and don't worry. I can take care of myself. If everything goes as planned, they'll never know who was behind their fall. In fact, their own actions will trip them up, leaving no trail that could point to my involvement, or yours." He stared meaningfully into her eyes. "That is, if you don't confide any of what I'm telling you to anyone. We can't appear to be in collusion. Do I have your promise?"

"You have my promise, Miguel. I'm not sure that I really have many options, except to proceed with business as usual for now." Amanda turned to glance back at the house. "Meanwhile, we'd better head back to the party or they'll be suspicious for sure."

As they entered the living room, Raffy walked up with a solicitous smile and encircled Amanda in his arms. "Where have you two been? Miguel, how dare you monopolize our guest of honor?"

Raffy's question, although charmingly light, was delivered with a faint overlay of irritation.

Miguel ignored his remark, bidding Amanda 'Goodnight' as he headed swiftly towards the front door.

"Testy devil." Raffy said as he drew her close. "You arrived just in time for the last of the dancing." Sweeping her into the beat of the music, it became obvious that, in spite of the close embrace, sweet nothings weren't what were on his mind. "Your conversation with Miguel—how did it go?"

"What do you mean by that?" Amanda turned on him a direct look of puzzled affront.

Raffy came back in a lighter vein. "Nothing important enough to cause those wrinkles on your brow. It's just that he's been mixing with a rough crowd these days. I'd distance myself from that one if I were you."

"I ran into Miguel on my way back from a walk to see Caro's rose-garden." The look on her face and her delivery conveyed indignation. "Hello and goodbye could hardly be construed as a conversation." She marveled at her knack for deception as he quickly recanted.

"Enough said then. Except about business; I do need to go over some important matters concerning the De La Serna accounts. Do you have some time this week?"

"I don't have my appointment book with me at the moment—" She stopped suddenly as she remembered Raffy's appointment book. Something in his look and her own sense of guilt made her hesitate. Act natural, she reminded herself. "Of course, Raffy. Call me tomorrow and we'll coordinate a time."

The music ended. Not a moment too soon, she thought. She could have sworn Raffy's renewed embrace was a touch too firm. "Fine. I'll await your call." He let her go and marched off quickly toward the bar. She found herself suddenly in the middle of the dance floor, dazed and alone.

Someone grabbed her from behind. "Whoa!" Derek reared back as she turned an angry look on him. "It's only me, here to tell you your carriage and driver await. Am I too late? That face is definitely not the Cinderella I brought here."

"Derek—sorry to scowl at you. I'm just tired."

"I tell you what then. How about a quick after-dinner drink in the hotel lounge? I'll have the bartender prepare a special drink with secret Irish ingredients; call it an antidote to Brad's elixir. It's guaranteed to send you off to dreamland." As she hesitated, he pressed on. "I'd be anxious to hear what Nigel had to say. So, how about it?"

Amanda didn't think she could take any more tête-à-têtes for one day and yet she felt too keyed up for sleep. She glanced about at the thinning crowd. Several of the remaining clients passed her with a quick abrazo as they bid goodnight to Brad and Caro.

She turned back to Derek, suddenly remembering the strange photos and her anting-anting hidden in his briefcase. The thought that she might get him to reveal something decided her. "Alright; I think I could handle maybe one drink."

"One should do it. My word on it. Shall we bid our host and hostess goodnight?"

Caro and Brad were in the center of a circle of departing friends and family, which opened to include them. The De La Serna clan, with the exception of Raffy, who was nowhere in view, were the last to bid their farewells. Amanda suddenly remembered she hadn't seen Vivi since soon after her arrival.

"Caro, has Vivi left?"

"She and Raffy slipped out a few minutes ago. What a female! I've never seen anyone that could have both the men and the women hanging on her every word." Caro turned to escort her last guests out the door. She and Brad watched as they drove away and then turned to walk Amanda and Derek out to their waiting car and driver. "Sorry we didn't get our last dance." Brad seemed contrite as he whispered: "Wednesday lunch. Don't forget."

Derek looked into her eyes with a puzzled expression, but withheld any comment.

The lounge of the hotel was deserted. One look at her watch told Amanda why. It was nearly one o'clock. She turned to Derek. "Are you certain you want to prolong the evening? You look a bit the worse for wear yourself." Derek answered by drawing her gently over to the farthest banquette.

They waited in silence until Derek's special Irish brew had been concocted and served. He reached across to take her hand in his. "Is everything all right, Amanda? You were gone a long while with Nigel's call and then were cornered by Brad, Miguel and Raffy for the rest of the evening. Anything I should know or can help with?"

The dark corner, potent drink formula and Derek's overpowering physicality all threatened to disarm her reticence. Almost, until it dawned on her that he knew a bit too much about her comings and goings. "Derek, I really feel muddled right now. It must be this drink of yours, plus my tiredness and the whole crazy evening, starting with Nigel."

"How'd he sound?"

"He was in a panic-plus state and must have taken Brad right along with him. This whole business has both of them seeing villains around every corner."

She remembered both Miguel's and Raffy's questions concerning Derek. She put her remaining drink aside as she darted him a wry grin. "It's just a bit too much high drama if you ask me."

Derek reached across the table and took hold of her hand as he stared into her eyes. "I'd discount a lot of those kinds of remarks if I were you. Frankly, I suspect everyone's running scared, not only because of the New York arrest, but also because of all the changes going on within the bank. Whenever there are new players there's an added amount of paranoia."

"I'm sure you're right. Nigel's afraid the new department-head might get wind of these funny-money rumors so I'm under the gun to produce a clean bill of health for FAB."

"Don't let him push you into anything rash." Derek seemed to take extra pains as he continued. "I'd suggest you err on the cautious side. Even if there was only a suspicion that one of your clients may be involved, it would be wise to proceed carefully."

"If you're about to say 'Don't trust anyone', I'll..." Her hands tightly twisted the napkin in her lap, noose fashion, as she thought, *Somebody had better lay his or her cards on the table right now, starting with this Judas.* "God damn it, Derek; level with me." The rage in her voice startled her. "Exactly what do you think is going on?"

Derek mouthed a soft 'shush' as he glared at her and ever so subtly moved his head as though looking for their waiter. She was shocked to discover someone had entered the bar area without her having noticed. How much had they heard? The group halted, staring in her direction.

Derek reached out and patted her hand, raising his voice. "He really sounds like a bastard, that boyfriend of yours. Lord knows what's going on with his type."

"Waiter." The group took a table and began their own conversations as Derek called out: "Waiter; our bill, please—and do you have any sleeping tablets for the lady?"

Derek was silent as they walked towards the elevator. Once the doors had glided closed, he turned to her. "As far as the 'don't trust anyone' maxim, I'd put it more positively. Trust yourself. You're intelligent, intuitive and a good judge of character. You're going to have to depend on those qualities."

As the elevator door opened, she glanced around to make sure no one was in view. She grinned up at him. "I guess that means I can't opt for telling the bank what they can do with this 'glamorous' job of theirs?"

"Like it or not, I see you standing up to whatever comes your way—but running away—never." As she put her key in the door she whispered: "Quiet; Vivi may be sound asleep."

"Vivi asleep?" Derek muffled his doubtful response, but drew Amanda back before she opened her door. "What's the story on Vivi; she is leaving soon, right?"

"Supposedly, but she's 'crazy in love' as she puts it, so nothing she does would surprise me."

A strange look came over Derek, but no response. He brushed her cheek with the lightest of kisses and turned away. "Good night, sleep well."

Stepping inside, she turned to find both beds empty. No sign of Vivi ever having been in the room. Too tired to explore the ramifications, she pulled off her dress, removed her make-up, brushed her teeth and was in bed in five minutes.

Her last thoughts as she drifted between wake and sleep were of Derek's last words. *Funny, but not a trace of his Irish accent leaks through when he's serious, she thought. In fact, there are times his 'Irish' blarney seems distinctly forced.* Feeling on uncertain ground, she returned to her conversation with Miguel. She felt a chill go through her.

She jumped when the phone rang.

"Derek here; sorry to disturb you, but it seems I'll have to leave Manila sooner than planned. Something's come up. One of my biggest trust clients is in Hong Kong and needs to meet with me. I've arranged a flight for eleven AM tomorrow."

"But what about our meeting with Don Emilio and his attorneys to set up his trust? I can't disappoint him."

"I have complete confidence that you can handle everything. If he asks for anything out of your depth, I'll arrange to meet with him sometime after my return."

"Which is?"

"If all goes well, I should return Wednesday. In the meantime, you can always leave word for me at the Regent Hotel if anything important does come up."

An urge to question his strange explanation of 'a big trust client?' was swallowed up by her heightened conviction that Derek couldn't be trusted. Amanda's long silence was broken by a response only thinly disguising her disbelief and irritation. She didn't like being thrown a curve in an already fast-moving playing field. "Well, if you must. It's not as if I haven't made a dozen of these trips all alone."

"Remember, Amanda—if anything comes up, you know where to reach me. Don't hesitate. Goodnight."

Her curt response of "Goodnight" warred with an overwhelming urge to blurt out: "And good riddance."

# EIGHTEEN

Amanda gingerly sidestepped her beautiful dress, tossed casually over the sofa's arm, and walked to the windows. She drew the draperies and peered out at the day. A small group of Filipinas, bright umbrellas raised, was strolling along the avenue.

Another hot and muggy day, she thought, but thankfully, a day of few meetings. Suddenly she remembered Derek's late-night call to announce his sudden departure. She shook his news aside as she focused on Emilio De La Serna and his need to meet 'soon.' Grabbing her appointment book, Amanda quickly dialed his number. Lani, his housekeeper, recognized her voice.

"Oh, Miss Amanda; Senor De La Serna had a very bad night." Her voice wavered. "Rafael was with him until just a half an hour ago. They've given him so much medication, but still he speaks. I hear him say to let him know when Amanda Evan calls. I check to see if he is able to talk."

Amanda frowned at the memory of Don Emilio's yellow-flecked eyes and darkened nails, his dehydrated features. "Please Lani, don't disturb him if he's asleep." No response came. As she held the phone, prepared to disconnect, she heard a feeble "Hello".

"Don Emilio, please don't try to talk. It's Amanda. Can I do something for you?"

"Urgent—put affairs—in order." His voice, faint and painfully labored, gained strength with his last word. "...soon" His heavily medicated voice repeated the word: "...soon."

"When? I can meet whenever you ask or, if you agree, I can try to meet with your attorneys today to begin a discussion." His silence prompted Amanda to halt. "Just rest now. Your health is all that matters."

"Too late...fate sealed." A resurgence of the choking ended with, "...call...tomorrow." The receiver bounced into its cradle, echoing the rattling sound of Don Emilio's barely audible words.

Amanda examined the few words he was able to get out. It wasn't the words she decided, but the emotion, a blend of determination underscored by a killing grief, which disturbed her. An ominous sense that she may not see him again overcame her. She made a quick decision to cancel her two meetings for the day. It seemed critical that she stay available to Don Emilio. She called and left word with her two scheduled clients.

As she hung up, she hesitated, wavering, with a strong impulse to go to him. Before she could shake the thought, the phone rang again.

"Good morning, Amanda. It's Raffy here; I hoped to catch you. Something's come up. Father has taken a turn for the worse. As I mentioned last night, we need to talk. What's your day looking like?"

Relief filled her at the thought that he didn't know she had already spoken with Don Emilio. Voice appropriately distressed, she responded: "How is he?"

"Not good. I'll tell you more when I see you. How soon can we get together?"

"This morning can work, when and where you wish. How about we meet at the house? I'd love a quick visit with your father."

'That's out of the question. His doctor has forbidden all visitors." Amanda detected sudden anxiety coating the firmness in his tone.

"Well then, I've not had breakfast. Can you join me at the hotel's coffee shop?"

"I'll meet you there in one hour."

Amanda headed for the bathroom, wondering if Vivi would accompany him.

As if on cue, a tap came at the door, followed by Vivi's voice. "Amanda, it's me, Viv." Vivi walked through the door with a look of such intense consternation that Amanda suspected the worse.

"What happened?" Amanda walked over and put her arm around her. "Is Raffy turning out not the knight in white armor, after all?"

"Raffy?" Vivi gave her a blank look. "No; it's not about Raffy. The guy's hooked." Her face suddenly reflected a mix of frustration and anger. "And now I have to leave."

"Are you returning to Hong Kong?"

"No; I thought I was...but read this. The hotel manager just handed it to me when I walked in." Vivi thrust out an envelope she'd kept tightly clenched in her hand. And just when I was starting to pack to go with Raffy back to Hong Kong."

Amanda glanced down at what appeared to be a summons. "Tax avoidance?" She looked down and read on. "A special audit to be held of Nova Creations on this Thursday!" Amanda dropped the paper. "But what...?"

"I just called the number on the bottom of the letter and this Symonds guy said I have to attend. You bet your sweet patootie I'll be there. No way could I owe the Feds forty eight thousand dollars!" Vivi leapt up from the sofa and grabbed the phone. "I'd better see if I can leave on the next flight out, then call my accountant to see what's going on."

"I'd like to stick around while you sort things out, but I have an appointment" Amanda looked at her watch; "...in two minutes."

"Yeah, I know, with Raffy. He dropped me off and went to the coffee-shop to meet with you." Vivi headed into the bathroom, stopping suddenly, a look of pained recall coming over her face. "Just wait till he hears this shocker. We were going to a special dinner tonight with—can you believe it—Imelda Marcos?" Her look of distress segued into anger as she picked up the phone.

Amanda threw on a cool shirt and linen pants, but before heading out the door, halted as Vivi spoke into the phone. Vivi's expression spoke volumes as she looked, eyebrows raised, from the phone to Amanda.

"Today; you have one seat only on the three o'clock flight? Yes, go ahead. Reserve the seat for "Vivian Nova". I know; I'll be there two hours ahead." She slammed down the phone.

"Doesn't that beat all?" She looked up for confirmation.

"Too bad you couldn't have known of this earlier. Derek is headed for the airport as we speak." Amanda looked down at her watch. "No, I take that back. His flight has just taken off for Hong Kong."

"Derek's gone to Hong Kong? Why didn't he let me know last night when I told him I was going to Hong Kong with Raffy? His plane easily seats ten." Vivi shrugged away all concern for Derek's plans to return to her own. "I'm going to call my accountant fast. If that bastard's done anything to sic the feds on me, I'll have his balls"

"I have to get down to the coffee shop, Viv. Shall I say anything to Raffy?"

"Yeah, sure. He'll come undone when he hears the latest. Ask him if he can meet me in the lobby at twelve thirty for a ride to the airport?" She began to dial, looking up as she completed the number. "Better make that twelve fifteen. I'll need to go by his place and get my luggage."

Amanda nodded as she sprinted out the door to the elevator. With three minutes to spare she walked into the coffee shop. Raffy's face was buried in a cup of coffee. He looked around with a distracted air, making an effort to assume his usual veneer of charming self-assurance. "Amanda, look, ah, there are just too many people here. Maybe we can use an empty conference room somewhere in the hotel?"

"Sure, the executive suite in the Business Center is open and usually empty around this time. Let's go check."

As they exited the coffee shop a messenger handed Amanda a phone message saying: "Mr. Santos asks you to please return his call."

Raffy was lost in thought, waiting at the elevator. As it made its way to the Business Center floor, Amanda mentioned Vivi's predicament. "Yes, poor girl; tell her I'll do my best to accompany her. If not, my car and driver are at her disposal. Twelve fifteen in the lobby."

She studied the back of his head as he swiftly turned away, returning to thoughts involving his own agenda. Underneath his role as a Casanova lay a highly disciplined and focused young man, consumed with assuming the full mantle of "Don de La Serna".

"After you, Amanda", Raffy said as he opened the double doors, to reveal an expansive suite of executive rooms leading off of a central reception area, all empty. As he held the door, his smile was a blend of practiced charm and focused intensity.

He headed towards a sofa drawn up in front of an expansive cocktail table. Putting his briefcase on the table, he collapsed into the cream silk cushions and directed a look of pain her way. "Father is very bad. So bad, I doubt he'll last the night. There are things he would like me to address with you." He pulled out a pen, hand poised over his notebook. "Just how far did he get with his instructions?" Raffy held her eyes until his own began to glisten and he glanced away, coughing and reaching for his handkerchief.

She felt herself start to go into a knee-jerk sympathy reaction and pulled back. "Raffy, are you sure you're not overly pessimistic? Don Emilio has such reserves of strength and will. I predict he'll bounce back full force. What do his doctors say?"

"Doctors, what do they know? I say he won't last the week out. They are with him now, but he's pretty well out of it." Raffy folded his hands and bowed his head, raising it slowly, a pleading look in his eyes. "Pray for his soul, dear Amanda."

"No… I won't believe it. I have to see him."

Raffy slammed his note-tablet closed, leaped up from the down confines of the sofa cushions, walked to the window and peered through the blinds. He turned abruptly. "He can have no visitors. The best way you can help him is to cooperate with me. Those are his wishes and that's what he asked me to do, to handle whatever he's begun with you." Raffy's voice grew in volume until even he registered the manic edge it was reaching. He drew a long breath, assumed a faint smile of boyish chagrin and offered up a semi-apology. "I've not had much sleep, what with father and all. I'm just doing my best to complete his wishes." He walked over to sit alongside Amanda, taking one hand in his. "Help me to help him. I know he was eager to conclude some dealings with you. I need to know just what's involved, so as to finalize his wishes."

Amanda hesitated, haunted by Don Emilio's words. She formed her response carefully. "I'd like to be able to help, but until I receive authorization from him regarding your assuming full power of attorney to act on his accounts, I can't discuss his business dealings with you."

A sudden vacuum of silence descended as Raffy dropped his head to his chest. Amanda, feeling unnerved, stood and walked to the bookcase. She picked up a large conch shell, smoothing its satiny peach curve. She slowly turned, surprised to find Raffy frozen in his posture. She rushed to get some response, any response. "I'd love to visit your father, Raffy—as a friend. He is very dear to me."

Raffy's head slowly came up; his eyes fixed on hers with a stare of contemptuous dismissal, his hands clenched tightly into fists. He rose deliberately, coming just that little bit too close so as to instill in her the momentary effect of being thrown off balance. "There will be no contact. My father would be shocked at your lack of cooperation in this matter." He turned and headed towards the door. "I shall deal with you as soon as the issue of his health is determined; until then, good-bye." He was gone before she could move.

She stared, dazed, and yet unable to feel guilt or discomfort at her response. The echo of Don de la Serna's grief-filled voice seemed to ring silently in the wake of his son's exit. What can I do, she wondered? She slowly retrieved her briefcase and headed towards the elevator.

Curious to see whether Vivi was still in the room, she tapped on the door before she inserted her key. No answering response. She opened the door onto an empty room. A note lay on the bedside table. "Amanda. Sorry to have missed you. I'll call you from the airport. Kisses, Vivi" Amanda looked down at the bedside clock: twenty five past twelve. Might they still be in the lobby? A quick call to the desk brought the response "Senor De La Serna and Miss Nova just pulled away, headed for the airport." A sudden thought filled her. Now is the time to see Don Emilio with Raffy gone. She picked up the phone and dialed.

Lani answered, sounding anxious as she said that the doctor was with Don De La Serna. "They think he has fallen into a coma, Miss Amanda." Lani sobbed her disbelief. Amanda hesitated, torn between going, coma or not, before responding. "Lani, everything will be alright." Her confident tone seemed to have eased Lani's sobs. "Promise you'll call me the moment Don Emilio awakens. He wants to see me. Any time, night or day, I'll be there." Amanda hung up, feeling not at all convinced he'd be all right. Her meetings canceled, her thoughts racing, her shoulders aching, she felt impelled to head for Don Emilio's home. Before she could begin to sort her decision through the phone rang. Miguel. She felt a momentary twinge of guilt at having forgotten his call. "What's going on, Miguel?"

"I have to talk to you. Something's come up. The dining room looked empty. Could I persuade you to join me there for lunch?"

"Sure, say ten minutes. Bye." Amanda hoped she was suitably dressed for the main dining room's hushed and elegant confines. Mostly she hoped whatever it was could be dealt with quickly. Now that she had decided to see Don Emilio, she felt anxious to get under way. She stopped at the desk to ask them to forward any calls for her to the dining room.

Miguel was the only one in the dining room, sitting at the far end. She scarcely recognized him. His face was etched with anger and his hand gripped his coffee cup as though it was the cause of his wrath. The second he spotted her he forced himself to smile. His Mr. Hyde image vanished.

As she took a chair, he glanced at her and, with a serious look, began. "Sorry for the intrusion, but this simply couldn't wait. I've discovered something you need to be aware of." His voice lowered and he glanced around to make certain they were still alone. The waitress was approaching to take their order. Amanda ordered a cheese and fruit plate. Miguel seconded it and asked that they not be disturbed. Amanda kept the conversation general for the few moments it took for their waitress to return with their order. She efficiently laid the plates in front of them and quickly disappeared, leaving them completely alone.

Miguel turned to Amanda before she could bring the first bite of pineapple to her mouth, and said, "Where is Derek Ashton?"

"He had to go to Hong Kong—to see a client, he said." She heard how hollow it sounded.

Miguel's expression surprised her as he gave a subtle nod of affirmation and murmured…'hmm' before continuing with: "Who's he seeing and what's he up to in Hong Kong?"

"He's meeting an important client and will return in a couple days. That's all he said." She stared at his cat with a canary smile. "What do you know?"

"Your Mr. Ashton is not who he pretends to be. He's involved with some pretty shady characters, here and in Hong Kong."

"But he's a trust officer, and maybe…"

"Maybe nothing; don't you think it's a bit too much of a coincidence that he happens to have easy access to moving money through all his paper banks in the Caymans? I have it on good authority that he's up to his eyeballs in the strange goings on here in the Philippines."

"Then why would he leave to go to Hong Kong?"

"My contact says he headed to Hong Kong to meet with one of the biggest Middle Eastern shysters around, a cohort of Marcos. This guy could smuggle a king's ransom out of any country, and do it so smoothly it would never be traced." Miguel leaned in closer to Amanda, stressing his next words; "Getting Derek Ashton close to all of your clients is like introducing them to a hand grenade." He paused, his forehead etched in furrows. "And it is very dangerous for you."

Amanda felt a sensation not unlike one would have when they haven't felt well, believed it to be something they ate and were given a verdict of cancer. "But exactly how is it dangerous, Miguel?"

"He intends to use you, at the very least, as a front to take the focus off all his dirty work in the wings. Derek's meeting with the guy on the plane should have tipped me off earlier. I've been able to do a lot of discreet checking since then and "Derek Ashton", if that really is his name, is definitely not who he pretends to be."

Amanda glanced at her barely touched plate, feeling sick to her stomach. "Derek's not done anything yet to tip his hand."

"I figure he plans to make his move before you leave for Hong Kong. At minimum, you may be used as a plant." He brought his head closer to hers, lowering his voice but increasing its emphasis. "Anything he, or anyone else, gives you to take back with you should be examined like a landmine."

Amanda tried to force some rational thought to what was becoming an unthinkable dialogue. "They're not about to be so stupid as to try that again with another U.S. banker."

"If my informant is right, they're about to try something and it will involve you. Watch yourself with everyone, but especially with this fake colleague of yours, 'Derek Ashton'. Trust me; this bunch could have Reagan taken out with nary a trace back to the source."

Amanda's face had gone ashen. "Miguel, you're scaring me."

"Sorry, but I meant to. You need to be on your guard. Meantime, I'll keep my informants on the trail. They have their own sources and will know the minute any action is planned."

Amanda had hung onto Miguel's every word, too astonished to know where to begin. "This leaves me feeling totally at their mercy."

Miguel reached over to take Amanda's hand. "It has to look that way, but I'll be available at all times if anything goes wrong. Call me. Just say, "I called to see how your Aunt Florencia is doing" and I'll be there as quickly as I can."

"Maybe I should leave Manila and head for Hong Kong early?"

"No." His emphatic response caused him to look around at the still empty room. "Don't do anything precipitous, especially leaving town early. That could cause them to act faster and sloppier."

Amanda stifled her fear with anger. How dare Derek Ashton be deceiving me all along? Her wrath seemed to generate a solid core of energy. "Thanks, Miguel. I can't tell you how much it means to me to have a friend like you." She reached her hand across the table, hoping to ease his worried frown. "Count on it. I won't do anything rash to tip their hand."

Miguel studied her closely, reassured by her determined look. "I've got an appointment. Keep me notified of anything you turn up." She watched him walk away, feeling unable to sit still for one moment longer. *Damned if I'll let myself be manipulated by powerful men, she thought, determined to get to Don Emilio's bedside as quickly as she could.*

# NINETEEN

As they neared the familiar entry to the De La Serna compound, Amanda's heart began to race and drops of perspiration formed in her hairline. Emotions flooded her; anxiety about how she would find Don Emilio, apprehension about not having been invited, fear that she might have guessed wrong and Raffy would open the door and slam it shut. All were offset by her need to be there for Don Emilio.

"Wait in the car for me, driver." She turned and approached the entry. The door swung open the instant she pressed the chime. Chaos greeted her. Lani was staring dumbfounded, bathed in tears. Another servant was rushing behind her, carrying a basin of water that slopped over its rim. He gave a quick nod and a 'Yes, Doctor' in the direction of a short, heavy-set gentleman who stood at a distance, deep in conversation with another man. Amanda fixed her attention on the doctor. His solemn demeanor transfixed her as she strained to overhear their conversation. The doctor ignored her intrusion, motioned to something on a clipboard he held, and spoke softly but firmly to the man with his back turned to Amanda. The man grabbed the clipboard just as the doctor paused and looked her way. His stare caused the man with whom he had been in deep discussion, to turn.

Raffy's jaw started to drop, then swiftly formed a shout. "Amanda. What are you doing here? I told you how serious my father's illness is." His lips curled in disdain as he continued. "You Americans think you can walk all over us. Think again as you return to your hotel, immediately."

Amanda stood her ground. "I must see him. He asked me to come." She softened her stance. "Please Raffy, I mean no harm. Now that I'm here, may I silently say my hellos—" She paused, her voice cracking, "—or good-byes?"

As in slow motion, Raffy's hand came out, flinging the clipboard in a swift arc up, over and down the opposite wall. All eyes followed it to stare in shock as it crashed to its resting-place at the foot of a large philodendron. Its mesmerizing effect was suddenly broken.

"You may silently leave—or not so silently—as you wish." Raffy's voice rose to a yell, barely obscuring the faint sound of Don Emilio calling Amanda's name.

The shock wore off. Amanda's features turned to rage. The soft strains of Don Emilio's cry of her name erased any emotion but concern for over him. The doctor looked from Amanda to Raffy. He fixed Raffy with a firm gaze as he spoke.

"In my professional opinion, Raphael, she could not do any harm." He hesitated, "Perhaps her visit would ease Don Emilio's stress. He has asked for her repeatedly."

Amanda rushed to the doctor's side, eyes pleading for some affirmative answer. "How is he, Doctor? He will be alright, won't he?"

The look on his face left little room for hope. Amanda turned away, only to confront the icy stare of Raffy. His features were contorted with rage. "I said you must leave—right now!" His fists made only the slightest motion as they curled into a tightly clenched ball. Amanda's shock was halted by a keening wail.

Lani began to cry in earnest. "Don't hurt Miss Amanda. Don Emilio wants her here. He says it over and over." She practically shouted the last statement. Its volume and her sobs unleashed a burst of activity from the back of the house. Suddenly someone she didn't recognize pushed open the doorway leading into the main part of the house. He rushed up to Raffy and thrust a sheet of paper in his hands.

Amanda stared at Raffy's face as he read. It slowly drained from deep red to pink to white as his eyes moved quickly over the document. He read it, crumpled it into his fist and, with some effort and hesitation, he turned a look, if not of contrition, at least of neutrality, on Amanda.

All eyes froze on Raffy. Amanda was in a direct line between the doctor and Raffy. She was shocked to see the doctor's practiced, professional demeanor reveal a flicker of thinly veiled repugnance. Lani's sobs had abated, but she remained a solid presence as she stood waiting. Her tear-streaked face tugged at Amanda's heart. *Behind Lani's softness, Amanda thought, lay her strong and immovable devotion to Don Emilio.*

"You may see father. Keep it brief. No more than ten minutes." Raffy's words stunned them, not only by his abrupt recanting, but also by their tone. They were delivered as if by rote. Only his forced biting back of their last syllable revealed the effort it cost him to disguise his bitterness. "Dr. Lamora, please accompany Miss Evans. Ten minutes. No more."

Eager to get to Don Emilio, Amanda turned to follow the doctor. Dr. Lamora moved swiftly and confidently. Amanda kept close as they wound their way though the corridor leading to an area of the house that she had never seen. She broke the silence as they approached a large wooden double door. "Are Brad and Caro with him?"

The doctor whispered. "Caro is sedated and Brad is at the office."

The large room was dark and cool and completely dominated by an ornately carved mahogany bed. Amanda had eyes only for the small form almost lost in the massive white pillows that cradled him. An image came to her of Lani, or a Lani sister-soul, lovingly placing each one just so in the hopes that one added pillow would somehow provide the support, the rest, and the peace necessary to heal him.

She approached softly, staring at his closed eyes and watching fixedly for the cool white sheet to move. She let out her own breath as the slight movement began. He looked so childlike and defenseless. His face was translucently pale, appallingly vulnerable in its frailty. She turned away from the unthinkable, that Raffy might be right in his prediction of the Don's inability to last another day through.

No! She thought, turning back to direct her own strength and will his way, oblivious to the tear that began to course down her cheek. The doctor, who had positioned himself discreetly by the doorway, began to move towards her side. The motion caused Don Emilio's eyes to flutter open.

"Amanda. You came." A matching tear accompanied his soft words.

"Don't speak." Amanda reached out to take his immovable hand and began to softly stroke its black and blue veining.

"Want you to...." He choked with a slurred attempt to get the words strung together. "...call attorney." A paroxysm of coughing overcame him, causing the doctor to move quickly to his side.

He ignored the doctor's offer of a drink of water. "Killing me." He said, gazing from the doctor to Amanda with the most poignant look of sorrowful disbelief. "Help stop..." The last word faded away in a silent mouthing as his eyelids fluttered closed.

Amanda stared in shocked disbelief, anger surfacing at the doctor's gentle touch. She shrugged his hand away as she counted the seconds between the sheet's hesitant lifting, willing life to keep coursing through her frail friend.

"I'm sorry, Miss Evans. Mr. Raffy says it's time to go." The entrance of the young maid had gone unnoticed. Her gentle words inflamed Amanda.

"I can't. He needs me." Amanda looked from the doctor to the maid. The one's eyes filled with pity, the other's with fear that her orders may not be followed.

The doctor placed a firm hold under Amanda's arm and lifted her to a stand. "There is nothing you can do for him right now, Miss Evans."

As they entered the corridor, she turned to him, eyes flaming in accusation. "And you? What can you do for him? What have you done to him?"

"I've done all I can. Nothing has helped." As the words left his mouth she heard in them the bewilderment and the pain such impotency caused him. He continued his explanation, more for his own answers than for hers. "It's beyond medicine to fix. It's a collapse of his heart and will, even more than his body."

"What do...?" Before she could get the question out, she saw the look of fear come over the nervously waiting maid. Amanda looked up. Raffy filled the corridor. With one last look backwards she sent a silent part-prayer, part-vow in the direction of her defenseless friend. Watching the willful set of Raffy's shoulders filled her with a vow to keep that image fresh in the forefront of her mind.

Lani was nowhere in sight as they reached the entryway. Raffy had obviously vanquished her as completely as he had commanded the hotel's driver to bring her car around. It idled quietly at the front of the portico. Raffy turned to Amanda with a look that broached no delays, nor questions.

Amanda returned his look with a raw look of accusation. Raffy pulled back as though physically struck, turning his head to avoid her eyes. Without a word, she walked in front of him, head held high, back straight. She entered the car and, eyes focused inward, sat silently as the driver pulled away.

The shock had yet to wear off by the time they had arrived back at the hotel. Amanda murmured her thanks and walked zombie-like up to the elevator and on to her room. She entered and sat staring out the window. Overwhelming sadness for Don Emilio was the first emotion to seep through. She forced her thoughts away from the burnt-on-her-brain-echo of his plea. Retreating from grief, she stoked her rage at such a thing having happened. Could it yet be reversed?

Oh my God, she thought, staring around her room as thoughts filled her of her missing talisman—*surely a mankukulam. Miguel's Aunt Florencia had the right diagnosis. They must have brought in a kukulam.* As the word 'they' presented itself, an image of Brad and Caro arose. *Why didn't they try to intervene? Or did they? What did the note say that caused Raffy to do such an about-face?*

She knew her focus couldn't be on what happened or even how. I need to know who and why and what I can do about it, she decided, taking a tablet in hand. Suddenly a plan presented itself. She turned towards her briefcase, reached for her appointment book and note tablet and began a review of Wednesday's schedule. One look at the names convinced her to clear the decks.

She phoned her scheduled appointments and eliminated all but two. Hesitating over lunch with Brad, she decided, given today's horror, to cancel. She called the office to learn that Brad had left early. Marisa said she'd give him the message and hoped everything was all right. Amanda tried to keep it light, hanging up rather quickly to return to her plan.

Amanda replayed her meeting with Don Emilio: Raffy's rage, Caro's absence, Brad's involvement and the next steps required to establish a trust for the Don. His words, 'killing me' echoed between every line she wrote, firming her decision to call Don Emilio's attorney.

She dialed the number, half-expecting, at ten minutes to five, to find no response.

"Good Morning. 'Amparo, Tang and Curzon.' How may I direct your call?"

"Ernesto Curzon, please. Amanda Evans calling in regards to Emilio de la Serna." She held long enough to be overcome by a growing sense of unease,

"Miss Evans? Ernesto Curzon here. Sorry our appointment was cancelled. I was looking forward to meeting you."

"I'm hoping we can yet arrange to get together. I met with Don Emilio today at his home. He urged me to meet with you concerning his new trust. I'd like to schedule an appointment tomorrow if possible."

"How much do you know about the trust he'd been working on?"

Amanda hesitated. "I know he had been in consultation with you to make changes and our meeting today is to firm up those changes."

"How much did he share with you about the nature of these changes?"

"Not much, I'm afraid, at least regarding the specific details. My sense is that he'd..." She froze as she heard a telltale click on her line.

"I'm sorry Mr. Curzon, but I'm not comfortable discussing anything further over the phone. Could we meet?"

"Yes. Fortunately a time-slot is open tomorrow morning at nine. Do you know where we are located?"

"Yes. I'll be there. Thank you." She hung up, slowly staring at the phone. A sense of relief filled her at having stopped before anything specific was divulged. 'Close' she whispered, shocked at how her anxiety over Don Emilio had nearly overcome her caution.

Brad? She paused, returning to memories of the lunch that was to cement them as allies, trying to understand just where and how he fitted into the larger plot. She shook her head in disbelief and fear at what that larger plot might entail.

Forgoing any dinner, she lay awake, her thoughts stoking the fires of conviction to do whatever it took to "Help stop…" as Don Emilio's cry beseeched her to do. Her meeting tomorrow with his attorney was the only thing that helped to counter-balance her sorrow.

\* \* \*

A rush of adrenaline propelled Amanda out of bed in a frenzied leap for the door. Anxiety-coated dreams of her upcoming meeting enveloped her as she grabbed for her notes. Closing her tablet with what could be damning notes, she dropped them into her briefcase and walked to the closet.

She pulled out her most conservative corporate suit. Her power look was complete with a new pair of Ferragamo pumps, a flawless manicure and her hair done up in a sleek chignon. Once dressed, she turned slowly, and, assured of her composure, dialed the front desk.

"Of course, Miss Evans; the car shall be available to you."

"Thank you." She walked to the elevator, reviewing her approach to the meeting. Her strategy would include a professional emphasis on finalizing the Don's trust, confident that with his attorney's help, it would be a fait accompli. The wild card was whether Curzon would be forthcoming enough to cooperate without the Don able to be there.

The driver seemed to know exactly where the attorney's office was. Amanda sat on the edge of her seat all the way, oblivious to the usual traffic jams, smog, smells and noise. Her mind was running with anticipation at what their meeting would reveal. That it had to do with Raffy she was certain. That it would incorporate some changes as to succession and/or, control over his companies, she suspected.

She frowned as she thought how important it was for her to clarify the extent of those controls and to assure the full breadth of the changes Don Emilio wanted implemented. *There wasn't a moment to waste if the look on Don Emilio's face is any indicator, she thought, as they pulled up to the entrance of the building.*

She didn't wait for the driver to open her door. She jumped out, asked the driver to please wait and dashed through the door and over to the elevator. As the elevator door opened to the eighth floor and the offices of Amparo, Tang and Curzon, Amanda kept in the forefront of her mind the sight and sound of Don Emilio as he pleaded for her help. The receptionist smiled as she dialed to let Mr. Curzon know Amanda was there.

The suddenness with which he appeared pleased her, until she registered the look on his face. It was not one of welcome. "Miss Evans. Please step into my office." He turned and walked as briskly as one could whose girth was equal to his height. They moved down a long corridor until he reached a corner office. Its glass doors bore his name, followed by a series of acronyms attesting to his impressive degrees. As he held out a chair, she had a sickening sense that this man, who so resembled Saint Nick himself, wasn't about to present her with a gift.

"I'm sorry, Miss Evans. I tried to reach you at your hotel. It seems our meeting has been made unnecessary." He reached over to his desk, taking one end of a document and handing it to her.

"Non compus mentus--Don Emilio?" She looked up, a slow dawning draining her face of color. "Does this mean what I think it means?"

"I'm afraid so." A look of surprise flooded Attorney Curzon's features. "An attorney for Raphael De La Serna just served this notice not twenty minutes ago. It seems a group of doctors has diagnosed Don Emilio as being unable to undertake any business due to his condition." Attorney Curzon took the document from her hand and began to read. "This condition is of a nature to make null and void any legal changes that may have been initiated by Don Emilio De La Serna prior to and up through the previous six weeks."

"But…" Amanda was on her feet. "He can't do that. Don Emilio's no more mentally unstable than, than…" She noticed a look stealing over Attorney Curzon's face that suggested a prelude to "Good Day". She quickly composed herself. "I saw Don Emilio yesterday and, although his health may be broken and his body overmedicated, his mind is functioning as clearly as ever. He fully expected you and I to work together to implement his desired changes to his trust."

"Off the record, I quite agree with you Miss Evans." He flicked his finger against the pages of the decree. "But this is a valid legal document and the record says I cannot continue with any plans Don Emilio may have put in place over the last six weeks. That includes any discussion with you of what those plans may have entailed." He stood and made a motion towards the door. "I'm sorry to have taken your time."

The elevator ride down, the walk out the door, the driver escorting her into the car, all took on a sense of unreality as Amanda's mind raced. "Damned if he's going to get away with this", she muttered under her breath as the car proceeded towards her meeting with Brad. She considered asking the driver to take her to the De La Serna home for a confrontation with Raffy. She quickly discarded any such action as being useless. Her thoughts followed a labyrinth of next steps, debating as to whether or not Brad might reveal something. He wasn't in the office this morning when she called to discuss her cancelled lunch.

Returning to her room, she dialed the Manila office. Brad came on the line, his manner distracted, so much so that the cancelled lunch seemed a non-event. "I'd decided to cancel it myself after Raffy told me of your visit yesterday. You acted a bit impetuous, poking your nose into things that don't concern you." His words were coated with more fear than upset. "Why didn't you leave everything to me?"

"Don Emilio's wishes of me as his banker do concern me."

"Not any longer. He's slipping fast. The new doctor says he's incapable of rational action. The Don's body may linger, but his mind's long gone." Amanda bristled at a recitation that sounded coached. She forced herself not to scream something to the effect of "You lily-livered limpet, clinging to De La Serna money by latching on to the next obvious provider." Instead she dissembled, hoping for some opening. "How does Caro feel about that prognosis?" Amanda listened carefully.

"She denies it of course—so much so that the new doctor had to give her a tranquilizer strong enough to keep her sleeping the rest of the day." He coughed after choking the sentence out. "I know she'll see reason once she's had a bit of rest."

She was silent for a moment. "As to the clients we were to have reviewed..."

"I can't think of that right now, except to give you one a bit of advice. Erase one name from your list: the De la Sernas." His voice grew in firmness. "That's one family whose accounts you needn't be concerned for." He hesitated and continued with a conspiratorial aside. "In fact, I wouldn't be a bit surprised if you didn't double your totals soon, now that Raffy has the reins." Her hesitancy in responding left no doubt that his remark gave offense. "Don't misunderstand me, Amanda. Of course we're all pulling for Father to rally round. But, let's face it, the old guy's had a good run; it's time for new blood. My advice is to play ball."

"It's time I go. I have an appointment." Amanda kept her voice neutral.

"Right; and I'm leaving the office for the day. But I'll call you tomorrow. We can tie up loose ends."

*You jerk, Amanda thought, hanging up the phone, incensed at his callous comment about an increase in De La Sernas accounts with me and his 'play ball' admonition.* She had to get out of her room, clear her head and decide: :Where to next?"

# TWENTY

As Amanda headed for lunch in the coffee shop, her thoughts returned to Derek and his abrupt trip to Hong Kong. He was supposed to return today, or at least that's what he had said. She stared at her barely touched fish—cold now—suddenly convinced he wouldn't show up.

Returning to her room, she retrieved two phone messages shoved under the door. Andrew Tang saying: "Are we on for dinner?" and Rob saying he'd try to catch her tomorrow.

As she dialed Andrew Tang's number to cancel dinner, she halted mid-dial and replaced the receiver. She repeated his name aloud. "Andrew Tang? Wasn't Tang one of Don Emilio's team of attorneys?" He might be able to add something to the Don Emilio enigma, she decided. In any event, she had to eat anyway, so dinner would stay. She dialed, got an answering machine and left word to confirm when and where.

Suddenly she remembered what she'd wanted to ask Brad. She had a packet to send via his inter-branch mail to Hong Kong. She fished out the manila envelope at the bottom of her briefcase. How could I have forgotten to ask Brad if he'd inter-office this to Hong Kong? Her presentation to the Hong Kong branch managers would go out the window if her transparencies and handouts for her meeting didn't arrive.

*Brad's edict be damned, she thought.* Knowing he was off for the day, she'd walk across to the Manila office and leave the envelope with Marisa.

Her suit and heels would never have done, she thought as she walked across the hot, gravel lot between the hotel and the bank's parking lot. She'd shed her corporate look for tan pants, a white blouse and flat shoes. Even so, she felt perspiration wending its way down her back as she reached the lobby of Brad's office.

Marisa greeted her with a blend of excitement and nervousness. "I just hung up from talking with one of your clients: Senor Estancio. Your ears must be ringing with all of the nice things he was saying." She stopped as she followed Amanda's glance around the office.

"Mr. Gregory isn't in. He left early, said he had some business to take care of. From the sounds of it, he won't be back for the day."

Amanda felt her shoulders lower and her smile return. "Actually I don't need to see Brad. I dropped by because I needed to give him an important envelope to inter-branch mail to our Hong Kong office." Amanda held out the packet of materials.

"No problem. I'll see to it that it goes out today." Marisa hesitated, her manner turning serious. "Now I need to ask you for a favor. A wire transfer order just came in that has to go out right away and Mr. Gregory didn't leave a phone number where I could reach him."

Amanda was struck by Marisa's nervousness and rushed to reassure her. "I'll do whatever I can."

"I just need you to review it for accuracy, and sign for approval in the authorized signature section." She grabbed the wire from her desk and shoved it into Amanda's hand. "Ernesto's the only other authorized signature besides Mr. Gregory—and he's on vacation." Her smile flickered. "It was an answer to a prayer to have you walk into the office."

"Let me have a look at it." A brief overview revealed the transfer as being made by Tennyson Trading Company Ltd., Philippines to be remitted to Milton Mfg. Corp., Ltd., Hong Kong, for further credit to Blue Sky Holdings in the Bahamas. Amanda carefully reviewed every detail, account numbers, routing instructions, bank addresses and codes. So precise was she in examining each box for complete information that it took a few seconds for the amount to register.

"Eight Million U.S. dollars? I thought it was eight million pesos." She shoved it across the desk towards Marisa. "That's way over my limit. I'm surprised it isn't over Brad's." She paused as she saw the look of fear in Marisa's eyes. "Even if it isn't, an amount this size requires two officers signatures for confirmation and approval. Sorry, I can't do you much good, Marisa."

"I don't think I can reach Mr. Gregory—and Ernesto is unavailable. The wire won't go out until Monday." Marisa's voice took on a note of panic. "Mr. Gregory will have to contact the client right away." She grabbed the phone. "I'd better try to reach him."

"Don't mention my being here."

"I guess it was a good thing you couldn't approve the wire after all. Not to worry, I won't even mention that you were here to ask." As Marisa held for a response, Amanda decided to go back to Brad's office and get a glass of filtered water from the refrigerated cooler he kept in back of his desk. She skirted the rooms where the remaining staff was busy at work. She didn't want to risk having them comment to Brad about having seen her. In the cool and private confines of Brad's office, she drew the door partially closed while she went to pour herself a drink.

The heat and the humidity took its toll on her. She reminded herself to drink more water as she gulped it down. She decanted another glass and then a third. As she reached to put the cup into the wastebasket, she saw a piece of crumpled paper with her name on it. Amanda furtively retrieved the piece of paper and dropped it into her purse.

Reentering the reception area, she was surprised to find Marisa still on the phone with Brad. Surprise turned to shock. Marisa's face was a painful blend of fear and anger, coupled with white knuckled resistance as she gripped the receiver. "Mr. Gregory, how can I do what you ask? It's against the bank's regulations." She was quiet for a long moment as she listened intently. "I understand, but I simply can't do such a thing. No, please." Her voice threatened tears. "I'm the sole support of my family. It would be difficult to find another job."

Marisa glanced up and saw Amanda. Embarrassment and shame colored her features, but quickly turned to hope and excitement. "Please, Mr. Gregory, maybe I have a solution. If you could come down to the office and sign it, you could call Miss Amanda to provide the other bank officer's signature." The relief that renewed her spirit faded fast as she listened. "But, I don't understand. Amanda is a more senior bank officer than Ernesto as far as counter-signing goes." She paused, glancing fearfully towards Amanda. "Yes, of course I won't call her. You have my word. Yes, Mr. Gregory, I'll be here, but I can't sign Ernesto's signature."

Her eyes widened, the tears ceased as she set her jaw. "Of course I'll wait." Marisa slowly hung up the receiver. One look at Marisa's crestfallen face wrenched Amanda's heart. She ran to her and held her as tears resumed their fall.

"Don't worry. Everything will be all right. You'll see." Amanda soothingly uttered the standard phrases until Marisa's sobs eased and she looked up.

"What can I do? He wants me to sign Ernesto's signature. He says the transfer must go out today." Marisa looked from the wire transfer and back to Amanda. "I couldn't live with myself if I did it." Her sobs resumed in earnest as the look on her face deepened its despair. "What about my job? My family depends on me."

Amanda walked over and turned her downcast face up to her own. "Listen carefully. First of all, I'm quite certain he won't fire you. He'd be much too concerned over your contacting his new chief, Lyle Carter, with the reasons behind your dismissal."

"But what can I do when Mr. Gregory shows up?"

Amanda took Marisa by the arm and walked her back over to her desk. "Follow my instructions to the letter." When she was certain Marisa was fully focused, she began. "Stick to your guns in a firm and professional way. Remember to take notes later of the date, time and content of your discussions. You should insist there be another bank employee present during these meetings. It's important because it's your word against his, and you know whose will carry more credibility."

"But he won't want anyone..."

"Of course he won't." Amanda finally got a slight smile out of Marisa. "That request alone will silence Brad. He'd be sure not to let even one word of this incident reach anyone's ears."

"You're positive?"

"You can count on his not wanting anyone, particularly me, involved; right?"

Marisa let out a laugh. "Are you kidding? He really panicked."

"He knows it's over my limit and certainly over Ernesto's as well." Amanda moved quickly as she walked towards the filing cabinets. "Do you have a copy of each employee's signing authorization?"

"Sure; in the vault. I'll go get it." Marisa walked briskly towards the hallway.

Amanda grabbed the wire transfer order, rushed behind the desk to the copier and ran off a quick copy. She had barely stuffed it into her briefcase when Marisa appeared, holding an envelope with the authorized signature list inside. She had waited to open it until Amanda could witness her doing so. She gasped.

"You're right. Ernesto can only sign or countersign up to one million U.S. dollars. I'm sure there have been larger amounts that he's signed. Should I go and pull the copies out to check to be certain?" A look of sorrow erased the disbelief. "Poor Ernesto; Mr. Gregory must have threatened him too."

"Don't do anything right now. Get that copy back exactly as it was before Brad gets here." Amanda glanced nervously towards her briefcase. "I need to get out of here before he decides to come back to the office."

She turned to find Marisa's eyes widening, and panic about to return. "Remember, stay cool, and simply decline. Brad won't fire you. He's going to need your support more than ever."

Marisa's panic left; but her voice held deep perplexity. "I don't understand what's going on. Mr. Gregory can't afford to offend his most powerful client—and a De La Serna at that."

"What did you say?"

"Tennyson Ltd.; I'm pretty sure it's one of the De La Serna accounts. You know how those offshore corporations are. They all have some kind of stand-in people signing on them so you never really know who owns them."

"Then what makes you think so?"

"One of the cousins brings packages for me to inter-branch. They're usually in the names of Tennyson Ltd. or one of those other names."

Amanda held her growing excitement in check, wondering just how far to risk Marisa's involvement. "If you find there were similar transactions, try to make copies when it's safe to do so." Amanda watched Marisa's eyes widen. "Don't leave them in the office. Put the originals back, take the copies home and call me. We'll meet and review the whole matter."

Marisa smiled her relief at the offer of help, but her smile faded. "Isn't that against bank policy?"

"Not if they're suspicious transactions. Anyway, I'll take full responsibility."

A hint of confidence returned to Marisa's face. "I'll do it."

"Good. Remember not a word about our discussions. Call me, but don't say too much over the hotel's phones. Good luck."

Amanda headed swiftly out the door and to the elevator. Her heart stuck in her throat as the elevator opened and a man got out. *Not Brad, thank God, she thought as she entered.* Exiting at lobby level her brisk stride took her out the revolving door and into the parking lot. She bolted in alarm just as she was about to strike out for the crossing median of gravel that separated the parking lot from the hotel. Brad's car was in his assigned spot and he was bent over to turn the key in the door lock.

In the space of a second she reviewed her options. Stand and brazen it out. Turn back inside and look for cover. Walk towards the street and hope not to be recognized. She took the latter, hoping that her angle and her change of clothes obscured his ability to recognize her. Ducking away, she cringed in anticipation of hearing him call her name. She resisted the temptation to glance back and didn't slow her stride until she had rounded the front of the building and turned right to cross at the light. Her heart was racing when she reached her hotel's foyer.

The sight of her room didn't reassure her as it usually did. She looked down at the two messages lying on the floor. One from Derek saying he'd call back. The other from Brad saying he needed to meet her in the morning, breakfast at eight at her hotel. Placing them aside, she felt a deep chill of vulnerability. Suddenly, being an American wasn't the insurance policy she'd always taken for granted. *Alien, exposed and at risk for God knows what, she thought?* From her growing terror it, was something tangible and something close.

"Get hold of yourself." She spoke aloud, reassured by the sound of her own voice. "You're letting your imagination carry you away." She kicked off her shoes, sank back into the chair and forced herself to slowly sip a glass of water. Replaying the scene in Brad's office stirred a memory of the note in his wastebasket. She was fishing through her purse when the phone rang. Jumping in panic, she dropped everything as she ran to answer it.

"This is my lucky day. I tried to call you yesterday with no luck. Didn't you get my message?" Derek's voice triggered an impulsive urge to dump everything into his lap. She caught herself, remembering whose camp—whoever he was—he was really in.

"I only just got your message a few minutes ago; where are you? How'd things go with your client?" She forced her voice to that of a professional colleague.

"Is everything all right back there? I'm still in Hong Kong. Not quite finished wrapping everything up, but I should be back Thursday at the latest. You sound a bit uptight. How'd it go with Senor De La Serna?"

Her silence prompted him. "Sorry; forget I asked. I know you can't talk now. Just answer me one thing." He paused, adding extra emphasis to his words. "Do you need me to hurry back for any reason?"

The silence seemed to hang on for just a touch too long before Amanda responded. "No, Derek. I'm fine, just a bit over-tired. Saturday can't get here soon enough. I'm ready to finish up, head for Hong Kong, do what I have to do and go home."

"If you're sure you don't need me back there."

I need you like I need a hole in the head, she thought, careful to keep her response professional and calm. "Don't change your schedule because of me. By the way, have you had time to call on our Hong Kong office?"

"Not yet. I'll save that pleasure for when we're both here on Saturday. That way you can properly introduce me. I'll try to call you once more when I've confirmed my arrival time. If you need to reach me before then, take down this number. I'm staying at The Regent in Kowloon."

Amanda wrote down the phone number and the hotel, hung up the phone and shook her head to try to clear it. Why is it he comes across so concerned, when I know whoever he really is, he's a scoundrel through and through? The anger at being made a fool of revved up her resolve to keep her own counsel. She felt her earlier fears begin to dissipate.

The spilled contents of her purse drew her back to an earlier focus—the note she'd retrieved from Brad's trash-basket. She lifted it from the pile and smoothed it out.

"Amanda; probe; what to do?" The words themselves were made more ominous by the emphasis. Her name was underlined over and over, as were the final three words. Brad was concerned over the meeting, but not simply concerned to 'find out what to do' to help me, she thought. His more important 'what to do' was to cover his ass quickly and thoroughly, she thought—given the size of his wire transfers. She was eager to see what Marina would turn up. Whether one or a dozen, collusion was apparent.

The thoughts that followed thrust her, like Alice, down the rabbit hole and up to the edge of an abyss. This was nothing that any cover your rear action could obscure. No one, not Carter, not Chairman Sorenson, not Fidelity American Bank, no one would remain untouched. Where did that leave Amanda Evans? She itched to see all the accounts involved and to trace each one of the principals. Her heart sank at the thought that it might involve Don Emilio.

The ring of the phone convinced her to avoid ,for the moment, the unthinkable. It was Andrew Tang calling. They arranged for an early dinner, an hour from now in the hotel's dining room. She tossed the scrap of paper into her briefcase as she headed for the shower, deciding to take a page from Scarlet O'Hara and "Think about it tomorrow".

Such a philosophy allowed her, if not to fully enjoy her dinner with Andrew Tang, at least to get through the evening with easy conversation. He wasn't at all involved, or wasn't willing to discuss, Don Emilio's legal affairs, but he did comment on how strange it was that Don Emilio's health has failed so quickly. His charm helped pass the hours away with wry tales of a Filipino film star and his multiple wives and families, all unaware of one another. She said "Goodnight", feeling a silent gratitude for his lightheartedness having helped in easing her earlier paranoia.

Amanda took the hotel elevator to her floor and strolled casually down the hall to her room. The moment she opened the door she froze, all senses acutely alert. Her room radiated a palpable aura of having recently been occupied. She tripped the master switch at the entryway, flooding the room with light. Her eyes raked every inch of the room from the safety of her open door. Leaving the door ajar, she gingerly approached the bathroom. Its pristine white marble expanse provided nowhere to hide except the shower stall. Heart pounding, she nudged the opaque glass door and bolted back towards the safety of the hallway exit. The silence shamed her into a sense of foolishness. No one was there.

Lulled by her routine dinner meeting, she fought to hold onto its aura of normalcy. She had almost talked herself around when her eyes caught sight of a stubbed-out cigarette in the toilet.

*It must be the maid's. But they're not allowed to smoke in the rooms, are they?* Her attempt to rationalize suddenly ebbed away. She jumped at the ring of the phone, letting out a cry. She eyed its ringing in fear, her hand hesitant as it lifted the receiver.

"Amanda? Amanda—is that you? Is anyone there?"

"Rob! Oh, Rob, it's so good to hear your voice." A sudden click on the line silenced what would have been her outburst of panic over her situation in Manila.

"I had to let you know that I'm off to New York tomorrow. I may not make it back in time to pick you up."

"Not to worry." She swallowed back her anxiety at all that lay between her return. "I've got my plate pretty full right now, but the minute I arrive in Hong Kong I'll call you to coordinate."

"Do that. If I make it back, you have a chauffeur. If not..."

"If not, I'll have to taxi it home. I..." She hesitated, wanting somehow to communicate something of what was going on.

"You what?"

"Nothing, Rob; I'm just glad you called. Have a good trip. See you soon." She felt a shiver at the finality of the disconnect tone.

Her uneasiness mounted at the dawning awareness that Rob's first concern was his own agenda. There's no one to turn to, she thought. Count Nigel out. He only wants good news. My ersatz colleague, Derek Ashton, whoever he is, is my enemy. Brad is up to no good. The only one I can really turn to is Miguel, but I can't unload all of the stuff concerning Brad and the bank onto him. Before putting out the light, a plan began to take shape.

Ten hours later she awoke feeling rested for the first time since she'd arrived in the Philippines. No aching muscles, no sleep-stuck eyes, no resistance to dragging her body out of the bed. She walked with a light step into the bathroom. Gone was the helpless terror of the night before. Whatever was going on, she determined to get at the heart of it. No more chasing phantoms and depending on will o' the wisps for support. She remembered Brad's message to meet him at breakfast at eight.

The coffee shop was full. She hesitated, eyes searching the room for Brad. He was sitting alone in the corner, nervously snuffing out a cigarette as she walked up. "Amanda, glad you could make it." His voice held a jitteriness, his eyes dark-rimmed from lack of sleep.

"What is it, Brad? Is it anything to do with Don Emilio?"

"Let's order first." He looked around and motioned for a waiter. "And no, Father's condition remains the same.

"Sliced mangoes and a poached egg on rye toast please." Amanda turned to Brad.

"Just coffee."

"Do you really think this is the place to review suspect clients?" Amanda glanced around the fast-filling coffee shop.

"It isn't your clients I'm concerned about. It's your colleague, Derek Adams." He waited until the waiter had placed their orders in front of them, lowered his voice and continued. "Something's fishy about that guy. I've been doing some digging on him, or at least, the De La Serna contacts have been busy." Brad paused as he met her eyes and waited for the effect of his words. "He stinks to high heaven. I don't care what you say about some referral via our Bank's chairman. The guy comes up as phony as a three dollar bill. I just hope you haven't spilled too much information to him."

Amanda, whose thoughts had been primed to deal with a defense of Miguel, was thrown. "Be specific. Exactly what did they turn up on Derek?"

"To begin with, he isn't 'Derek Ashton'."

"He *isn't* Derek Ashton?" Amanda's eyes widened as a sudden sinking sickness filled her. "Who is he?"

"No one could trace exactly who he really is. There is, or was, a Derek Ashton, who had a solid career in offshore banking in the Channel Islands, but it wasn't your phony Irish friend. The real Derek Ashton died a natural death two years ago."

"Derek's wife died Brad. They must have picked up on that information."

"They were quite clear. The real Derek Ashton is dead. The most suspicious part though is that no one can figure out just who the fake Derek Ashton really is. Not one single bit of information." He looked for one long moment into Amanda's eyes. "For God's sake, don't tell him anything about your clients."

"I'd say it's a bit late for that. You know he's met many of my clients on this trip already."

"Yeah, well I'd move slowly with providing him any further information." Suddenly his face turned white. "You haven't revealed anything to him about the rep office, have you?"

Amanda froze, still trying to absorb his news about Derek Ashton. "The rep office?" She responded as though from the bottom of a well, suddenly wary about her discoveries concerning Brad's irregular wire transfers. "I'm not sure what you mean. I haven't said a thing about the rep office, except what you heard when we came to your office on our first day."

"Good. Keep it that way. I don't know all of the characters he's involved with; but I do know that he has been seen with the real scum of the Philippines. By the way, they traced him to a flight to Hong Kong. What do you know about this sudden trip of his?

"Nothing much. He just said something had come up with one of his important trust clients and he needed to meet with him in Hong Kong. He'll be back in a couple of days."

The contempt in Brad's answering guffaw stung. "God, Amanda, you don't really believe that?" At that moment someone approached their table.

"Brad Gregory? Just the man I wanted to see." The man made a move as though he intended to stay awhile.

Brad seemed frozen. Amanda glanced at her watch, pushed back her chair and moved towards the door. "I have an appointment. Thanks for letting me know." Amanda was out the door before he could respond.

As she left the coffee shop, a messenger handed her two phone messages that had just come in. The first was a message from Paco Ramirez, asking her to call him regarding her availability for dinner tonight. The thought of ending the day in Paco's company cheered her. She returned back to her room, picked up the phone and called Paco to leave a "Yes" message on his answering machine.

She stared at the receiver, her hopes growing that she'd to be able to explore with him Don Emilio's strange and sudden illness. Her conviction grew that Paco knew more about the De La Serna family secrets. She hoped to persuade him to share them.

Her hand returned to the phone as she began dialing Don Emilio's number.

Lani answered, a little nervous at identifying Amanda as the caller. "Don de la Serna is in a coma, Miss Amanda. He called out for you once though. His new doctor is with him now." She held back a sniffling cry. "No one knows if he'll awake."

"And Raffy?"

"Senor Raffy is not here. He had to go to Hong Kong." Amanda detected rage in Lani's voice. "An emergency came up with one of the De La Serna businesses. He did not say when he is expected back." She hesitated. "If you wish to come by, I must inform you that Mr. Raffy has forbidden it. He gave the new doctor strict orders." She let out a half-sob, half-angry sound. "And me."

"That's alright, Lani. From the sounds of it, my coming there would serve no purpose. I would appreciate one favor however. Could you let me know when Don Emilio comes out of the coma?" She hesitated before considering the worse. "Or, if there are any changes at all? I'd ask his doctor, but, I--"

"Senor Raffy forbids the doctors to discuss Don Emilio's condition with anyone but himself." Her voice took on a tone of defiance. "He'd be furious if he knew, but I don't care; I will call you if there's any change."

Amanda hung up the phone, deep in thought. Why would Raffy head to Hong Kong with his father at death's door? She decided she'd call Brad if she hadn't heard anything by tonight. It would take a bit of fence-mending on her part, but she needed Brad to level with her about Don de la Serna. Her spirits lifted as she thought that maybe Caro would answer.

Her hand hesitated over the second message, a sealed envelope. She tore it open.

"Call me immediately. I must see you today, earliest. Urgent! Miguel." She reached back towards the phone when the phone rang.

"Look, I can't talk. Did you get my message? How soon can we meet?" Never had Amanda heard Miguel's voice sound so strained. He spoke with the urgency and quiet breathlessness of someone who'd been running.

"I only just now opened your message."

"I'll be there in ten minutes. Be down in the lobby."

"I'll be there." Her tan pants and white blouse should do, she decided. She grabbed the ringing phone as she moved towards the door. Paco's voice filled the room.

"Lovely, my dear Amanda; we're on for dinner at seven thirty at the Manila Pen. I have a meeting there for Rotary tonight. I'll send my car over for you around seven twenty or so. Look forward to seeing you."

Great, she thought, as she hung up. The loud slam of her door caused the cleaning woman to look in surprise as Amanda strode briskly towards the elevator.

Miguel, looking disheveled, was pacing in the lobby. He rushed forward, ushered her through the door and into the car without a word. Only when they pulled away, did it dawn on her that he was doing the driving.

"What happened to Luis or Tomas?"

"I can't take the chance of anyone hearing what I have to say. I thought we'd drive over to the botanical gardens where we can walk and talk unheard." One look as his haunted expression and Amanda felt her bravado begin to sink.

"What is it?"

"Listen carefully. You're in danger. You're being set up as the target to take the heat off the real money launderers."

"Me! In danger? How?" Her hands felt hot and moist as she twisted them in her lap. She instinctively reached for her door handle, unconsciously impelled to leap out. She turned back to Miguel, hoping for some reprieve.

"Could your informants be mistaken?" Her heart seemed to halt its beat as she studied every nuance of his expression.

"I'd like to answer yes, but it's worse than I thought. Soft-pedaling it would only expose you to an even greater threat. They must be convinced that something could blow the lid off, because they're desperate enough to risk anything, including setting you up as the scapegoat." His hands gripped the steering wheel as he swung the car into an alleyway fast enough to squeal the tires.

Amanda held tight to the door, looking anxiously out the windows, totally lost as to where they were, and feeling at the mercy of a madman. 'Desperate' and 'scapegoat' hung in the air.

"Who's setting me up? And how?"

Miguel turned, his face contorted by a deep scowl of derision. "Derek Ashton." He spit the name out. "He's up to his neck in this dirty business. All signs point to his being the mastermind behind the plan to snare you."

Amanda felt a sudden sinking in the pit of her stomach. She turned her head from side to side, looking everywhere and nowhere. She felt cornered. "Derek? But he's in Hong Kong?"

"In Hong Kong where he's stirring the pot with another one of the masterminds. Their plans call for you to be sacrificed—and soon."

'Sacrificed' did it. Amanda reached for what she considered her wild card. "What about the American Embassy?"

Miguel's look was that of a parent telling his child there was no Santa Claus. "They have a mole at the top. You'd be as good as dead."

"If Derek's trying to position me as a sacrificial scapegoat, I need to know when and how." Amanda's voice held a firmness that caused Miguel to turn abruptly. She stared back with eyes turned the blue of steel.

"That it's being planned, I'm certain. With whom and how, I've almost figured out. As to 'whom', near the top is my old friend, Raffy. He's in it up to his eyeballs."

"No wonder you've been like a dog with a bone with Raffy. I wondered if it was, you know…"

"I've got an old score to settle with him, sure, but apart from that, every whiff of corruption that came my way was traced to his direction. I now have evidence that he's one of the key figures behind one of the biggest money laundering schemes that was ever designed. I won't stop until I see him behind bars."

"It sounds as though he may have bitten off more than he can chew."

"Maybe by himself, but he's not alone. He's getting a lot of help from a middle-Eastern shyster named Masta Wunari. Old M.W. is hand in hand with the corrupt of the world." Miguel seemed to warm to his next revelation like a lion to cornered prey. His eyes held hatred and anticipation. "Including a U.S. senator, without a doubt. But there's even bigger fish in the wings." He turned to Amanda and lowered his voice, even though they were safely inside the car. "A more senior U.S. politician has benefited from the Marcos largesse as well. With a promise of more to come, rumor has it he'll look the other way as this deal goes through."

"A senior U.S. politician; meaning...?"

"Where do you think the millions in campaign donations are coming from?"

"But.... How and why would anyone chance it?"

"Not millions, but billions of reasons. Dollars yes, but mainly gold, lots of gold. Yamashita's gold. It's steadily being drained out of the country and many hands want a share in it. I've got proof that a huge haul is soon to be headed out via Hong Kong, thanks to M.W.'s yacht and phony clearances."

"I thought Yamashita's gold was just fodder for the lunch time gossips. Something like the Loch Ness Monster."

"It's real and it's disappearing if our friends, Derek and Raffy, succeed. They're both there in Hong Kong with M.W, right now."

"Back to Derek— no, back to me. What should I do?" Amanda studied Miguel as he turned. His look was one of grief, the kind of grief seen on faces at funeral parlors. "Miguel!" She shouted, not to erase the image but to turn his attention back to driving. He slammed on the brakes as a car cut sharply in front of them. The traffic slowed to a halt, giving him time to form a response. "Derek was sent over under an alias to center-post a plan to throw the heat off their trail. Word has gotten out that whatever methods they were using are in danger of exposure. They can't risk that happening. They have to keep their conduit open."

"Derek center-posting a plan to throw them off the trail" kept ringing in Amanda's ears. *I'm damned if he'll get away with it*, Amanda thought. "Derek Ashton should have learned by now that there's no way I'm about to launder money."

Miguel snorted. "Of course not; but it's enough for him to make it look that way. The Marcos press then becomes focused on the venality of the American banks and their criminal activities, making you the target."

"And Brad; do you really think he'd go along with it and let me hang?"

"What do you think?" Miguel turned a look of chagrin on her. "Everything points to Brad being too deep to ever back-peddle. He's thick as thieves with the De La Serna clan—golf, dinners, and an unbelievable marriage to Caro, the apple of his father's eye."

Amanda was on the verge of sharing what she'd discovered about Brad when a chilling thought intruded. "Not Don De La Serna. He couldn't have known."

"Calm down. I'm not saying that Don Emilio is involved. His father's sudden failing health, probably fostered by Raffy himself, has conveniently set Raffy up for this opportunity to push his own power to the hilt."

Amanda fought to take it all in. "Alright, let's go over what we know. Derek and Raffy are orchestrating Marcos' money movements and they plan to use me as a scapegoat to take the focus off of what's really going on." She turned to Miguel, pausing for emphasis. "I need to know exactly how they intend to go about it."

"What will they do? Listen carefully. I'd watch for..." Miguel halted his reply and began staring intently into the rear-view mirror. He slammed his foot down on the accelerator and whipped the car around the traffic ahead, making an abrupt left-hand turn across two lanes of oncoming traffic, over a divider and onto a service path leading behind the buildings of the botanical gardens. They'd nearly rounded the shelter of the large buildings when a shot rang out. Amanda fell to the floor. When she recovered and looked up, Miguel was slumped forward over the dash, blood streaming from the back of his head.

Amanda grabbed the steering wheel, keeping her head low as she fought to bring the car under control. She pressed the brake pedal to the floor, barely managing to stop it just short of impact with one of the buildings. Pushing the door open, she dropped to the ground, expecting to experience the source of the gunshot as someone approached from the direction of the building.

She leaped to her feet, prepared to run. Her focus cleared, revealing an elderly man, stooped and white-haired and dressed in a gardener's uniform. She relaxed her guarded stance, shocked at the strangeness in her voice as she heard herself say, "Call an ambulance. He's hurt badly. We have to get him to a hospital right away!"

# TWENTY-ONE

The wait was torment. Amanda sat beside Miguel as the curator went to call the police and the ambulance. With each glance at Miguel's face, growing paler by the moment and streaked with drying blood, Amanda wanted to scream. Her rage at their not getting there fast enough consumed her.

Finally the sound of sirens filled the air. Action exploded with the medic's arrival. Her eyes followed their every move. Fast, but not fast enough, she thought as she watched them slowly and carefully position Miguel's body on the gurney and place it within the ambulance. "Is he going to be alright?" She heard someone keep asking, not connecting it with her. Only the strong grip on her arms, drawing her away from the ambulance as, sirens screaming, it tore away, brought her back to reality.

"I have to go with him." She pleaded with the policeman who held her arms. With one hand he held her firmly, while with the other he held her wallet opened to her driver's license.

"Not yet. We can let you go after a few questions." He glanced down at her photo and name. "The car following you suddenly fired on Sr. Santos, your driver? Is that correct, Miss Evans?"

"He's not my driver. He's my friend."

"He's not your driver?" He gave his partner a raised eyebrow as he continued. "What would the owner be doing driving a car like this —without his regular driver?"

Amanda hesitated before responding. "Miguel sometimes chooses to drive himself."

"Not a smart decision. A luxury car is always a target for theft or for the kidnapping of its occupants. We'll make our usual report, but chances are, whoever it was has vanished into the back alleys of Manila by now." He snapped his notepad closed and motioned to another policeman who was photographing the car. "We'll have to impound the car until claimed by the owner." Turning back to Amanda he gave her a sympathetic look. "They've taken Sr. Santos to Manila General Hospital. We can drop you off there on our way back to the station. If we need any more information we'll call you. Where are you staying?"

"The Mandarin Hotel in Makati." She kept repeating the phrase in her mind all the way to the hospital. It served as a mantra to wall off any other thoughts.

Walking into the lobby of the hospital with a police escort caused faces to turn. It also allowed for her swift escort to the emergency room floor. He was in surgery someone said. The same someone took her by the hand and led her over to a sagging chair to wait. Amanda fought against the smothering surreal sensations of the hospital environment. The neutral color of the walls, the scent of antiseptic, the noncommittal expressions on the faces of the nurses, the endless agony of waiting and not knowing, all conspired to unleash the screams she was painfully holding at bay.

An hour in the emergency room and four hours in surgery elapsed before they rolled him into the elevator leading to the intensive care floor. Amanda didn't let Miguel out of her sight, following their course in spite of their refusal to allow her in the restricted access elevator. She ran to the visitor elevator, pressed the button to the seventh floor and walked out to find them pushing his gurney into room seven forty one. A nurse approached swiftly, looking ready to do battle.

"May I see Senor Santos in room seven forty one?"

"Are you a family member?" The nurse raised her eyebrow with a look daring her to claim such a thing.

"No, but I was with him during the accident. My name is Amanda Evans. I'm certain that Sr. Santos would be anxious to see me." Amanda's logic dwindled at the impermeability it had met. "He's a good friend. Please just tell me how he is."

"We can only give information to a blood relative of Sr. Santos." The large, gray-haired, matronly looking nurse delivered her message with a tone of finality and a stern look of self-righteousness. Another one, a tiny, dark-haired, young nurse, gave much the same reply, but with sorrow and compassion filling her eyes as she gave an apologetic shrug of helplessness.

Amanda jumped up and headed for the phone. During the past four hours she'd tried to reach someone at Miguel's home, to no avail. It suddenly occurred to her to try to reach Paco. He'd be puzzled if she failed to keep their dinner meeting.

The phone at his office rang several times before anyone picked it up. Finally a harried voice answered. "International Communications Systems, will you hold please?" Before she could ask for Paco, she found herself listening to some ad for Asia American Airlines. Who else should she call? Miguel's Aunt Florencia, or his office number again? His sister was his closest relative, but poor Ortie was sequestered behind convent walls since her broken engagement to Raffy. Amanda hesitated over Miguel's Aunt Florencia before deciding she was much too emotional where Miguel was concerned and could fall apart at the news. Her sense of frustration escalated. She started to give up on her endless hold for Paco.

Reaching to depress the receiver, she was startled to hear a voice saying, "Sorry to keep you holding. The ambassador is still in a meeting. How may he reach you?"

She left the number for the hospital and left word that she would be unable to meet Senor Ramirez for dinner this evening. Re-dialing

Miguel's number, she was surprised when someone answered. It was Miguel's cousin, Felipe. She vaguely remembered having met him at one of the family dinners. An image surfaced of a brash, young artsy rebel. A silence fell as she gave him the details of Miguel's having been shot.

"Who'd you say this is...the hospital? How is he? When can I see him? Why didn't somebody call me sooner? "

"I'm so sorry, Felipe. My name is Amanda Evans, with Fidelity American Bank. You may not remember me, but we have met before. I was with Miguel in his car when he was shot. I've been trying to reach you." She paused, listening carefully to his repeated questions. "He's out of surgery and in intensive care now. No one will tell me anything. They keep saying that they will only discuss his condition with a relative." Amanda had raised her voce and turned to direct a venomous glare at the older nurse.

"Yes, of course. Manila General, room seven forty one. Seventh floor; turn right when you exit the elevator and walk all the way back to the nurses' station. I'll be waiting for you." She hesitated before adding, "You'll notify the others?"

"I'm not saying a thing until I get there and see what there is to tell them. We'll talk when I get there. Goodbye." The force with which Felipe replaced the receiver left her rubbing her right ear.

Amanda drummed her fingers on the phone book, feeling more brain dead than she had thought. A sense of disbelief penetrated the numb paralysis that had shielded her. She considered calling the office and leaving Nigel a two-word message: "I quit." Being shot at wasn't in her job description. When she had made her choice of a career in the banking world, she figured that the only risks were paper-based.

"Who are you kidding?" Rob responded when she told him why she chose boring merchant banking. "You instantly sought out the one place in banking that sends you to trouble spots to woo millions in flight capital in countries whose foreign exchange laws forbid such activity." She remembered his laugh as he accused her of being a closet-risk-taker if he ever saw one.

If so, she decided, it began with her mother insisting she emulate a super-nice television child whose autographed photo was the only adornment permitted on her bedroom wall. She'd tried to some extent to be as amiable and to smile as sweetly, but felt a sudden fondness for her long-dormant dark side. She stared at the phone. Of course she couldn't call Nigel and leave such a message, but she could savor the image of his response. Put that in your bloody diary, Nigel, she thought, recognizing that anger was her attempt to hold fear at bay.

Her fingers remained inert on the receiver, brow furrowed in thought. Why couldn't she think of anyone to call, and if she were to, what could she say from bugged phones?

Her hand released the receiver and went to her forehead. What about this is connected with her erstwhile colleague, Derek Ashton? The thought stopped her in her tracks. Oh no. He's undoubtedly behind this. She shivered as the image of Miguel lying so pale, hair matted with blood—body so cold and breath so still—filled her. *If Derek is behind this, I won't stop until I make him pay for it, she thought.* Her teeth clenched in rage. She felt resolve move like cold steel up her spine. The intensity of her emotions made the waiting agony.

She reviewed her list of someone she could turn to for support. Not Nigel, not Brad, not Rob, not Vivi, not Mai—and certainly not Derek. The only one that could have helped was lying in the emergency room at death's door. She walked back to the nurse's station to demand information on Miguel's condition.

Like a chorus from Hell, they responded with flatly rehearsed lines: "Miss Evans, as we've told you before, Mr. Santos is restricted to visits by family members only. The doctors can discuss his status only with them. We must insist you follow the rules."

She gritted her teeth and turned away just as the door of the elevator opened on someone looking a lot like Miguel, only edgier. He moved quickly in her direction.

"Amanda? Felipe." He gave her a brief look. "Sure, I remember you." He turned and looked around. "Where's Miguel?"

Without waiting for Amanda's response, he turned towards the nurse. "Take me to him." He short-circuited her look with "I am Felipe de la Garza, Mr. Santos' nearest relative. Take me to him immediately."

"Of course, Senor de la Garza; your cousin is just down the hall." She lowered her voice. "He is not conscious. Doctor Garcia is with him now. He will have to answer your questions. Come right this way please."

Amanda flashed him a look that communicated all the emotion words couldn't express. "Please tell him I'm pulling for him" she whispered to Felipe's retreating back. Seeing her tears, the young, dark-haired nurse came over to her.

"Miss Evans, there is an empty room down the hall if you would like to be alone and rest awhile. I promise I will come for you when Sr. De La Garza is out of Sr. Santos room."

Amanda was grateful for privacy. She tried to frame a prayer for Miguel, but her thoughts kept returning to revenge. She paced the room, giving her emotions full rein. Let him be all right and let me find the person behind it, and, and--. With each replay she felt unable to wait one minute longer. She stopped her pacing, heading towards the door when her name was called.

"Miss Evans?" A soft tap at the door accompanied her name.

"Yes?" She opened the door and saw Felipe standing beside the young nurse.

"Let's go down to the hospital cafeteria and I'll fill you in."

"Tell me now!" He responded slowly, offering her the bare facts.

"His prognosis is guarded. The bullet nearly severed a main artery."

"No!" Amanda turned her face away, refusing to cry.

Felipe put his hand awkwardly on her shoulder. When he spoke it was with all the reassurance his anger would allow. "The doctor says he has a good chance. The next twenty four hours will tell the tale." He steered her gently into the elevator.

"A good chance; what does that mean?" The door opened onto the cafeteria.

Felipe pulled out a chair at the most isolated table. "Sit down. No more details until you get something to eat."

Amanda was surprised at her hunger when he returned with a big bowl of soup and a large pot of chamomile tea.

Felipe began: "The bullet went into the neck from the back and exited the front. It came close to the spinal cord and a main artery to the heart; but, thank God, not close enough to sever either."

Amanda blanched at the picture. "But the surgery; will it impact any part of his spinal cord?"

"Time will tell. Dr. Garcia succeeded in removing as many as possible of the splintered bone fragments, but it's still touch and go."

"Has he come out of the anesthetic? Can I see him?"

"Miguel's still groggy, but he did mumble a few words: "Is Amanda OK?" was all I could make out. When I said "Yes" he was gone again."

Amanda hesitated. "Even so, could I just look in on him?"

"Dr. Garcia said no visitors, not even family, at least not for the time he's in intensive care. It'll be a week before he's stabilized, he said –and then rehab for God knows how long."

A look of total desolation came over Amanda. Felipe squirmed in his chair as he searched for a response. "I tried to get the doc to give his OK for you to see Miguel, but the doc wouldn't hear of it." 'It's critical his neck should heal', he said, 'the slightest movement could kill him.' "That's what convinced me." Felipe shrugged as he held his hands open in a 'What can I say' gesture.

"What's the prognosis?" Amanda turned to Felipe with a look of such questioning intensity that he rushed to answer. "It's too early to tell. He says Miguel has a good chance of coming through this, but…" Felipe couldn't finish the thought. "I'd just love to get my hands on the bastard responsible." His fury echoed Amanda's own. "Did you get a look at the guy that shot him?"

"It happened so fast and I couldn't look back until he was long gone." Images and emotions flooded her mind, forcing her to focus on facts. "I ducked, got up and then was too busy reacting, checking on myself, checking on Miguel and trying to steer the car to a stop."

"Yeah well… if Miguel has any clue, he'll let me know. Right now the trick is to keep him from moving; 'perfectly still', that's the phrase the doc kept using."

"Is there anything I can do?" Amanda's look of frustration mirrored his.

"Nothing for now; how about I drive you back to your hotel. Good thing I didn't take my motorcycle." Felipe stared, pushing his hands nervously down into his pockets as Amanda remained silent. "I'll gladly ask the doc to give you some sleeping pills or something. You must still be in shock." Felipe gave her a boyish look that reminded her of the late James Dean. "I'm damn sorry you had to go through this. There are just too many crazy bastards in my country."

"Thanks, Felipe. I'm going to try to tough it out. And if not, I can always get a sedative from the front desk." Before he could ask again the car had pulled up to the hotel.

"You're sure you'll be alright?" Felipe turned to leave. "I have to get back to the hospital. I'm not leaving Miguel's door tonight."

"Good. I'll gladly spell you tomorrow."

"Maybe I'll take you up on it. I have to go and break the news to the family soon." Felipe left, driving away with a squeal of brakes that caused the doorman's eyebrows to rise.

The door to Amanda's room revealed messages slid below. She picked them up and looked around. No sign of anything unusual. She took it as confirmation that she'd be as safe staying here as anywhere. She set aside the two messages from clients and turned to the one from Paco. His said he'd called the hospital and would call her this evening at seven. There were no messages regarding Don Emilio's status. She tried to put aside a sinking feeling. The remaining message was from Marisa. She'd called only twenty minutes ago, leaving a message to ask Amanda to call her at home as soon as possible.

Amanda took a moment to shed her disheveled outfit and slip into the soft, white, terry-cloth bathrobe. She went over to the mini-bar and poured a glass of wine and settled into the big chair by the phone. Drawing a deep breath, she began to feel that she'd actually pulled out of her shock—or perhaps, just sank even deeper into it. Whatever it was, she felt enough concern over Marisa's message that she pulled the phone closer and dialed.

Marisa grabbed it on the first ring. "I have to talk to you. I brought home—" she paused at the soft click on the line. "You know. Can we meet?" Marisa's voice began to crack.

"Can you come to the hotel now? Bring what you have, we'll order room service and talk." Amanda waited. "Great. I'll look for you in about thirty minutes."

The minute she hung up, the phone rang again. It was Paco. "Amanda, I was worried. I called the number you had left and the hospital answered. What's going on? They wouldn't give me any information except to say that you were not admitted as a patient."

Paco's concerned voice shattered her. Tears started to roll unbidden down her cheeks as she felt an emotional dam begin to break. "I don't know where to begin, Paco. It's such a nightmare." Aware of the need for dissembling on the phone, she somehow managed to communicate Miguel's situation.

"Is Miguel all right? What's the prognosis? " Paco's concern reminded her that, not only did he know him, he had referred him to her as a client.

"He has a good chance, but—"

"From the way you described his maneuvers when he spotted the other car, I'd venture a guess that Miguel may well have recognized the car and its driver."

"How Miguel could have recognized anyone, I'll never know. Everything happened so fast. By the time I turned to look, they'd pulled away." She paused as a thought came to her. "The police said it may have been an attempted kidnapping."

"Maybe." He paused long enough for Amanda to hear his unspoken 'maybe not.' "I don't want to alarm you, but, whatever it was, I want you to consider terminating your trip." Hesitancy had entered his voice. "Your sense that he knew them would suggest something more than a robbery or a kidnapping. Promise me that you'll give serious consideration to leaving Manila as soon as possible."

Amanda hesitated, wondering if she should tell him of Miguel's comment that she'd never make it to the airport. "I promise I'll give it serious thought." She floundered, riveted by the intensity of his concern. Suddenly a well of anxiety flooded her. "Do you think someone might try to finish the job on Miguel? Or me?" She rushed out these last few words, her heart pounding in her throat.

Paco's response was slow and deliberate. "Calm down, Amanda. You've just been through a big shock. Chances are the assailant was just after the car or cash by kidnapping Miguel for ransom." At the echo of shock and fear in her chocked gasp, he rushed to reassure her. "I tell you what. I'll have a look at what the police have found out. In the meantime, please act on my advice. After you hang up from my call, pick up the phone and book your flight out now. That will give me peace of mind as to your security."

"But I can't leave with Miguel..."

"As to Miguel's security, I'll arrange for a series of guards—twenty four hours— posted at his hospital room door."

Amanda led out a sigh of relief. "If you knew how much your words help." At the mention of 'words' Amanda froze. "Oh no, Paco; I'm afraid I've already said too much over this phone, but thank you my friend. Your actions will help me sleep tonight."

"Are you sure you want to stay at the hotel tonight? Ana and I would be honored to have you stay with us. I'll put my car and driver at your disposal. It's completely bulletproof and my driver is the best bodyguard in Manila. Say you'll take me up on it."

"Can I let you know sometime tomorrow? I should be fine for one more night here in the hotel and I'll need to tie up some loose ends, especially if I decide to leave. As far as tomorrow goes, I promise that I'll seriously consider your suggestion and get back to you."

"Very good, my dear." She could detect the note of relief in his voice. "Get a good night's rest and call me as soon as you know your plans. They'll put your call through to me at any time. Good night."

Amanda reluctantly hung up the receiver. If she were to take him up on his offer to stay at his home she'd be afraid that she'd come close to spilling everything into Paco's sympathetic ear. She couldn't do that, for many reasons, chief among them the repercussions such revelations could precipitate. *Just how much had she implied, she wondered?* The ring of the phone interrupted her thoughts.

"Marisa. Come right up." Amanda just had time to pick up her briefcase and draw the other chair up to the coffee table before the knock came.

Amanda opened the door. Marisa stepped in, nervously looking all around. "Are you sure this is all right? I know how busy you are, but I have something important to show you." Marisa hesitatingly placed a large file folder on the table.

"Don't worry about time. I'm glad you came." Amanda turned to the folder and back to a worried look on Marisa's face. "I'm sure this is important, but let's relax just for a bit, shall we? Take a chair and let's decide what sounds good for dinner? She handed Marisa the Room Service menu. "The seafood is excellent. We'll have a glass of wine and enjoy our dinner before we get into the serious stuff." Amanda suddenly slowed the pace of her pitch as she saw it wasn't getting the response she'd expected. Marisa had yet to sit down and was staring, not at the menu, but at the folder. Her expression was that of one knowing that it contained a boa constrictor.

"I can see you're anxious to get down to business. How about if we order something first, and while we're waiting, we'll have a glass of wine and get right into what you've brought? Agreed?"

Marisa smiled, walked over to the chair and sat down. She glanced at the room-service menu, saying, "Very little wine for me please, Miss Amanda."

Do call me "Amanda", between friends; OK?" Amanda smiled as she walked to the mini-bar and took out a bottle of white wine. "While I open this, will you call and order for us? Just order me some sort of fish. Thanks."

Amanda poured two glasses, both three-quarters full. She sipped slowly at hers before Marisa turned back from the phone.

"I hope you like spinach salad. I thought we might share one. I ordered the prawn brochette."

"That sounds perfect. Cheers." Amanda raised her glass. "Now; let's drink to everything working out perfectly." Marisa smiled at Amanda's lighthearted toast and took a healthy swallow of wine before reaching for the file.

"I don't know if I did the right thing. I was so upset when Mr. Gregory threatened to fire me. Anyway, I decided to go back and pull all the copies of the other wire transfers for these accounts."

"How many were there?"

"There were fourteen; for a total of one hundred and ten million dollars."

"One hundred and ten million dollars!" Amanda fought to bring her shock and the level of her voice down.

"I made two copies. They're all here." Marisa pointed to the file with pride as Amanda reached for it. "It was lucky I did." Marisa said, her voice taking on an air of perplexity that caused Amanda to look up from the file and listen closely. "Mr. Gregory has been acting so strange. He came back to the office right after you left, shouted at me, then apologized and said he didn't mean it about firing me. He said that he was just worried about losing this business and he swore he never meant to suggest that I do anything against bank policy."

Amanda slowly shook her head. "But that should have put you more at ease."

"Yes, but there's more. Today, just before I left, he had a phone call come in on his private line. He was on it for so long and looked terrible when he finally came out. He immediately started to tear through all the wire-transfer files. It looked like he removed the originals of every wire transfer relating to these customers."

"Lucky you'd already made copies."

"I was worried when he started going through them, but I'd been careful to put the originals back exactly as I found them."

"I'm sure his actions aren't to do with you."

"Good." Marisa let out a long sigh. "I copied all of the Authorized Signature forms too. Do you think I did wrong?"

"No, Marisa; please don't worry. You did everything right. To take original documents would be wrong, but to have copies of something that the bank may need is very helpful."

"What should I do now?" The level of anxiety in Marisa's long look told Amanda just how much she needed her guidance.

"Go about your business exactly as before. Keep your eyes and ears open. If those originals vanish, let me know. Oh, one more thing. Can you find out more about the principals behind Tennyson Ltd. and Milton Ltd.?"

Before she could answer, a knock, followed by "Room Service", caused them both to jump. Amanda opened the door to the scent of seafood. Marisa was silent until the waiter had left. She turned to Amanda with a frown.

"I think I know how to get that information, or some of it. I'll call you when I have it and you can let me know when to meet with you to go over it."

"Good; but let's postpone that discussion before our dinner is cold."

When they both had savored the salad and were well into finishing their seafood, Amanda turned to Marisa. "Are these copies the only ones you have?"

"Yes. I'll be happy to be rid of both of them."

Amanda fell silent, thinking of who she could trust to receive the envelope's contents. Brad didn't report to Nigel, but the whole mess seemed to tie in with IPB's clients. At any rate, she decided, Nigel would know to whom and how and when to reveal the envelope's contents.

"I was thinking that, just to be on the safe side, one copy should be sent out right away via courier to Nigel Taylor. You always get into the office before anyone else, right? Could you prepare a courier envelope to Mr. Taylor's mail code and get it off in the early morning mail pick up tomorrow?"

"I can do better than that. I'll take it right downstairs to the express-mail company office and send it out separately. That way, just in case Mr. Gregory wants to send something to head office, he won't put it in the same envelope and ask me what I'm sending to Nigel Taylor. But what about the other copy? I'd be worried sick if they were in the office." She hesitated. "Maybe you want to take the second copy with you?" Marisa looked beseechingly at Amanda.

"Hmm… let me sleep on what to do with the second copy. In the meantime could you hide them safely at your home?"

Marisa's frown belied her slow response. "I guess; but if you decide not to take them with you, please let me know that Nigel Taylor received his copy so I can destroy the second set. I don't want to be responsible for them one minute longer than I have to." She changed the subject, but not her level of concern. Her voice shook as she asked: "What do you think might happen to our office? I really need to keep my job."

Amanda reached out to take her hand. "Don't worry, Marisa. In the worst case Mr. Gregory would be the one to go. You and the office would certainly remain. The new department head, Mr. Carter, may make some changes, but I very much doubt that it would mean closing the Manila operations."

Marisa's deepening frown prompted Amanda to continue. "In any event, I'll be sure to give you a strong recommendation in writing, with emphasis on your honesty, your focus on doing a good job and your loyalty to the bank and its policies."

"Thank you, Amanda. When will you be leaving?"

"That's the big question. I'm scheduled to depart Saturday. But I may leave for Hong Kong as early as tomorrow night if I can book space. There are a few things I need to take care of first." She withheld any mention of Miguel, aware that Marisa had all the anxiety she could handle. "I'll call you before I leave. If I do decide to take the second copy, I'll arrange to meet you to pick them up. Meanwhile, don't hesitate to call me if Brad gives you any worries. I'll be in Hong Kong through next Thursday before I fly back to San Francisco on Friday night." She paused to see how Marisa was taking it all in.

Marisa seemed in deep thought. "You do have my home phone number, Amanda. I mean, just in case you need to discuss anything you don't want Mr. Gregory to know."

Amanda glared over at the telephone. "I know your concern over trusting these phones, but if you get any more information on those accounts—especially the names of the principals—make a copy of them and inter-office mail anything suspicious to Nigel Taylor."

Marisa let out a deep sigh, seeming to release her anxiety in favor of sudden exhaustion as she loosened a deep yawn before standing.

Amanda found herself duplicating those yawns with a sudden awareness of her own overwhelming exhaustion. "What say we call it a night?"

Marisa gathered up the file copies and moved towards the door. Amanda followed, pausing to give her, not the light social kisses, but a firm handshake. "Good job! Remember, call me and just say, 'Let's have lunch', if anything comes up."

Too tired to shower, Amanda climbed into bed, certain she'd be sound asleep the minute her head hit the pillow. She was—until she awoke with a racing heart and a rush of fear. Her bedside clock registered three AM. The dark silence of her room seemed ominously oppressive, the sleepless hours until dawn endless. Not even the thought of booking an early departure could soothe her growing uneasiness.

Amanda jumped up, startled at having forgotten to call the airlines and check on a flight out. She dialed Philippine Airlines, only to get a response that said they'd be happy to reconfirm her Saturday flight to Hong Kong, but no seats were available before then.

Amanda's spirit's plummeted. She hadn't realized how much she'd counted on being able to leave early. "Would you please waitlist me on your next Hong Kong flight?"

"Our next flight to Hong Kong shows nineteen people wait-listed ahead of you. I've added your name, but I would suggest you call later today to check on any cancellations."

*I might as well have waited until morning*, Amanda thought, as she tossed and turned. And yet she must have dosed, for she awoke with a start from a nightmare of Miguel.

She glanced at the clock: six AM. Grabbing the phone she dialed the hospital. "I'll be there in an hour, Felipe. How is Miguel doing?"

"No change in Miguel. See you whenever you get here."

She hung up and looked at the room service tray with its remnants of last night's dinner. Marisa's revelations tantalized her. I'm going to need a double dose of caffeine to handle this morning, she decided. She dialed room service.

A cold shower helped. Her tan linen pantsuit would have to do for one more day, she thought, as she slipped it on, feeling relieved that she'd cleared the deck of any client calls. Miguel's shooting incident and the Manila office wire-transfers were uppermost in her mind, but not erasing her major concern for Don Emilio. She began to go over her options, leaving her wondering just what to tell Nigel—and when?

She'd have to prepare him before he received Marisa's package in his courier mail. She let loose long, deep breath thinking: *That gives me nearly three whole days. I can either try to reach him at home or wait until the courier mail hits his desk.* Opting for expediency, she decided to call him as soon as she arrived in Hong Kong, convinced he'd have apoplexy right at his desk if she sprung it on him at work.

Amanda shuddered at the repercussions her disclosures would precipitate, feeling an icy lump form in her solar plexus. Whatever the consequences, she knew she was going to have to go the mile.

She gave a startled jump at the knock on the door. Her heart slowed to normal when she remembered she'd ordered room service. After the smiling waiter removed last nights' remnants and spread a white linen table-setting and departed, she looked at the mini-breakfast, surprised that, for the first time ever, she'd not ordered mangoes. She gulped down two quick cups of coffee and a few bites of pastry before forcing her mind to some semblance of rationality.

Staring off into space, she carefully reviewed all that had taken place. She knew that her opponents must not be underestimated. Her first decision would be to take Paco up on his offer of a safe car and driver. She picked up the phone and dialed his number. While it rang, she nervously folded and refolded the scrap of paper she had written his private number on and idly stuck it in her pocket.

"Of course, my dear, I'd be happy to see to it." His prompt response revealed his relief. "I'll have Mickey over there in ten minutes. Now, to reassure your old friend, I trust you've booked your flight."

"I tried Philippine Airlines last night with no luck. Looks as though I'm meant to stay on and tie up a few loose ends."

"Leave Manila as soon as you can." Amanda couldn't remember ever hearing Paco sound so firm. "I'm on the board of Pan Am. Let me see what accommodations I can get for you."

"Well I..."

"No ifs, ands or buts. How about First Class to Hong Kong and on to San Francisco, courtesy of your good friend Paco? I'll check on the availability of flights for tonight and tomorrow. How long do you plan on being in Hong Kong before departing for San Francisco?"

"Dear Paco, you are such a special friend; but you know that I couldn't accept such a favor. Conflict of interest, as the bank would call it."

"I'll not hear of your declining. It's nothing for them to provide me with an empty seat in First Class in place of your coach seat, and at no expense to me, so don't even consider it a gift. Just reserve judgment until we see what they can do."

Amanda let out a sigh, relief filling her response: "What would I do without you?"

Within fifteen minutes, Mickey rang to say he was at her service and would be in the lobby when she needed him. The sight of his burly figure, his no-nonsense face with its ever-present smile, filled Amanda with a sense of ease.

"We're headed for Manila General Hospital, Mickey. Let me leave word with the desk as to where I'll be, in case someone needs to reach me." She walked over and gave the concierge the phone number of the hospital and turned to Miguel as they walked to the car. "Did you know that your namesake, Miguel Santos, had been shot yesterday?"

"Yes; the Ambassador told me. He said it was someone following him in a car, right? And you were there with him." He shook his head. "I think your bank had better consider paying you—what do they call it—hazard pay?" He laughed at the cleverness of his joke. The sight and sound brought a smile to her face. "Well, Miss Evans, you can relax; you're with me in a car that is attack proof." Mickey grinned. "And its driver is even more so." As he walked out of the lobby door ahead of her, he was careful to check every direction before escorting her swiftly into the back seat, locking all doors with one quick movement.

The hospital parking lot was full as Mickey pulled up to the front door and swiftly escorted Amanda to the entryway. She thanked him, saying: "I plan to be here until around two o'clock, Mickey. You can take off or do whatever you need to until then. Thanks for your excellent chauffeuring."

"Yeah, well I noticed that you only looked over your shoulder twenty or thirty times during the ride here." He laughed again and reassured her that he'd be around all day just in case she needed him.

*I can see how expatriates like Brad could become addicted to this level of service,* she thought as she rode up in the elevator. She walked briskly out of the elevator and up to the nurse's station, relieved to see that even the prissy matron was obsequious today.

"Oh yes, Miss Evans, Sr. De La Garza is expecting you."

Felipe walked up to her, eyes twinkling in spite of no sleep. He brushed her cheeks with light kisses of greeting, taking a moment to step back and give her a long look. "You're a mighty powerful lady. Dr. Garcia has actually agreed to let you have five minutes with Miguel."

"Thank you, thank you." Amanda grabbed him in a warm hug, planting a non-Filipino, non-sedate kiss firmly on his cheek.

"Don't thank me." He shrugged, looking down to hide his confusion. "Miguel somehow must have browbeaten Garcia into agreeing. Oh, by the way, I'd hold off on those kisses with Miguel if I were you." It was said lightly but Amanda recognized concern behind his words.

"Trust me. Five minutes. No kisses and no movement of any kind for Miguel."

"Well then, what's keeping you? Off with you." He opened the door and softly walked away, leaving her to enter into a veritable bower of greenery and scents. Her eyes lit up as she saw Miguel's eyes flutter and open.

"How are you, my dear friend?" She whispered, batting away tears as she pulled a chair up close to his bed. .

"They can't kill me." His faint voice belied his assertion. It so obviously pained him to make even these few guarded movements of his mouth. "Promise—go home." His eyes fought to convey the urgency and emphasis his voice could not.

"Please don't try to talk anymore, Miguel. I promise; someone is checking the airline schedules for me even now." Her eyes went to the tubes, the large brace holding his head so rigid, the paleness of his face as his eyes closed. "How can I leave you in this condition though?" His eyes fluttered open. "Please don't try to answer and don't open your eyes. Just hear my words. I promise you that I'll make that decision to depart right away." She began to move back toward the door. "But if you need me, I'll be back— no matter what. Rest now, my friend." She turned to leave before Miguel could hear the sob that stuck in her throat, begging for relief. Softly closing the door to his room she let loose the painful thought that this could be her last look at him.

"They're keeping him pretty doped up." Felipe said as she walked back to the waiting area. "When I was in the room it seemed like he wanted to say something important, but his life depends on his not even trying to speak."

"I know. It was the same with me. He got out only a couple of words, namely 'Go, Now'. I promised I'd leave as soon as I could book a flight."

"Maybe, with a week of total immobility, he'll be out of the woods." He saw that his words hadn't lessened the look of anxiety on Amanda's face. "I second the motion you should leave right away. You can't do a thing except keep him worried if you stay in Manila."

"You're right, Felipe. The first minute with him convinced me of that."

"Good. He'll rest easy and begin to recover fast when he knows you're safely on an airplane headed for home." His look turned even more anxious. "Well, I have to get going. I have to break the news to Aunt Florencia and Ortie. If you can hold the fort for an hour or two I'd really appreciate it."

"It's yours. Take as much time out as you need." Amanda followed as Felipe headed for the elevator. The door opened and a crazed looking man got out. One glance at his retreating back as he lumbered up to the nurse's station reminded Amanda of Paco's suggestion. She drew Felipe aside just before he could enter the elevator.

"What do you think about having a guard posted at Miguel's door? I know it might only have been attempted theft, but what if it was Miguel's death they were after?" She lowered her voice as she glanced back to see if anyone was in earshot.

"You might be on to something." His eyebrows went up. "And I know just the fellow, a former cop out on medical leave. He's as tough as they come. I'll line it up while I'm out today."

Amanda let loose a sigh of relief as she stretched up to plant a quick kiss on his cheek. "Thanks. You know I dearly love your cousin." She turned before tears could come and headed back to the chair in front of Miguel's room.

She was lost in thought when the soft sound from the gummed soles of the nurse's shoes caused her to look up. The young, dark-haired woman smiled at her and whispered that she needed to change Miguel's bedpan and could Amanda step away while she went in. Amanda nodded, whispering back that she'd go down and bring up a juice from the cafeteria.

When she returned she found that the older nurse had been looking for her. "Oh, Miss Evans, there you are. Sorry to bother you, but you had two calls while you were gone. A Mr. Derek Ashton, on the line from Hong Kong, was the first caller. He said he'd call back in ten minutes. When his call comes in, I can transfer it to the phone in the empty room that Sr. Felipe Santos had been working in. The second call was from your hotel. They said a Mr. Ramirez called to say you were reserved on Pan AM's four o'clock flight to Hong Kong this afternoon. He asked you to call as soon as you could to confirm the reservation.

"Thank you", Amanda peered closer to read her name badge: 'Senora Perez'."

"De nada, senorita." She said before turning back to her duties, leaving Amanda feeling a rush of emotions as to whether she wanted any calls, certainly not calls from Derek Ashton, forwarded to her. Too late; no sooner had she arrived at that decision when Nurse Perez returned to say Mr. Ashton was on the line.

"What gives? Why are you in a hospital?" Before she could decide if that was fear in his voice, he'd reverted to sarcasm. "One of your dear clients on their way out, I presume. Hope you've signed them up for a trust before they gasp their last." Derek's comments sounded strained. He silently awaited her reply. His act was definitely wearing thin, she thought, and totally inappropriate for a murderer.

*God damn him*! She thought as she bit back the accusation. "You might say that. It's Miguel Santos who's at death's door. Someone shot him while he and I were driving to a meeting. I don't suppose you'd know anything about such matters, would you?"

"Wait a minute; say that again! Slow down and tell me exactly what happened. When? And who was involved? Are you all right?"

"As to your first question, you probably know better than I do the answers to what happened and why and exactly who was involved, 'Mr. Ashton', or whoever you are. As far as my being alright, I'll be a lot more alright as soon as my plane lifts off the tarmac at four o'clock today."

"Hold everything. You can't just take off like that. We have to talk. You know it's impossible over these phones. Don't leave until I get there."

"I don't owe you anything. In fact, whatever house of cards you've built for yourself here in the Philippines, you had better get ready for it to come crashing down upon your ears; and I'm just the one who'll give it that final nudge."

"Stop right now. Don't say another word. Promise you won't make any rash moves until I get there and can sort things out."

"Right; like assuring me of the room next to Miguel's maybe? Thanks, but no thanks. The staff here is OK, but I wouldn't want to get to know them any better." She was just warming up when he interrupted her.

"I have to take a later flight from Hong Kong. That should put me in Manila tomorrow night. Promise you won't do anything rash. At least postpone your decision until we've talked. Just stay put. I'll see you soon!"

*Not on your life. No, not on my life*, Amanda thought as she hung up. With a surge of rage and renewed determination she dialed PAN AM to confirm her four o'clock departure for Hong Kong.

# TWENTY-TWO

Felipe no sooner had walked through the door than Amanda told him of her decision to leave for Hong Kong at four o'clock. "I'm glad. I'm convinced that just knowing that will help Miguel more than anything will. You'd better run, though, if you're going to make it. It takes nearly an hour to drive to the airport." Felipe nudged her in the direction of the door. She gave one last glance towards Miguel's closed door and a quick farewell abrazo to Felipe.

Mickey was waiting in front, lounging in the shade while flirting with a young nurse who had taken a cigarette break. As Amanda approached he quickly opened the car door. "Where to next?"

"Take me back to the hotel, Mickey. I've decided to leave for Hong Kong this afternoon. How much time will you need to get me to the airport for a four o'clock flight?"

"That time of the afternoon, hmm...say around fifty minutes or so. If you need to check luggage and purchase tickets we should leave your hotel by two thirty. Will that leave you enough time?"

The car pulled smoothly up in front of the hotel's entrance as Amanda reviewed her remaining task list before responding. "I can do it. Wait in the lobby. I'll be down by two thirty." She hurried towards the reservation desk.

"Please have my room bill ready for a two fifteen check out."

The hotel manager walked up with a look of concern. "You're leaving, Miss Evans? But we show you reserved through Saturday morning. Any problems?"

"Everything's fine. I'd appreciate it if you would please have my bill ready. I have to make a four o'clock flight. Thank you." At his polite agreement, she dashed to the elevator, reviewing her remaining 'To Do's', remembering that she'd promised to call Marisa and Paco when she'd made her departure decision.

Opening the closet and the drawers, she began tossing everything into her suitcase. She'd worry about getting everything sorted after arriving in Hong Kong. Her tan pantsuit was looking a bit tired, but she decided to keep it on anyway. As soon as everything was packed and the suitcase closed, she dialed the Manila office.

"Amanda, I was about to call you." Marisa lowered her voice. "Mr. Gregory is out of the office for lunch with one of our clients from Tennyson Ltd." Marisa's voice dropped to a whisper. "It's exactly who I thought. I mean the family and all. The clients we discussed."

Amanda got it—the principals on the wire transfer accounts. Convinced her phone was being tapped, she responded reassuringly, "That's nice, Marisa. I appreciate your efforts, but I won't have any time to meet with any more friends this trip. I'm leaving for Hong Kong at four. I'll phone when I've settled into my hotel in Hong Kong. Thanks for everything."

Marisa sounded more than a little nonplussed. "Could you call in on Mr. Gregory's direct line, around two Manila time? It's his lunchtime and we'd have the use of a private phone." She rushed to erase any peremptory tone, "Whatever you decide, I'll be waiting for your call."

"Perfect! How about my shipment of courier mail?"

"It went out first thing this morning, direct from the courier company office." Marisa hesitated before adding; "I sent the copies to your hotel. I was worried about keeping them at home. Is that OK?"

Amanda tried to hide her uneasiness. "Yes, of course. I'll check with the desk to see if they've arrived. Thanks for all your help. If anyone should call, please tell them I had to leave earlier than expected for Hong Kong."

"Yes, of course." Marisa's voice held a strange blend of polite farewell with an overtone of anxiety. "Have a safe journey, Miss Amanda. Be sure to let me know how things are going with you while in Hong Kong and upon your return to San Francisco."

Amanda reassured her she would be in touch, hung up and promptly dialed Paco. "Paco; I'm so glad you're in. I'm on my way out the door and will be headed for Hong Kong on the four o'clock flight. Thanks to you, my friend. And thanks for the loan of Mickey. He's waiting to get me to my flight on time."

"That's exactly what I wanted to hear, my dear. Make sure that Mickey waits until your plane has left. I want to know you're safely off the tarmac and on your way. Get going so you don't miss it and be sure to call me as soon as soon as you reach Hong Kong."

Amanda gave one last look around the hotel room and made for the lobby. Emilio, the manager, had her bill ready.

"I didn't charge you for any part day, Miss Evans." He seemed eager to reassure one of the hotel's steady clients as he continued: "We shall be sorry to see you go. Do come back soon. Shall I give any forwarding number if calls come in for you?"

"Refer them to Marisa at the local office of Fidelity American Bank if you would please." As she wrote down the rep office's general phone number, she remembered the envelope Marisa was to have sent. "Oh, and I'm expecting a package. Has it arrived?"

Emilio looked a bit sheepish. "How could I have forgotten? Something just came in." He walked back into his office, returning with a sealed manila envelope. She glanced over at Mickey who was nervously pacing in the background. "I'm sorry, but I must dash or I'll miss my plane." She grabbed the envelope. "Thank you. Good-bye."

The bellman had already placed her luggage in the trunk of Paco's Mercedes. As soon as she entered, Mickey pulled her car door closed, made certain all were locked and smoothly drove away.

It was a wild ride through peak Manila traffic so Amanda didn't interrupt Mickey's concentration with idle chatter. She was much too busy reviewing her decision to leave. She would have promised Miguel anything, but her decision to leave had been cemented with the evidence she now had. *It should be enough for the bank and the FBI to take it from there,* she thought. She let the image of the plane lifting off, leaving Manila behind, sink in as a reality. After landing in Hong Kong, the first thing she'd do would be to let Nigel know everything that had transpired. She had copies of the illegal wire transfer documentation and the other copies should reach him soon. An image of his reaction, and the potential repercussions to their department, suddenly filled her.

She shook her head, forcing her thoughts just on the moment. It's Nigel's problem as to how he takes it and what he does. Her own accountability ended when she divulged all that she knew to him. She let out a sigh of relief.

A sudden squeal of brakes as a car jockeyed around their car, tipped her thoughts from rational to panic. *Oh my God, what if I don't make it? I could end up like Miguel, only worse.* She turned her head, looking right, left and back. The memory of the shot that felled Miguel reverberated through her. No sounds followed as their car continued on its course. She mentally replayed her internal mantra: *"Just one more hour and I'll be gone."*

Mickey sensed her nervousness. He turned with a reassuring look. "Almost there Miss Evans; relax—you're in good hands. Don't worry. The traffic is lighter than usual and it's only three twenty."

She forced herself to smile and lean back into her seat. "I couldn't have made it without you, Mickey."

Mickey grinned wide as he turned off the main highway. Billboards advertising airline services announced that they were just entering the airport departure area. Her heart lifted at the thought of nearly being home free. The minute those wheels lift off the tarmac I'm going to order champagne and celebrate, she decided, letting out her breath.

The airline's counter marked "First Class" had no line. The smiling attendant swiftly handled the processing of her documents.

Amanda could feel Paco's hand in the extra efficiency. Their assured manner helped to calm her. The woman finished her explanation of the proper boarding gate, airport tax and preferred boarding for First Class. With a broad smile and a little flourish she reached to one side and produced a colorful, cellophane-wrapped package. "This is a little something special from your biggest admirer. He told me how much you loved mangos, and since you couldn't take the fresh ones into the States—Voila!"

Amanda looked down at the label clearly showing through the packaging: "Luxury Grade-Dried Mangos". *What a dear Paco was to send them, she thought.* She thanked the attendant, turned to Mickey and said, "Please tell Ambassador Ramirez how happy I was at his thoughtful gift." She held out her hand. "Thank you and good-bye."

Mickey reached for her remaining carry-on bag. "Hold on there, Miss Amanda. I have instructions to stay with you until you're on that plane. Let's get going over to the airport tax window. Do you have the customs and immigration forms filled out?"

"I'm afraid not. If you'll take this money and pay my airport tax, I'll fill out the forms right next to you." The tax window had a couple people in line. Mickey waited as Amanda walked to an empty counter alongside and began the routine filling out of her customs forms. "List total of all goods purchased, quantities of alcohol, etc." It was the usual stuff. The critical section was the part that read: "Are you taking more than ten thousand U.S. dollars (or peso equivalent) in currency or negotiable items, out of the country? If so, you must declare all details." With a sigh of relief and the fleeting thought, *do they think I'd really be so stupid?* She checked "No" with a flourish.

Mickey had completed the payment of her airport tax with its official stamp. They headed towards the customs and immigration line, the last hurdle before boarding the plane.

"This is where we part, then." Amanda's eyes, as she turned to Mickey, filled with gratitude and relief.

"Not yet. Usually they don't let anyone come through those gates except passengers, but the Ambassador said if we ask for Adrian he'll let me see you right through and onto the plane."

"The Ambassador thinks of everything. Tell him he's my hero." She was still smiling, looking up into the face of the somber looking customs official, when someone grabbed her arms from behind and drew her away from the line. "Mickey, what …?" She shouted as she turned to see that two men, burlier than Mickey himself, were laboring to keep him from freeing his hands from their grasp.

Mickey struggled valiantly, scowling as he said: "Let her go now, or you'll be sorry you ever laid hands on her."

Amanda looked up at her captors as they swiftly propelled her and Mickey through a door marked "Private-No Admittance". She gasped in shock as she walked through the door and the man turned to face her. His mouth curled into a contemptuous snarl.

"What right do you have to treat me like this? Release me this instant. Let Mickey go. He hasn't done anything and neither have I!"

"Let her go, Pablo. As to the driver, take him out of here. Get rid of him." Noticing the over-zealous look in their eyes, he amended his order. "Take care to do nothing that'll raise any suspicions, but take him as far out of the city as you can—and deal with him. Now, get going!"

As they opened the door to leave, Amanda saw her chance. She rushed towards it, shouting: "Help! Don't kill him!" In the next second she felt herself hurled against the wall with a blow that sent her reeling towards the edge of unconsciousness.

"No more of that! Understand? One more such stupid outburst and I'll have to take things into my own hands."

Her vision began to clear enough to register the seriousness of his threat. His eyes were slits of steely determination, his jaw rigid with cold disdain.

"Who are you? What do you want with me? I have a plane to catch. If I'm not on it, people will become alarmed."

"I'm Inspector Horne of the Espionage Division of the Philippine Federal Law Enforcement Agency, formerly with the Green Berets." His next words were edged with disgust as he spit them out. "And you are a stupid thief." He continued in a more matter-of-fact tone. "We had a report that you were illegally moving large quantities of foreign currency out of the country."

"That's not true."

"While my assistants were detaining you, a customs official went through all of your belongings and confiscated the illegal item. Stupid female! Did you really think you could get away with hiding a million dollar check in the bottom of a box of dried fruit?"

"A check? I never put any check anywhere." Her thoughts were racing nearly as fast as her heart. *If Paco didn't send the dried mangoes, then...* "Who sent that fruit? How did it get there? And whose check is it?"

"Shut up; I've heard enough of your useless denials! I'm here to take you into custody. You'll have a chance to bore someone else with your stupid questions when you get booked."

"Booked? But..." He took a step towards her. One look into his eyes told her she wasn't dealing with a man to be reasoned with. She quieted down, indicating an acceptance of whatever was to come next. Inspector Horne took her arm roughly and in one quick move clasped handcuffs on her. She stifled a gasp of shock and pain.

The drive back into Manila was a blur as her thoughts volleyed between Mickey and prayers for his safety, and herself and dread at what lay in store for her. She tried to make sense of it. Closing her eyes and putting her head back, she attempted a logical review.

*Who planted that check—and why? Could it possibly be Raffy and his thugs? Then Brad would have to be in on it. But Brad wouldn't go along with anything that would subject me to such brutal behavior. Would he?* She shuddered as her mind raced for a solution. What can I do? Who should I call? Do they let prisoners have one call here? Horror began to edge out all rationality. I could disappear and no one would be the wiser. She forced herself to hold at bay any such thoughts. I'll be damned if I'll let this fascist thug know he intimidates me. She drew herself up, gathering every shred of dignity about her as the car pulled up behind a monolithic, once regal, but now decaying, government building. It looked as though they were in one of the seedier parts of Central Manila.

"All out; get moving'!" He steered her briskly through a rear door of the building. They seemed to be expecting her. Someone walked up and took her other arm.

"OK Jake; your part is done. We'll be taking over from here." A uniformed man, less brusque but equally firm, took hold of her elbow.

"It's alright by me. She's all yours. Idiot American; what gall!" He swaggered up to her, defiling her with a look of abject contempt before turning and walking out the door.

"Step into the booking office and we'll take your statement." Her new captor led her into a drearily gray office. There were two other men, one sitting behind a massive desk and another off to his left side with an ancient Dictaphone machine in front of him.

"Please, sir." She addressed herself to the man behind the desk, the man whose nameplate identified him as Inspector Gregorio Garza. He looked up, surprising her by his stern, but wise and intrinsically kind, expression. He reminded her of Father Precipio, the benevolent Filipino priest of Paco's parish. "If you'd remove these handcuffs, I promise I won't try to leave." He was silent as he stared at her with curiosity.

"Why a young woman such as you would risk taking large checks out of our country I can't imagine." He turned to address the man who had accompanied her. "Release those handcuffs. She couldn't get further than three feet, even if she were foolish enough to try." Turning back to Amanda, he continued in a tone of weariness and disillusionment. "Now, let's hear your story. Remember that every word you say will be taken down and could be used against you."

Amanda began with a recitation of the bare facts. She had been visiting the Philippines and was called to a meeting in Hong Kong. She arrived at the airport and was given the box of fruit by the airport attendant. There was no card, but she assumed it was from a friend.

The man glanced down at a piece of paper on his desk. "Do you know someone by the name of "Miguel Santos"? There was a note with the envelope containing the check." He drew out a piece of paper and began reading. "Amanda, be sure to keep this with you. It should take care of you always." It's signed: 'Your friend, Miguel Santos.' Sounds like a pretty generous payoff to me. What do you have to say for yourself?"

"But, but, but..." The familiar words suddenly registered. "Oh no; that note was on my gift!" Amanda watched as his eyebrow rose in shock. "Not the mangoes. Miguel had sent me this special thing, something you call an 'anting-anting'." She saw the inspector's face change expression to one of intense puzzlement. "A strange man had stared at me so viciously that..." She began again. "It was just that Miguel wanted to be sure it wasn't the evil eye, so he sent this necklace thing to my room. With it was this note."

"This note?" Inspector Garza examined the note more closely.

"Both the note and the charm vanished out of my room the next day. Someone took it. Don't you see? You can call the Mandarin Hotel and ask. I had them looking everywhere for it"

"This Miguel might be thoughtful enough to send a necklace, but to write a check for a million dollars on one of his own accounts seems a bit excessive as a token of friendship. Not to mention that it's completely against the foreign exchange laws of the Philippines." He paused as he reached towards a familiar manila envelope. Amanda's stomach lurched as she recognized her wire transfer copies. "I suppose he gave you this as well? Some friend he is to think of putting you at such a risk. As to the note, it sounds pretty far-fetched for you to try to link it to missing jewelry. We're going to be bringing Senior Santos, your generous partner, in tonight. We'll see if your stories add up." He turned to respond to a whispered message. "What's that, Jaime; a phone call from Manila General concerning Senior Santos? I'll take it. Yes, on this phone."

He turned away as Amanda strained to catch some sense of his conversation. He hung up and turned to her with a strange look. "It seems your friend Santos is in the hospital's intensive-care ward with a bullet to the head." He let out a sigh. "Most curious; seems that someone may want you both out of the way." He gave Amanda a more probing look at this latest bit of news.

"No, you idiot, don't take that down!" He turned to the transcriber, who had been diligently taking down every word. "Whatever you may think young lady, we are a civilized country. Our law is based on your own, and is adhered to just as scrupulously. In that respect you are allowed one phone call before you are booked and held pending trial. Give some thought to whom that call should be directed. I shall give you…" He glanced at his watch, "until six fifteen to make up your mind."

He glanced down at the papers in front of him. Amanda's mind swung wildly through a mental list of who to call. *Brad, to get the rep office's attorney to defend her? No, if he were in on this, that call would be wasted. Nigel, to contact the Consulate here to arrange a defense for me? It's the middle of the night there, and even if Nigel didn't have a heart attack, his call to the consulate here would produce nothing. It's nearly six and only minimal staff would be there. I need someone right here, right now, someone powerful enough to pull some strings for me. Paco… I'll call Paco. He'll know what to do. Anyway, I'll need to tell him about Mickey.* A sudden urgency overtook her at the thought as she turned to the inspector. "I've decided who to call. What if no one answers? May I redial?"

"A reasonable period of time will be allowed for you to place this one call to only one phone number. There is a cubicle right over there. You will be observed at all times, so don't be so foolish as to attempt anything."

"I won't. Thank you." She was escorted to a cubicle containing one small rectangular table, one chair and one telephone. Her hands shook as she tried to remember Paco's phone number. She suddenly remembered stuffing the note with his number into her pant's pocket. She sighed in relief at its reassuring crackle as she drew it out and began to dial. "Please God. Let him answer" she prayed under her breath. His private line rang and rang. Why isn't someone answering, she wondered? Her heart sank as she remembered that he had told her that no one answered his private line but himself. Where could he be at this hour? After fifteen hollow rings, she slowly replaced the receiver.

She gazed nervously at the man assigned to make certain she was under surveillance at all times. He stood close by the entrance to her cubicle, staring noncommittally back at her. She mouthed "no answer" to his unheeding, uncaring presence and turned to redial. Maybe I miscalled his number. She stared penetratingly at each separate digit as she painstakingly dialed their exact sequence. Her heart lifted at the thought that this time it would be picked up by the third ring, the fifth, or surely by the eighth. After the twenty-second ring, she reluctantly let go of her lifeline.

"Time's up. We'll book you and assign you a cell now. You may try to place that same number you just called in the morning." The priest look-alike seemed to soften a bit as he saw the anguish on her face. Her booking was worse than any bad movie. At the sight of a woman entering the room, her guard shoved something towards her and said in a bored tone of voice, "Take this garment and follow Miss Cisco. She'll show you to the extermination room and the showers and return you here for your prisoner registration number."

*This can't be real,* Amanda kept thinking. The woman that took her firmly by the arm made the head nurse at the hospital seem like Little Mary Sunshine. She gave her a glance as contemptuous as someone spotting a cockroach, held her tightly to her sweaty armpit and dragged her in the direction of a room marked: "Sanitation and Showers."

"Here's the program. Strip down completely for an internal search. When I'm through searching you, get under that showerhead marked "Disinfectant." After you've been under it for a full five minutes, step right across here and into that shower there. Got that? Strip— Now!"

"But my clothes? What happens to them-- and to my luggage?" Amanda couldn't bring herself to confront the real question: *What happens to me?*

"That's not my problem. Get undressed now. They want you back in there in ten minutes." She started to reach for Amanda's jacket.

"I'll do it." Amanda stepped out of her clothes, but not before making certain she had memorized Paco's phone number. She placed the crumpled piece of paper carefully back inside her pants pocket, carried her clothes over to the wooden bench and positioned her shoes neatly alongside. Somehow she'd managed to block out the 'Search' part. When the matron shoved her onto a cold steel gurney and began her brutal probing Amanda recoiled, both physically and mentally. Her psyche quickly found escape by staring fixedly into the tiny holes of the ceiling's insulation. The matron yanked her off the table and pointed in the direction marked "Sanitation". Amanda's mind longed to retain its state of disassociation, but to no avail. It reluctantly reappeared, only to confront grim images of Dachau triggered by the showers.

A hideous, burning sensation overcame her. It smelled and felt like pure chlorine. She tried to hold her breath for as many of the five minutes as she could, all the while praying for it to wash away the nightmarish examination.

"Time's up!" The matron shouted. "Into the shower across the way. Make it quick. Here's your uniform. Put it on, along with those shoes. I'll be watching you when you're done."

The cold water barely penetrated Amanda's thoughts. *Surely someone will discover that I wasn't on the plane. They'll investigate and find me. By morning I'm sure to reach Paco. Just let me make it through until then.* As she stepped out, the matron shoved a thin, bleached out, gray uniform at her, barking an expletive.

"Damn bitch! Put it on fast. We're late. Don't you think anyone wants to go home around here?"

The question pushed Amanda towards hysteria. She bit her cheek to keep from breaking down. As the uniform slid around her, she struggled to hold her breath at the overpowering scent of stale sweat and chlorine. The shoes were at least two sizes too big, but she slip-slopped her way, firmly tugged by the vise-like grip of the matron's powerful biceps.

Inspector Garza had gone. The guard was waiting. He roughly pinned to her uniform a badge with her name and a number printed on it, took her photo and fingerprints and, without pausing, led her down a corridor, out a door and across to an even seedier looking building. Amanda gagged as she stepped across its threshold. Overpowering smells of urine, excrement and vomit, mingled with an ineffective overlay of bleach, saturated her senses. Sounds reached her, threatening calls coming from behind the cells they passed. The small barred window, high in the doors of each cell, didn't allow any view of the occupants. Men, she decided, as she registered the chilling sounds of obscene catcalls.

Her head swerved and her heart chilled as she repeated 'No' to herself, thinking: *This can't be real.* Her guard walked her onwards, turning at the end of the corridor as he steered her to the left and down to the far end. The cell doors they were passing now were quieter, although she thought she made out a female voice saying, "Welcome, Sweetie."

They stopped two doors down from her greeter's doorway. The guard took out his large key chain and opened an identical door. He motioned her inside. Her cell was dimly lit by one bulb hanging from the ceiling. She felt a second of relief as she saw that no one else was inside, only a small cot and a combination washstand and toilet. Their sagging dreariness seemed to whisper a weary greeting: "Abandon hope all ye who enter here."

"Breakfast is at eight. When you're taken out, they'll take you to Inspector Garza's office to try your call again." His voice carried neither pity nor disdain. It was chillingly devoid of anything but boredom. Much worse than its sound was the sound of the door clanging shut. She stared at her windowless walls, moving her gaze to the dim bulb overhead and over to the tightly sealed door with its minuscule window too high to reach. An icy terror at being helplessly confined overcame her.

# TWENTY-THREE

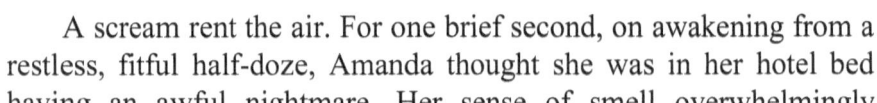

A scream rent the air. For one brief second, on awakening from a restless, fitful half-doze, Amanda thought she was in her hotel bed having an awful nightmare. Her sense of smell overwhelmingly confirmed reality, causing her stomach to recoil.

She shut her eyes as she quickly rallied defenses to ward off the unthinkable. Painstakingly she willed herself to review logical next steps. Surely Paco will find out I didn't make my flight, or the Hong Kong office will begin to worry... except... She suddenly remembered that she hadn't notified the Hong Kong office of her changed arrival time. "My office will begin to worry when I haven't called." She spoke out-loud, trying to drum up every last ounce of resolve before she opened her eyes.

She opened them to a view of the dangling light bulb. Images of prisoners who hung themselves in their cells flooded her thoughts. Her gaze raked the circumference of her cell. It was even more of a hellhole than she remembered. She had no idea if it was morning yet. A dim glow of the hall light shone feebly through her small barred window, but there was no way to tell whether it was night or day, summer or fall. The silence was complete except for the scuttling sound of a cockroach rushing towards the toilet pipe. The phrase "Kafkaesque nightmare" threatened to unleash a scream from her painfully constricted throat.

*How could she have slept, she* wondered? For ten minutes, or ten hours? She looked automatically at her naked wrist. It struck her that stripping a human of all identity was calculated to quickly erode one's will. She determined not to fall into a well of helplessness. It would have to be nearing morning. Soon they'd have to come and take her to make her call.

Forcing herself to review the sequence of events leading up to her current state, she had gotten all the way up to her last conversation with Derek Ashton, re-experiencing each line of dialogue, thinking *Damn him if he's responsible for this hell!"* Suddenly she began hallucinating—actually thinking she heard Derek's voice.

"It can't be; not here. I'm afraid I'm fast losing my grip on reality." The sound of her voice, as it struggled against succumbing to a mental state bordering on that of psychosis, seemed to elicit a response. But real or imagined, she wondered?

"Get her out of there—right now!" It was Derek's voice, accompanied by the sound of a key turning in the lock. The door suddenly filled with Derek's massive form. Flaming eyes scanned her cell as he took in a dazed figure sitting on the cot. With one step he scooped her into his arms. "They'll pay for this! Are you OK?"

"She'll be a lot more OK when she's out of here." Amanda suddenly recognized the smaller form standing behind Derek.

"Paco; I tried to reach you, but no one answered!" Amanda reluctantly stepped out of Derek's embrace to wrap her arms around Paco. Tears of relief began to flow.

"I'm sorry I wasn't there, my friend. It took me awhile to connect with Derek. His flight was canceled and he barely got on a later flight. After his plane landed, he checked with me to see whether or not you'd confirmed or canceled your flight. When the Pan AM staff responded to his inquiry and described the incident that took place to deny you access to your flight, they also mentioned someone having just left the airport after asking about the same incident. It was Derek.

He soon caught up with me and...but...." One look at Amanda's bewildered stare silenced Paco. "Never mind all that now. Let's get you back to the Inspector's office."

Legs wobbling with relief, Amanda retraced her agonizing route. The Inspector awaited them with the look of someone who had been brusquely dragged out of sleep. The wall clock showed six thirty AM. There were two other people in the office. One was introduced as Colonel Sanderson from the U.S. Consulate in the Philippines. The other was Adam Laing of the Central Intelligence Agency. Who they were, why they were there, and what they said, didn't quite register to Amanda. The only thing that penetrated was the miraculous news that she was to be released, freed of any charges—by orders of someone named General Kevin Logan.

Amanda glanced from face to face, gratitude beaming in her smile as it settled on Derek. "I don't know what's going on, but I want to meet this General Logan and give him a big kiss. He's my undying hero, sight unseen. I owe him my life!"

"Well, we'll begin with the kiss and negotiate the life part of the deal later" Derek said as he pulled her into his arms and began a kiss that seemed to explore eternity, drowning her in its delectable eroticism.

"Why is it that Kev always gets to kiss the girl?" Adam Laing's voice intruded. "I get to do the hard parts, slugging away at the research, tailing people, making arrests and you get to kiss the girl. It's all bloody unfair if I do say so myself!"

Amanda looked dazedly from one to the other, finally beginning to see the light. "Kevin Logan?" She glared at Derek. "So that's your real name. But who are you; General of whose army?"

"I promise I'll tell you all about it, but this atmosphere cramps my style. What say we go back to Paco's house? He's become privy to some of the stuff through our endless night together. I can add the finishing touches over breakfast."

"Ana's fixed all of your favorites. When did you last eat?" Paco's eyes turned from compassion to steely contempt as he turned a devastating look at her jailers. "Please accept my apologies for your brutal mistreatment from my countrymen." He directed an especially scathing look into the eyes of a now-cringing Inspector Garza.

Derek—she couldn't think of him as Kevin yet—glanced at the matron entering the office. "There, they've brought your clothes. Go quickly and change. We'll finish up a couple of things and get you out of here. Ten minutes or less, I promise."

Amanda felt a tiny shiver of fear at the thought of leaving their presence, even briefly, but the prison matron nodded encouragingly. She led her to a doorway opening directly off of the Inspector's office. "This is Inspector Garza's private bathroom. He insists that you feel free to use his shower. There are plenty of towels and soap inside."

What was not inside suddenly hit her. No awful smells of chlorine—or worse. She tugged off the offensive uniform and stepped under the warm flow of water. It felt delicious, but not enough to keep her any longer than it took to wash away the aroma of jail. The residue of fear would take longer. She rushed to get back in the company of friends; the very thought caused her to murmur, "Thank You" as she drew on her wrinkled tan pantsuit. Hair wet and make-up ignored, she rushed back through the door. With one savior at each side, Derek and Paco escorted her out of the grim building and into the breaking dawn of what looked to be another hot, humid, smoggy, but glorious, day.

Suddenly she stopped. "Oh Paco, how could I have forgotten Mickey? Is he all right?"

"He will be. They messed him up pretty bad, believing they'd finished him off. They did succeed in finishing off the car. I still don't know how he managed to get himself four miles to the nearest phone. He was unconscious for hours before he could drag himself away. In the meantime, Derek, I mean, General Logan and I, were comparing notes on the sequence of events that led up to your disappearance."

Derek picked up the beat. "Right; we called both the Makati and the Metro Manila Police Stations and got a negative on your having been arrested. These guys are so powerful that the whole police force bows to their orders—and the whole army too, for that matter. I began to make a few calls state-side."

Paco rushed to allay Amanda's quizzical look. "It wasn't until the call came in from Mickey at five o'clock this morning that we knew what had become of you. We took him to the emergency room at Manila General and headed here. A stateside call from Kevin, and more than a little strong-arming from the U.S. government, convinced the Philippine authorities that it would definitely be in their best interest to have you released immediately." Paco hesitated as they approached the familiar street leading to his home. "That's enough for now until we get some food into you."

Amanda looked up as the car drove through the guard gate of Paco's compound. The familiar sight of its beautiful grounds and Ana's smiling face at the door, filled her with relief and joy.

"Ah chica, how tired you look—and hungry, I hope—very hungry even." Ana guided her into the cool expanse of the sunroom terrace, where the tinkling waterfalls, the bright parrots and glowing orchids were eclipsed by the bountiful array of food.

"You've outdone yourself." Amanda turned to Ana with a grateful grin. "I'm absolutely famished. I just thought back to when I last ate anything. It seems ages." She turned to see a smiling servant quietly guiding her to a chair beside a plate piled high with eggs, cheese, pastries and heaps of Paco's homegrown mangos. Her stomach recoiled. She may never be able to enjoy them again. "The sight of those mangos reminds me. How in the world did a check from Miguel get into a box of mangos?" She put down her fork and stared at Derek and Paco.

"Not now, remember? Eat first and all will be explained." Paco drew up a chair for Derek along one side of Amanda and one for himself on the other. Amanda didn't feel quite so bad at the volume of food she was putting away when she noticed Derek shoveling it in even faster. He saw her glance his way.

"Worry always makes me hungry. Why didn't you do as I said and stay in Manila until I arrived? Your actions tipped their hand."

'Why did you go to Hong Kong?"

"To tie up loose ends; I had to be sure you weren't the one helping to funnel money out of the Philippines. When I'd ruled you out, it became a matter of following up on our other leads. They made it an easy trail to follow, especially Brad Gregory's."

"Brad. He told you…"

"God, did that guy talk when we got to him. It never occurred to him that he'd better hope we lock him away forever before one of the De La Serna clan blows him away. He seemed relieved to come clean about the whole business. Typical banker type; I've seen it before. When they go bad they can't wait to be found out. The relief for his conservative conscience must have been euphoric."

"Speaking of 'typical banker type', what about your bank in the Cayman Islands?" Paco directed a cautionary look as he pushed more food towards Amanda.

"Thanks Paco, but I've eaten all I can hold. Can I get the whole story now?"

"What do you say Derek, ah, I mean Captain Logan." Paco smiled encouragingly in Derek/Kevin's direction. "She definitely deserves to know." He turned back to Amanda, offering his arm. "Let's go in my study where we won't be disturbed. I wasn't overly shocked when Derek—he paused; let's agree to stick with the name "Derek" for awhile or I'll stumble each time." As "Derek" nodded, Paco continued. "Anyway, Derek laid it out for me; at least as much as he could reveal. But then, he'd already determined that I wasn't their target either."

As Paco concluded and nodded in Derek's direction, pointing out a soft black leather chair, Derek declined, choosing to stand and pace. Amanda flashed on an old war movie where the commanding general gathers his team to give them a briefing. She expected him to broach no interruptions and to just tell it as it happened. He surprised her.

"All right Amanda, begin at the beginning. Feel free to ask whatever questions occur to you and I'll try to fill in the missing blanks." He hesitated, "At least to the degree I can."

"At the beginning, hmm" She thought back to her arrival. "The staring man on the plane; how does he fit in?"

"Benjie Amparo? That was downright stupid of him. At that stage we were convinced it must be you that was in cahoots with helping one of your clients launder the money."

Paco joined in. "Benjie Amparo, besides being one of Derek's local operatives, comes from a long line of Filipino mankukulams."

"Yeah, I guess he figured his added contribution would be to give you the evil eye." Derek's expression held fury. "I had to straighten him out fast on that one."

"So that's why I saw you having breakfast with him early one morning. You didn't see me, but I didn't trust you from that minute on." She frowned at the memory. "Next question: "Who are you? Are you really a general?"

"Let's just say that I work with the CIA at the highest level. My specialty is espionage, anything that threatens our government, whether directly, or, as is the case with the Marcos regime, indirectly."

"But your knowledge of trusts…"

"I'm fortunate enough to have had some background in banking. That, coupled with the cooperation of your bank's chairman, made me the perfect choice for this assignment."

"To trap me." Amanda glared at him.

"It was becoming critical to try to staunch the flow of dirty money coming from the Philippines. Especially when word got out that Marcos was playing it smart and about to get the really big money out." He stopped, spread his hands and smiled. "It was either you or Brad orchestrating the moves."

"Brad." Amanda spat out the name.

"Brad Gregory's role was a small, yet critical, piece. One they didn't want to have to close down. It all started with his marriage to Caro. Well, actually it started a bit before. They were setting him up even then. Their agreeing to the marriage was designed to secure his complete allegiance to the family. For that he'd be paid well, be a big man in the Philippines, etc. You get the picture."

Paco noticed Amanda's disbelieving stare. "I'm with you. Never would I have thought the Don would go along with that marriage."

"It was Brad's going along that actually weakened their scheme." Derek stopped his pacing as a frown stole over his face. "He was pretty skillful at covering his trail though. In fact, when we searched the office, he'd destroyed virtually every transaction that the De La Serna group, specifically Raffy De La Serna, was involved in."

"Hold it a minute. The wire transfers! I made duplicates of all of them. Unless... I bet they confiscated them in jail." Her mouth went from frown to a sudden grin. "A wasted effort though, because I had Marisa send one set off to Nigel."

Derek almost choked on his mango. "Marisa? You trusted Marisa to mail those copies? How could you be sure she wasn't part of the cover up?"

"No way; Marisa rebelled when Brad insisted on her forging an officer's signature to them. He'd strong-armed his assistant, Ernesto, all along into co-signing earlier ones; but Marisa wouldn't budge."

"Good for her—and for you. Having those copies will help immensely." He shook his head, giving Amanda a look mingled with surprise, admiration and respect. "Now, back to Brad; he knew the word was out that some major bank was involved in moving money. He then got the news of the Bank's new department head. Carter's assignment filled him with fear that his number would soon be up. Raffy helped put together a plan that would not only throw everyone off Brad's trail, but would make him a hero besides. Their plan was to fan all the rumors that the International Private Banking departments of major U.S. banks in the Philippines were under suspicion. That gave him the excuse to warn you off any trip to the Philippines. It also gave him license to 'help' you to discover more info on your big clients. Their strategy was to eliminate any evidence implicating them. While all the while, skillfully setting you, and one of your clients, up to be the scapegoat."

"I get the picture." Amanda's eyes turned frosty. "My good buddy, Brad, would deflect attention away from the actual persons involved by sacrificing me."

"Righto—and become a hero in your bank's books."

"But where does Miguel come into the picture?" A look of total recall filled her eyes. "How is Miguel; is he out of the hospital?" Amanda felt a rush of guilt at having only just remembered poor Miguel.

"It was Raffy's idea to implicate Miguel, his old enemy. Miguel got wind of it. When it began to look as though Miguel was getting close to discovering the broader extent of Raffy's involvement, he decided to have him killed. After that plan aborted and ended up putting Miguel in the hospital, he hit on a plan to incriminate both of you in a manner that would render you both worse than dead. The penalty for your crime—and Miguel's role in it—would have been a lifetime in prison for you both."

"But the mangos with that note; who was it that masterminded that?" An ah-hah look came over Amanda's face. "I think I understand. They raided my hotel room—more than once. When they got my anting-anting and Miguel's note, they decided to use its wording to implicate him." She hesitated, looking to Derek. "But how about the check on Miguel's account, complete with his signature? How'd they manage that?"

"Easy. Several members of the De La Serna family own a controlling interest in three of Manila's largest banks. One of them just happens to be where Miguel has a major account. With his signature on your note and the collusion of the bank manager, it was easily forged. The check was never really meant to be cashed anyway, only to be obtained as incriminating evidence."

Amanda stood up, deep in thought as she walked over to one of the caged birds before turning suddenly. "But what about the 'making Brad a hero' part? Just how were they going to pull that one off.?" Amanda looked from Derek/Kevin to Paco in complete puzzlement.

Derek looked down at his hands and over to Paco before responding. "Have a chair before I continue; you may need it." He paused as Amanda returned to her chair. "Right about now Nigel would have been notified of your death, as well as the revelation that you had been laundering money on behalf of one of your clients. Brad was ready to call him and produce evidence of what had happened."

"My death!" Amanda nearly upset the table as she jumped up. "How could they have gotten away with such a thing?"

"It was already set up." Paco reached out and took her hand as he described the condition of the car and the ease with which her death would remain unsolved. "It was important to know they had set it up convincingly before you would have been actually done away with."

"And Brad knew that? He actually would have gone along with it?"

Paco took her hand, looking so distressed at her pain at such a thought that he nodded for Derek to continue. "Brad claims he didn't know of any plans to kill you, only discredit you and implicate you in the money laundering. He had already prepared a memo to Fidelity Bank, offering his services in any way to help them sort out the whole mess. I wouldn't be a bit surprised if he hadn't implemented a couple of other ways to put the last nail in your coffin, professionally at least. But he swears that he never expected them to kill you."

"I can't believe he'd do such a thing." She continued to stare at Derek, a look of shock stealing over her face. "Nigel! If Nigel thinks I'm involved in money laundering this will definitely push him over the top. I've got to call him right now." Amanda jumped up as she looked around for a phone.

"Hold on there; Nigel's being handled." Derek walked over to her. "I've been in constant touch with your bank's chairman. Sorenson knows the whole story and is preparing extra compensation for your ordeal. I wouldn't be surprised if that doesn't include a promotion on top of it. Nigel will be filled in sometime today."

"What about Lyle Carter? Even though Brad's mess doesn't involve IPB, he'll definitely want to take the path of greatest caution and axe our department—especially when the papers get hold of it!"

"I very much doubt it. It all depends on what Sorenson wants. As to the papers, I'm sure the story won't break just yet. We still have bigger fish to fry."

"More?" Amanda studied Derek's solemn look.

"The millions that washed through your Manila office were just a drop in the bucket. I went to Hong Kong to stop the shipment of four billion in gold bullion about to leave for Switzerland, all under a phony bill of lading for prawns. Raffy was up to his eyeballs in that one, thanks to a big pay-off to one of the most powerful Saudis. Fortunately we caught them both red handed. But the CIA is after bigger game yet; seems that large amounts of that money were earmarked for some pretty shady goings on, including the benefit of some pretty important politicians in Washington." Derek/Kevin suddenly fell silent, deep in thought before he continued. "I've already said more than I am at liberty to say. Just don't be surprised if Raffy, et al, manages to pull out all the stops to avoid indictments—and we let him. Still, we did confiscate all that gold. It wouldn't surprise me if some of it isn't used for bait to persuade these guys to lead us to our big catch."

"Gold? Yamashita's gold? Then it wasn't just a myth after all." Amanda turned to look beseechingly at Paco.

"We can't be sure, or Derek can't, to hear him tell it. But just between you and me, Amanda, I never once believed that the story was just folklore." He gave Derek/Kevin a knowing look as he moved closer to Amanda. "It's probably the truth, whether or not the U.S. wants to label it as such." Paco reached over and gave her hand a pat.

Derek's General Logan persona assumed a stern look. "You can believe whatever story you like, as long as you keep it between yourselves. I can't have any mention of any of this getting out, not to anyone. Your lives could depend on it." Gone was any trace of Irish whimsy.

"But why; if we know it could help us to understand. After all you've put me through, can't you trust me with the big picture?" Amanda gave him a steady look.

Derek's frown deepened. "Raffy's pal in Hong Kong is a mighty big fish, with unsavory side alignments. The Mafia and the cocaine cartels also have their hooks in this mess. Marcos' government is so corrupt and the pay-off is so big, that trying to trace all of the tentacles of those involved leads to everyone connected with big money and power—major U.S. politicians included."

"The Kraken is what Miguel called it."

Derek froze at the word. His look hardened. "How far I'll be encouraged to go with this monster, I'm not certain. But for now, and, as to your involvement, say nothing to any one. Above all, don't use that phrase ever again."

"But..." Amanda was stopped by the look in Derek's eyes.

"For your safety, forget everything. Trust me to mop up the trail of everyone involved, right down to the Marisa's and Miguel's of the world."

"If you say so, but remembering what he did to Miguel, it just frosts me to think that Raffy might get off free." A look of sadness overtook her. "On the other hand, any news of Raffy's having been arrested would kill his father. How is Don Emilio doing? You did imply that the Don wasn't personally involved, right Derek; I mean, Kevin. Sorry, it will take me awhile with the Kevin bit."

"Don Emilio wasn't involved, although he was definitely getting wind of Raffy's plans. It wouldn't surprise me if his sudden illness wasn't provoked by even more than such awareness. He's managed to remain alive, but barely. The longer his coma endures the poorer his prognosis." Derek looked from Paco to Amanda with a "Let's wrap this up and move on" expression.

"End of story. All will be handled discreetly, quietly, and with all memory of your involvement erased from the records. No more discussion, speculation, or gossip whatsoever can be allowed. It never happened—none of it. Got that?"

"None of it?" Amanda looked puzzled. "How are you going to explain away your role? New banker comes and goes?"

"Why not? Derek Ashton goes back to his office in the Cayman Islands, and the last you heard, had buyers remorse with the corporate world. So he chucked it all and aimed his sailboat towards the South Pacific."

His comment brought a frown to her face and concern to her voice. "And so you vanish, just like that?" Her heart gave a squeeze of pain, but her look remained steady.

"Let's just say that you and I need to get re-acquainted on different terms. I won't be free from this entanglement and you wouldn't be safe, even indirectly, associated with me, until it's finished. How long that'll take, I can't say. In the meantime, promise me that you'll get on with your life." He looked expectantly in her direction, taken aback at the strange expression on her face. Misinterpreting its message, he pressed on. "My career doesn't make me promising relationship material. You've come a long way since we set out on this trip. I like the new dimension you've revealed, that tough, take-no-nonsense-from-anyone side. Keep it up."

"How dare you patronize me?" Amanda's look was fierce in its anger. "I don't need your validation Mr. Derek Ashton-Kevin Logan, or whoever you are. And I don't wait around for a man whose life involves a love of cops and robbers and aliases and game playing. If you ever decide to give up war games and look me up, you might get lucky and find me around to take your call." She took a deep breath, her shoulders squaring and her tone of voice escalating its power. "In the meantime, I'm going to focus on someone who really has my interests at heart—and that's Me."

Paco had been all ears until his eyes took over, widening in surprise and support. "Let him have it, Amanda; foolish man, not to see something far more valuable than Yamashita's gold when it's right under his nose!" Paco drew her into his embrace as he turned and raised one eyebrow. "Take note of that, General Logan."

# TWENTY-FOUR

Two weeks later- Los Angeles, California

"Amanda! Are you ready? Nigel says the meeting will begin in exactly twenty minutes." Mai Wong Lee was agitated and excited as she approached Amanda in the hotel lobby. She knew there was a big announcement in store concerning Amanda's promotion. Her agitation came from wondering what, if any, fallout might accrue to her.

"I'll be there soon. Why don't you go in and save a spot for me?" Mai gave a firm and smiling nod of agreement and darted off towards the doors of the Los Angeles' Sheraton Grande's largest conference room. Amanda silently wished her well. Over breakfast this morning, Amanda had shared with Mai the main focus of the Bank's Annual International Private Banking Conference. She'd been given an advance notice that Nigel would announce that Amanda Evans would be the new Senior Vice President in charge of International Marketing and Product Management. What she couldn't tell Mai as yet was that she had strongly recommended that Nigel appoint Mai manager of the San Francisco office as her replacement.

Mai deserved it. Amanda remembered the surprise she'd felt on learning that the "M.W." notations in Raffy's appointment book referred to Masta Wunaire, the Middle Eastern contact, not Mai. Raffy had, in fact, attempted to subtly enlist Mai in providing information and assistance—to no avail. Mai's loyalty and attempts to warn Amanda away reassured Amanda that Mai would always put the bank first. There'd been a few reservations on Nigel's part, until Amanda reminded him that Mai was the type of dedicated employee that would always produce the profits he wanted. Amanda smiled as she anticipated that Nigel's announcements today would include Mai's promotion as well.

Putting her concerns for Mai on the back burner, Amanda let the mixture of sorrow and excitement she was feeling come to the fore. Her deepest emotion was sadness at leaving San Francisco, her office team and her clients. She sighed deeply at the memory of how hard she'd worked to build the office and how close were the client relationships she'd forged. After the debacle over Brad and the mess in the Philippines, Nigel decided she shouldn't go back. Nigel's relief at having won the approbation of the Bank's Chairman mellowed his willingness to offer Amanda any assignment she wanted. Especially since the accolades he and his department received were "due to the professional skill his San Francisco Manager, Amanda Evans, had displayed." The fallout was so favorable it even prompted Lyle Carter to commit to expanding Nigel's role. Amanda smiled at the knowledge that Nigel was already salivating over plans to bring the Domestic Private Banking Group under his International Division's control. She'd never known him to be so obliging. In that respect her move was shaping up well.

Even the Rob situation was made easier by her promotion. She turned her head to one side, smiling at the memory of their cool reunion. Soon after returning from Hong Kong, she'd made it clear to Rob that their relationship would have to revert to that of friendship as professional colleagues. Not too surprisingly, he was too busy with his new assignment to show much remorse. Still, she trusted that the actual physical move back to LA would help ease any residue of awkwardness for her.

The sorrow that lingered was one of having to separate from the people and the situation in the Philippines. She recalled her last phone call with Miguel Santos. As soon as his recovery had allowed for it, he'd made sure to keep her up to date on all of the dramatic happenings since she left. Things were moving to a critical point. So much had happened so fast, events that no one could ever have anticipated.

It had begun back in December with the Benigno 'Ninoy' Acquino assassination trial. The jury concluded that Galman, working alone, managed to move unnoticed through a phalanx of one thousand soldiers guarding Acquino, and shoot him as he came down the ramp. That decision ignored completely the evidence that Galman himself had actually been shot some time earlier. The following day, Aquino's widow, Cory, a soft-spoken housewife—ostensibly committed to family and to religious pursuits—announced her candidacy for the Presidency.

Everything moved so quickly after that, snowballing on the heels of Amanda's return. She hung on every bit of news as the election approached on February seventh. There was a heavy turnout of the country's twenty-six million voters. In spite of extreme harassment, stolen ballot boxes and altered voter lists, a determinedly accurate tally of votes showed Cory Acquino the winner. Her success was largely due to the zealous guarding of the ballot boxes by nuns. An unprecedented act of bravery, they actually defied the soldier's attempts to confiscate the votes and replace them with thousands of fictitious ones. In spite of Cory's obvious win, President Marcos announced the results of the polls as showing his own victory. The whole world, even President Reagan, who'd tempered his censure with the implication that both sides may have been culpable, was appalled. Amanda had been devastated at the news of Cory's ignoble defeat after such a valiant victory.

Miguel, barely rallied from death's door himself, had been quick to notify Amanda of Don Emilio De La Serna's having slipped into a gentle death just two days after she had left Manila.

She felt a sharp pang of sorrow, tempered only by his having been spared any further grief at the revelations of his son's betrayal of his family honor.

A few days ago Miguel had called to let her in on a secret strategy which, with the implied approval of the U.S., backed Ramos and Enrile. With the help of some of the Philippine Army they'd implemented a plan to attack the Malacanang Palace and force President Marcos to accede to Cory Aquino's rightful victory.

Amanda smiled as she recalled Miguel describing Enrile's panic over the outcome. He laughingly described Enrile as "Saying his rosary in anticipation of his own death". Miguel was quick to second the notion; sure that Enrile's suicidal force of several hundred soldiers would quickly be annihilated by the tens of thousands of Ver's army.

All of it was coming to a head today. *Whatever her Bank was doing took a back seat to what was happening in the Philippines today, she thought.* She couldn't go into the meeting without knowing the outcome.

She needed to get to a phone fast. The thought propelled her towards the ladies room. She crossed the lobby and pushed through the restroom doors. One glance in the bathroom mirrors reflected multiple images of her furrowed brow. Her stomach lurched in fear at the thought of what was certain to be a blood-bath in the Philippines.

"Damn! Aren't there any phones in here?" She aimed her frustrated question at the back of the only other woman in the room. The dark-haired figure turned. Anne gasped at the sight of a tiny Filipina maid, streaks of tears running down her cheeks.

"What's the matter? Is it Manila? What's happening there?" Anne reached out her hand towards the grief-stricken woman, whose only decipherable response was a briskly nodded "Yes." Images of Miguel dead ran through Amanda's thoughts as she searched the woman's eyes. "Please." Her own tears started to flow. "I have to know what is happening. I have good friends in the Philippines."

The woman blubbered out a stuttering reply. "Look. I, I—" She couldn't continue to speak as she fumbled to reach into her apron's large pocket and pull out a crumpled fax paper. It was a copy of the front page of a late-night special edition of The Manila Times. Its alliterative headline brought a disbelieving gasp from Amanda.

PEOPLE POWER AND PRAYER PREVAIL IN PHILIPPINES "One hundred and twenty five thousand Filipinos, nuns and children included, kneel and pray as they block the army's tanks...." The unthinkable had happened. Amanda felt a wave of shivers run up and down her spine at the miraculous relief flooding through her.

"Amanda, are you in there?" Mai's panicked shout as she pushed through the doorway was quickly stifled. She stared at the sight of the two women locked in a sisterly embrace, faces wreathed in joy.

"It's all right, Mai. It's very much all right." She reached out to link arms. "Let's get to that meeting." As Amanda hurried through the conference room door, eyes sparkling, she brushed a hand across her face—erasing a tear's moist path. Hesitating, she turned to locate Nigel out of the crowd and stopped suddenly, staring in disbelief at the smiling figure approaching alongside him.

"Come on now... no tears. Or let me be the one to dry them."

"Derek! I mean, Kevin, what are you doing here?" She looked him up and down, struck by the awareness that, not even in her wildest dreams, did his remembered image come close to the real one.

"How could I miss your promotion?" He lifted his arm to give her a comradely salute. "Congratulations. We made a good team. You fumble the ball and I catch it." He grinned as her expression clouded. "Just kidding—I thought I'd put in an appearance; maybe give you some moral support."

"Sure—and disappear over cake and champagne maybe?"

"Maybe." His grin widened.

"Maybe? You're definitely not the maybe sort." She gave him a questioning look as Nigel nervously raced up to them. Squaring her shoulders, she began a strong stride in the direction of Nigel's frantic urgings for her to go quickly up to the podium.

Stopping mid-pace, she turned at Derek/Kevin's raised voice. "Right you are. I'm definitely not the 'maybe' sort. How about you?"

Amanda grinned as she responded: "Neither am I!"

**THE END**

# ABOUT THE AUTHOR

Nita Hughes was for many years a Vice President at Security Pacific Bank (now merged with Bank of America)

As a global executive in the International Private Banking division, she provided financial services to high net worth clients in Asia, South America, and Europe.

She draws on diverse passions, including her love for teaching, singing, and traveling between homes in France and Hawaii.

Her writing includes historical fiction and political thrillers as well as contributions to books on childhood autism, corporate training and marketing.

When not involved in her personal pursuits, Nita is a partner with *Hughes Associates,* a team of professionals committed to helping entrepreneurs and artists profit from their creative endeavors.

For more information, visit the author's website at:

*www.NitaHughes.com*

# PAST RECALL
## When Love and Wisdom Transcend Time

In the novel, *Past Recall*, Nita Hughes blends an ancient story of terrifying persecution with a vision of hope for the world today.

The tale is told by a photographer who unexpectedly discovers information from the past about a spiritual secret, a treasure so coveted that an entire culture was massacred in an attempt to control it.

Her search for answers propels the characters of this romantic thriller through time as history threatens to repeat itself.

We meet Clotilde and Jean de Mirepoix, devout Cathars in 13th century France. Their world of growing enlightenment is being extinguished by a reign of terror. Clotilde and Jean seek refuge in Montsegur, a Cathar sanctuary thought to be impregnable. But their focus on safety fades as they attempt to secure the Cathar treasure, described in the archives of the Catholic church as "*so powerful as to transform the world.*" Vowing to safeguard the treasure throughout time, their souls commit to return and unveil it at "worlds end".

Now that time has come, as photographer Dana Palmer and writer Eric Taylor collaborate on a story whose secret may provide the world's salvation ... or its destruction.

For more information, visit the website: ***www.PastRecall.com***

www.ingramcontent.com/pod-product-compliance
Lightning Source LLC
Chambersburg PA
CBHW020551260626
47157CB00003B/655